"What's wrong?" Gib prompted.

He had seen the darkness cloud Kuchana's eyes at the mention of Geronimo's name.

"I miss my tribe," the young woman admitted softly.

"I know it wasn't easy for you to leave them, but you'll be reunited soon," he comforted her.

"No," she whispered. "That will never be."

"Geronimo can't keep running forever. There are too many people after him."

"You don't understand. It does not matter." Tears rushed into her eyes, and Kuchana bowed her head, struggling to control her emotions.

Gib reached out, placing a finger beneath her chin, forcing her to look up at him. As her lashes lifted, he saw for the first time the full extent of the terrible pain she carried.

"To them, I no longer exist," she explained. "Before I left, Geronimo pronounced me dead."

Dear Reader,

Welcome to the world of Harlequin Historicals, where April promises to be another exciting month.

In *Sun Woman,* by Lindsay McKenna, a young Apache woman becomes an army scout in a desperate attempt to save the last of her band of Geronimo's followers. On a lighter note, Kate Kingsley has written *Ransom of the Heart,* a fanciful tale of a penniless Louisiana belle and her swashbuckling rescuer.

Mari, by Donna Anders, is the first of two books set in exotic Hawaii, so be sure to look for the sequel, *Ketti,* in June. And with *Mission of Mercy,* Kathryn Belmont brings to life the whaling industry as we travel with Mercy Randall on a voyage of discovery and danger in the South Seas.

You'll have to wait until next month to read our May books, but I can at least tell you that you have stories from Lynda Trent, Patricia Potter, Marjorie Burrows and Peggy Bechko to look forward to. Don't miss them!

Yours,

Tracy Farrell
Senior Editor

Sun Woman

Lindsay McKenna

Harlequin Books

TORONTO • NEW YORK • LONDON
AMSTERDAM • PARIS • SYDNEY • HAMBURG
STOCKHOLM • ATHENS • TOKYO • MILAN

Harlequin Historicals first edition April 1991

ISBN 0-373-28671-6

SUN WOMAN

***LINDSAY McKENNA*'s**

native American background spurred her interest in history, which she feels is a reflection of what goes on in the present and an indication of what the future will be like. Most interesting to Lindsay are the women of history. She feels their strength of spirit can be an inspiration to the women of today. Her three favorite historical periods are the Old West, medieval times and the Roman era.

Lindsay, an avid rock hound and hiker, lives with her husband of fifteen years in Arizona.

Chapter One

September 1, 1885, Sonora Desert, Mexico

It is a good day to die, Kuchana thought, standing at one end of the Apache encampment at Rio Aros. She listened to the women wailing out their grief. Hot, blinding tears filled her eyes, and she shut them, hanging her head so that no one would see her weep. Her sister's last child had died minutes ago from starvation. The Mexican soldiers, *soldatos,* had been hunting Geronimo's group relentlessly for the past two weeks. There had been no time to hunt. Although the warriors, twenty in all, had given their families what little food they could find along the trail, it hadn't been enough. Ealae's four-year-old daughter had now gone to the Big Sleep.

Sniffing, Kuchana wiped away the tears with the back of her thin cotton sleeve. She was a warrior. Warriors showed only bravery and fearlessness in the face of their enemies. Opening her eyes, she raised her head again. Holos, the sun, was about to brim the craggy mountains that stood in silent testimony to the scene before them. For his people, Holos was the symbol of life. Just as he greeted them, without fail, each morning, so would the Apache continue to survive. Kuchana's heart felt torn, and she placed her hand against her breast.

So many of her people had died as the *soldatos* and U.S. Army had mercilessly hunted them down after they'd escaped the reservation near Fort Apache. As she knelt on the dry, arid ground, Kuchana's black hair fell across her shoulders, acting as a curtain to hide the haunted expression on her face. If Geronimo caught her shedding tears, he would be disgusted with her. After all, she was his best tracker, and one of four women riding with him who wore the third braid of a warrior.

What could she do to stop the slaughter of her people? There were few Chiricahua left. Why couldn't Geronimo see the wisdom of going back to the reservation? The screeching wail of her sister, Ealae, made Kuchana flinch. In her eighteen years of life, all she could recall was the continued death and murder of her people.

It is a good day to die. The words cartwheeled through her grief-stricken mind. Her people were being slowly starved to death. They were being pursued and cold-bloodedly murdered. Lifting her chin, Kuchana stared out across the sparse encampment. Groups of families huddled here and there, the horses weary, their heads hanging. She saw Geronimo walking to each family, giving encouragement to those who had chosen to flee into the desert with him.

Something must be done. Kuchana raised her face to the sun, watching the first brilliant rays top the rocky, desolate crags to the east. Just as the rays struck her, she heard the shrill cry of a golden eagle. Looking up, she saw the huge bird circling high above them. A cold shiver wound up her spine. Painted Woman had answered her prayers. Slowly, she got to her feet, singling out Geronimo. Her hand clutching the butt of the knife she carried at her waist, Kuchana moved grimly toward the Apache leader. It didn't matter if Geronimo killed her or not, she must speak her heart regarding the plight of her people.

"Geronimo?"

"Eh?" He turned, his flinty black eyes settling on the woman warrior. "Kuchana? What is it?"

She came to a halt, realizing they stood in the center of the encampment. Did it matter? Within minutes her people would know of her decision. "I've prayed long and hard on what I should do," Kuchana croaked, her mouth dry.

Geronimo scowled. "What do you say?"

Her hand tightening on the knife, Kuchana knew she must be strong. "I have lost another cousin. My sister lost her husband and now, she has no more children left."

"We have all lost family," Geronimo said hoarsely. "My own wife and children were murdered by the *culo-gordos*. Those Mexican bandits would kill us all if they were given the chance."

Kuchana nodded. "I've made a decision. I cannot watch our people being slowly starved to death or murdered any longer. Please, stop this fight."

"Surrender?" Geronimo exploded. "And let them send us to Florida where we will sicken and die like the others? Has Owl Man rattled your brain? You are a warrior! You have taken an oath to protect the people. Surrender for us means to give over to a power stronger than ourselves. The white eyes and *culo-gordos* are not stronger than we are! I will not surrender to them!"

Her heart was pounding like a water drum in her breast. Kuchana wondered if Geronimo could hear it. She feared this medicine man, for he had the power to turn her into a donkey if he chose. But the plight of her people drove her beyond regard for her own safety. Moistening her chapped lips, Kuchana said slowly, "Then I must leave."

Geronimo hissed a curse. "If you leave, we lose our best animal tracker. I need you here to help supply food for us."

Tears stung her eyes but Kuchana stood her ground. "I will go to my enemy and help him track you down and bring you back to the reservation. At least, what few of our people are left will then be protected. I have lost all of my family. Only my sister remains. If nothing is done, she will also die. At least on the reservation, there was food."

Geronimo stood thunderstruck. He stared up at the tall, thin warrior. Her brown eyes watered with tears, but her voice was low and strong with feeling. "Surely you remember the food we received from our so-called *pindah* friends. The white men promised us beef, and we got none. They promised us blankets to warm our people, and we received none. All we were given were beans and hard, dry biscuits." He punched his finger into Kuchana's chest. "You," he rattled, "of all people, know what happened. You were there. That was why we stole off the reservation and came to hide in Mexico."

Kuchana was vaguely aware that people were gathering around them, standing blank-faced, watching. She refused to back down from his tirade. "I would rather eat biscuits than starve to death," she answered, gesturing at the inhospitable mountains. "I would rather my sister survive than be murdered by *culo-gordos!*"

"Your memory is short," Geronimo snarled, his lips lifting away from his teeth. "You think the *pindah* army is going to keep us alive? They were the ones slowly starving us to death. Don't make the mistake of thinking the *pindah* soldiers are your friends. They are not. They have lied to us. They have stolen what was rightfully ours and broken the treaty." He looked around. "I would rather die out here, like a warrior, than sit on a reservation accepting my fate like a stupid donkey. Think this through, Kuchana. Stay here with us. We need you."

Kuchana's breath came in heaving gulps, all her carefully closeted emotions unraveling. "I will not change my mind. I am leaving, Geronimo. If you want to kill me, then do so. I will join the army as a scout and hunt you down. Our only hope is the *pindah* reservation."

The flinty anger in Geronimo's eyes grew. "Get out of my sight, Kuchana. You are a coward. I would not stain my knife with your traitorous blood." He raised his arm, jabbing a finger toward the northwest. "Go. From this moment on, you are no longer one of the people."

Kuchana gulped, a sharp breath issuing from between her lips. Geronimo had just delivered a sentence worse than death. Even if she was able to save the last of her band, they would all consider her dead. No one would ever speak to her again, not even Ealae, her sister. Her stomach knotted, and she longed to sob out her grief.

"Go!" Geronimo roared. "In your next life, you will turn into a donkey. You have deserted us. Take your horse and leave."

Kuchana whirled on the heel of her boot, blindly moving toward the hobbled horses just outside the camp. The crowd parted, their faces long and saddened. None of them understood her actions. It didn't matter.

"Kuchana!" Ealae reached out, gripping her sister's arm. "Do not do this..."

Halting, Kuchana looked down at her older sister. Ealae had cut off her hair and painted her face black over the death of her daughter. There were tears streaking down her features. Choking back a sob, Kuchana whispered, "Let me go, sister. You will be punished for speaking to me. I no longer exist to the people."

Her hand tightening on Kuchana's arm, Ealae sobbed. "You cannot do this. If you go, I have no one. No one."

Kuchana groaned as her sister flung herself into her arms. She must not show her feelings. No matter what, she was a warrior, and a warrior must face life with courage. "Hush, Ealae, hush. You will be all right." Gripping her sister, she gave Ealae a long, hard embrace.

"I will lose you, too. Oh, think, Kuchana. Think of what you have chosen to do. The army will kill us if we are recaptured."

"No." Fiercely, Kuchana gripped her sister, giving her a small shake. "Listen to me, Ealae. Geronimo will watch our people dwindle away until we are only a memory on the wind. This is our only chance to survive."

Her cheeks glistening with spent tears, Ealae stared at her sister. "But to go to our enemy for help? You will be a traitor."

She must go—now. Kuchana reluctantly released Ealae. "I must do what I feel is right. My heart is broken over the loss of your daughter. I will not see you go to the Big Sleep because of Geronimo."

Ealae sniffed and took a step back, her dark chocolate-colored eyes mirroring her misery and confusion. "Kuchana, you shame me. You shame us just like the other Apache warriors who have gone to the army to become scouts to track us down. My own sister..."

Kuchana swallowed against the lump that was forming in her chest. "Ealae, I love you. Always know that. May Usen protect you."

Kuchana turned away. She spotted her black mustang, Wind, among the herd. Moving between the horses, she knelt down by the mare and released her hobbles.

Patting the hardy pony, Kuchana slipped the leather jaw cord into her mouth. Looking back toward the camp, she saw that everyone had returned to their duties. Even now, she was a ghost. Taking a deep, shaky breath, Kuchana swung up onto the horse's back.

Kuchana walked the mare into the camp and dismounted. The only item she owned beside her weapons was a ragged wool blanket. Picking it up, she laid it near Ealae, who was quietly sobbing. Then she placed her quiver of arrows on her back and picked up her bow. It was done. She was now an outcast. Mounting, Kuchana walked the mare through the camp and down a narrow, rocky path that would take her out into the flat, arid Sonora Desert.

Holos burned hot and bright against her back. Though it was early morning, the heat was beginning to build. Her mind was clogged with grief, but Kuchana knew she had to think clearly. There were few watering holes, and in order to make the long trek across the Mexican desert, she would have to remember their location, or die of thirst. Her mind turned northward.

Geronimo had raided many ranches along the Arizona border, and a number of military forts had been built there. Praying to Painted Woman, she asked to be guided to a fort that would give her protection and allow her to become a scout.

There was much danger between Rio Aros and the nearest army outpost. The *culo-gordos* could capture her. If they did, they would murder her and take her scalp. The possibility of running into an army patrol could also claim her life. Many of the *pindah* would shoot her on sight. She would have to find the right man to help her. A man who would not raise his revolver in hatred. Painted Woman was the spirit of all women among the Apache. Kuchana's faith in her power helped allay some of her fears. Within four days she would reach a U.S. Army fort. What waited for her at the end of her journey?

"Look," Claudia Carter whispered behind her fan, "there's that rogue officer, Sergeant Gib McCoy!"

"I declare," Melissa Polk, wife of the commander of Fort Huachuca, "I can see why that colonel's wife at Fort Apache ran off with him."

Both women giggled beneath their gloved hands. They stood on the wooden walkway of the headquarters building. Though it was barely ten in the morning, they carried parasols to protect their skin from the blazing Arizona sun. Melissa's green eyes narrowed as she watched Sergeant Gib McCoy walk across the flat and dusty parade ground in front of them.

Barely twenty-one, Claudia was the wife of Lieutenant Dodd Carter. She leaned over to question her friend. "Melissa, do you really think he lost his commission?"

"Of course he did!" Melissa's blond curls moved with her bobbing head. She delicately touched the bow and ribbon at the side of her neck, making sure her straw bonnet was in place. "Why, I overheard my husband talking about Sergeant McCoy."

"What did he say? What did he say?"

Melissa smiled, fanning herself rapidly, hating the heat. Having to wear a corset, all those petticoats, plus a long-sleeved cotton dress, was simply too much. "According to my husband, Sergeant McCoy was a lieutenant up at Fort Apache. He ran off with Juliet Harper, wife of the commandant."

"Did he love her?" Claudia asked, batting her eyelashes.

"It was something," Melissa agreed coyly. And judging from McCoy's lean, powerful build, she could see why Juliet Harper had wanted to run off with him. So would she. Yes, McCoy was definitely a stallion. She kept her thoughts to herself, realizing Claudia, who had been gently reared in Boston, would faint if she voiced them out loud. She was like any other brass-button bride: naive. And having come to the West only three months before, she was still adjusting to post life.

"He's positively handsome, don't you think?"

"He'll do in a pinch," Melissa said with a shrug. Beneath the surface, she seethed with anger. A week after arriving at the fort, she had purposely caught McCoy alone in the stable. When she'd approached him and ran her hand along his sweaty bronzed arm, his eyes had turned a glacial blue. And when she'd pressed herself to his hard, tense body, McCoy had stepped back. Murmuring something about enlisted men not fraternizing with officers or their wives, he'd turned on his heel, leaving her humiliated.

Melissa snorted. Any time she approached Claudia's husband, Dodd, he was more than willing to meet her in the hay mow. And so was any other man at the post she wanted. She hated the fact that McCoy had snubbed her advance. No man ever had before. One way or another, Melissa promised herself that he would come begging to bed her.

Giggling, Claudia added, "Pinch, my foot! My husband tells me that McCoy has been out in the Southwest for seven years. He's rough-looking."

"Probably every laundress on the post is ogling him," Melissa stated, pretending not to be watching McCoy. He had been busted because he'd tried to help Juliet Harper escape and return to her home in the East. Melissa had heard about McCoy from time to time, because he'd been an officer at Fort Apache and responsible for the Apache reservation nearby.

Studying McCoy, Melissa decided he was ten times the man that her flabby, fifty-five-year-old husband was. She smiled to herself. Harvey was such a dolt. He never realized she hadn't been a virgin when she'd married him. Of course, she'd made him think otherwise. After having young men who were truly studs in comparison to Harvey, she ached to find a man to match her hungry desire. Harvey certainly couldn't. Dodd wasn't bad, but was unexciting in comparison to McCoy. She fumed, fanning herself more rapidly. She was utterly frustrated by the fact her husband made love to her once a month and treated her like delicate porcelain, afraid she'd break beneath his weight.

McCoy had been at the post for three months now. Most of the cavalry soldiers were unmarried. The only way these men relieved their urges was with some of the single laundresses or white women who posed as such, but were on their backs day and night. According to the colored laundress, Poppy, McCoy stayed to himself.

"Outcast," she muttered.

"What?" Claudia asked.

"Oh . . . nothing."

Claudia, who had red hair and dancing gray eyes, pouted. She stood restlessly on the squeaky wooden expanse, tapping her fingers against her lavender gingham gown. "Oh, pshaw. I wish there was something to do. Post life is so boring, Mellie. The men are always gone, hunting those dreadful Apaches. We've nothing but sand and heat to keep us company. I can't keep our quarters clean for the sand. How I long for some green trees and hills.''

Melissa shrugged her shapely shoulders. ''There's no use complaining about it, Claudia. You know they only stick men out West that the army has no use for. Out of sight, out of mind.''

''Ohhh,'' Claudia whined, ''don't say that. Why, Dodd dreams of getting orders to go back East.''

With a grimace, Melissa flicked a fly away from her face. ''You're new here, Claudia. Believe me, the only men the army sends West are those they consider misfits, and of no potential use to the military system.''

Moaning, Claudia rolled her eyes upward. ''You've only been married for five years and already you know so much about the army.''

Too bad I didn't learn it sooner, Melissa thought. Harvey Polk had presented a bold and swaggering picture in uniform at a ball in Washington, D.C. He had been a hero coming out of the Civil War, and was an attaché to the Secretary of War. How could she have known he was such a loser about to be sent West and forgotten? Her marriage was one scheme that had fallen through.

She had married Harvey thinking that he was in line for a much more prestigious job in Washington. Instead, four days after the ceremony, he'd received orders to Fort Huachuca, Arizona. Melissa knitted her fine, thin eyebrows in vexation. There was nothing but sand, scorpions, heat and loneliness at the post. At first, she'd been one of three wives. Over the years, colored laundresses had moved West to escape the South and married the Negro cavalrymen of the Fourth stationed here. What few white laundresses there were, were nothing but soiled doves, as far as she was concerned. No self-respecting white woman would wash laundry like a colored. Of course, laundresses, and their families were considered little more than just necessities to post life, but they were certainly not included in it. They were animals of toil, in Melissa's opinion.

Still, she held out hope that Harvey would leave the army and run for governor or senator. There was power in either of those positions. Melissa's wandering gaze moved back to McCoy, who was now checking with the guards at the main gate of the post.

Since that day she had flaunted herself in front of him, Melissa's further plans to meet him again had failed miserably. He was always polite when he had to confront her on occasion, but she'd seen the amusement in his icy blue eyes. It was as if he could read her mind. With an unladylike snort, Melissa decided that was impossible. A man's brains hung between his legs. She stepped off the porch, her feet sinking into an inch of dust. She intended to intercept the sergeant and force him to take notice of her.

"Come, Claudia. Let's walk around the parade ground. I need my morning exercise."

Picking up her skirt, Claudia scrambled to catch up with the older woman as she glided across the parade ground. "Dear me, Mellie! Why are you in such a hurry?"

"Sergeant McCoy?"

Gib turned to the sentry standing by the opened gates, Private Lemuel Ladler, a Negro boy of eighteen. "What is it, Ladler?"

"I see something out there, suh. Take a look." He pointed to beyond the wavering curtains of heat across the desert.

Squinting, Gib turned and directed his attention to the cactus-strewn desert. Sure enough, he saw a lone rider. And if he wasn't mistaken, it was an Indian.

"Looks like an Apache," he muttered.

Ladler's eyes rounded, and he quickly pulled the rifle off his shoulder, holding it ready to fire.

Gib pushed the rifle barrel down toward the sand. "Take it easy, son. That's one Indian, not a party of them."

"B-but, sergeant—"

"At ease, Ladler. We don't shoot Indians. For all we know, it could be a scout from one of the other forts. Relax." Gib rested his hands on his hips, watching the progress of the rider. The Fourth Cavalry resided here, the only all-Negro outfit in the West. Ladler had recently come from the East after signing up and had never seen action. The few Indians he had met were scouts. Deciding to stay because Ladler was nervous and might shoot first and ask questions later, Gib waited with the sentry.

"What's going on here?" Lieutenant Carter demanded, coming up to them.

McCoy kept his face neutral. The young shavetail lieutenant had recently graduated from West Point and was pushing his weight around the post. "Not much, sir. Just an Indian. Apache." Gib could see the lean, black horse, its head hanging low with exhaustion, and its rider, who didn't appear to be in much better shape.

Carter stared at the Indian who was still a good distance away. "A scout?"

"Dunno, sir." McCoy disliked having to address Carter as "sir." The young blond-haired officer hated the Negroes who served under him. The only thing Carter liked was white men of rank—and any white woman. Gib found himself wishing he had his commission back. The Fourth deserved better leadership than this tall, gangling officer from Georgia who went around with a lace handkerchief stuck under his aristocratic nose because he couldn't stand the dust.

Carter glared at McCoy. Impudent bastard! He almost uttered the words, but hesitated. McCoy was a veteran of the West. His skin was deeply bronzed by years in the sun, his flesh tough and his body hard. The set of McCoy's square jaw did nothing but annoy Carter. An ex-officer who still thought and acted like an officer. Even the enlisted coloreds worshiped the ground McCoy walked on, preferring to go to the sergeant instead of him.

"I think you do know, Sergeant," Carter ground out, casting a furious look in McCoy's direction.

Gib's eyes narrowed. "No, sir, I don't."

"You've got eyes like an eagle. Surely you can tell who it is by now."

Clenching his teeth, McCoy watched the approaching horse and rider. "It isn't a scout. He's wearing Apache clothing, not our blue uniform."

Excited, Carter withdrew his revolver from its holster. "Maybe it's one of Geronimo's people."

Wanting to shake his head but deciding it wasn't a wise idea, Gib muttered, "Don't get trigger-happy, Lieutenant. That's one Indian. I don't see any weapons on him except a bow and arrow." Gib looked significantly at Carter's weapon. "I'd put it away, sir."

"When I want your two cents' worth, Sergeant, I'll ask for it."

Ladler glanced at McCoy, nervously fingering the rifle. "Sergeant?"

"Keep the rifle down," Gib intoned coldly, glaring at Carter. The officer was such a dandy. His features were delicate, his skin white as an Englishman's and easily sun-burned. The white lace handkerchief his wife, Claudia, had made for him made him look effeminate, and three months in Arizona had baked him red as a beet.

"What's going on?" Melissa cooed, stepping up to McCoy, giving him a flirting smile.

"Nothing, ma'am. Just an Indian coming in," he drawled. Now the worst busybody on the post was here along with Carter, who was acting as if he wanted to shoot the Indian.

Claudia rushed to her husband's side. "Oh, my, Dodd! Look out there! Why, it's our enemy."

Gib clenched his teeth again. "Not all Indians are our enemies, Mrs. Carter."

"If that buck's off a reservation," Carter said emphatically, "he's our enemy." He lifted his revolver and cocked it.

"Why, I do declare," Melissa said, remaining next to McCoy, "we're finally getting some excitement." She looked up at the sergeant through her lashes. The unforgiving line of his mouth excited her. What made this man's blood run hot? His face was glistening with sweat and there were deep lines at the corners of his eyes and mouth. His blue eyes were frigid and off-limits. Whatever the sergeant's true thoughts, he kept them to himself.

McCoy calculated all the possible scenarios that could happen. Ladler was nervous because he knew so little about the Indians. Carter wanted to kill one just to brag about it to his fellow officers. Claudia was a romantic wanting to see her husband kill one of the dreaded Apaches. And Melissa stood there looking like a bloodthirsty wolf ready to pounce on the Indian herself for the sheer excitement of seeing one killed.

As the rider drew close, Gib was the first to realize it was a woman on the mustang. In his seven years in the Southwest, he had met a number of Apache women, but never one who wore the third braid of a warrior. Swallowing hard, Gib wondered how in the hell he was going to handle the situation. He was the only one who knew that Apache women could be warriors right alongside their men.

Tensing, McCoy took a few steps forward, separating himself from the group as the rider approached. Private Ladler would obey him, but Carter wouldn't. He prayed that the officer, once he realized it was a woman, would put his weapon away.

Gib focused on the Apache woman. Her face was square, her features delicate, almost beautiful. She was Chiricahua, judging from her dress. She wore a faded red cotton headband that kept her long, waist-length black hair out of her face. A quiver of arrows was slung across her back. She wore a pale blue shirt and a leather belt around her small waist. A knife hung next to her long, curved thigh. Her dark green corduroy pants were faded and threadbare, and the distinctively tipped *kabun* boots fitted snugly to just below her knees.

As she came nearer, Gib recognized the shaft on the arrows as that belonging to Geronimo's people. His heartbeat quickened as he met and held her weary brown eyes. The woman was near starvation, her flesh sunken against the bone. She held her chin high and rode with her shoulders proudly thrown back, although he knew she must be light-headed and hungry. There was a magnificent dignity about her, and Gib took a few more steps away from the group, toward her. Whoever she was, she **was** courageous, riding alone out in this terrifying heat and waterless country in the midst of many who would murder her on sight.

Maybe it was the slenderness of her hands and fingers that made Gib relax. He sensed somehow that she wasn't going to try foolishly to kill him. His gaze moved to her lips, and he felt an immediate hardening within his body. There was a lushness to her mouth, coupled with a gentle upward curve at the corners. Despite the harshness that life had demanded of her, Gib knew there was a softer side to this woman.

He shook his head. What was she doing here? Was she an emissary from Geronimo? He kept his hands relaxed at his sides, not wanting to broadcast any movement that might make her think he was an enemy. In his seven years of working closely with the Apache people and scouts, he knew they read the silent body language of another with the sense of a wild animal.

"Oh, Lord!" shrieked Melissa hysterically. "It's a woman!"

Chapter Two

Kuchana jerked Wind to a halt when the *pindah* woman in the pink dress shrieked. Her eyes went wide as a yellow-headed officer rushed forward brandishing his revolver at her. She froze, her gaze seeking out the other man, the one with black hair and startling blue eyes. Her instincts told her this was a man of honor.

Gib cursed as he reached out and jerked Carter's arm down. "She's unarmed," he said at the officer, pulling him to a halt.

"Let go of me," Carter snarled.

"Not until you promise to put that gun away—sir."

Carter gestured at the woman. "She's Apache."

"And unarmed." Gib's fingers increased their pressure around Carter's wrist. "Put the gun away before you shoot yourself in the foot."

A dull red flush crawled across the lieutenant's taut features. Yanking out of McCoy's hold, he belligerently aimed the revolver at the woman.

"Who are you?" Carter demanded, his voice, high, off pitch.

Kuchana sucked in a breath of air, staring at the ugly muzzle of the revolver no more than fifty feet from where she sat astride her mare. Was Yellow Hair crazy?

"Come on. Tell me who you are and what you want," Carter repeated.

The English words all tumbled together, and although Kuchana had an excellent grasp of *pindah* language from her time spent on the reservation, she hesitated. The revolver was threatening. She raised her hands above her head, looking desperately to the other soldier, pleading silently with him to intervene on her behalf.

"I come as friend . . ." she stumbled in their language.

"Dammit, Lieutenant, put that gun away," McCoy roared. If Carter didn't holster that weapon, he was going to do it for him. Melissa giggled behind him, and Gib wanted to turn around and put the spoiled brat of a woman over his knee.

Kuchana watched the angry words between the two men. Her heart was pounding without respite. Light-headed with hunger, she forced herself to keep her hands held high.

With a glare at McCoy, Carter holstered the revolver and turned back to the Indian. "Just who the hell are you?"

"I come as friend . . ." Kuchana repeated, directing her attention at the dark-haired man.

Gib held up his hand in a show of peace and walked toward her. He switched easily from English to her language. "I'm Sergeant Gib McCoy. Tell me who you are and what you want before that fool over there shoots all of us."

A wry smile split Kuchana's features and she lowered her hands. He spoke her people's language. The fear she'd felt melted away beneath his husky tone. "I am Kuchana, of Geronimo's party. I have come to offer myself as a scout for the army." She couldn't tear her gaze from his probing eyes, and a trickle of heat stirred in her, reminding her that she was a woman.

"What are you saying?" Carter snapped, striding up to McCoy. "Dammit, you speak English so that I can understand."

McCoy struggled to compose his features. Carter was making a total ass of himself, but that was nothing new. He told the officer what Kuchana had said.

"She wants to be a scout?" Carter uttered in amazement, studying the Apache.

Gib kept his eyes on Kuchana. She was weak from hunger, if he was any judge of the situation. "She's a warrior, Lieutenant." But still a woman. An incredibly beautiful one with haunting brown eyes, which were warm and inviting.

"I didn't know the Apaches had women who were warriors," said Carter.

"There're a few." McCoy switched back to her language. "Kuchana, how many other women warriors ride with Geronimo?" Her name flowed from his lips like sweet honey. There was nothing masculine about her, not even her name. Again, he saw the wariness melt from her gaze as he held it. Something was happening between them.

"Three others."

"Why did you leave?"

Lowering her lashes, Kuchana whispered, "I left because I want to save what is left of our people." Despite the danger surrounding her, she couldn't help the response McCoy pulled from her each time he held her gaze. Each look was charged with a heat and excitement she had never experienced before.

"I see—"

"No," she said swiftly, her voice cracking with emotion, "you do not see. I once had ten members in my family. Now, only my sister is left. I watched her daughter die of starvation four days ago. Then I came here to help the army find Geronimo and take him back to San Carlos Reservation." Tears marred her vision as she saw the soldier's face melt with tenderness. He understood. "I—I must work for you. I must save what is left of my people. Please . . . help me . . ."

McCoy approached her horse, placing his hand on its mane. "Easy now. I'll do what I can. The army isn't used to having women as scouts. All we have are men."

"You must take me," she cried in desperation. "I am Geronimo's best tracker. You must believe me. I will find them for you. I must save my sister."

"I'll do what I can," he repeated, reaching out to touch her hand where it clenched the mustang's mane.

Kuchana felt his hand momentarily on hers. His flesh was roughened and weather-worn. Drowning in the look she saw in his blue eyes, she nodded her head. "I will trust you." It was more than that, but so much was happening, she didn't have time to dwell on her awakening feelings.

"Good. Now, come on, get off the horse." Gib forced a slight smile and stood back, watching her slip off the mustang. There was an effortless grace to her that underscored her femininity. Kuchana was weak, but she forced herself to stand straight and tall. There was pride in her carriage and in the golden blaze of her eyes as she fearlessly surveyed the group who stood openmouthed before her.

Gib gestured toward the tall, two-story adobe building that housed headquarters. "This way."

Kuchana hesitated, placing a hand on her weary mare. "My horse..."

"Private Ladler," Gib ordered, "take her horse over to the stable. Get one of the men to curry it down and give it a little hay and a bit of water, nothing more. Understand?"

Ladler picked up the jaw cord. "Yes, suh, sergeant."

Kuchana looked closely at the dark-skinned soldier, then turned to McCoy. "This man's skin is the color of the night. I have never seen such as him before."

Nodding, Gib offered, "His people come from across a great sea." He pointed toward the east.

Ladler hesitated, realizing Gib was speaking about him. His mouth split into a smile. "She's wondering about my color, suh?"

McCoy smiled over at Ladler. "I told her you came from across the ocean."

"That's right, suh. My grandparents came from Africa." He shouldered his rifle and tipped his hat respectfully toward Kuchana.

Unsure of what was being said, Kuchana made a slight bow toward Ladler. He appeared friendly enough, and that was all she cared about.

"You're letting her come into the post?" Melissa demanded, stamping her foot haughtily. How dared they treat her like a white woman. After all, she was an Apache, and therefore, their enemy.

McCoy shot Melissa a hooded look. "She's surrendering to us, Mrs. Polk. What would you have us do? Shoot her on the spot?"

Heat nettled Melissa's cheeks. In that moment, she hated McCoy. He was laughing at her again. "Well, she's wearing men's pants, of all things." She turned to the lieutenant, who had more authority than McCoy. "Surely, Dodd, you aren't going to let this filthy woman on the post?"

Kuchana stood apart from the group, carefully listening to the conversation. She noticed McCoy watching her from beneath the brim of his hat. Looking down at herself, she realized her clothes were dusty from the four-day ride. But every morning she had brushed her hair and kept it neatly tied with the scarf around her head. Nightly, she had cut open cactus and used the juice to wash her face, neck, arms and hands, so that she was free of dirt and odor.

Gib watched the play of emotions cross Kuchana's features. She had more dignity than all of them put together, standing there with her feet slightly apart for balance, shoulders back and chin lifted. Her lips were badly chapped and split. She weaved, but caught herself. Anger stirred in him as Dodd continued speaking at length with Melissa.

"Lieutenant, while you discuss army regulations with the ladies, I'll get this woman some water."

Gib reached out, wrapping his fingers around Kuchana's arm and gently pulling her forward. "Come on," he coaxed, "you look thirsty." Her flesh was firm beneath the shirt, but still soft and inviting.

Kuchana stared up at him. She saw the hard line of his mouth soften, and she surrendered to the tumult of feelings he had loosened by simply touching her. Grateful, she went with him. The *pindah* women gawked at her, disbelief and disgust clearly written in their eyes.

When he had escorted her through the gate, McCoy's hand dropped from her arm. A part of her lamented the loss of contact. Wearily, she looked around. The post was huge, with rows of two-story barracks and nearly two hundred sun-bleached canvas tents. Kuchana was astounded by the number of blue-coated soldiers, as McCoy led her to a watering trough in front of headquarters.

Gib reached for a tin cup that was always kept on the trough. He filled it with water, then handed it to Kuchana. Her hands shook as she took the cup. Frowning, he studied her as she drank. Thin trickles of water escaped from the corners of her mouth, winding their way down her long, slender neck and soaking into the fabric of her shirt. An ache seized him, and he wondered how she would respond if he stroked her lovely neck, trailing his fingers down its length and tracing her collarbones hidden beneath the shirt she wore. The thought was jolting, completely unexpected. Gib placed a tight clamp on his fevered imaginings. What the hell was happening to him?

"Take it easy," he cautioned. "A little goes a long way." When he saw her frown, he added, "You'll throw it up if you drink too much too fast."

"I understand. Thank you, Sergeant." For the first time, Kuchana had a chance to study the soldier. His raven hair was short and neatly cut. The dark blue hat he wore emphasized the intensity of his azure eyes. They were wide, intelligent eyes filled with wisdom. That was good. His nose appeared to have been broken more than once, and a thin, almost invisible white scar cut across one of his high-boned cheeks. His mouth was strong. When McCoy glanced up at her, one corner of his mouth curved upward, easing the rugged planes of his face.

"Call me Gib." He took the cup from her fingers, placing it back on the trough.

"You speak our language."

"I've been out here for seven years. Most of my duties have been with the Apache scouts. They taught me."

"I'm glad," Kuchana admitted in a lowered tone. She turned, steeling herself against the dizziness.

"How long have you been riding?"

"Four days."

"Have you had any food?"

Kuchana shook her head. "No, I left what little I had."

"How about sleep?" He knew most Apaches feared the night and would never ride, thinking that Owl Man would grab them.

"I slept each night."

She was just this side of starvation, Gib realized. His protective side was working overtime. He tried to figure out why. At the reservation near Fort Apache, he had many dealings with Apache women. But this woman was different. He was curious about what kind of woman rode to war alongside the men.

He noticed a number of small scars on her fingers and a faint scar that ran the length of her neck. He wondered how she'd gotten it. He liked the idea of a woman being able to take care of herself. He always had. His French-and-Indian mother had owned her own millinery shop in New Orleans before marrying his father.

"Thank you for saving my life," Kuchana said. "Yellow Hair would have killed me if you hadn't been there."

Gib said in English, "Yellow Hair is Lieutenant Carter. And he can't hit the broad side of a barn, much less you." He saw Carter and the two women hurrying toward them. "Whatever happens, just stay at my side and don't say anything. Understand?"

She gave him a confused look. "You are more Apache than *pindah*."

McCoy's smile broadened. "Don't let our lieutenant hear you say that. I'm already a pariah here at the post."

Not knowing what "pariah" meant, Kuchana stood patiently. Carter strode up, his face flushed.

"Sergeant, strip her of her weapons. I want her taken in to see Colonel Polk for interrogation. Pronto."

"Don't you think," Gib said, trying his best to sound reasonable, "that we ought to get her something to eat and some rest first? She's half-starved."

Melissa picked up her pale pink silk skirt and gingerly climbed the wooden steps, sweeping past them and into the building. She spotted Corporal Ryan McClusky sitting at his desk outside her husband's office. Lifting her chin at a saucy angle, she sailed by him and went directly into Harvey's office. Of course, she wasn't supposed to, but when necessary, army etiquette was something to be bent to her will.

"Harvey, darling," Melissa cooed, closing the door to the inner office. She smiled beguilingly over at her white-haired husband who sat behind the ponderous oak desk scattered with papers.

"Mellie. What a surprise." Harvey beamed and put the papers aside. "What brings you here, pet?"

"Darling," she began in a conspiratorial tone, rushing to his desk, "you won't believe what just happened. There's an Apache woman warrior from Geronimo's party outside. She says she wants to be a scout." Melissa wrinkled her nose. "She's wearing men's clothing. Why, she even has boots on. And stink. Lord save us all, but she smells to high heaven. I think it's a trap. I think she's lying." Besides, Melissa didn't like the way McCoy had treated the savage. She wanted McCoy to show interest in *her,* not in some heathen.

Scowling, Polk rose ponderously from behind his desk. "Mellie, what on earth did you just say? A woman warrior from Geronimo's party?" His hopes rose. If he could capture Geronimo, he was sure that General Crook would give him an assignment back East, thereby salvaging what was left of his thirty-year military career.

"Oh, fluff," Melissa muttered, fanning herself. The heat in the room was nearly intolerable. The wooden-frame building had one small window, and Harvey had it closed, probably to keep out the sand and the dust. "You didn't hear what I just said. This...this woman, if you can call her that, is wearing men's clothing. She's carrying a knife, and a bow and arrow. Really, Harvey, she's disgusting. I really don't believe she's a woman warrior. This may be a ruse. If it is, Sergeant McCoy has stupidly fallen for it. He's outside with her right now."

Moving as quickly as his bulk would allow, Harvey came around the desk. "Pet, there are women warriors among the Apaches. I'm sure I've mentioned that to you from time to time." He headed toward the door.

"But," Melissa wailed plaintively, "aren't you going to make her stay down at the scout camp?"

Harvey turned, his hand on the brass doorknob. "My dear, you really ought not be here. This is army business. And I understand your disgust for this woman. They're all savages in my opinion, too. Come, come." He held out his hand toward her.

Pouting, Melissa moved slowly toward her husband. "What are you going to do, Harvey?"

"Well," he said, raising his thick, white eyebrows, "if she was indeed with Geronimo, we'll interrogate her on his whereabouts."

"And then?"

Shrugging, he opened the door. "If she wants to be a scout and help hunt Geronimo down, I don't care."

"But, a woman in an all-male camp of scouts?"

"Tut, tut, pet. I know all this is a shock to your gentle sensibilities. These savages live differently than we do. If this redskin can lead us to Geronimo, I don't care if she's a woman dressed in men's clothing or not." He smiled and led her into the outer office. McClusky leaped to attention, straight and tall.

Melissa rested her gloved hand on her husband's arm and he led her out onto the porch.

"Lieutenant Carter, what's going on?" Polk demanded, sizing up the Apache woman as he spoke.

Sputtering, Carter told his commanding officer the series of events.

Kuchana stared up at the large, overweight man in the dark blue uniform trimmed with gold and rows of brass buttons. His hair was thick and white. A mustache partially hid his thin lips. His silver sideburns drooped, following the line of his jaw, making his face look fat and round. When the colonel came forward, she tensed.

Harvey peered into the woman's face. Typical of all savages, she displayed no emotion except wariness. Looking her up and down, he muttered, "How can you be sure she's from Geronimo's party?" His question was directed to McCoy who had the most experience with the Apaches.

"The shaft on the arrows she carries, sir." Gib brought one out for the officer to examine. Polk was a lazy bastard at best, he knew, shunning his duties as commanding officer except when necessary. Most of his work fell to the majors and captains below him. McCoy doubted if Polk knew one tribe's shaft from another, but he said nothing.

"Hmph. Interesting." Polk handed back the arrow to McCoy, his gaze settling again on Kuchana.

Bristling at his inspection, her lips tightened. She vividly recalled similar inspections by soldiers at the San Carlos Reservation.

Straightening, Polk turned and headed for his office. "Get her in here, Lieutenant Carter. I want to question her at length."

"Sir," McCoy said, "I think she needs to eat and rest first. She hasn't had food for four days."

Carter turned angrily on McCoy. "That's enough, Sergeant. She looks perfectly fine to me. Now, get her in here."

Polk smiled at his wife. "I'll take care of this, Mellie. Why don't you and Claudia visit Ellen? I understand she's faint from this heat again. I'm sure she'd like to see you."

Dismissed, Melissa stood there, glaring at Kuchana. She hated the woman. And McCoy's protectiveness toward her nettled her even more. How dared he. "Come, Claudia," she demanded, "I can't stand the stench around here. My poor nose is about ready to fall off."

McCoy gave the two white women a look that spoke volumes. In the army, the men were required to take a bath every third day. Clothes were washed once a week by the many laundresses. Everyone smelled at the post. Except for the officer's wives, who went daily to Draper's Pool, a secluded pond with a stream located two miles from the post at the end of a box canyon. They were the only ones with time for such a luxury.

Kuchana hesitantly followed McCoy into the large adobe building. Her eyes rounded as she studied the interior. Thirty rifles hung on one wall. Geronimo stood no chance against so many guns. Once in Polk's office, she was forced to stand in front of the desk while the colonel sat down.

Polk looked at McCoy. "Sergeant, I understand she knows some English, but for the sake of speed, I want you to interpret."

Gib stood next to the Indian woman, refusing to sit down. "Yes, sir."

Kuchana noted the tightening of McCoy's face. She wished mightily that the *pindahs* wouldn't speak so quickly. If they slowed their speech, she'd be able to understand what they said. Dizziness assailed her. She planted her booted feet apart so as not to appear weak in front of them and waited for her inquisitors to begin their questioning.

Gib's patience thinned. For the past two hours Polk and Carter had relentlessly questioned Kuchana. Polk seemed oblivious to the fact she was weak with hunger. If the fat bastard had gone one day without food, he'd be baying like a coyote. Their treatment of Kuchana was unconscionable.

Risking another blistering tirade from Carter, Gib came to attention. "Colonel Polk, I request this session end. The woman is obviously tired and in a weakened condition. I'd like permission to take her to the cook's tent, feed her, and then find her quarters over at the scout area."

Carter glared at the sergeant. "We're not done interrogating her. After all, these Apaches are tough as nails."

Polk chuckled in agreement. "I've never seen such endurance."

Kuchana closed her eyes as another wave of dizziness nearly overwhelmed her. She was dying of thirst and wanted to sit down. McCoy's hand settled on her arm. She quickly opened her eyes and realized she was swaying. Heat flooded her face and she looked away from the concern in the sergeant's eyes.

Gib glared at Polk. "You'll get more out of her on a full stomach than an empty one, sir." He hated putting it in that context, but Polk's regard of Apaches as little more than animals was well-known.

"Very well," Polk muttered. "Get her out of here, Sergeant."

Carter leaped to his feet. "You're in charge of her, McCoy. If she escapes, you're responsible."

Gib nodded. "Yes, sir." Carter would like to see him drummed out of the army for allowing one of Geronimo's warriors to escape. Turning his attention to Kuchana, Carter released her, telling her to follow McCoy.

Relief fled through Kuchana once they were away from the building and walking across the arid parade ground. The sun was hot overhead, but it felt good. She noticed a number of tents to the left with women inside them scrubbing clothes on corrugated tin washboards.

"What's that?"

"Our laundry facilities," he explained.

"The dark ones are there, too."

He smiled. "They're called Negroes, Kuchana."

"And these women come from across the great sea, too?"

"Yes." And then Gib amended his statement. "They were brought here as slaves. Twenty years ago, they were set free and allowed to pursue whatever they wanted, just like white people."

Kuchana noticed a large black woman in a yellow calico dress and a thinner, younger one in a dark green dress who were openly staring at her. Their stares weren't like those of the *pindah* women, however. There was only curiosity in their eyes.

"They are different from the *pindahs*."

"They're good people," said Gib. "The older one's husband is a lance-corporal here at the post. I'm sure you'll be meeting all of them sooner or later."

"Then, I am to be a scout?"

He nodded, watching her eyes widen with happiness. "That's what Colonel Polk said. I'm in charge of the scouts, so you'll be working directly with me, not Carter." *Thank God.* Gib saw her flush, and he realized that whatever he felt toward Kuchana, it was mutual.

Kuchana wanted to give a cry of triumph, but resisted the urge. Instead, she sent prayers of thanks to Painted Woman. "I will be a good scout. I will not shame you."

"I'm not worried," Gib said. He pointed to a large tent that had been bleached white by the burning sun. Its flaps were open at both ends to catch what little air moved sluggishly across the post. Inside were two big black kettles bubbling with beans, and a table filled with hardtack. "This is the enlisted men's chow tent. Why don't you go and sit down under that cottonwood and let me get you something to eat?" Gib pointed to one of the few trees that managed to survive on the post.

Not needing another invitation, Kuchana gladly headed toward the shade of the tree. She noticed the two men in the tent watching her. One, a big man with a black mustache and brown eyes, sent a shiver of warning up her spine.

"Who's that, Sergeant?" Private Odie Faulkner asked, with a leer at Kuchana.

Scowling, Gib took a tin plate from the stack on the table. "Our newest scout," he growled. Gib took the ladle and dished up the food from the kettle. Beans, moldy bacon and weevil-infested hardtack was the usual fare for a soldier or scout.

"That there's a woman, ain't it?" Odie asked, licking his full lower lip.

"That's right. One of Geronimo's warriors."

"I'll be go to hell," Odie murmured. "I heard about them women warriors, but never saw one. She looks starvin'. That why she crawled into our post?"

Adding three hardtack biscuits, McCoy kept his anger at Faulkner in check. "She didn't come here because she was starving. She came to offer her services as a scout."

"Right purty," Odie noted, craning his thick neck out the side of the tent, watching her.

"Mind your own business, Private."

Faulkner's bushy black brows drew up in surprise over his heavy German features. "Yes, sir."

Kuchana watched McCoy saunter in her direction. He was dressed like most of the other soldiers: a pair of yellow suspenders holding up his dark blue trousers, and a dark blue shirt that was damp with sweat, clinging to his upper body. There was much to admire about McCoy. Everything about his demeanor claimed him to be a warrior. There was an economy to his movements, and he carried himself proudly. There was no doubt that he was a leader of men.

Her attention shifted to the food he handed her. Eagerly, Kuchana took the plate, amazed at how much was on it. In seconds, she was using her fingers, eating ravenously.

Gib crouched in front of her. "Take it easy," he cautioned. Kuchana was wolfing down the food. Dammit, he shouldn't have filled the plate so full. "Why don't you eat the biscuits first," he suggested, trying to get her to slow down. "Your stomach isn't used to this kind of food...."

His husky warning came too late. Kuchana had eaten half the food when her stomach violently rebelled. With a cry, she leapt to her feet and turned away. Within seconds, everything she had eaten had been thrown up. Sweat covered her features as she knelt on the ground, her arms pressed against her stomach. Kuchana stayed that way, her head bowed with embarrassment and shame.

"Dammit," Gib whispered, moving quickly to her side, "I should've known better." Instinctively, he reached down, placing his hands on Kuchana's shoulders. She was trembling badly. "Come on, let's get you over to the tree." He pulled Kuchana to her feet. Her face was flushed and she could barely walk. Anger at Polk's and Carter's insensitivity to her physical condition raged through him.

Gently, he settled her back against the trunk of the tree. "Stay here," he ordered quietly, his hand remaining on her slumped shoulder.

Feeling dizzy and weak, Kuchana nodded. Just the touch of his hand on her shoulder stabilized her whirling world. She shut her eyes, feeling as if she would die.

Gib came back with a cup of tepid water. He knelt and placed his arm around her shoulders. "Here, take a swallow and then spit it out," he ordered.

Kuchana opened her eyes, sipping the water from the cup he pressed to her lower lip. Following his instructions, she rinsed her mouth.

"Good," Gib praised, setting the water aside. He picked up a biscuit from the plate and broke off a small portion of it. "Now, chew on this, and do it slowly."

Her eyes never left his harsh features. McCoy had a face like the rugged mountains in Sonora, yet he was treating her as a mother would a sick child. Gratefully, she took the proffered piece of biscuit.

Despite her condition, Kuchana was a proud and independent warrior. Gib knew that to coddle her too much

would make her look weak in the eyes of others. He removed his arm and sat back on his boot heels.

"Good," he rasped unsteadily, watching her chew the
biscuit thoroughly before swallowing it. He offered her the
cup. "Now a little swallow of water."

Kuchana managed a grimace, then sipped the water and
put it aside. McCoy handed her another bit of biscuit.

"How's your stomach feeling now?" he asked.

Placing her hand on it, she said, "Better."

"Any rolling feeling?"

She shook her head.

"Just take your time," Gib soothed. "A bite of biscuit
and a sip of water. You've been without food a lot longer
than four days, haven't you?"

Kuchana avoided his piercing look. "Warriors must give
their food to their families," she said.

Relaxing, Gib placed his arms on his knees. "Looks like
you've had more giveaways than most," he teased gently.
Indians believed in giving away all that they owned, especially food, to those who were poor or incapable of hunting
for themselves. He saw the corners of her mouth turn up in
the barest hint of a smile. Kuchana had a magical effect on
him.

"The Old Ones and the children will not starve," Kuchana said stubbornly. Her stomach was settling down, and
the biscuit tasted good. "How do you know so much about
my people?" she asked McCoy.

"I made a point of learning about them when I was assigned to Fort Apache," Gib answered.

"Many *pindahs* know nothing of us."

His mouth twitched. "I don't have any prejudice against
your people, Kuchana."

Her name rolled off his tongue like a reverent prayer.
Kuchana could feel the power of the emotions behind his
words. She searched his face. "What is 'prejudice'?"

"It's when one person hates another because he might
believe or look differently than himself."

"*Pindahs* have prejudice against us because we are different?"

"Yes."

She tilted her head, watching a group of Negro soldiers marching off in the distance. She held up her hand, gesturing toward the soldiers. "The dark ones are also different. Do *pindahs* have prejudice against them, too?"

Pushing the hat back on his head, Gib mulled over his answer. "There are many *pindahs* who don't like any other color except their own."

"You are not like them."

Gib shook his head. "Color means nothing to me. How a man or woman treats others is what's important."

"You are like an Apache!" she said excitedly. Touching her breast, Kuchana regarded him somberly. "You are a man who talks from his heart. That is good."

"I try to, Kuchana." Gib grimaced, his gaze restless. As a sergeant, his duties and responsibilities were many. There was a decided prejudice against the Negro enlisted soldiers. In the month he'd been at the fort, he'd realized that he was the only buffer between them and the white officers. The Civil War might be over, but the Negro was far from free. He felt it wise to keep his eyes and ears open, be alert at all times.

Aware that the sergeant surveyed the post, Kuchana remained silent, continuing to eat the biscuit. The strain of the past few hours was catching up with her. Her eyelids were becoming heavy, and she sighed, placing the rest of the biscuit back on the plate.

McCoy noticed the weariness in her eyes. "Tired?"

"Yes."

"Feel like standing?"

Kuchana tested her legs carefully, finding new strength in them. Gib remained at a distance, allowing her to stand on her own. "Where do we go now?"

"The scout area," Gib said. "I'll show you where you're going to live." Silently, he wondered how she was going to fit in with the other Indians who worked for the army. Many tribes didn't get along with one another. Even among the various Apache segments, some tribes were friendlier than others. The Chiricahua, Kuchana's tribe, had few friends.

Chapter Three

The scout section sat behind the rows of laundry tents where the women washed the clothes and bedding for the entire post. Kuchana surveyed the bone-colored canvas tents that stood, with flaps open, in neat, orderly lines. Huge tin tubs filled with hot, soapy water sat on wooden tables. The dark-skinned women who toiled laboriously over their duties had sweaty faces and their dresses clung to them from the heat. These women reminded her of the diligent Apache women, who worked nonstop for their families.

Turning her gaze in another direction, Kuchana saw several Indian men crouched in a circle, speaking in low guttural tones. The hackles on the back of her neck raised as Chee, a huge Apache of Tonto ancestry, stood up at her approach.

Chee was dressed in a blue army jacket and dark brown twill pants along with his *kabun* boots. He was the chief scout, and judging from his deepening scowl, McCoy knew there were going to be fireworks. The other four scouts, wearing cotton shirts, army trousers and black leather boots, stood also. Their faces were wary, inspecting Kuchana behind a wall of formidable silence as she and Gib came to a halt. Chee stared down at the woman for a long moment. "You are Geronimo's warrior," he spat.

Girding herself, Kuchana stared at him defiantly. "I am Chiricahua. My name is Kuchana."

Chee stuck out his chest and thumped it with his fist. "I am in charge. You Chiricahua think you are superior. Well, you are not. I am Tonto."

Gib grimaced inwardly. There was little that could be done to settle the friction between the Tonto tribe and the Chiricahua. That was one reason the Apache hadn't been able to push the whites out of Arizona; they'd fought too much among themselves and not presented a united front. Even here Gib was seeing evidence of the same hostility. And if he had any doubts about Kuchana's bravery, now that she stood in front of the huge, huffing Indian, they disappeared.

Kuchana thumped her breast, thrusting out her chin in Chee's direction. "You may be chief scout, but I'm Chiricahua, and we are better trackers."

McCoy watched as Two Toes moved forward. The Yavapai's face was lean in comparison to the fuller Apache face. He saw Kuchana's anger turn to hatred as she noticed the scout's approach.

"Yavapai," she hissed. Glaring at Chee, she demanded, "How can you work with our enemy? This tribe sneaks onto our reservation and into our wickiups at night, killing our women and children with clubs."

Chee's massive features, lined with forty years of life, worked into a sneer. "We all work for the army against Geronimo. Yavapai are now our friends."

Kuchana was the only Chiricahua present. The other scouts were also of Tonto heritage. With a sinking feeling, Kuchana realized that even as a scout, she was going to be an outcast. Although members of Chiricahua and Tonto were brothers, they did not get along. Often, there were blood feuds between the tribes.

Gib cleared his throat. "Chee, it's up to you to make sure she is trained properly to take over scouting duties when called upon."

Chee nodded, assuming an air of importance. "She is a scout, Sergeant. I'll give her a tent and tell her the rules."

"Good. Tomorrow morning, I'll be back over here and issue her a kit and weapons."

Kuchana moved uneasily. She had no choice but to trust Chee. All her weapons had been taken earlier, but no warrior, even without weapons, was defenseless. She had courage and strength born of the knowledge that she would survive where others had died.

Gib glanced at her. "If Chee can't help you, or answer a question, you come and see me over at the barracks. Understand?"

She nodded, moistening her lips, looking in the direction he pointed. The two-story barracks stood in rows several hundred feet from the scout area.

Pointing to the building closest to the scout area, Gib added, "I have a small office in there. The scouts are free to come and go to the laundry, chow tent, or to the enlisted barracks, but that's all. Don't be caught unescorted up by headquarters or on the parade ground."

"I will stay here," Kuchana said, pointing to the ground.

"Get some rest. I'll come for you tomorrow morning and we'll fill out the rest of your billet."

Kuchana gave him a small smile of appreciation and whispered, "A-co-'d." The word meant 'thank you.' And it wasn't often that an Apache spoke it. Gib's face changed and softened for a moment.

"You're welcome," he acknowledged.

Without any further word, he turned and left. Kuchana's pleasant features wavered in his mind's eye as he crossed the parade ground, dodging a troop of cavalry coming back in from an assignment. She stirred his senses and feelings as no other woman ever had. He wondered if Polk would allow her to continue as a scout, or send her back to the reservation. If she was going to stay, Kuchana was going to have to prove herself to everyone, and quickly.

Lieutenant Carter hated anyone who wasn't white or an officer. He didn't care one whit if a scout was killed in the line of duty. Too often, while on assignment, the scouts were

fired upon by civilians who thought they were Geronimo's
people. Carter wasn't cautious enough about protecting the
scouts in that kind of situation. Gib was damned if Kuchana
was going to be gunned down by a jumpy silver miner just
because Carter chose to ignore certain directives that would
keep her safe. He'd have to remain vigilant.

Wiping the sweat off his upper lip with the back of his
hand, Gib climbed the wooden stairs. All his life, he'd protected the underdog. That's what had gotten him in trouble
in Fort Apache. With a sigh, he took off his hat and entered headquarters.

Kuchana presented some potentially damaging problems
to his own floundering career. The last time he'd placed
himself in jeopardy for a woman he'd lost his officer's
commission. Many felt he should have left with his tail between his legs, but he hadn't. In his heart, he knew what he
had done had been right. Instead of retiring, he'd forced the
army to give him sergeant's stripes and retain his services for
the duration of his twenty-year enlistment.

Stopping at Corporal McClusky's desk, Gib picked up
several sets of orders that would involve his scouts on future
expeditions. Once a month, Polk set out riding assignments for the Fourth, and McCoy was responsible for as-
signing scouts to the Negro columns.

As he perused the orders, his mind dwelled on Kuchana.
He wondered if she was going to get along with the other
scouts. With a mental shrug, Gib swung his focus back to his
duties. He couldn't afford to keep thinking about Kuchana.
But whether he wanted to admit it or not, his heart was still
lingering on her sweet, soft smile.

The sky was crimson with the rising of the sun. Gib settled the hat on his head and gingerly touched the spot on his
chin where he'd cut himself with the razor this morning.
Swinging off the barracks steps, he headed for the scout
area. The mountains to the north were dark, rugged shapes
carved with deep ravines. Juniper and piñon clung to the

lower reaches of the slopes like a scraggly green skirt above the sandy-yellow reaches of the desert floor.

Sentries on horseback rode slowly around the huge rectangular area that comprised the buildings and grounds of the fort. As he passed the bustling laundry facilities, he saw Poppy and waved.

"Sergeant McCoy, come over here!" she called out in her booming voice.

Gib smiled and changed direction. As he approached she wrung out a shirt and handed it to her daughter, Nettie, to rinse.

"Why, you look fit as a fiddle this morning, Sergeant McCoy."

Tipping his hat, Gib halted at the front of the huge tent, now open to the breeze. "Thanks, Poppy. Looks like you're hard at work." Most of the laundresses washed from dawn until noon, and then pressed and folded the clothes throughout the hottest part of the day.

Poppy's hair was wrapped in a bright blue turban, and sweat streaked her face. "Word's flying around here that the army hired a *woman* Apache scout."

Nettie looked up from her tub. The girl's hair hung in two neat pigtails and she was rail-thin compared to her mother. "I saw her, Sergeant McCoy, yesterday when I took some clothes back to the enlisted barracks." Her eyes grew merry. "She's a purty thing, ain't she? I never knew Apaches to have gold-colored eyes."

"Some do," Gib said.

"Lordy me," Poppy gushed, "what's this gonna do to the post? Why, I heard from Clarissa, that Miz Melissa is livid about this woman being here. Is that so?"

Gib kept his face neutral. The laundresses were a gossipy bunch. Anytime he wanted to know what was really going on at the post, he came to Poppy. He wasn't surprised Melissa Polk was throwing a fit over Kuchana's presence. Melissa was jealous, that was all; Kuchana was a hell of a lot prettier than the snobbish banker's daughter.

"Ladies, you know I don't have much to do with the officers or their wives. I'm afraid you're asking the wrong person."

Poppy pushed her lips together, eyeing him with laughter in her eyes. "You're a wolf among sheep, Sergeant McCoy." She made a jab with one thick finger toward the officer's quarters in the distance. "And they all know it, too. You might be wearing sergeant's stripes, but the men of the Fourth trust you."

That was part of the problem, Gib thought. He hadn't let color dissuade him from becoming a protective buffer between the men of the Fourth and the likes of Lieutenant Carter. "Poppy, have you got a couple of cups of coffee hidden somewhere in that tent of yours?" She always had some forbidden officers' supplies stashed away.

She grinned, placing her hands on her ample hips. "Two cups, Sergeant? Usually, you only want one. By any chance, you heading for the scout tents?"

Gib rubbed his jaw. "Can't fool you, can I, Poppy?" The laundress didn't miss much, but then, Poppy could be trusted with knowing things like this and keeping it secret.

Cackling, Poppy asked Nettie to fetch the coffee. "Ain't like you to take the scouts coffee. They know they can come here and get it from me."

"The second cup is for Kuchana," he said, trying hard not to smile.

"I thought so."

"Mind if I bring her over here and introduce her to you ladies later? I think she could use some friends."

Nettie handed Gib the tin cups filled with steaming coffee and clapped her palms together. "Oh, would you? Why, Clarissa is just dying to get a look at her."

"Ladies, she needs some friends, not curiosity seekers." Gib held Poppy's knowing gaze. "Kuchana isn't liked by the scouts because she's Chiricahua. And I know the officers' wives will snub her."

"Just stop your worrying, Sergeant McCoy. You send that purty little thing over here and we'll take good care of her." Poppy beamed. "She's scrawny..."

Gib nodded grimly. "Yeah, she hasn't had enough to eat for a long time."

"Well, you just never mind, Poppy will fix her up. I'll take care of that poor chile. She'll be a part of our family, just like you are, Sergeant McCoy."

"Thanks, it means a lot to me."

The laundress grinned. "I know it does. I can see she's something special to you."

Gib nodded and turned away, heading for the scout area. The scouts on duty that day were usually up by this time, working on their weapons. Today, it was Two Toes and Jemez who had the duty.

Chee had assigned the last tent nearest the horse line to Kuchana. Gib came to a halt at the head of the tent where the flap had been drawn aside and saw that Kuchana was still soundly asleep, clutching a fist-size rock.

It bothered him that she felt she had to have some kind of weapon to protect herself even here, but he couldn't blame her. The Yavapai hated the Apache and had a reputation for slitting the throats of their enemy under the cover of darkness.

As he crouched down, Gib eyed Kuchana's sleeping features. Her flesh wasn't as taut, and there was some color in her cheeks. Her thick, black hair, no longer bound by the cotton headband, lay about her shoulders like a blanket. She reminded him of a finely bred horse—lean, proud and delicate. Her lips were parted in sleep, and he wondered what it would be like to kiss her, to explore the texture of her mouth beneath his.

Chee had issued her only one blanket, and he frowned, knowing she should have been given at least three. Kuchana had placed the blanket on the ground and curled up in a fetal position to remain warm during the cool night. Today, he would make sure she was issued a full billet.

He was about to awaken Kuchana when he saw tears bead and form on her lashes. Putting the mugs aside, he reached down and gave her shoulder a shake.

Kuchana hissed, jerking upright, rock poised in hand. Her eyes widened when she realized it was McCoy. "I—I'm sorry," she rasped, her voice thick with sleep. She dropped the rock. Tears trailed down her cheeks and she tried to wipe them away before the sergeant saw them.

"Hold on," he ordered quietly. "What's the reason for the tears?"

Embarrassed, Kuchana kept her eyes on the ground between them. "It was a dream."

Gib took one of the cups and handed it to her. "Here's some chicory coffee. Go on, take it." The high color in her cheeks told him that she was shamed by her tears. Gib picked up the second cup and sipped the liquid, remaining in his crouched position.

Chicory coffee was a rare treat for Kuchana. She managed a nod of thanks, holding the cup with both hands. Why hadn't she heard the sergeant approach? Had her sleep been so profound that Two Toes could have sneaked into her tent and killed her? Usually, her sleep was light and watchful.

"Looks like you were sleeping hard," Gib said conversationally. He had an urge to reach out and tunnel his fingers through her shining ebony hair.

"Too hard," she muttered unhappily, drinking the coffee with relish.

"You were tired." Tired from months of running, he thought. The army and the Mexican *soldatos* had been pursuing Geronimo and his people without rest for nearly six months. And Kuchana was proof of that.

"It is no excuse. I should not sleep like that. It could get me killed." In the distance Kuchana heard the soft snort of horses, the clank of bits, the creak of saddles. A number of soldiers were up and about performing their daily duties. Chee and one of the other scouts came up to the horse line, saddling their mounts. There wasn't much to like about Chee, Kuchana had decided. He was a swaggering, bragging male, more wind than courage, in her estimation. Chee was not a warrior. In fact, none of the scouts wore the third braid.

The tears were drying on her cheeks, and Gib searched for a way to find out more about their cause. "You said there wasn't much of your family left since Geronimo escaped the reservation."

A pain stabbed deeply into her heart at his words, and Kuchana bowed her head. "I have only one sister left." The words came out low and strained.

"Was that what you were dreaming about?"

The question was gently put, and Kuchana lifted her chin, holding his gaze. McCoy had harsh features, but he was truly sensitive to others' feelings. "I...it was of her daughter that I dreamed."

"Oh?"

"Her daughter went to the Big Sleep just before I left."

"And that's the reason you came here?"

"Yes. There was not enough food..." She sniffed, taking her sleeve and wiping the tears off her face. Kuchana prayed that none of the other scouts saw her behaving like this. Looking at McCoy, she wondered at the tenderness she saw burning in the depths of his blue eyes. His look gave her a sense of safety she had never known. With a wry grimace, she muttered, "You pull my feelings out of me, Sergeant. I am not used to a man doing this."

"I'm sorry the child died, Kuchana." He held her wavering gaze. "As for drawing feelings out of you, all I can say is that's good, as far as I'm concerned. I want to know how my scouts feel." When he saw her nod, he added, "When we're alone like this, call me Gib. I don't like a lot of formality."

The compassion in his voice told her much. "Does your name mean something?"

He smiled and shook his head. "I'm afraid not. My mother named me after my grandfather and great-grandfather."

Just talking with Gib eased the pain and anxiety she carried for her people. The warmth of his husky voice was balm to her grieving heart. "Tell me your family name."

"Gibson Justin McCoy."

"You carry the spirit of your family with you?"

"Yes, I guess I do." He paused. "Kuchana has something to do with water."

She felt heat flood her cheeks and she lowered her lashes. The warmth Gib established with her was profound and new. He made her heart open like a blossom in the spring. "It means 'woman of the waters.'"

"Then you must feel things strongly and deeply, like water."

With a little laugh, Kuchana said, "Too deep."

She was beautiful when she laughed. Her eyes, dark brown with gold flecks in their depths, sparkled. And her mouth... Gib took a deep, steadying breath. When her lips curved upward, she reminded him of a sunrise.

"I don't think it's wrong to feel things deeply," he countered thickly.

The burning light in his eyes made Kuchana vividly aware of herself as a woman. Just the way Gib looked at her, she felt special—and beautiful.

"Well," he said, straightening, "you're a woman of the waters. I think it's a good thing. Feelings are not a sign of weakness."

She shook her head. How odd, a man who approved of feelings.

"We've got plenty of things to do this morning," Gib began. "Why don't you get something to eat over at the chow tent and then meet me at the stables? I'm having your mare shod and then we'll find a saddle that fits her."

"I'll see you at the stables," Kuchana agreed.

Wind had already been shod with her first set of shoes by the time Kuchana made her way to the massive stabling area. There were buildings housing dried hay and grain for the hundreds of horses that milled in the huge corrals at the rear of the buildings. She found Gib with a red-haired giant of a man who had a worn leather apron draped around his thick middle.

"This is Kuchana," McCoy told the farrier, Kelly McManus.

McManus thrust his big meaty hand in her direction. "Right nice to meet you."

Kuchana hesitantly placed her hand in the farrier's, unfamiliar with the greeting. She'd seen *pindahs* do this before on the reservation. McManus had dancing green eyes, a red mustache that drooped like twisted ropes down the sides of his mouth. As she reclaimed her hand, his smile made her relax.

"Your mare is over there," the farrier said, pointing down the aisle of the open building where at least twenty horses were tethered.

The black mare wore a halter, and the rope was tied to an iron ring that hung from a stout wall. She pricked up her ears as Kuchana thanked the farrier and walked down the well-swept aisle.

Gib escorted her down the center of the building, walking at her shoulder. On either side were roomy box stalls, and other rooms at the rear that held tack and barrels of grain. He noticed that Kuchana had washed and neatly combed her hair. The faint scent of soap lingered around her. Memory of Melissa's cutting remarks yesterday that Kuchana smelled came back to him. It was obvious she had tried her best to look neat and clean under the circumstances. The clothes she wore were threadbare and would have to be replaced. It crossed his mind that he would like to give her a pretty dress to wear, instead. He laughed at himself. It was the first time in his life he'd ever wanted to give a woman gifts. Kuchana invited that kind of response.

"Has your horse ever worn a saddle?"

"Yes, I had a cottonwood saddle for many years until the *culo-gordos* attacked our camp and I had to leave it behind."

Wind nickered as Kuchana walked up to her. She patted the mare fondly as she inspected the new iron shoes on her hooves.

McCoy took a blue wool blanket edged with yellow and threw it across the mare's back. "From now on, you've got to ride with army gear." He pulled a black, bull-hide-covered McClellan saddle off the rack and settled it on the animal's back. In no time, he showed Kuchana how to cinch the double girth. Next came the military-issue bridle. Wind wasn't very happy about having a metal bit in her mouth, but she accepted it with grace after attempting to chew on it.

Kuchana stood back, amazed at all the items that McCoy had piled in front of the pommel and behind the cantle of the saddle. There were canteens, pouches for ammunition, a blanket, and containers to carry food and even grain for Wind.

"When you're assigned to ride with a column, you'll come over here and saddle the mare up just like this." He saw the stunned expression in Kuchana's eyes. "Something wrong?"

"No." She stepped up to Wind, placing her hand on the mare's neck. "There is so much."

"When a column goes out, we usually patrol for five to ten days at a time." Gib gestured to the saddle that had been created for endurance riding. "We have a saying in the army. We ride forty miles a day on beans and hay. The pack mules carry the hay and most of the food, but sometimes, on a forced march, we have to rely on what we can carry on our saddle."

"*Pindah* horses can never keep up with our horses," Kuchana noted proudly. She pointed to a bay gelding tied next to Wind. "Look at him. He is grain fed. I have seen many army horses unable to stand the heat or the distance."

"You're right. I told the officers here they shouldn't feed our animals grain." He grinned, giving the mare a pat on the shoulder. "We ought to train our horses to eat cactus like you do yours."

"Wind will not die on a march. She knows to eat cactus for food and also water in order to stay alive."

"The Apache know how to survive," Gib agreed with a smile. "Come on, let's go over to Supply. We'll be coming back to do some hunting, so leave Wind saddled."

Kuchana's eyes shone with excitement as she walked with Gib toward another large two-story adobe building. "We hunt four-leggeds?"

"Yep. I figure the only way to get Chee and the colonel to believe in you is to prove your worth as a tracker. Lieutenant Carter ordered Chee to send someone out to the mountains over there—" he pointed to the north "—and kill some deer or bighorn for the officers' families."

"I will prove myself worthy."

Gib saw the challenging fire in her eyes. "Well, whatever we kill, some of it is going to be dropped off to Poppy so she can distribute it among the laundry families."

"Who is Poppy?"

"One of the women who washes clothes."

"A dark-skinned one?"

Gib smiled "Yes."

As they climbed the steps of Supply, Gib noticed the soldiers giving Kuchana discreet looks. He led her inside the building where clothing, weapons and tack were kept. Sergeant Mulrooney, head of Supply, nodded a good-morning to them.

"Kuchana needs a scout's issue, Sergeant," Gib told the gray-haired man.

"Right away, Gib."

Kuchana turned around, looking at the columns of boxes stacked around the room. There were huge piles of green wool blankets, canteens, saddles and row upon row of rifles.

McCoy was sure that she'd never seen so many new things. Her face glowed with excitement when Mulrooney led her to the clothing section.

A blue wool uniform jacket was finally found to fit her slender build. When she gently ran her fingers reverently over the brass buttons, Gib found himself wondering what her touch would feel like on his skin. The unexpected thought was inviting.

Mulrooney gave her a set of blue kersey pants to replace the thin ones she wore. When he tried to give her a set of black boots, she adamantly refused them, saying that her hardy *kabun* boots were better. The distinctive curled toes on the boots were good for picking up and moving poisonous snakes or Gila monsters out of her path with ease and safety. The black boots had a rounded toe and were, in her opinion, worthless.

Gib watched Mulrooney's reaction to Kuchana. The old supply sergeant couldn't seem to do enough for her. Crossing his arms on his chest, Gib leaned against a rough beam and watched them with pleasure. He was sure it was Kuchana's winsome smile and her bubbling gasps of delight that spurred Mulrooney to hunt for just the right items.

When Mulrooney brought out five brightly colored cotton shirts, Kuchana gasped. Her fingers moved lovingly across the shirts. The supply sergeant blushed fiercely when he gave them to her.

"These are all mine, Sergeant?" she whispered in disbelief, holding them in her arms as if they were a babe.

"Why, sure, Kuchana. Every scout gets five of 'em. Don't look like I just gave ya the world, girl. Go on, take 'em!" he ordered gruffly with a wave of his hand.

Gib suppressed a smile as Mulrooney colored even more deeply when Kuchana gave him a smile.

"A-co-'d," Kuchana whispered, hugging the beautiful shirts to her breast.

"Ahh, don't get sentimental on me, girl." Mulrooney slanted a glance at McCoy. "Git her outa here before she cries."

Smiling, Gib nodded and, picking up the rest of Kuchana's issue, walked to the door. She came to his side, marveling at the cotton shirts.

"Come on, let's get this gear back to your tent," he told her.

Chapter Four

Melissa was just coming out of her quarters in the officers' building when she spotted Sergeant McCoy and Kuchana. This morning Clarissa had fashioned her blond hair in a cascade of curls that grazed her shoulders. With her straw bonnet decorated with brightly colored ribbons and her apple-green dress, she knew that she presented a comely picture. She'd brushed her bangs, making sure they were in place across her wing-shaped brows.

A beautiful woman was a rarity at any post, and Melissa reveled in the wishful and admiring glances the hard-bitten army men gave her. Why hadn't the sergeant looked at her that way, too? He acted as if she didn't exist, and that made her angry. Her gaze followed McCoy. If her eyes didn't deceive her, he looked almost happy. And he was carrying most of the Apache's issue for her. Envy of Kuchana rippled through her. Tapping her fan furiously in her opened palm, Melissa fixed a smile on her face as they approached.

"I declare, Sergeant, you look more like a pack animal than a man beneath that load."

McCoy halted. Normally, he'd have tipped his hat to the wife of any man, but both arms were full. "Good morning, Mrs. Polk."

Melissa hated the impervious look he gave her. The Indian woman halted at his side, gawking up at her like a child, obviously enthralled with the dress she wore. "Why, Kuchana—that is your name, isn't it?"

Kuchana nodded. "Yes, it is."

McCoy scowled, sensing the coldness behind Melissa's smile. "Mrs. Polk, as you can see, we're loaded down. I've got—"

"Nonsense, Sergeant." She smiled warmly at Kuchana and stepped off the wooden porch. With her fan, she tapped the variety of cotton shirts Kuchana held in her arms. "My, my, what do we have here?"

Eagerly holding up the shirts for inspection, Kuchana said, "Look, the army has given me the colors of the rainbow."

Wrinkling her nose, Melissa leaned over. "Why, I believe they have, Kuchana." She giggled. "A rainbow of colors. First time I've ever heard that expression applied to army issue."

Gib gritted his teeth. Kuchana was too trusting of others. Honesty and truth were the Apache way of life. Greed, envy and jealousy were not tolerated, because they threatened the existence of the tribe as a unit. Kuchana had no experience identifying or dealing with Melissa's type of woman. She needed to be protected. She was being led to slaughter. "Mrs. Polk—" he began.

Melissa glared at him. "Sergeant, why don't you just toddle on over to your favorite place, the scouting area? You seem to enjoy the savages much more than your own kind. I insist upon talking with Kuchana."

Holding on to very real anger, Gib studied the officer's wife. "I'm sure you're aware that if Kuchana is caught in a restricted area without the regulation escort, she can be punished."

"Oh, my!" Melissa shrugged delicately. "Of course, you're right, Sergeant. Well, just a few more minutes, then. You look brawny enough to carry that load. You're such a gentleman, after all." She swung her attention back to Kuchana, hating McCoy for his accurate appraisal of the situation. If he had left, Melissa would have made sure Kuchana was placed on report for being in the officers' area unescorted. Harvey didn't stand still for such infractions by coloreds or savages. Damn McCoy, anyway!

"So, you like colors?" Melissa asked the Indian sweetly.

Kuchana nodded, not understanding the tension between McCoy and the *pindah*. "You also wear rainbow-colored clothes."

Melissa tilted her head and gestured to the frock she wore. "I just knew that beneath that Apache skin of yours, there was a woman. I'm delighted to know you like dresses. But I'd use these rags to dry off my horse after a long run."

The insult was lost on Kuchana, but Gib tensed. "Mrs. Polk, I've never seen you rub down a horse after you've run it into the ground. Matter of fact, I don't believe I've ever seen you around the stabling area. Josh always brings your mount to your front door." Melissa was known to ride hell-bent-for-leather, purposely losing her army escort to gallop freely off the post whenever she pleased. The only problem with that was that someday, if she wasn't careful, she could get killed or captured by marauding Indians or *comancheros*. All that, however, was lost on Melissa, who viewed the world as one dramatic and exciting event after another.

Fire flashed in Melissa's eyes. "That will be all, Sergeant." She smiled coldly at him, noting the tight, angry lines in his sweaty features. "Or are you planning on running off with this helpless female, too?" She whipped the fan outward, hiding her lower face, batting her lashes, and moved with slow, measured steps toward headquarters.

"That brat," Gib whispered under his breath after she was out of earshot. He turned to assess the damage Melissa had done to Kuchana. Her face was free of any anger or upset. Instead, he saw confusion in the depths of her eyes.

"Come on," Gib ordered tightly.

Kuchana had long legs and was able to keep up with his striding pace. Frowning, she asked, "What does she mean, running off?"

"I'll tell you on the trail, Kuchana. Right now, all I want to do is get away from this post." Specifically, away from the scheming Melissa Polk. Why Melissa had him earmarked as a target for her cutting tongue was beyond him. She flirted outrageously with him whenever she got the chance. Gib knew his actions at Fort Apache had been carried here along with his transfer. He didn't dare openly challenge Melissa, because she'd run to that spineless husband of hers and complain. And then he could be brought up on charges again. Women were definitely a problem in his life.

The mountains above the valley were sitting silent, waiting for the sun to rise over their peaks. Once she was in the rolling hills above the fort, Kuchana trotted her mare abreast of McCoy's bay gelding. Gib had a rope in his gloved hand and two brown mules in tow behind his horse. If he and Kuchana made a kill, the mules would carry it back.

As Holos's first rays tipped the mountains, Kuchana nudged Wind closer to Gib's mount, not wanting her voice to carry and frighten off any wild animals in the vicinity. "You said you would speak of running off."

"I did, didn't I?" Kuchana rode as if born to the animal. Apaches, however, were equally at ease on foot, covering up to thirty or forty miles a day. Sometimes, when being pursued by the army, they would run their horses until they died, and then continue on foot, handily outdistancing the cavalry.

He cleared his throat, his gaze scanning the juniper and piñon coming into view as they climbed higher out of the desert.

"Juliet Harper is the wife of the commander of Fort Apache," he began. "Her husband, Colonel Phillip Harper, drinks too much alcohol." When he saw that Kuchana didn't understand the term, he used the term "firewater," instead.

Kuchana wrinkled her nose. "I saw what firewater did to our people when we were on the reservation. Men go *heyoke,* crazy."

"Yes, and that's what Harper did. Almost every day," Gib added grimly.

"And Juliet was upset?" She knew how irritated the wives of the warriors became after their men stumbled around drunk and incoherent for days on end.

"It was worse than that, Kuchana. Harper would drink at night in his home, and then he'd beat his wife."

Her eyes widened. "Beat her?"

"Yes."

She frowned. "A warrior does not hurt women and children. They are bound by the laws of Usen to protect them."

"I wish we had such laws, but we don't," Gib muttered. "Juliet was taking a beating almost every night. One time, she ran from her home and I happened to be out checking sentry posts. I heard someone sobbing and found her hiding in a dark corner with her hands covering her head. I held her until she quieted. That was when I found out about the beatings and Harper's drinking problem. Anyway, after that, Juliet would confide in me. I was the only one on the post who knew that she was slowly being beaten to death."

"If you knew, didn't you challenge Harper?"

"Kuchana, it's different in the army than in your world. I was a lieutenant, and Harvey was a colonel. If I tried to interfere, he'd have crucified me." Gib laughed derisively. "A month later, Juliet came to me, begging me to help her run away. She wanted an escort to the stage line thirty miles away. She planned on running away from her husband and going back East to her parents." He lifted his hat, wiping the sweat on his brow with the back of his sleeve, then settled it back on his head. "It would have ruined Harper's career, but Juliet was desperate."

"To see a woman hurt by a man must have bothered you greatly," said Kuchana. "You're not the kind of warrior to stand aside and allow it to happen."

"You're right, I couldn't."

"You helped this woman?"

"I finally agreed to escort her to the stage. We worked out the plan, and one night, a week later, we made our escape. Halfway to the stage, Harvey intercepted us with a troop of cavalry. Apparently he'd overheard Juliet talking with one of the other officers' wives. That woman turned Juliet in to her husband. He knew all along of Juliet's plan of escape."

Her eyes rounded. Gib was grim. "You're a man of bravery."

"In *pindah* society, you're not rewarded for trying to help in a situation like that. I got hauled up on charges and busted from officer to enlisted status." Gib managed a thin smile. The wind played with strands of Kuchana's ebony hair, lifting and settling them back on her shoulder. Her red cotton shirt brought out the smooth planes of her high cheekbones.

"They punished you? How could they?" Kuchana's indignation was impassioned. "What you did was good and right."

"Not in the army's eyes. Things are different between *pindahs* and your people, Kuchana."

"You are more like an Apache than a *pindah*."

Laughing, Gib placed his hand on her shoulder. "Maybe I am." Her eyes widened at his gesture and he cursed himself. What the hell had gotten into him? Withdrawing his hand, he tried to break the bond of warmth that existed between them. No woman had reached inside him as she had. It was disconcerting. "Up there," he said gruffly, pointing to the top of a hill, "is where the deer and bighorn have a trail. There's a watering hole down on the other side where we can put your tracking skills to use."

Kuchana nodded. She saw that Gib was embarrassed by his gesture. Trying to ease his discomfort, she asked, "Why does Melissa dislike you?"

Kuchana hadn't missed a thing. Gib wasn't really surprised. "Some *pindah* women," he said, "think they are better than other people, Kuchana."

"She wears very beautiful dresses." Kuchana sighed and then smiled.

A grin edged Gib's mouth. "Yes, she does. But be careful of her—her friendship is not sincere."

Shrugging, Kuchana began to look for animal trails at the crest of the hill. "She wasn't unkind to me." The area was dotted with small, scraggly piñon, which were good food for her people, when they could get to them. In the month of Many Leaves, the sticky green cones were filled with delicious nuts. "She liked the shirts the army gave me," she added with a smile.

Halting his horse, Gib watched her study the ground. Her mouth became pursed, her eyes hooded. "Look, Melissa wasn't being complimentary about your shirts," he warned.

Looking in his direction, Kuchana said, "She was smiling."

Uncomfortable, Gib chose not to pursue the topic. Kuchana was naive to the wiles of women like Melissa. "Well," he muttered, "just try and stay as far away from her as you can." He knew from experience that the backbiting that went on among white females did not exist within the Apache community. And if it did occur, the guilty woman was pressured to resume a more humble demeanor in order to get along with the other people of the tribe.

Kuchana had no idea how wicked Melissa could be. Gib realized that the colonel's wife was going to continue to snub and insult her. He didn't care if she went after him, but Kuchana was innocent. As Gib studied the fresh tracks on the ground, he realized that Juliet Harper had been innocent, too. *Damn.* Kuchana was too trusting. She had no reason not to be. *Pindah* women hadn't made war on her, the men had.

"Come," Kuchana said, moving Wind down the ridge line, "I see bighorn tracks." She flashed him a triumphant look. "They are nearby. Four of them. I think young bucks."

Rousing himself from his worry, McCoy nodded. "You lead the way, and I'll bring the mules."

Dodd Carter's day got worse when he saw the female scout and Sergeant McCoy return late in the afternoon with the mules laden with bighorn kills. He stood on the porch of headquarters, hands on his hips, watching as they slowly rode by in the direction of the chow tents.

He fumed and raised his arm. "Halt, Sergeant." Stepping off the porch, he hurried out and intercepted them. Dodd was sure that McCoy had shot all the bighorn with a rifle. This female savage was worthless. No woman could track, much less scout.

"How many?" Carter demanded.

"Four bighorn, sir." Gib saw the displeasure in Carter's red face. The officer glared up at Kuchana.

"Who killed them?"

Gib settled in a comfortable slouch on the saddle. "Kuchana not only tracked the herd, but killed two with arrows. I got the other two with my rifle."

Scowling, Carter muttered, "Impossible," and walked up to the mules.

Sure enough, there were arrows in two of the bighorn. Angrily, Carter strode back, noting that Kuchana seemed unconcerned about his fury. She was just like the rest of those savages: no emotion registered on her face. As he rounded the horses, he saw laughter in McCoy's eyes, although the man's face was like granite.

"Get this meat over to the officers' mess, Sergeant," he snapped, spinning on his heel and making his way back to headquarters.

Gib clucked to his horse, chuckling to himself. Word of Kuchana's ability would spread quickly through the post, and that was good. He aimed his horse between the city of tents. The laundresses looked up, smiling and greeting him.

Their eyes widened with envy when they saw the fresh meat on the mules. Only the officers got such food.

Kuchana followed Gib as he led them from the officers' area toward the enlisted men's chow tent. Stopping behind the largest tent, Gib ordered two of the cooks to untie the largest bighorn from the mules. Eagerly, the men took the carcass into the tent. Then Gib continued toward the officers' mess.

Kuchana waited patiently as the other three bucks were delivered. They were heading back to the stabling area before she spoke.

"You said only officers got the meat. Why did you give a buck to the dark-skinned ones?"

"Just between you and me, Kuchana, I've always sneaked some of the fresh kills I've made to the Negro families. They don't get any fresh meat otherwise."

Her brows arched. "A giveaway." That she understood. Giveaways were always a sign of generosity on the part of those who had much to those who had little. "I will give away every time I make kills."

He threw her a warning glance. "Don't get caught doing it, Kuchana. You'd lose your scout status and have to go back to the reservation. Understand?"

Frowning, Kuchana pulled her mare to a halt in front of the stable. It was a busy place in midafternoon. A large group of horses waited to be shod by Kelly McManus. The huge farrier worked beneath an open shed, his anvil ringing with the sound of the striking hammer clenched in his massive fist.

"Then why do you do it if you will get in trouble?" she asked, dismounting.

Gib got off his own horse and strode around to face Kuchana. She stood there, hands on her hips. "I do it," he said, "because those people deserve better food than what they're given. They aren't animals. They're human beings."

Kuchana admired him for taking such a risk. "I will do the same." When she saw Gib's darkening expression, she added, "I will not get caught."

That worried him. "The enlisted people will never tell on you, but if an officer or one of their wives catches you, you'll be in more trouble than you ever thought possible."

Her smile was wry. "No one is as clever as an Apache, Gib. No one."

The challenging fire in her eyes made him ache. There was such courage in her tall, proud body. "I know that better than most. Let's unsaddle our horses, rub them down, and get back to work. Colonel Polk wants you to study the maps we have in headquarters so we can track Geronimo down."

Kuchana's triumph over the bighorn kills ebbed. For a few hours, she'd forgotten about Geronimo and the plight of her people. She went about unsaddling Wind, feeling the pain of separation from those she loved.

"What's wrong?" Gib prompted. He had seen darkness cloud her eyes at the mention of Geronimo's name.

With a sigh, Kuchana rested her hands on Wind's back and looked at Gib. "My heart is breaking," she admitted softly.

"You've a right to feel that way," Gib said. "Leaving your tribe to become a scout wasn't easy for you."

His understanding made tears rush to Kuchana's eyes. She forced back the reaction, managing a shrug. "I—yes, I miss them."

"One of these days, you'll be reunited," Gib told her, wishing he could comfort her. The tears in Kuchana's eyes tore at him.

"No," she whispered, "that will never be."

"Sure it will. Geronimo can't keep running forever. There're just too many people after him."

"You do not understand," Kuchana said, pausing to gather her emotions. "Before I left, Geronimo pronounced me dead." Her voice cracked. "I no longer exist to them— not even to my sister, Ealae."

"What?" Gib stared at her suffering features. Kuchana couldn't be more than eighteen, her skin was so flawless and unlined. Yet, he knew her life had been a harsh one. To be an outcast was worse than being killed. Without thinking, Gib gripped her arm and gently pulled her around to face him.

Tears beaded her thick lashes. "Look at me," he whispered thickly. When she bowed her head, he placed a finger beneath her chin, forcing her to look up at him. As her lashes lifted, he saw for the first time the full extent of the terrible pain she carried.

"I can never go back," she murmured. "I am dead. No one will ever speak to me again, Gib. I am a ghost..." A sob caught in her throat, and with a little cry, she turned away from him burying her face in her hands.

Gib stood there helplessly. He didn't dare touch Kuchana again or take her into his arms to comfort her as he wanted to. Searching, he tried to find words that would heal her, but it was impossible. "I didn't realize any of this." Kuchana would never fit into white society, either. Once Geronimo surrendered, he'd be sent back to the reservation. And most probably, so would Kuchana. Her own people would ignore her. That would gradually kill her. Gib had seen it happen before.

"You've paid a hell of a price to come here."

Kuchana turned toward him. She longed to lean against Gib, instinctively realizing that she would find solace in his arms. The fierce blue fire in his eyes told her he understood. "I believe in what I did, Gib. I have watched my family dying for the past two years. I have only one sister left. What else could I do? Geronimo has filled the heads of my people with impossible dreams." With a trembling hand, she touched her brow. "I had no choice but to offer myself to the army. Geronimo must be brought in to save those who blindly follow him."

Studying Kuchana in the silence that followed, Gib held her softened gaze. She was incredibly vulnerable in ways that most women would never be. The desire to slide his fingers across her smooth cheeks, frame her face and kiss away the pain he saw there was unbearable. "Such courage," he whispered, managing an unsteady smile. "You've got more than any ten men I know."

Kuchana took a ragged breath. "I do not see myself as courageous. I see only my people slowly dying of starvation."

The urge to comfort Kuchana was overwhelming. If Gib didn't move to break the spell between them, he'd do something he'd regret. She confronted too much adversity to be humiliated by him in front of all these men. Knowing the truth of her decision to become a scout only served to make him that much more protective of her.

"Somehow, things will work out for you," he told her. "I don't know how yet, but I've got a feeling they will." When he saw her rally, he smiled. "Come on, let's get to work. First things first. Let's go study those maps. Afterward, I need to go over to Laundry and pick up my clothes."

Never had a woman held his heart as gently in her hands as Kuchana. Gib wrestled with his feelings toward her. He'd been in love before, but never had such an intense or all-consuming emotion taken him so completely. He studied her closely. Love? *Impossible.* Forcing himself to shove his discovery aside until later, when he could think straight, Gib headed toward headquarters with Kuchana at his side.

Grateful for his unspoken support, she looked up at him. "I want to see your maps. Geronimo must be caught soon."

"Look, she's coming!" Nettie squealed, up to her skinny elbows in hot water and suds. She stood just outside one of the many laundry tents, washing clothes. "Mama!"

"I'm coming," Poppy grunted, bent over a pot in the tent. One of the cooks had just made a delivery of fresh bighorn meat to the rear of their tent. Poppy had thanked the soldier and promptly dropped the meat into a large black kettle with onions and beans. She rubbed her hands together and straightened.

"Mama!" Nettie's high, excited voice warbled again.

Wiping her hands on a worn towel, Poppy trundled forward. She saw Sergeant McCoy and Kuchana walking her way. Beaming, she stepped outside and into their path.

Kuchana had never seen such a huge woman in all her life. There was warmth in the woman's big brown eyes and an even warmer smile on her thick lips. She heard Gib chuckle.

"Poppy, you look like a sly fox."

"Sergeant McCoy, I just wanted to thank you."

Gib glanced at Kuchana who was politely trying not to stare at the Negro woman. "Better thank Kuchana, then. That was her kill we dropped off."

Picking up her blue calico skirts, Poppy barreled toward the Apache woman. She grinned broadly and gripped Kuchana's hand. "My name is Poppy, chile. We just got the meat and wanted to thank you."

Kuchana was overwhelmed by Poppy's gushing warmth. She stared down at the woman's ebony skin, amazed at how pink her palms were in comparison. "The food is for all," she said. Poppy's callused palms dwarfed her own slender hands.

"And we'll use it, chile." Poppy released her hands and grinned at her. "You're a purty thing. Isn't she, Sergeant McCoy?"

"Yes she is," he agreed.

Poppy saw a dull red color creep into Kuchana's cheeks. "The girl's blushing."

Gib grinned. "She's not used to such personal remarks from strangers, Poppy. Her people are very reserved in comparison to us."

Nettie leaned forward then, gingerly touching Kuchana's outstretched hand.

"And I thought Apaches were tough as nails," Nettie said.

"They're people just like us," Gib said with a chuckle.

"They've got heart," Poppy corrected her daughter, relinquishing Kuchana's hand. "They ain't got thick skin, Nettie." A rumbling laugh erupted from her. "I know some officers that are thick-headed as mules, though."

Gib laughed as he watched the rapport between the three women grow. He saw the glow in Kuchana's features and her eyes sparkling with new life. Poppy's motherly nature was making her feel at ease for the first time.

"Nettie, fetch Sergeant McCoy's pressed clothes. And Kuchana, you come with me, chile." She grabbed her hand again and led her into the tent.

Poppy opened one of the large, battered leather trunks. "Now, you just stand there, chile. I've got something for you."

Kuchana strained to look over Poppy's shoulder—difficult, for the woman was as large as a mountain. And Poppy's friendliness was genuine. She came from the heart.

Poppy threw several pieces of clothing to one side, digging deeper in the trunk. "Now, I know I've got them here. Unless Nettie gave them away to the children..."

Kuchana saw Gib saunter to the front of the tent. Nettie came rushing back from another tent, his pressed and folded clothes in her arms. Gib took them and thanked her. He dug out some coins from his pocket and gave them to her.

"Sergeant McCoy, you always pay us too much."

"Keep it, Nettie." Ten cents was a lot of money. It could buy a pound of food, and Gib knew that Poppy would put it to good use. The woman was forever feeding the scouts and the other enlisted men who couldn't afford to buy enough food for themselves. Malnutrition was a real problem within the cavalry. Poppy was always making deals with men who hawked fresh food at the post. She kept it on hand in her large trunks to dole out to the men.

"I found it!" Poppy crowed. She brandished a stick of candy she'd pulled from the trunk. Turning, she gave it to Kuchana. "Here, chile, you suck on this. I bet you never had peppermint before.'' Her eyes danced as she watched Kuchana stare at the candy. "Go on, now, eat it."

Sniffing it cautiously, Kuchana noted it smelled wonderful. Poppy stood there, grinning, as Kuchana put the stick in her mouth. It was pleasantly minty and sweet. Surprised, Kuchana took it out of her mouth and studied it more closely.

"It is sweet, but it is not honey."

Chuckling, Poppy clapped her on the back. "Chile, you just come around once a day, and Poppy here will fatten you up."

Kuchana needed some care, Gib thought. And he couldn't give it to her without being accused of favoritism. Poppy gave him a knowing look, and Gib breathed a sigh of relief. Kuchana might not have a place among the Apaches or the white world, but if he was any judge of the situation, Poppy had just adopted her as part of her own family.

Chapter Five

❦

"Sergeant, I want you to go pick up the food supplies from Jacobsen's Mine," Carter ordered, triumph blazing in his eyes. During the two weeks since that woman savage arrived, Dodd had been giving her every detail he could think of. Although she had brought in fresh meat twice, he still didn't believe she could track. McCoy must have brought down the game and lied for her, he was certain. He saw the disgust in the sergeant's eyes at his command.

"And take Kuchana with you. You'll need help with that string of mules to and from the mine. Go get a voucher over at Supply to pay for it."

What was Carter trying to do? Get Kuchana shot? Gib had watched a pattern develop the past couple of weeks. Carter was trying to get Kuchana in trouble. If Gib hadn't been as alert as he was with his enlisted men, Carter might have gotten his way. Kuchana was rapidly learning about army and post life, but her naïveté could be her downfall.

Holding on to his temper, Gib drilled the officer with a scathing look. "Sir, it isn't wise to send a scout up to Jacobsen's. Those miners are constantly getting raided by Apaches. If I take Kuchana along, there could be real trouble."

Carter shrugged. The day was just beginning and the sun was already sending hot streamers across the arid land.

"Sergeant, just do as you're ordered. Pick up the ten mules and get up to Jacobsen's."

"Sir, those miners hate Apaches."

"I don't care," he said irritably.

"You've never ordered one of our scouts along on this supply trip before. Why now?" Sweat was forming on McCoy's upper lip. He longed to wipe it away with the back of his hand. Carter stiffened, his eyes blazing with anger.

"Sergeant, are you questioning my orders?" he snarled.

"Sir," McCoy said evenly, "I'm not questioning your orders, just your choice of who should go with me. Normally, one of the cooks goes along to help pick up the officers' supplies."

Setting his mouth, Dodd glared up at the tall sergeant. He hated McCoy. The Negroes jumped to carry out the sergeant's orders. While, when he gave orders, the men were sullen and slow about obeying them. "You may have been considered a brilliant Indian campaigner at Fort Apache, Sergeant, and you may have more medals than I'll ever get, but you're not an officer any longer. What you think isn't important. It's my responsibility to give orders." He punched McCoy in the chest. "It's your job to carry them out. Or do you want to be drawn up on charges of disobeying a direct order?"

The urge to reach out and pin Carter against the headquarters building was very strong. West Point had swelled Carter's already arrogant head. Worse, McCoy realized, was that Carter had been in the Southwest less than a year and didn't have a flea's intelligence about Indians. Nor did he care.

"For the record," McCoy ground out, "I protest Kuchana being chosen to go along. She's an Apache, and the miners aren't going to like her presence in their camp."

With a wave of his hand, Carter turned away. "Go file your protest, Sergeant. Those miners know we have scouts. Nothing's going to happen." He turned on his heel, stalking off toward the stabling area.

With a curse, Gib stood there, mulling over the options. Kuchana was going to be in danger. Over the years, the miners had killed a lot of Apaches. They were trigger-happy and liked to collect black-haired Indian scalps for the twenty-five dollars apiece they got from scalpers. Turning, McCoy went into the office to file his protest. If anything did happen, he'd at least be able to protect Kuchana and himself from any further charges by Carter. The snot-nosed officer was out to get him, and was using Kuchana as a lever to do it.

Kuchana was visiting Poppy's tent when Gib located her. The laundress and her daughter were hard at work, scrubbing clothes on the corrugated tin washerboards set in tubs filled with hot, soapy water. He hid his worry and anxiety over the forthcoming trip to the mine as he approached. Kuchana was helping out by hanging clothes on a line.

"Morning, Sergeant McCoy," Poppy greeted, her features shiny with perspiration. She wore a bright red scarf around her head, and a voluminous red dress. The sleeves were folded up to her elbows but the material was soaked, anyway.

Gib tipped his hat. "Morning, Poppy. I see you have Kuchana hard at work."

"No-o-o, Sergeant McCoy. Why, I told that chile she didn't have to help us, but she got it in her head to do just that."

Kuchana smiled and waved to Gib. Hanging the last two items of clothes on the line, she brought the woven basket over to the laundress and set it down.

Every time Kuchana smiled, an ache shot through Gib. The past two weeks had wrought a miracle of sorts in her. With Poppy's feeding her three times a day and making her feel at home, Kuchana had blossomed from a silent, suspicious woman into one with a ready smile.

And every night, he dreamed of her in his arms. Gib tried to tell himself it was infatuation, not love, that he was feeling for Kuchana. It was agony to be with her and not reach out and make contact with her. This urge to touch her was a hunger he was barely able to control. Kuchana was in his blood and he was helpless to do anything about it.

Gib nodded in her direction. "We've got orders to get up to Jacobsen's," he told Kuchana.

Poppy gasped. "You aren't going to take this chile up there! Why, that's plumb stupid, Sergeant McCoy."

Kuchana frowned at the alarm in Poppy's voice. "Who is Jacobsen?"

Uncomfortable, and wishing he could express his anger and concern just as the laundress had, Gib explained, "It's a mining community about five miles from here. Lieutenant Carter usually sends the cooks up with the mules to get supplies for the officers and their wives once a month." Trying to hide his worry, he added, "Carter has ordered us to do it this time."

"Oh, Sergeant McCoy," Poppy pleaded, "you know that's foolish. Kuchana's Apache. Oh, Lordy, something awful could happen."

"It won't," Gib answered tightly. He could see Kuchana becoming upset over Poppy's dramatic display. Taking Kuchana by the arm, he gently pulled her to his side. "Come on, we've got a long day ahead of us. I'm sure Lieutenant Carter expects us to be back in time for the officers to get fresh food for dinner tonight."

Poppy gave him a helpless look. "You be careful," she warned.

Kuchana remained at Gib's side. The time spent with him had been rare. If she saw him once a day, that was a lot. To be able to spend a day in his company answered her prayers. She looked at Poppy's distraught features.

"Painted Woman will protect us, Poppy."

"Somebody better," Nettie wailed. She wrung her hands, giving Gib an anxious look.

"We'll see you late this afternoon," he promised the ladies. Kuchana's gold eyes shone with happiness. He'd wanted time alone with her, but not like this. Not under these circumstances. "Come on, Kuchana, let's get our horses saddled."

In no time, the pack-mule train was assembled. Kuchana sat on Wind, watching as McCoy checked the long string of harnessed brown mules carrying a huge canvas sheet on their strong backs. Each mule's halter rope was tied to the next mule's tail.

Holos was barely above the horizon, and excitement thrummed through Kuchana. A whole day with Gib. True, he'd be at the head of the mule train and she'd be bringing up the rear, but that didn't matter.

They left the post, working their way slowly up and out of the valley. The breeze was warm and the only sour note to the day was that Gib had insisted that Kuchana wear the heavy wool army jacket to identify her as a scout. The blue jacket was cumbersome. Gib had never made her wear it before, although the other scouts proudly walked around wearing their jackets all day long.

Kuchana felt happiness sing through her as she watched Gib up ahead of her. Ealae had once confided in her that love made her feel like a cloud—light and happy. That was how she felt toward Gib. She'd had no experience with the wonderful feelings that lived within her heart since meeting him.

Frowning, Kuchana wondered if it was the love Ealae had spoken of. Her vow to bring her people to safety must override such a personal need. And yet, every time Gib looked at her, she felt like warm honey. Confused, she refused to hide her feelings from herself. Perhaps she was wrong. In time, this beautiful emotion toward Gib would dim. Perhaps...

Jacobsen's Mine was a thriving mining community comprising fifty silver mines in the rugged mountains north of the fort. Gib went on internal guard as the city of gray tents and spindly wooden shacks came into view. Bearded miners with floppy, sweat-stained hats and small gray donkeys moved in tow up and down the main street.

Kuchana's joy over the beauty of the mountains and being with Gib disappeared. She watched his back become ramrod straight, his hand resting across the flap of the pistol holster at his side. As she brought up the rear of the mule train, she saw her presence in the mining community ripple like wind across the water.

Several miners halted, gawking at her as the mule train swung down the street. She saw surprise and then hatred in their accusing eyes.

Gib looked over his shoulder and saw Kuchana's face become expressionless. A number of miners had stopped to stare at her. Damn! Turning, he kicked his horse into a trot, forcing the train to amble along a little more quickly. The butcher shop was at the other end of the town.

There was a long hitching rail at the butcher shop. Gib dismounted, giving orders to Kuchana to start tying the mules to it. Ordinarily, he'd have gone straight into the butcher shop, but he didn't trust the gathering miners who had followed them down the dusty street. He and Kuchana tied the mules, one after another, to the rail.

Kuchana met Gib at the center rail. She saw the hardness in his eyes, his attention directed to a small group of miners who were approaching them.

"Whatever happens, you stay behind me," he warned her.

"But—"

Gib pushed her behind him as a big miner with a long, scraggly black beard stopped a few feet away, his face plumcolored with anger.

"My name is Barstow. What the hell's going on here?" he rumbled. "That's a redskin."

"She's a scout for our post," Gib said, keeping his voice low and calm.

"Right nice scalp she's got," a second miner crowed, his eyes shining with excitement. "Why, I could get thirty dollars for it."

Gib's hand moved to the pistol. "Don't even think about it, men," he warned them. "She's been hired by the army."

The black-bearded miner spat to one side. "Don't make no difference. Who the hell do you think you are, bringing one of those bastards up here?" He waved his hairy arm at Kuchana. "You boys in blue think you can rub our noses in it. Hell, you don't get up here often enough. Just two days ago a bunch of renegade Apaches robbed Bob King's mine of two mules."

The murmurs of the gathering miners joined the confrontation. McCoy turned to Kuchana. In Apache he told her, "Get in that building and stay there. These men aren't going to listen to reason."

Her eyes narrowed on the miner with the black beard. "I will not run like a coward and leave you here to fight alone."

Gib wanted to strangle her. "I said, get the hell in there and don't give me an argument. These men mean business."

"No."

Frustrated, Gib returned his attention to the ten miners who stood in a small, tense group in front of them. Damn Kuchana for disobeying his orders. But what had he expected? She was a warrior, and he'd never seen one run yet from a battle. It was then, in those seconds before Barstow lifted his rifle, that Gib realized just how very much Kuchana meant to him. The festering situation had ripped away all his defenses against his feelings toward her. He loved her. God, how could it have happened so quickly?

Kuchana saw the miner lift the rifle to pump a round into its chamber. It would take Gib precious moments to unholster the pistol beneath the flap of leather. Without thinking, she pulled the bowie knife from her side and stepped from behind McCoy.

Just as the miner lifted the rifle in both hands, Kuchana lunged those few feet, sticking the point of the knife into the stock of the rifle.

Barstow gave a croak and leapt back. Kuchana kept the tension on the knife, not allowing him to get a shell in the chamber of the rifle. If he did, he might shoot and kill Gib.

Stunned by her attack, the miners scattered, widening the circle. Gib pulled the pistol from the holster. "Hold it!" he shouted. "Put down your weapons."

Kuchana glared at Barstow, all her strength put into the knife that held the rifle against the man. He smelled sourly of sweat, and his clothes were stiff with filth. She saw his small eyes burn with hatred, and she realized he was physically much stronger than she. It didn't matter. No man was going to lift a weapon against Gib or herself.

"We come in peace," she rasped in his face.

McCoy stepped forward, settling his hand on Kuchana's tense shoulder. "That's enough," he told her in Apache.

Glancing out of the corner of her eye, she saw McCoy had his gun drawn. With a hiss, she jerked the point of the knife out of the stock of the rifle and stepped back. She didn't trust the rest of the miners. They stood in a semicircle, their mouths hanging open and shock in their eyes. Keeping her knife ready, she waited for Gib's next order.

"All right, Barstow, you're on report," McCoy snarled, jerking the rifle away from the miner. "You don't raise firearms against us."

"But," the man sputtered, "she's Apache."

"It doesn't matter!" McCoy roared back. "She's right. We came here in peace to do army business. You were the one who raised the rifle against us."

"Just her," he grumbled, backing off a few feet, "not you."

Placing the rifle under his left arm, Gib surveyed the lot of miners. "You've got a choice," he said commandingly. "Either disperse, or line up and I'll put all your names on report. Once that report gets to the judge, you'll have to come down to the post for trial.''

More grumbling erupted. Some of the miners shook their heads, moving off and dispersing. McCoy settled his gaze on Barstow. ''What do you want to do?''

''Give me my rifle and I'll get outa here,'' he muttered, giving Kuchana a contemptuous look.

''I don't want to see your face the rest of the day. Understand?''

''I'll leave. Just give me my rifle.''

Gib holstered his own gun and then made sure all the bullets were released from the rifle. He tossed the empty weapon back to the miner. Without a word, Barstow wheeled around, grabbing the halter rope to his donkey and left.

Kuchana relaxed slightly and placed the knife back in the sheath at her waist.

''Next time I give you an order to leave, you do it,'' Gib ground out, gripping her by the arm.

She stared at his hard, sweaty features. ''But—''

''No buts, Kuchana. You're in the army now. You follow orders whether you think they're right or not.''

His hand on her arm was firm without hurting her. She was confused by what she saw in his blue gaze. There was so much there he wasn't saying. ''You saved my life weeks ago. A warrior does not run when her friend is going to be attacked.''

Gib's heart was still pounding like a sledgehammer from the fear of Kuchana's being hurt by Barstow. He clenched his teeth and gave her a small shake. ''Dammit, Kuchana, I'm not going to have you hurt by these men. I don't care whether you're a warrior or not.''

Her eyes flaring with sudden anger, she pulled from his grip. ''If I were a man warrior, you would not have told me to leave and hide.''

''You're probably right,'' he admitted.

With a cutting motion, Kuchana shook her head, her black hair moving in ebony ripples around her shoulders. "I *am* right. You cannot treat me like a *pindah* woman." She pointed to her eyes. "I see how *pindah* men treat their women. They think them weak and incapable. I am not. Apache women are as strong as their men, and their men know that."

The confrontation with the miners had left Gib shaky. Any kind of danger did that to him. "You aren't among Apaches any longer," he rasped patiently. "There are some things you won't be able to do because the *pindahs* see women differently than the Apaches do."

Hurt because he was scolding her for helping defend them against a common enemy, Kuchana continued to argue. "I will never run if you are facing the enemy. I will not follow your orders."

Gib winced at the tears in her eyes. They were tears of anger, he realized, and of being hurt by his actions. Damn Carter for sending her along. All this could have been avoided. Wiping his brow with the back of his hand, he said, "You will always follow whatever orders I give you, Kuchana. Lieutenant Carter is waiting to get you in trouble. If he found out you'd disobeyed my order, he'd have you stripped of your scout status. Is that what you want? Isn't finding Geronimo more important?"

Hanging her head, Kuchana fought back a barrage of mixed feelings. "I—yes, my vow to get my people to the safety of the reservation is more important." She shut her eyes for a moment to calm herself before continuing. "But I also care for you. How can I let the *pindahs* raise their weapons against you while I am standing at your side?"

Her words struck him hard. Gib savagely rubbed his chest, where his heart lay. For Kuchana to openly admit her feeling for him was something an Apache rarely did. Helpless, he tried to think what was best to say under the circumstances. "Look," he said in a low voice that no one else could possibly hear, "don't let your heart speak for your head. Your vow is more important than I am." Gib wanted to touch her drawn face as she looked up at him. He didn't dare tell her he felt similarly about her. That he loved her. All that would do was complicate her life even more, and perhaps make her more protective.

With a shake of her head, Kuchana admitted in a small voice, "You are right. My people come first."

"Your people are worth saving, Kuchana. I want that as much as you do. That's what we have to work toward. Always remember that, no matter what situations we find ourselves in."

"You are a wise man."

Gib gave a self-derisive laugh, feeling the tension between them break. "Not really. Come on, let's get these supplies and get out of here. This isn't a safe place for you."

For a split second, Kuchana saw an emotion in Gib's eyes she couldn't decipher. Her heart took a violent leap in her breast as his husky voice grew powerful with emotion. His smile was just for her. She nodded and followed him into the butcher shop, but the feelings in her heart clamored to be noticed. What had possessed her to admit she cared for him? But it was the truth, and her people always said what they felt. The past few minutes had stunned her. When Gib had been threatened, she had realized that she loved him. She knew without a doubt that she would have given her life for him if necessary.

Her mother had told her long ago that love made one do things without regard for one's self. She lowered her head, her heart alive with feeling for Gib. She wanted to cry. To love him was not wrong. It was simply the wrong time. And she did not know how he felt toward her. Somehow, she was going to have to live with the knowledge, yet fulfill her vow. When a warrior took a vow, all else in her life became secondary. Even love. But could she do that? Would her heart let her?

Gib greeted the Chinese butcher and within minutes he was haggling over the price of the beef. Kuchana wisely remained in the background as they went from shop to shop. A Negro carried fresh fruits and vegetables that came from Mexico. He managed to get onions for five cents a pound, potatoes for four cents, and some overripe bananas for almost nothing. At the pork butcher, he wrangled the price of bacon down to fifteen cents a pound.

Kuchana helped load the supplies, and by noon they were leaving Jacobsen's. None too soon, thought Gib. A knot of miners had remained at the saloon, watching them like hungry wolves. Would they attack them outside town? Gib wasn't sure. This time, he had Kuchana take the lead, and he rode in the rear. If there was going to be an attack, Kuchana would at least have a fighting chance of getting away.

Sourly, Gib reminded himself that Kuchana wouldn't ride away if trouble started. He constantly surveyed the rocky walls that rose on either side as they traversed the well-worn sandy path down out of the mountains. Kuchana wouldn't run. She'd come back and help him fight off the miners. Rubbing his jaw, he felt more frustrated than ever before. Kuchana drew out such powerful emotions within him that he barely stopped to think before he spoke. Today, he'd almost told her that he'd fallen in love with her.

Damn, but this was complicating everything. Gib watched the graceful movement of Kuchana's waist-length hair as she rode ahead of him. Nothing could have prepared him for her. Kuchana had captured his heart from the moment they'd met. Only it had taken him more than two weeks to own up to it. Their love was mutual, there was no doubt. But Kuchana's vow stood in their way. And so did a lot of other things. Gib didn't know what to do.

One thing was for sure: Kuchana must never know how he really felt toward her. He had to make way for her to fulfill her vow. Somehow, he was going to have to hide his feelings, his need of her.

The trip out of the mountains proved uneventful. As the mule train wended its way down the juniper-laden hills, Gib relaxed. He could see the post in the desert valley below, shimmering waves of heat making it look like a mirage. Spurring his gelding, he cantered toward her.

Kuchana smiled as Gib rode up beside her. "You were lonely back there?"

He nodded, reaching into his saddlebag. "Yes. We're safe now, and the mules are on the way home. They won't break loose and try to run away. They know there's grain waiting for them down at the post as soon as they get rid of their loads."

"I'm glad we can ride together."

Gib didn't react to her statement as much as he wanted to. "Here," he said, handing her a small orange, "I got this for you. Go on, try it."

Delighted with the unexpected gift, Kuchana dropped the reins on Wind's neck and inspected the fruit. "I have never seen one before." She sniffed it. "I like the smell."

"You'll like the taste, too." Gib chuckled. "Peel off the skin and try it." He watched her work at peeling the orange, her brows drawn in concentration. Her long fingers moved delicately across the surface of the fruit, and a shaft of heat suffused Gib. How would her fingers feel against his skin? The jolting thought made him frown.

"This smells good," Kuchana confided, surveying the peeled fruit.

"Try a bite," he urged, watching as she placed her tongue against the flesh of the orange and then took a bite of it.

He grinned as the juice trickled from the corner of her mouth. Kuchana had no idea how juicy the fruit was, and had taken too big of a bite. Before the liquid could slide much farther, he leaned over, brushing it away from her chin with his thumb. Kuchana's eyes grew large and her lips parted in the aftermath of his touch. Gib saw a luster come to her eyes, and his loins tightened. Her flesh had been smooth and soft, and he ached to lean down and kiss away the juice on her lips.

Clearing his throat, he scowled and straightened in the saddle. "Oranges can be messy," he muttered, digging for the handkerchief in his back pocket.

Kuchana took the proffered handkerchief. Gib's thumb had barely grazed the corner of her mouth, yet the sensation had been overwhelmingly pleasurable. She had seen the hunger and longing in his eyes as he'd reached for her. Never had someone grazed her skin like that. Kuchana was aware of a strange, pleasant sensation in her breasts and lower body. Gib's touch was magical. Lowering her lashes, she looked away, using the handkerchief to blot her lips. She had no one to ask about these strange sensations she was experiencing. It was probably a part of love, but she wasn't sure. Her only friends were Poppy and Nettie. Ordinarily, such things would be discussed with the grandmothers of the tribe, but perhaps Poppy could serve that purpose.

Just before they entered the gates of the sprawling post, Gib said, "I'm going to drop the last mule off at the enlisted men's chow tent. You keep going with the others toward the officers' mess."

"You are a fair man, Gib. Let me do it. If you get caught, Lieutenant Carter will have his chance to get you."

"No, you just slowly work your way toward the officers' area with the train. I'll catch up with you before they miss any food off the last mule."

"We are a good team," she said. "Many warriors travel in pairs and take care of one another, protecting them from danger."

The glow in her cheeks was unmistakable. Gib nodded. "We are a team," he acknowledged.

Kuchana smiled happily. By this evening, Poppy would receive part of the fresh food and be able to distribute it under the cover of night among the laundry families. No one would report them. Only the wife of an officer, or one of the officers' children would do such a cowardly thing. Everyone was careful because a person caught stealing food meant for the officers faced a court-martial.

After leaving the train at the officers' mess and ordering Kuchana to help with the unloading of supplies, Gib headed to headquarters. Taking off his hat, he entered the outer office. His uniform was dusty from the day's ride.

Lieutenant Carter looked up from his desk. He scowled. "What do you want, Sergeant?"

Gib handed him the supply papers that had been signed by the various merchants up at Jacobsen's Mine, verifying the money spent and items bought. "I'm reporting an incident that happened up there, sir." Gib let the papers drop on the desk. Carter squinted, his full lips working into a crooked line. "What incident?" he growled.

Gib told him about the miners' threat to kill him and Kuchana. As he stood there giving the details, he could see a feral gleam in Carter's eyes. The officer sat back, his fists clenched on his desk. When Gib had finished, Carter shrugged.

"Kuchana's on report, then," he snapped, pulling open a drawer to take out the proper papers. "A scout shouldn't lift a weapon unless ordered to do so."

"Sir, I believe you're jumping the gun. I filed a report with Colonel Polk before I left, containing what I told you earlier—that ordering any Apache scout to escort a mule train up to Jacobsen's was potentially dangerous." Gib smiled grimly to himself. He had checkmated Carter's attempt to put Kuchana on report by filing his opinion earlier in the day.

Carter glared at the corporal sitting at his desk nearby pretending to be very busy. "O'Reilly. Did Sergeant McCoy give you any papers before he left this morning?"

O'Reilly looked at the lieutenant sheepishly and got up from his desk, handing McCoy's handwritten report to him. "Yes, sir. As you can see, Colonel Polk read and initialed the report."

Dammit! Carter glared down at the paper outlining McCoy's objection to sending a scout with the train. He'd been outfoxed by the bastard. Tossing the report aside, Carter muttered, "Get the hell out of here, McCoy."

Gib remained at attention. "Then Kuchana is not going to be reported . . . sir?"

Nostrils flaring, Carter jerked up his head to look at the sergeant. "Nothing will be done. Now get out of my sight."

Making an about-face, Gib headed out the door, a cat-like smile on his mouth.

Dodd stood up, pacing the length of the outer office. Corporal O'Reilly moved rapidly to his desk, sticking his head in the abundant paperwork. Placing his hands behind his back, Carter felt the anger eating him up. McCoy was too damn savvy about this army business.

Something had to be done to give McCoy a black eye, Dodd thought. The men liked him far too much. It was obvious that Kuchana was fitting in nicely with the men on the post. The Negroes accepted her. Hell, the laundry families loved her. When Chee couldn't find anything else for her to do, she was always over at Poppy's tent, helping out.

Worse, Kuchana was making herself indispensable, Dodd fumed as he glared out the window and across the parade field. On a number of occasions, Dodd had found her taking care of ten or fifteen of the little Negro children, playing games with them, making them laugh.

The door opened and closed. Dodd looked up. Melissa gave him a disgruntled look from behind her fan.

"Melissa, how are you today?" He smiled and went over, picking up her gloved hand and pressing a kiss into it.

"Not very well," she complained. "Is my husband here?"

"No. He's down at Supply."

Good, that would mean he was choosing the choicest cuts of meat and fresh vegetables for their personal cook to prepare. Harvey loved his food, of that there was no doubt. Pouting, she gave Dodd a long look. "I have a problem and need to discuss it with someone in charge."

"Of course. Corporal O'Reilly, leave us. Come back in half an hour."

"Yes, sir." O'Reilly got up, took his hat off the rack and disappeared out the door.

Quickly, Dodd brought a chair out for Melissa. She looked lovely in her pale blue dress with ruffles around the neck. "Please, sit down. How may I help you?" In Carter's mind, it never hurt to be of assistance to the wife of the post commander; it could only help his career.

Folding the fan, Melissa sat down, smoothing the folds of her dress. "It's that woman savage," she began, hating to even call her by name, because it had such a lovely sound.

"Oh. Kuchana."

"Yes, her."

"Has she broken a regulation?" Dodd asked eagerly, thinking that he still might get her on report.

"I wish." Then Melissa added, "She's simply getting too popular with the trash, Dodd. I mean, Claudia saw her the other day playing with those Negro children. Can you imagine? Playing tag with them? She's a savage and shouldn't be allowed to bother them."

"I know, I know." Dodd began pacing, hands behind his back. "I heard about it, too."

"Isn't there a regulation that prevents her from becoming too friendly with the laundry trash?"

Unhappily, Carter shook his head. "I wish there was."

"Well, I wanted to speak to Harvey about this. After all, she is an Apache and, Lord knows, she used to raid and kill people before she gave up and became a scout. How do we know she won't slit the throats of one of our people?"

"I agree with you, Melissa," he said with great feeling.

Kuchana was the talk of the post, Melissa thought enviously. In two weeks the savage had all the men, women and children wrapped around her little finger. "She's just too friendly," she muttered. "She ought to stay in the perimeter of the scout area and mind her own business. Every time I go out for a walk with the ladies, I see her over at Poppy's tent. Why, she even helps to hang the wash and fold it. That's not her job. Who does she think she is?''

"I think," Dodd said, "that someone needs to tell her what is expected of her."

"That's Sergeant McCoy's responsibility," Melissa said. "He's not doing his job." She snapped the fan open. "What an arrogant, pompous man he is. It's as if he still considers himself an officer, the way he presents himself."

Dodd would give her no argument on that. "I'll have a talk with McCoy." He gave her an enchanting smile meant to make her feel as if the problem would be handled properly. Melissa gave him a smile in return and stood up.

"Oh, Dodd, would you? Harvey sometimes gets so busy with other problems that he forgets about these small, but insidious things." She reached over, patting his arm. "You're such a gentleman. I'll be sure to mention to Harvey how well you've dealt with it. Thank you."

Chapter Six

Kuchana could taste the disappointment in her mouth. With the rest of the dark-skinned column, she slowly dismounted from Wind in front of the stables. For the second time in a month, they had tried to catch Geronimo without success. Worse, she could see that Gib's exhausted, dust-covered features mirrored how she felt. Shame flowed through her. Lieutenant Carter had goaded her into promising that this time they would find Geronimo.

There wasn't much talk among the men as they unsaddled their tired mounts and rubbed them down. Kuchana led Wind to the water trough, for a small drink, then led her to a large holding corral in back of the stables. On her return, Kuchana caught a glimpse of Melissa Polk in a riding habit standing expectantly at the door to the officers' building. The thought that the officer's wife was going to the pool to bathe made her wish that she could get permission to do the same thing.

Chee rarely sent a request to headquarters for permission for her to bathe in the pool. And when he did, it was always turned down. No one, as far as she could tell, except white men, women and children, were allowed to use the pool. She'd never seen it, but now and then had heard Poppy and Nettie speak of it in glowing terms.

Feeling saddened that she hadn't been able to fulfill her promise to Lieutenant Carter, Kuchana headed toward the scout tents. At least she could clean the grit from her skin and change her badly smelling clothes.

"Kuchana."

She halted and raised her head. Two Toes was hurrying toward her, a smile that looked more like a coyote's snarl on his thin mouth. Automatically, Kuchana went on guard, her hand moving to the butt of her knife.

"What do you want?" she demanded irritably, longing only for a wash and some sleep.

Two Toes sniggered, pointing toward the officers' building. "Corporal Hodges tells you to find Sergeant McCoy. He's to take Mrs. Polk to Draper's pool to wash."

In the time Kuchana had spent at the post, she had become familiar with the way of life here. Whatever Melissa wanted, Melissa got. She nodded. "I will tell him," and she turned back toward the stables.

Gib was putting away his tack when Kuchana found him in the large room. Despite the baggy, dusty clothes she wore, she looked beautiful. The past two months had done nothing but made him vibrantly aware that he loved Kuchana more than any other woman he'd ever known.

"What's wrong?" he asked, hanging up the bridle and wiping the bit with a clean cloth.

"Two Toes just stopped me. He said Corporal Hodges wants you to escort Mrs. Polk to the pool so she can bathe." She watched Gib's mouth thin with displeasure.

"She ought to be taken over someone's knee and be given a good paddling," Gib muttered. He flashed a look at Kuchana, longing to reach out and caress her smooth cheek and the clean line of her jaw. "I've been gone ten days and she's already up to her games again."

Kuchana leaned against the wall, her arms crossed over her breasts. "She stalks you like a coyote stalks prey. Why?"

Taking off his hat, he slapped it against his thigh to remove some of the dust and settled it on the floor at his booted feet. "Some women like to needle a man."

"I think it is more than that." Kuchana knew that Gib liked her to speak her mind when they were alone. Most of the column was still unsaddling their horses and few men were down at this end of the building yet. Keeping her voice low, she watched as he used his hands to beat the dust off his uniform.

"Poppy and Nettie think Melissa is after you." The idea made Kuchana angry because of the powerful feelings she herself held for Gib. Each day was a special agony for her, as she was unable to tell him what lay in her heart because the vow came first—and knowing that in trying to achieve her goal, she might die. The thought of never being able to tell Gib of her love nearly overwhelmed her at times. But the words must never be spoken. "I do not know why. She is married. A married woman should not try to capture another man."

Gib grinned at the angry fire in Kuchana's eyes. "I think you may be right."

"And you like this?" There was accusation in her voice, and Kuchana quickly lowered her lashes, embarrassed that he would know her feelings on this matter.

Straightening, Gib settled the hat back on his head. So, Kuchana was jealous. He walked over to where she stood leaning against the wall. Her head was bowed, her hair hiding her expression. Placing a finger beneath her chin, he gently raised it.

"Look at me," he commanded quietly, removing his hand.

Mutinously, Kuchana raised her lashes, drowning in the brilliant blue of his eyes. Again, she saw that strange, undeniable look that made her go weak and shaky inside with something she couldn't define. "Yes?"

"Does it upset you that Melissa chases me?"

She nodded. "Of course."

"Why?"

"B-because she is married." Her heart was beginning a slow pound, but it wasn't from fear, it was from Gib's closeness. Long ago, Poppy had told her that Gib did not have a woman close by. But perhaps, like many other soldiers, he corresponded with one from back East. The question ate at her.

"I see," Gib commented, resting his hands on his narrow hips. He wanted to lean down and kiss the provocative lips that were now pouty with indignation. There was such simplicity to Kuchana. "I thought you might be upset because you like me," he added.

Swallowing, Kuchana stared up at his sweaty features in surprise. "I do like you," she blurted. And then she looked away, ashamed of her admission. Scrambling to save herself from further embarrassment, she quickly added, "I have always said you were a warrior in the Apache tradition. You are brave and generous."

Fighting his need for her, Gib reached out and grazed her cheek with the back of his hand. "I'm more interested in how your heart feels about me."

The butterfly caress of his hand on her cheek made Kuchana draw in a startled breath of air. She savored the unexpected action, heat pooling and simmering throughout her lower body like fire. Risking everything, Kuchana slowly raised her chin, forcing herself to hold his burning stare. His face was free of the tension it usually carried, and the set of his mouth sent another tremor of hunger through her. So often, Kuchana had to force herself not to stare at his strong mouth.

"I..." Her voice was a bare whisper. "My heart has always cared for you." She shut her eyes, wondering if such a private admission would destroy what she felt for Gib. Kuchana still hadn't gotten up enough courage to ask Poppy about all the emotions she experienced when she was around him. Now, they were shearing through her like a fertile rain on a parched desert, making her wildly aware that she was a woman.

Gib stepped away, watching Kuchana's cheeks become pink with her blush. He groaned to himself. She licked her lower lip nervously, highlighting it, and he wanted to lean over and kiss it. Checking the rest of his escaping emotions, he scowled. What was he doing? How could he tease Kuchana like this? Her entire life was devoted to finding Geronimo, as she had proven in her two months at the post. He had no business, no right, to step in her path. Not now, and probably not ever.

"I'm sorry," he said thickly. "I didn't mean to..." Damn! Gib knew he was exhausted from the ten-day trip to and from the Sonora area. As a sergeant, his responsibilities were far more than any officer's, and Carter was lazy out on expedition. That meant little sleep for McCoy. Rubbing his face savagely, Gib walked to the door.

Kuchana's head snapped up, her eyes wide and lustrous and confused.

She stood there, her body trembling with a storm of incredible emotions. She could hear the heels of Gib's boots striking the wooden floor growing fainter and fainter. Placing her hand against her heart, she closed her eyes, feeling bathed in a rainbow of dizzying colors. Only love could make her feel this. With a shaky breath, she realized she'd nearly told him everything. Somehow, she had to take better command of her emotions.

Forcing herself to move, Kuchana left the tack room. Her mind and heart were on Gib's fleeting touch. He had been so gentle with her, his voice drawing such overwhelming feelings from deep within her. Avoiding several of the soldiers, she wove her way out of the stables. Across the parade ground, she saw Gib talking on the porch of headquarters with Corporal Hodges.

"Corporal, why can't you assign someone else to escort Mrs. Polk to the pool? I just returned from ten days out in the desert."

Hodges, a man in his early thirties, shrugged. "Mrs. Polk requested you, Sergeant. I'm sorry."

The writing was on the wall. "Very well, Hodges." Melissa couldn't wait. She had to stir the pot the moment he returned. Ever since he'd arrived at the post, Melissa had been a pesky fly in his life. This time, he was going to thwart her plan. "Corporal, send a runner over to the scout tents. Order Kuchana to get over to the stables. She's going with me on this escort."

"Right away, Sergeant."

Gib turned and smiled to himself. There was more than one way to parry Melissa's thrusts. He hated to bring Kuchana along, but it was better that another woman was present. Normally, a private or a scout would escort the ladies to the pool. Not a sergeant. Chuckling, he wondered what Melissa's reaction would be to Kuchana's coming along.

Melissa's eyes flared with anger when McCoy rode up with the Indian woman, and a fat, grain-fed bay mare for Melissa to ride.

"What's this?" she demanded, waving her crop at Kuchana.

McCoy kept his face carefully arranged, the brim of his hat so low that his eyes could barely be seen. "Kuchana will be with you down at the pool, Mrs. Polk. I'll be guarding you from up above." *And out of sight,* Gib added mentally. He wouldn't put it past Melissa to undress and flaunt herself before him. If she did, he could be put on report, and this time, the court-martial would drum him out of the army for good.

Pouting and furious, Melissa mounted the sidesaddle, delicately arranging the folds of her dark blue riding skirt. She had taken extra pains with her appearance for McCoy's benefit. Glaring at Kuchana, she snapped, "This is ridiculous. I only need one escort, not two!"

Kuchana watched the *pindah* woman jerk the bay mare around and charge between them, galloping across the parade ground and toward the gates of the post. Kuchana followed on a gray gelding that responded sluggishly to her commands.

"I think she's angry," Gib said, smiling and trotting beside Kuchana.

Kuchana tilted her head, unsure why he was grinning. "You are happy she is angry?"

Gib kept an eye on Melissa, who was now laying the crop to the poor mare. "No. Let's canter," he ordered. To let Melissa ride out in front without escort could mean a chewing-out by Carter, and he didn't want either of them to endure his tirade.

They easily caught up with Melissa. Kuchana saw Gib ride abreast of the woman and lean down, pulling the bay mare to a walk. Melissa was furious, her cheeks a fiery red and her eyes flashing. Kuchana decided it was best to hang back at the rear.

Despite her tiredness, Kuchana was eager to see the pool. The landscape changed rapidly from desert to hills and they entered a narrow canyon with huge gray rocks rising like rugged spires on either side of them. In her heart, she felt a stirring of jealousy as she saw Melissa reach out time and again and touch Gib's arm as she chatted airily with him. Melissa was beautiful. She always wore such brilliantly colored dresses and hats. Kuchana recognized how much Melissa liked Gib.

Her hand tightening on the reins, Kuchana looked down at herself. She wore men's clothing. Melissa always carried a dainty fan or a parasol to shade her skin from the burning sun. Looking at her hand, Kuchana thought of how dark she was in comparison to Melissa. Her nails were short, her hands roughened from the weather and daily outdoor activity. Compared to Melissa's curved body, hers was as straight as a stick. Her breasts were small while Melissa's full ones were proudly outlined by every outfit she wore.

The beauty of the canyon escaped Kuchana for another twenty minutes as they rode more deeply into the area. Her mind and heart were reflecting on what she did not have compared to Melissa. Gib's voice haunted her, and so had his provocative touch on her cheek. Kuchana lifted her hand, her fingers pressing the spot.

Her thoughts were broken when Gib and Melissa came to a halt. Kuchana's eyes widened with surprise. In front of them was a big, circular pool of blue-green water at the bottom of the box canyon. White-barked sycamores crowded the shore, their leaves shiny and huge, creating large areas of shade. There was even grass along the bank. The walls of the canyon formed a natural defense around the pool. It appeared to be a very safe place to bathe.

Gib turned to Kuchana. "You stay here and guard Mrs. Polk." He pointed to an area far above them. "I'll be up there on guard. If I see anything, I'll give a whistle."

Kuchana nodded, relieved that Gib would be leaving. She saw Melissa's eyes flash.

"Sergeant McCoy!" the woman screeched. "I demand that you stay here and send her up there."

McCoy reined in his horse, looking over his shoulder. "Kuchana is an able and worthy escort, Mrs. Polk. You couldn't be in safer hands." He nudged the gelding forward, smiling to himself at Melissa's snort of derision. Giving Kuchana a wink as he passed her, he saw her sad eyes suddenly lighten with hope. Why was Kuchana sad? He thought she'd enjoy seeing this place.

"Come on," Melissa ordered angrily, dismounting and dropping the reins on the ground.

Kuchana dismounted, taking both horses toward the bank to feed on the rare green grass.

"Don't you dare do that!" Melissa cried, waving her whip imperiously. "That grass beautifies this place. Don't let the horses eat it."

Stunned by Melissa's anger, Kuchana said nothing. She led the horses to the nearest sycamore and tied their reins to a low branch. She watched as Melissa stormed off to another tree and began undressing, throwing each piece of clothing to the ground. Finding a large gray rock beneath the shade where the horses were tied, Kuchana cradled her rifle in her arms, remaining attentive to her surroundings.

Melissa looked up, searching the top of the box canyon. She saw McCoy sitting up above them, rifle in hand, his back to them. The bastard. How she'd plotted and planned this special escapade! Because he was a sergeant, she couldn't just sally forth and flirt with him. Enlisted men and officers had lines of demarcation that they never crossed. Despite all she had done to get close to McCoy, the army regulations had prevented it. Except for this time.

Melissa jerked at the strings that held her corset in place. With a groan, she threw it down. The nerve of him to bring Kuchana! How dared he! McCoy had known all along what she was planning and he'd thwarted her plan by bringing this damned woman scout to protect himself.

Kuchana watched with interest as layer after layer of clothes peeled off Melissa. She was amazed at how many clothes a *pindah* woman wore. The funny things with staves interested her, but Kuchana knew better than to speak to Melissa unless spoken to. Poppy had warned her that Melissa was a rattler waiting to bite.

The water looked inviting. Kuchana's gaze ranged around the canyon to the entrance, and then back to Melissa. Her blond hair was piled up in a nest of curls on her head. When she shed the last of her clothing and stood there gloriously naked, Kuchana gawked. She had never seen a *pindah* woman stripped before.

Melissa smiled, noticing Kuchana's undivided interest. She walked toward the Apache, placing her hands beneath her full breasts.

"Beautiful, aren't they?"

Kuchana blinked as Melissa approached. The officer's wife was a full-bodied woman, with large breasts, a tiny waist and wide hips that swayed provocatively from side to side. Words fled from Kuchana's mouth, so she nodded.

Looking up, Melissa studied McCoy, who still had his back to them. "You know, men love women like me." She caressed her breasts, holding Kuchana's wide-eyed gaze. "They like large breasts. Reminds them of their mothers." And then she laughed, allowing her hands to slide down her torso, across her rounded belly to her curved thighs. "They're all little boys, you know."

"Oh?" Kuchana croaked, watching Melissa dabble a toe in the water. Her skin was alabaster, and she looked strangely out of place against the natural grays, greens, blues and browns of the canyon.

Giggling, Melissa stepped into the sandy pool, the water closing over her ankles. "Sure. All they want to do is crawl up to you and suckle off your breasts like a babe in his mother's arms." She turned and gave Kuchana a scalding look. "But I'm sure you know all about that. I've heard stories about you Apaches. How you sleep with any man who comes along."

Alarmed, Kuchana sat up. "No, that's not true. Our men value each of us. A woman is pure until she takes a husband. Until then, she is respected and untouched."

Leaning down, Melissa cupped some water, running it over her thighs. "I've heard stories from the miners that an Apache man often has two or three wives."

"Well—" Kuchana stumbled, thinking "—sometimes the husband of a woman is killed and she will then become a second wife to that man's family."

"Terrible," Melissa clucked. "A man with more than one wife. Why, that's scandalous. You and the Mormons. They practice the same kind of savagery." She walked out into the pool, the water lapping around her waist.

Kuchana frowned. Poppy's warning came back to her. Biting her lower lip, she sat watching Melissa bathe. The woman seemed to enjoy being watched as she washed, taking a great deal of time with her breasts. The nipples grew hard each time she touched them. She giggled, glancing at Kuchana.

"And are you still a virgin?"

"Virgin?"

Melissa frowned. "Yes, you know. Have you ever slept with a man?"

"No, I am pure."

Snorting, Melissa leaned over, rinsing the soap off her flesh. "Well," she said lightly, "I don't know how any man would want you, anyway. After all, you wear their clothes and act just like them. You'll probably be a virgin until the day you die."

Hurt wove through Kuchana. "In my tribe, what a woman wears is not a measure of her true worth. I was looked upon with respect by my people."

"Respect." Melissa laughed and walked out of the pool. She retrieved a towel, patting her skin dry. "My dear, no man wants to respect a woman. They like to pant and grovel like animals with her, have their way with her." She saw the blank look on Kuchana's features. If she ever did dress up, she thought, and get rid of those awful men's clothes, she might be pretty.

Tossing the towel to the grassy earth, Melissa began to dress. "You do know that men are nothing but lusting animals in bed with us, don't you?"

Kuchana shook her head. "There is great regard between husband and wife," Kuchana said. She had never heard any of the married women refer to their husbands as animals. Were *pindah* men brutal and cruel to their wives? It sounded like it.

"You're so naive," Melissa tittered. She gestured for Kuchana to get up and come near. "Help me with this awful corset. I need you to truss me up."

For the next fifteen minutes, Kuchana learned about a corset and how to pull the strings tight to give the wearer an even smaller waist. When she was finished, she went back to her rock, keeping the rifle in her arms.

"In some ways, I envy you," Melissa went on as she finished dressing. "You don't have to wear these awful corsets, petticoats and all this other stuff."

"Can you die from a corset?"

With a laugh, Melissa buttoned her jacket and placed her hat on her head with several large pins. "Sometimes I feel as if I'm going to. I've seen women faint dead away from wearing one that was too tight."

With a shake of her head, Kuchana said nothing further.

"Tell me," Melissa said, picking up her crop, "are you engaged?"

"Engaged?" Kuchana had visions of combat between two enemy warriors.

Stamping her foot, Melissa muttered, "You are so stupid! You know, has a man asked for your hand in marriage?"

"Oh...no..."

Slyly, Melissa smiled, tapping the crop impatiently against her boot. "What about at the post? Who has caught your fancy?"

Heat flew into Kuchana's cheeks and she averted her eyes from Melissa's probing gaze.

"Ah, I see your heart is set on someone," she teased, coming closer. "Could it be one of those fine-looking colored bucks? They're built magnificently."

Kuchana shook her head, completely baffled. Among her people, such talk was taboo.

Raising her brows, Melissa thought for a moment. "I know! It must be one of those Mexican farmers who come to the post every week to sell their wares."

"No..."

Thinking for a long moment, Melissa studied Kuchana. The Apache woman was obviously uncomfortable. "Then it has to be a white man." The words came out low and accusing. She saw Kuchana wince. So, it was true. Who? Suddenly, Melissa looked upward. No! It couldn't be! Her mind raced. Since Kuchana had come to the post, McCoy had avoided her even more. Melissa tapped the crop with even more fervor.

"It's Sergeant McCoy, isn't it?" she demanded tightly. Kuchana didn't speak. Melissa hated that her face betrayed nothing of what she was thinking or feeling. Raising the crop, she struck Kuchana hard and snapped, "Tell me the truth!"

Anger wove with the shock at Melissa's attack. The skin of Kuchana's upper arm stung from the crop. She saw the hatred in Melissa's flashing eyes.

Kuchana got slowly to her feet and stepped back, putting a large rock between them. The barrel of her rifle pointed down. "Sergeant McCoy is a good man," she whispered.

"How good?" Melissa demanded angrily.

Knowing that Melissa could cause her to lose her job as a scout, Kuchana struggled to keep her anger under control. "Among my people, he would be considered a warrior."

"And what about as husband material?"

"He has a good heart, Mrs. Polk."

Melissa's eyes narrowed in fury. "Why you little upstart. It's in your eyes and in your voice. You're sweet on him, aren't you? No wonder he's been avoiding me—" She snapped her mouth shut, glaring at the Apache woman. "Do you deny this?"

Kuchana stood tensely. Some of what Melissa had said was beyond her comprehension. She didn't know what "sweet on him" meant. "He is a man of honor and fairness," she said at last.

Exploding with a curse, Melissa slapped the rock with her crop. "How dare you!" she screeched, her voice echoing off the canyon walls. Shaking the crop in Kuchana's face, Melissa shrilled, "You stay away from him! He's mine! Do you understand me? He's mine!"

Stunned, Kuchana watched the *pindah* woman run to her mare, mount, and then whirl the animal around. In moments, Melissa was beating her mare unmercifully across its withers with the crop as she galloped out of the canyon. Looking up, Kuchana saw McCoy stand and look down at her. Frustrated, she stalked over to her mount. What had she done or said to cause Melissa to behave like this?

Mounting, Kuchana urged the gelding into a trot. It was army regulations that no woman be unescorted. And Melissa had a head start on her. In the mood the *pindah* woman was in, she would not only get Kuchana in trouble, but Gib, as well. Compressing her lips, Kuchana hurried to catch up with the wife of the post commander. She knew Gib would follow.

Chapter Seven

By the time Gib arrived back at the post some fifteen minutes later, Melissa was on the porch of the officers' building, angrily shouting and pointing at Kuchana. He urged his horse into a canter across the parade ground, disregarding the regulation that all animals must be kept at a walk in the area. Harvey Polk was standing beside his shrieking wife, glaring down at Kuchana who stood tensely at the bottom of the stairs.

McCoy brought his horse to a halt, walking up to Kuchana. "What's going on?" he demanded.

Melissa sobbed into the lacy handkerchief, stealing a look up at her husband. Harvey was livid, his cheeks flushed against the whiteness of his long sideburns.

"Sergeant, I'm appalled. My wife is thoroughly upset. How dare you use your escort duties as a time to leave my wife undefended in that canyon."

Kuchana was breathing hard, anger and frustration boiling up through her. "He did not," she stated. Trembling, she turned to Gib. "She accuses you of leaving her alone at the pool."

In Apache, Gib said, "Kuchana, he's an officer. Remember why you're here. Remember your sister you're trying to save." He immediately saw the anger leave her eyes and she gave a barely perceptible nod of her head. McCoy wanted to wrap his hands around Melissa's neck. She was pretending to weep unabatedly into the handkerchief. "Sir," Gib said, "I left your wife in Kuchana's hands. I went to the top of the canyon to keep a watch for renegades." His eyes hardened on Melissa. "At no time was your wife left undefended. Kuchana has proven her hunting and tracking abilities. She's as good a shot with a rifle as any man on this post."

Polk put his arm around his weeping wife. "There, there, pet. Now don't take on so. I know how the savages frighten you. There, there..."

Kuchana's mouth tightened. It was all she could do to stand there and watch the charade Melissa was playing for her husband. Poppy was right: she was a rattler. Worse than one.

"My wife also said this woman savage made lewd and disgraceful remarks to her," Polk rumbled, glaring down at McCoy.

Helpless, Gib knew it was a lie. If anything, Kuchana was the epitome of silence most of the time. And she wasn't that familiar with English or the myriad slang words. Melissa sobbed louder. He wanted to haul her across his knees, but right now, Kuchana's scout status was in peril.

"Exactly," Gib growled, "what was said, sir?"

Polk flushed. "Not out here, Sergeant." He turned to Corporal Hodges, who stood nervously in the background. "Hodges, take my wife home. She's terribly upset. Call the post surgeon and have him treat her for shock."

"Yes, sir." Hodges leapt forward, taking Melissa by the elbow and escorting her off the porch.

McCoy nearly gagged on Polk's inability to see through Melissa's act. Something had passed between the two women, of that he was sure. Kuchana's brown eyes flashed with indignation.

"You, Sergeant, come with me." Polk jabbed a finger at Kuchana. "And you, take care of the horses. As of now, you are on report. When you're finished with the horses, get over to your tent and stay there."

She was on report! What had she done? Looking at McCoy, Kuchana realized he was just as upset over this turn of events as she was. Nodding, she turned and gathered up the reins on all three horses, leaving the men on the porch.

"Follow me, Sergeant," Polk ordered heavily, heading back into headquarters.

Gib braced himself for whatever Polk might say. Inside Polk's office, he remained at attention while the colonel sat behind his desk.

"My wife came back from the bathing pool in tears, Sergeant," Polk began furiously. "She said that Kuchana watched her undress and then made fun of her body. Not only that, but that savage had the gall to tell my wife that all men were animals in bed." Polk slammed his fist down on the desk. "This is despicable conduct by your scout, Sergeant! I don't care if she is a woman, she has no right to speak to my wife in such terms. Melissa is sweet and kind. She's not accustomed to that kind of talk."

"Sir, I don't believe Kuchana knows enough English to have said such things to your wife. She's also unmarried and, therefore, a virgin. The Apache moral code is very strict." McCoy took several deep breaths, trying to read between the lines. To accuse Melissa of saying those things to Kuchana would be foolhardy. Somehow, he had to get Kuchana off report. Polk would never believe his "sweet" wife was a weasel, capable of spreading malicious and damaging lies.

Glaring at McCoy, the commander rapped out, "Then you get to the bottom of this, Sergeant. I won't have my wife in tears, no matter what that savage said. As a matter of fact, she has no right to speak to Melissa, at all."

"Sir, may I have permission to question Kuchana? If you're placing her on report, shouldn't we get all the facts? Perhaps your wife only thought she heard Kuchana say something. Remember, they live in different worlds, and see things differently."

Polk sat back in his chair, his lips pursed. "My wife does not lie."

Controlling his anger, McCoy said, "Sir, your wife said I was remiss in my escort duties, too. And I wasn't." He struggled to be diplomatic, watching Polk's face flush again. "All I'm saying is that there could have been simply a misunderstanding, or perhaps a cultural difference. I'm sure your wife isn't lying, but I know that Kuchana, when faced with our language barrier, will usually remain silent instead of talking back."

Pacified to a degree, Polk grabbed a pen, tapping it on the desk. "You find out what was said, Sergeant. And then I'll decide if that savage is to stay on report or not. The fact my wife came back in tears should mean some kind of punishment for the Indian."

"Yes, sir," McCoy replied. "Permission to leave sir?"

"Dismissed," Polk growled. "And I expect to know the full story within the hour, McCoy. Understand?"

Gib stood at the door, hand on the brass knob. "Don't worry, sir, you will."

Kuchana threw the last saddle on the peg, venting her anger on it. The nerve of that woman! She had lied and shamed her in front of the men. Worse, she was on report for something she had not done.

"Kuchana?"

She whirled, her hair flying around her shoulders. Gib stood grimly in the doorway of the tack room. His eyes were dark and narrowed.

"She lied, Gib."

Calmly, he shut the door, leaving them alone in the tack room. "I know she did." He saw the hurt and fury in her face. "Now listen to me, I need to know exactly what was said."

Startled, Kuchana stood there. "You do?"

Gib sat down on a tack box. "Yes."

Heat sped up her neck and into her cheeks. Kuchana touched her brow. "She said many things, things I would never think a woman would say."

"Sit down," he coaxed quietly. Kuchana sat on a box opposite him. "Start from the beginning. I realize this is going to be painful for you, Kuchana, but I have to know. Polk has you on report and I've got to somehow clear your name."

Kuchana whispered, "My people would never speak as she did."

"I know that," Gib entreated gently. "But Melissa is mean and often gets people in trouble by making up tales."

"She is angry with me, but I don't know why."

"Tell me what she said and maybe I can figure it out." Gib wasn't so sure. Melissa's antics were sometimes for a reason, but other times seemed created just to bring excitement to the otherwise boring post.

Taking a deep breath, Kuchana forced out, "She undressed and then placed her hands here—" she motioned to her own breasts "—and said they were beautiful."

McCoy saw how painful it was for Kuchana to talk of such intimate things. "And what did you say?"

Shrugging, Kuchana muttered, "Nothing. But I thought they looked like a milking cow's."

Curbing a smile, Gib asked, "Then what?"

Embarrassed, she stared down at her dusty boots, avoiding his amused gaze. "She said that men loved women like her, that they liked those cow breasts." Her voice was barely above a squeak. "She said her breasts reminded the men of their mothers, and that they were all little boys."

"She what?"

Kuchana jerked a look up in Gib's direction. She saw him shake his head. Feeling terribly vulnerable at having to discuss such things with him, she placed a hand across her eyes.

Gib stood up and moved to crouch in front of her. Gently he pulled her hands away from her reddened features. "I'm sorry," he told her huskily. "I'm not upset with you,

Kuchana. I'm angry with Melissa. She had no right to say those things to you or anyone. I know how tough it is for you to repeat her words. You're an Apache maid, someone who is pure."

His words were a cooling waterfall to her heated emotions and her shame. McCoy's hands remained on hers as she lowered them to her lap. "I have never heard such things," she murmured.

"Did she say anything else?" Gib tried to brace himself for whatever else had come out of Melissa's foul mouth.

Closing her eyes, Kuchana was unable to hold his tender look. "She said that all these men wanted to do was crawl into her arms and suckle her like a baby would its mother. Then, she accused Apache women of sleeping with any man that comes along."

Gib's hands tightened around hers. Damn Melissa! What the stupid woman didn't realize was that Kuchana was a warrior, not just an ordinary Apache woman. Those kinds of accusations could have been enough to cause Kuchana to react in a combative way. "What did you do?"

Slowly, Kuchana opened her eyes, keeping them on his hands. "I told her that sometimes, if a woman's husband died in battle, she would go to his brother's wickiup."

That was true. Gib knew that most white people thought it was wrong, but the Apache and other tribes existed by banding together. A woman without a husband would die without help from her family. And sometimes, that meant becoming a second wife to her husband's brother.

Just having Gib's gentle attention unstrung all her withheld emotions. "She asked if I was a virgin, and I didn't know what that was. When she explained it differently, I said yes." Surprised at the tears that formed in her eyes, Kuchana forced them back. "She said that no man would have me because I dressed like a man and did a man's things."

Groaning, McCoy released her hands and framed her face. "Listen to me," he said harshly. "Among your people, you are honored and respected."

McCoy's roughened hands against her face caused a storm of longing to break loose within Kuchana. She ached to fall against his strong and powerful chest, and hide there. "That was what I told her. And then she said no man wants to respect a woman, that they pant and grovel like animals in her bed."

Gib's fingers pressed harder against her flesh. Kuchana's eyes filled with confusion and fear. Her lips were parted, and Gib wanted to kiss away her pain. "Damn her to hell," he muttered. "Listen to me, Kuchana. She is wrong. Do you understand?"

Sniffing, Kuchana shrugged. "I have never heard the wives of the warriors say things like that about them. The husband respects the wife. He does not treat her like an animal."

"Exactly," Gib whispered rawly. "Don't believe what Melissa is telling you. Not all men hurt women. Among the Apache, the husbands revere their wives."

"Then *pindah* men do this to their wives?"

Groaning, Gib wiped away her tears with his thumbs. "Most don't, but some do. It's obvious Melissa has that kind of relationship with her husband." *Or others,* he thought. She hunted men beneath her station, rutting with them like an animal in heat. Poppy had told him on three different occasions that she'd seen Melissa with Dodd Carter slipping into the hospital building when it was empty of personnel. McCoy didn't care what kind of tangled web Melissa wove, as long as she didn't trap Kuchana in it.

"She said I was naive. What does that mean?"

He gave her a slight smile. Her skin was soft and firm, and Gib longed to tell her just how much he loved her. "It means that you're an innocent woman. Something Melissa has never been."

Strengthened by Gib's support, Kuchana went on, "She asked if I was engaged, and I did not understand. When she explained, I told her no. She asked me if a dark-skinned man had caught my fancy." Miserably, Kuchana looked at Gib. "I did not understand the word 'fancy,' so I said nothing. She took my answer to be no. Next, she asked me if I liked one of the *culo-gordos* who come to the post. I said no."

"I would imagine," Gib said, knowing how much the Apaches hated the Mexicans.

"Then she stared at me, getting very upset. She looked up at where you sat, and then struck me with her crop."

Scowling, Gib asked, "Where?" It was against regulations to strike an enlisted man.

"It is nothing," Kuchana insisted, pointing to her arm.

Releasing her, Gib said, "Roll up your sleeve and let me look at it." The idea that Melissa struck Kuchana made him shake with anger. He waited, hiding his impatience as she awkwardly rolled up the sleeve. Her arm was smooth and firm. Gib clenched his teeth, examining the long purple bruise that ran the length of her upper arm. The skin wasn't broken, but it was puffy. It looked as though Melissa had used the crop with all her strength.

"Why did she strike you?" he demanded hoarsely, getting up and retrieving a bottle of horse liniment.

Kuchana avoided his sharpened look as he came and sat down next to her. "She...asked me if my heart was on you."

Gib was going to apply the liniment to her bruise, but his hand froze in midair. There was such shame in Kuchana's face. He knew they shared something good, something that might be a dream come true. But he didn't dare hope. Not right now. Not until Geronimo was caught and her vow to help her people was fulfilled. Until then, he knew Kuchana's entire existence centered on that aim, not on him or of falling in love. He forced himself to apply the liniment as gently as possible. Kuchana didn't wince, although he'd seen men take less of a beating and howl like a wounded wolf when liniment was applied. Only the tightening of her lips told him of the magnitude of her pain. Damn Melissa Polk.

"What did you tell her?" he asked finally after applying the liniment. Setting the bottle aside, he carefully unrolled the sleeve, buttoning it around her slender wrist.

"I . . . said nothing. She got very angry and slashed at me with the crop."

"And did you strike back?" Gib prayed Kuchana had held on to her control.

"No. I said that you were a warrior. She got angrier and asked me if you were husband material. I said you had a good heart." With a sigh, Kuchana looked over at the wooden door hanging on its leather hinges. "She called me an upstart and said I was 'sweet' on you and no wonder you were avoiding her. I didn't know what 'sweet' meant, so all I said was that you were a man of honor and fairness."

"That's when I heard her shrieking from below," Gib growled. "She was yelling at you to stay away from me, wasn't she?"

Hanging her head, Kuchana murmured yes. She felt completely drained. "She told me that you were hers. Then she ran to her horse and galloped out of the canyon. I mounted quickly and managed to catch up with her halfway to the post. When I rode up beside her, she struck me again with the crop, screaming at me to leave her alone."

McCoy sighed. Without thinking, he placed his hand on her shoulder. "I'm sorry, Kuchana. You didn't do anything wrong. None of this was your fault."

Kuchana's heart leapt as his hand settled on her. The urge to turn and throw her arms around McCoy's strong shoulders was excruciating. "I—I feel she wants me gone."

"She does," Gib said, giving her hand one last squeeze before standing up. His mind whirled with options and plans. "She's jealous of you."

Lifting her chin, Kuchana whispered, "Why?"

He managed a faint smile, holding her vulnerable gaze. "Because Melissa wants me in her bed."

"But she is married!" Kuchana sputtered indignantly.

"That doesn't matter to her."

Fear struck Kuchana's heart. "Does it matter to you?" Perhaps Gib liked Melissa. She prayed to Painted Woman that he didn't. Somewhere in her dreams, she held the hope that Gib would like her, Kuchana—not as a scout or warrior, but as a woman. It was a silly dream. She didn't wear a dress or appear womanly. And that, according to Melissa, was what *pindah* men preferred. Sadness serrated her heart as she watched McCoy's face soften.

"I'm like the Apache," he told her quietly. "My heart has room for only one woman, and that's the one whom I love. The woman whom I will someday marry." He wanted to tell her his heart wanted her, but he didn't dare. "I don't like women like Melissa. They're vindictive and cruel. The woman I love will be kind."

She hung her head, suffering because she would never be that woman. It was not her destiny. "I see."

Gib opened the door. "I want you to go back to the scout area and rest. I'll handle this report with Colonel Polk."

"Then you can let me stay as scout?"

McCoy nodded. "I think so. But wait until you hear from me before counting on it. I have an idea that ought to help the situation."

Tears filled Kuchana's eyes. "If you could, Gib, I would be grateful. Every day I think of my sister and wonder if she is starving to death, or if any more of the little ones have gone to the Big Sleep."

Hope burned like sunlight in her eyes. Digesting her new trust in him, he smiled. "Don't worry, Kuchana. Now, go on, get over to your tent and get some sleep. You've earned it."

Kuchana rose, her heart open and welcoming McCoy's smile. She saw so much in his blue eyes in that moment. "I must go to Poppy for fresh bedding, and then I will go to sleep."

"Fine."

* * *

"Mama," Nettie whispered, running back into their laundry tent, "Kuchana's coming."

"Lordy!" Poppy exploded, hefting herself off the stool where she was pressing clothes with a heavy iron. It was all over the post that Kuchana was on report. Bad news always traveled fast.

Kuchana was smiling when she sauntered up to the laundress. "I have come for my clothes, Poppy."

Grabbing her, Poppy dragged her into the tent. "You come here, chile. Now what's all this about a report?"

Surprised, Kuchana saw that both women were terribly concerned. She was too embarrassed to repeat what had happened to anyone. In her tribe, gossip was considered evil. Instead, Kuchana said that Melissa was upset, that was all. "Sergeant McCoy said he would take care of it." As much as Kuchana loved the women, she dreaded the whole story getting out and further shaming her.

"Whew!" Poppy expostulated, wiping her brow with the back of her pudgy hand. "Then I know it's going to be fine." She poked Kuchana in the ribs. "You feel skinny again."

The warmth of the laundresses washed away the remaining fear Kuchana felt in the aftermath of the confrontation with Melissa. "I did not eat as well on the trail as here in your tent."

Grinning, Poppy pulled Kuchana into the tent. "Chile, you're in luck. Chee just dropped off a haunch of a deer to us earlier." She made Kuchana sit on the three-legged stool in the midst of the ironing. Going to a black kettle that bubbled with venison soup, Poppy ladled out a huge bowl for Kuchana.

"Here, you eat this. All of it," she ordered her sternly, wagging her finger in Kuchana's face. Giving her the spoon, Poppy sat down with a groan opposite her.

While Kuchana ate, Poppy and Nettie kept her company. The heat of the day made all of them sweat profusely, even though both ends of the tent were pulled open. Poppy watched the young woman in silence for a minute before speaking.

"Chile, you're going have to defend yourself against Miz Melissa. Word's gone around that she's the one who got you on report."

Kuchana nodded, finding the stew rich and salty. After ten days on hardtack and tough, stringy beef jerky, Poppy's food was delicious.

"Kuchana, you just gotta be careful around that woman," Nettie said.

"She's jealous of you," Poppy decided. "You went to the pool with the sergeant, didn't you?"

Uncomfortable that Poppy could read so much into what little she'd divulged, Kuchana nodded again.

"I thought so," Poppy muttered. She glanced at her daughter. "Someone needs to tell her the truth, Nettie."

The girl shrugged her slim shoulders. The calico dress she wore was threadbare and faded from use. "Mama, I told you all along you should warn her."

The stew disappeared and Kuchana thanked Poppy, handing back the empty bowl.

"More?"

"No."

Poppy grimaced, refilling the bowl. "You Apaches are a funny lot. Starving, and yet you won't ask for second helpings."

Gratefully, Kuchana took the bowl, murmuring her thanks.

"Mama," Nettie reminded her, "tell Kuchana the truth about Miz Melissa. She's got her in trouble once, so ain't that reason enough to tell her?"

Poppy nodded. "Girl, you go keep watch. If any officers come by, you warn me in time so they don't hear me talking."

Delighted, Nettie raced out to the front of the tent. "Go ahead, Mama," she crowed, "tell her."

Curious, Kuchana awaited Poppy's explanation.

"Chile, now you listen well, you hear? I've been at this fort nearly five years. When Colonel Polk came out with his new bride, Melissa, she took advantage of him." Poppy's eyes narrowed. "Josh, the stableman, beds her down whenever she wants."

Kuchana's eyes widened enormously. Melissa's comment about the dark-skinned men being magnificent came back to her.

"It's common knowledge to us, because one of our own kind is involved with that soiled woman. She's bedded down enlisted men and officers alike. Never seems to have enough." Poppy scooted the chair closer, lowering her voice. "Ever since Sergeant McCoy arrived, she's put her sights on him. He won't have nothing to do with her. He knows she's trouble. The more he ignores her, the more she chases him. What happened today is a good example. Nettie and I bet that you made her angry because he's sweet on you, not her. She's a jealous bitch in heat, that one. You gotta be careful from here on out, Kuchana."

Shaken, Kuchana sat there going over everything Poppy had told her. Her stomach churning, she realized there was truth to the woman's impassioned words. Her appetite gone, she placed the bowl beside the stool, frowning.

"What does the word 'sweet' mean, Poppy?"

Patting her hand, Poppy grinned. "Chile, that means a man's in love with you."

Her heart took a violent leap in her breast. Kuchana blinked belatedly. Gib was in love with her? She held Poppy's misty gaze.

"You don't see it, do you?" the laundress asked, holding her hand gently. With a shake of her head, she continued, "Chile, you must see that the sergeant is head over heels for you."

The English words were confusing. Kuchana opened her mouth to speak, but nothing came out. She saw Poppy chuckle, her familiar, hearty laughter coming from deep within. "I—I did not know."

"He's courting you right and proper. But you just gotta understand why Miz Melissa is gunning for you. She wants your man and she won't stop at nothing to get him."

This was all too much for Kuchana. "Among my people, if a maid likes a young warrior, she goes through her parents, who in turn, tell his parents. It is an honorable way to tell one another what lies in their hearts."

Poppy nodded. "It's done a little different here, chile. But you can't be blind anymore. If Miz Melissa was able to get you wrote up on report, she won't stop at that. If you're caught doing something wrong, you could get a horsewhipping or, worse, put in front of a firing squad and shot. You just can't trust her."

Kuchana didn't know which upset her worse: Melissa's plotting to get her thrown out of the army as a scout, or Gib's courting her. "Our women do not do this kind of thing," she began with an effort. "How can I know what Melissa will do?"

"We'll watch for you, chile. Old Poppy here knows what's going on at this post. Be careful of anything having to do with her. She smiles to your face and then bites you when you've got your back to her. You've got friends here, Kuchana, so wipe that worry off you brow."

Grateful for their help and honesty, Kuchana slowly got to her feet. Nettie came back and handed her the clean laundry. Ordinarily, scouts did their own washing, but they had insisted on doing hers for her. Thanking them, she left.

Poppy watched Kuchana walk away. "I hope Miz Melissa learns from this," she told her daughter with a scowl.

"What if she don't, Mama?"

Placing two irons on the small stove outside the tent to heat, Poppy said, "I don't know how far that woman will go to get her way."

Chapter Eight

Kuchana stood by Draper's Pool, absorbing the silence around her. At last, Chee had gotten her permission to bathe in the water at the foot of the box canyon. He had promised her the rare gift if she would supply ten deer or bighorn for the families on the post. Kuchana knew he didn't think she was capable of fulfilling such a task, but she had. Savoring the look on Chee's large face when she had brought in the last animal, she grinned. As she shed the leather belt that carried her knife, her heart turned to other matters.

Lieutenant Carter had sent Gib out with a small patrol to investigate a rancher's complaint that Apaches had stolen some of his cattle. He had been gone three days, and she missed him acutely. Sitting on the bank, she placed her rifle next to her knife. The canyon was considered safe since cavalry patrols regularly checked the pool. It was also a place to water thirsty army horses coming in off the desert expeditions.

It was late, and the rays of the afternoon sun slanted through the rugged canyon, sending streamers into the pool and making the surface dance with light. Bees buzzed nearby, and she could hear birds chattering in the trees. For once, Kuchana allowed her heightened guard to dissolve in the quiet beauty that surrounded her. She gave thanks to Painted Woman for the opportunity.

As she pulled the *kabun* boots off her feet, her thoughts moved to Geronimo. Colonel Polk was working with General Crook to locate the elusive Apache leader. Geronimo was still raising havoc on both sides of the border, stealing food from ranchers in order to keep his people from starving to death. Setting the boots aside, Kuchana stood up and shed the regulation blue kersey pants. The trousers were made for a man's shape and they fit her poorly.

In early December, Colonel Polk would mount a ten-day effort to find Geronimo. According to the reports, the renegade Indian leader was in Sonora, and Polk had made it abundantly clear that he expected Kuchana to track and find him this time. With a sigh, she unwrapped her red headband, allowing it to drop from her fingers and fall to her feet.

Moving to the edge of the water, she tested the temperature with her toes. The pool was warm and inviting despite the November weather. The day was perfect, except that Gib wasn't here. How much she'd missed him these past three interminable days. Since the day Melissa had tried to frame her, Gib had subtly withdrawn. She still saw him at least once a day, but it was as if he was shielding his feelings.

She looked down and stared into the ripples created by the movements of her foot in the still water of the pool. That was how Gib affected her. Each time he gave her that heated, silent look, her heart bounded in her breast like a startled deer. Sometimes she would catch him watching her. In those split seconds, she saw raw hunger in his blue eyes, and it made her go weak with longing for something she had no experience with.

Unbuttoning the shirt, she felt the coolness lap her ankles. Tipping back her head, allowing the light of Holos to bathe her face, Kuchana slid her fingers through the heavy folds of her hair. The day was cool, but the warm pool invited her to come into its depths. Smiling, Kuchana slipped out of the shirt, tossing it on shore, and stood naked in the water.

Without hesitation, she walked forward and then glided into the deeper water. Her long, thick hair streamed about her as she dived and resurfaced.

Poppy had given her a special bar of soap made with lavender scent. Standing in waist-deep water, she lathered her hair, and then her entire body with the wonderful soap. Never had she smelled anything so good! Tossing the soap on to the bank, Kuchana turned and dived back into the pool to rinse off.

As she resurfaced, treading water, Kuchana heard an unfamiliar sound. Water streamed from her hair into her face, blurring her vision. Wiping the water away from her eyes, she twisted her head in the direction of the sound. A gasp escaped her lips. Private Odie Faulkner, the hulking German cook, was standing naked in the shallows, grinning like a wolf who had cornered its quarry.

"Now, ain't this somethin'," he shouted, his voice echoing off the canyon walls. "I just happened to come by for a swim and who should be here?" His thick lips pulled into a huge smile.

Fear stabbed through Kuchana. Faulkner's skin was a pasty white compared to the men who patrolled under the desert sun. The cook never left the shaded safety of the chow tent. Disgust came on the heels of her fear. She was shocked by the cook's nakedness. An Apache warrior would never appear like this in front of a maid. Never!

Angrily, Kuchana shouted, "Leave! You have no business here!"

Odie sniggered and moved slowly toward her, the water up to his knees. "Chee told me you were here. Come here, girl. Come and let Odie sample your goods."

Kuchana moved quickly, striking out toward shore where her clothes and weapons lay. The instant her feet dug into the sandy bottom, she hurled herself forward, taking leaping strides toward the grassy bank.

"Come here!" Odie roared, flailing after her. He bounced awkwardly through the shallows, veils of water flying up around him.

Her breath coming in sharp gasps, Kuchana lunged for her clothes. Her hands were steady as she reached for the knife. She heard the cook approaching, his grunt sounding like one of the pigs kept in a shaded pen behind the stables at the post.

Whirling around, her wet hair plastered to her body, she held the knife ready. The cook's face was the color of a ripe plum, his mouth open and his breath coming in punctuated gasps. He halted in the ankle-deep water, eyeing her and then the knife.

"Don't ya know your place, girl? Ya don't draw a knife on Odie." He grinned, rubbing his crotch. "I've got somethin' ya been wantin' for a long time. Kept my eye on ya, I have."

Kuchana felt heat in her cheeks and realized she was blushing. Grabbing her shirt, she jerked it over her shoulders, wanting to hide her nudity from the cook's eyes.

"Leave," she rattled in a low voice.

Leering, Odie took another step toward her. "Look at this, girl. I'll pleasure ya. Ain't nothin' to be afeared of."

"Come one step closer and I'll cut off that worm between your legs."

Odie jerked to a halt, scowling. He looked down at his crotch, his face reddening. "Why you slut of a redskin, I'll show ya what a real man is all about."

Kuchana braced herself for Odie's charge out of the water. She brought the knife close to her side, keeping her other hand outstretched.

A rifle was fired once, twice, three times. The water between Kuchana and the cook shot up in geysers. Odie croaked and leapt back, falling into the water with a huge splash. Kuchana turned to pick up her rifle.

"Gib!" His name was torn from her lips as she saw the sergeant on his horse at the entrance to the area. She straightened, the damp tails of her red shirt clinging to her thighs. His face was dark with anger as he rode up, pulling his horse to a stop beside her.

"Are you all right?" Gib kept his eyes on Faulkner, who was blundering about trying to stand up.

"Y-yes, I'm fine," Kuchana said with a quaver, allowing the knife to hang at her side.

Gib shifted his attention to the cook. "Faulkner," he roared, "get your ass out of here. Now! You're on report, mister."

Odie stood in the knee-deep water, his mouth hanging open, staring at the soldier. "But, Sergeant, I was just comin' here to wash." He stabbed a finger in Kuchana's direction. "Why, she came down here and started flauntin' herself at me. What could I do?"

Holding on to very real anger, McCoy grated, "I don't believe a word you're saying, Private." He lifted his rifle menacingly. "Now get the hell out of here and back to the post. When I get there, you're going on report for misconduct."

Whining, Odie trudged out of the water. Kuchana quickly put on her trousers and buttoned her shirt. She noticed that Gib had turned his horse so that his back was to her, and she could dress with some privacy.

Gib walked his weary horse over to where Faulkner was getting back into his clothes. Thank God Poppy had told him that Kuchana was at the pool after he'd arrived back at the post. Chee had shrugged, pretending to know nothing. Frowning, McCoy realized that Kuchana still had many enemies on the post. After the colonel had been made aware that his wife had struck Kuchana with a crop, she had been vindicated. Gib had thought things might cool down, but he'd been wrong.

"Hurry up," McCoy ordered the cook. Faulkner pulled on his boots, his feet still wet.

"I swear she did this to me," he whined.

Resting the rifle across his thighs, Gib remained immune to the cook's lament.

"She did!" Odie cried, moving toward his horse, which he'd hidden behind a wall of mesquite. He clambered into the saddle, and the horse groaned from his weight. When he realized the grim-faced sergeant wasn't going to say anything more, Odie spurred his horse and galloped out of the canyon.

Gib sheathed the rifle and turned his horse around. Kuchana was sitting on the bank, pulling her wet hair from beneath the damp red shirt she wore. He reined the animal to a halt and dismounted.

Kuchana sat and watched his approach. In her eyes and heart, no man had the stature of Gib McCoy. His skin was burned bronze by years of exposure to the sun. His build was powerful and lean, like that of a cougar. When he gave her a welcoming smile, it went straight to her heart.

Crouching in front of her, Gib reached out, moving several wet strands of hair that were stuck to her flushed cheek. "Are you all right?" he asked. He saw her brown eyes grow warm and golden, and all the need he'd held so long deep within exploded like summer lightning.

Kuchana nodded, closing her eyes as he caressed her hair. His gesture was thrilling. "I . . . yes."

"Tell me what happened." Gib knew Faulkner would be raising hell with Lieutenant Carter, telling lies to the officer as soon as he got back to the post. He'd have to defend Kuchana once again, just as he had protected her from Melissa's vicious attack.

Kuchana's pulse leaped violently as Gib continued to run strands of her long hair through his callused fingers. She absorbed Gib's caring gesture, understanding that they were alone as never before. "I . . . Chee gave me permission to come to the pool because I killed ten deer. He promised this to me if I did."

Gib smiled, drowning in her eyes. "He didn't think you could track down that many."

Laughter bubbled up her throat, and Kuchana relaxed beneath his ministrations. There was something beautiful and clean in the way Gib touched her. "Well, I did. He said I could come here today. I was alone, and I was not on guard, either. I thought this place was safe."

Gib's hand stilled on her shoulder. Her hair was drying quickly in the heat of the sun and the slight breeze. He shook his head. "No place is ever completely safe, Kuchana."

Gib was so close that his sweaty features were open to her inspection. Kuchana nodded, her lips parting as she saw a fierce longing come into his eyes. "My heart was empty while you were gone," she admitted softly. "These past three days were without life."

His smile was very tender. "So, you missed me?"

She rested her cheek against his hand as he brought it upward. Just once, she wanted to give in to her feelings for Gib, to show him her love. "Just as Mother Moon misses Holos."

The magic of Kuchana's honesty unstrung McCoy. All his good intentions of staying away from her, of holding his feelings of love for her at bay, dissolved in the seriousness of her gaze. He watched as her lips parted unconsciously. Without meaning to, without even thinking, Gib leaned down, framing her face with his hands.

The instant Gib's mouth touched hers, Kuchana closed her eyes. She inhaled his scent as his lips settled warmly against hers. The sensation struck her like lightning. Heat and moistness collected between her thighs. Her hand moving from her side, she placed it against his chest. Beneath the dampness of his shirt, she could feel the pound of his heart as his kiss deepened.

McCoy groaned, his fingers tightening on her face as her lips blossomed beneath his. She smelled of lavender laced with her own special scent. Her hair was thick and flowed across his hands as he tilted her chin slightly, hungrily seeking more contact with her lips. Just the grazing touch of her

hand tentatively resting against his chest drove Gib beyond
all the barriers he'd erected to remain immune to Kuchana.
It was impossible. Her lips were yielding as he gently taught
her how to kiss him in return. Her attempt was humbling as
she returned his searching movement with equal hunger.

Kuchana felt bereft when Gib ended the heated kiss. They
sat there, breathing raggedly, and staring deeply into one
another's eyes. Her lips tingled with the fire of his mouth.
She stared childlike at him, feeling the unsettled heat roil-
ing through her like an unexpected summer storm.

"You're so sweet," Gib said hoarsely, forcing himself to
sit back on his heels. He saw Kuchana's eyes grow concerned when he removed his hands from her face. "I'm
sorry. I didn't plan on kissing you."

Touching her lips, Kuchana whispered, "I am not."

He smiled, taking off his hat, wiping the sweat from his
brow. Giving her a tender look, he said, "Good." Gib knew
the Apache's morals were the strictest of all tribes. A maid
losing her virginity before marriage was not tolerated. She
would view his kiss as a commitment. He'd made a silent
one to her long ago, but it was too soon to tell her of his
love, of his need for her. Still, the circumstances had
changed—dramatically.

Lowering her lashes, Kuchana sat in the lulling silence.
Poppy's words about Gib courting her came to mind.
Gathering her courage, she looked at him and found his eyes
filled with happiness. It gave her the impetus to speak.
"What does a kiss mean between a man and a woman in the
pindah world?"

He sat down and crossed his legs. A few feet separated
them. It was time to talk. He couldn't lie to her. "A kiss is
a sacred thing between a man and woman," he told her in a
low voice.

Relief snagged through Kuchana. "It is sacred. That's
good, then."

Toying with a blade of grass, Gib held her gaze, then frowned. Odie's attack on Kuchana had changed everything. "I need to know a couple of things, Kuchana."

"Yes?"

"You've never spoken much about your life with Geronimo's tribe. Is there a special man who rides with him that holds your heart?" McCoy held his breath, waiting for her answer. Often an Apache maid was courted for a year or more, with both families deeply involved in the elaborate customs that preceded the marriage. To the Apache, marriage was the most sacred of all ceremonies.

Kuchana shook her head. "My heart has not been given," she whispered. Then she felt a slow pounding of dread. To lie was unthinkable. "And what of you?" Poppy had said he was not married, but she wanted to hear it from him. "Is your heart given to another woman?"

Gib grinned. No white woman he knew would be so bold as to ask that question of a man. "No."

Again relief fled through Kuchana and she nodded, compressing her lips.

"Listen to me, Kuchana," he said, capturing her hand and holding it. "My intentions toward you are honorable."

"Poppy said that."

His mouth quirked. So much for hiding his feelings for Kuchana. "What's she been filling your head with?" he teased.

Kuchana's smile was tentative. She didn't know what the 'honorable' intentions of a *pindah* man meant. Did it mean marriage? "When Melissa accused me of being sweet on you, I did not know what that meant. So I asked Poppy. She said that it meant a man had serious intentions of the heart toward the woman he was sweet on."

"That's right," Gib said. As he held her naive gaze, he knew he had to protect her. Although her kiss had been warm with welcome, it didn't necessarily mean she loved him. And even if she did, the very fact that she was Apache and he was in the army would cause terrible problems. Problems he didn't want Kuchana to endure.

Turning her hand over, he lightly traced the lines in her palm. "Until Geronimo is captured, I think it best that how we feel toward one another be our secret, Kuchana."

Delightful sensations rippled up her arm at Gib's touch. Never had she felt such pleasure at such a simple act. "Is that why you have avoided me since Melissa accused me?"

He nodded, lifting her palm and placing a moist kiss on it. Damn, it wasn't going to be easy keeping his hands off her. She invited exploration, and he ached to teach her the beauty of love between a man and woman. "It is the only way I can protect you from certain people at the post. If Melissa could prove how I felt toward you, she'd mount another campaign and try to get you in trouble."

"But at times like this, when we are alone, it is all right to show our true feelings of the heart?"

Gib reluctantly released her hand. She was incredibly responsive to even his slightest touch. "That won't be very often, I'm afraid."

"My mother said that love was like the saguaro cactus— slow and yet enduring, becoming stronger with each year after marriage."

"She's right," Gib said seriously. "You know how I feel about you. Now tell me how you feel about me."

Licking her lips, Kuchana was unable to hold his probing gaze. "Ever since I met you at the gate the day I rode to the post, my heart has felt differently toward you." Her voice was husky with feeling.

"What kind of different?" he asked.

With a shrug, Kuchana grimaced, looking toward the pool, which appeared much calmer than she felt. "What I feel here—" she pressed her hand to her breast "—is something I have never felt before. A joy that feels as if it will leap out of my heart and sing to the four directions." Kuchana's mouth pulled into a softened smile. "You make me happy."

"Tell no one of it," Gib warned.

"I told Poppy and Nettie of this feeling. Was that wrong?"

With a laugh, Gib got to his feet. He held out his hand, helping Kuchana to stand. "That's why she's been dropping all these bald hints lately. Poppy and her family can be trusted." He held her hand, wanting to draw her those few inches to him and crush her smiling mouth against his once again. "Just don't tell anyone else. Promise?"

"I promise."

McCoy let go of her hand and picked up the reins of his horse. "Come on, we've got to be getting back, or the tongues at the post will start wagging."

Kuchana nodded and hurriedly put on her boots and wrapped the red cloth around her brow. Her heart sang with a newfound happiness, while Gib's kiss hovered in her memory.

Gib mounted and slouched comfortably in his saddle, watching as Kuchana gathered her things and placed them in the saddlebag. Worry now erased the happiness he felt. More than ever, he wanted to protect her from the whites who hated her because she was an Apache. Lately, Melissa had been quiet, and that bothered him. According to Poppy, when the wife of the commander was silent, she was usually up to something. And then, there was Two Toes, the Yavapai, whose hatred of Kuchana was no secret.

Rubbing his chin, Gib watched Kuchana mount her mare. They left the canyon at a walk. He wasn't in that much of a hurry to return to the post. The precious moments he and Kuchana could spend together were rare, and he savored every one of them.

"A week from now, we go on expedition," Kuchana said, breaking the silence.

"This time, Lieutenant Carter will be in charge."

"He is going around the post bragging that he will capture Geronimo this time."

"Carter couldn't capture a grasshopper, much less your leader. Geronimo has evaded everyone."

"So far," Kuchana whispered. Her concern for her sister and the people who rode with Geronimo was never far from her mind or heart. The other ten-day expeditions in which she had taken part had been with Major Dobbins, a veteran like Gib. It took careful planning and, more importantly, good judgment to cross the Sonora desert without incident. The army animals were not accustomed to the heat and sand, and they refused to eat cactus for nourishment. The pack mules had to be loaded down with water and grain for the expedition, which slowed up the column.

Frustration marked McCoy's features. As they rode out of the canyon, in the distance ahead of them the post wavered in veils of heat. "This is Carter's first ten-day expedition, and unfortunately, I'm in charge of the men and animals."

"Will he listen to your counsel?"

"I doubt it."

Kuchana snorted. "Then, he will lose many animals and he will never get close to Geronimo."

"I know."

Chapter Nine

"Sergeant," Carter said angrily, "these men are lazy. The color of their skin guarantees that. We ought to be at least at a slow trot across this living hell, not a damn walk!"

Once again, Gib tried to placate the officer. Carter had whined about the broiling heat nonstop for the past four days. "Sir, if we push these horses beyond a walk in this kind of temperature, they're going to die. The men have been on these expeditions before, and they know enough not to force the horses into a trot, or they'll be walking back to the post." McCoy rode with the lieutenant at the head of the thirty-man column. He held on to his fraying patience. The trek across the desert into Mexico had been hot as always, burning up the men's patience. Carter wasn't handling it well at all.

Irritably, Carter rubbed his sunburned face. He glared at the jagged-looking mountains of Sonora coming up in the distance. The peaks wavered like a mirage, from the heat dancing across the surface of the desert. The sky was a pale blue with clouds like white horse tails feathered across it. There was no escape from the insufferable and intolerable sun. He glowered at the sergeant, noting that his uniform, like his own, was coated with layers of dust. McCoy was slouched in his saddle, his hat drawn down across his eyes, seemingly immune to the inferno. The yellow bandanna at his throat was soaked with sweat. Fingering his own neck-

erchief, Carter was disgusted with the filth he had to endure.
At the post, he bathed twice a day. Out here, all he could do
was collect more and more dust and sand on his sensitive
skin.

"Dammit, Kuchana had better be right about this new
trail she picked up. This is ridiculous. No one should have
to stand this kind of heat." Carter rose in the saddle and
twisted around. There were forty heavily loaded mules
bearing barrels of water, grain and food rations for the men.
The soldiers rode with their heads down, shoulders slumped,
their uniforms clinging to their bodies. Carter sat back down
in the saddle, glaring. At least at the post, during the hottest part of the day, he remained in his office, where it was
much cooler.

"I still think you ought to let her track with Charlie,"
McCoy protested. This morning, Carter had ordered Two
Toes to ride with Kuchana. She distrusted the Yavapai, who
made it known at every opportunity how he felt about her.
Normally, Gib was responsible for the scout assignments,
but Carter was pushing his weight around, canceling out his
orders. Big Elk and Chee were not compatible. Chee worked
better with Two Toes, and Kuchana did well with Big Elk,
Charlie or Bigfoot. Why Carter wanted to meddle in the affairs of his corporals and sergeants was beyond Gib. The
officer didn't have any sensitivity about the Indians and the
fact that some tribes were rivals, some friends.

"I was right to put her with Two Toes," Carter snapped,
giving Gib a triumphant look. "Didn't they pick up Geronimo's new trail this morning?"

Any of the scouts could have discovered the trail, but
McCoy said nothing. "Sir, no one knows yet if it is Geronimo's trail."

"Kuchana said it was."

McCoy gave Carter a deadly look. "No, sir, she did not."
He was all too aware that Carter was constantly trying to
maneuver Kuchana into a position where she could be
placed on report. Clarissa, Melissa's personal maid, had told

Poppy that she had overheard the commander's wife talking to Carter about placing Kuchana on report at any opportunity. Of course, Clarissa had pretended not to hear the conversation and walked quietly back to the door and made enough noise for them to stop their conversation when she made her second entrance.

"Sergeant, I heard her say exactly that."

"She said it might be Geronimo's trail, but couldn't be sure. Corporal Highland, who was with us when she discovered the trail, will tell you that, sir."

Angrily, Carter clamped his mouth shut and stared straight ahead. When it came to loyalty, the coloreds would side with McCoy every time. They'd lie to save his white skin. If Highland stuck to his guns and faithfully repeated what McCoy had just said, Carter couldn't place Kuchana on report. He'd have to wait until another opportunity arose and try again. Damn, but the sergeant was protective of that woman savage.

Carter glanced at the sergeant. "What do you think of Kuchana?"

The question caught McCoy off guard. "Sir?"

"As a woman," he added, watching the sergeant closely. Melissa swore on her instincts that McCoy was in love with Kuchana. There was no proof, of course. Kuchana could barely speak English, and she was so damn simple in comparison to the cultured and well-educated ladies of the post. Not even a mule could hold a decent conversation with her. Who would want to bed down with a woman warrior? That was like bedding down with a poisonous Gila monster!

"She's an excellent tracker," Gib said, watching the lieutenant's eyes light up with feral interest. This was the first time an officer had ever asked anything about Kuchana. Did Carter suspect his growing involvement with her? Appraising the lieutenant critically, McCoy didn't think so. Carter hated her so much that he was probably casting around for anything to hang on her head.

"I didn't mean *that* way, Sergeant."

Gib feigned surprise. "Oh?"

"Yes, you know. Man to man. She's a very attractive woman with certain, er, attributes that might draw a man to her bed."

Holding on to a chuckle, Gib lowered his head, pretending to tighten the strap on the bedroll anchored in front of his saddle so that Carter couldn't read the expression on his face. "Sir, my only concern with the scouts, whether they are male or female, is to help them do what they do best—track. In my opinion, Kuchana is our best tracker."

Simmering with frustration, Carter asked, "Do any of the other scouts find her worthy of their attention?"

Choking back laughter, McCoy took a deep breath before he answered. "I wouldn't know," he answered lightly. "Why don't you ask her, sir?"

"A gentleman doesn't stoop to those kinds of questions."

McCoy said nothing as he spotted Kuchana and Two Toes in the distance. They must have found something of interest in order to wait for the column to catch up with them. Normally, the scouts ranged one to two miles ahead of the main body of cavalry. As they approached, he couldn't take his eyes off Kuchana. When on patrol, Gib forced her to wear the cumbersome army jacket. It was hot and miserable, but at least it identified her as a scout. Down in Mexico, groups of undisciplined Mexicans and Indians who hunted Geronimo would shoot first and ask questions later. If the scouts didn't wear the jackets identifying them as friends, they might be instantly shot and killed by the murdering *soldatos*.

Kuchana met and held McCoy's gaze as the column ground to a halt. For an instant, she saw his eyes soften, and she felt joy riffle through her like a cooling night wind across a heated desert. Carter blew his nose noisily into a handkerchief, breaking the silence.

"Well, Two Toes, what did you find?" Carter demanded, stuffing the handkerchief back into the rear pocket of his trousers.

The Yavapai shrugged. "She found it."

Damn! Carter looked at Kuchana. The woman sat straight and tall in the saddle, and her small mustang looked fresh compared to the rest of the animals. His own horse, one that he had brought with him from the East, was standing with its head bowed, its nose almost touching the ground. "What did you find?"

"I saw a track that tells me it is Geronimo we hunt," Kuchana said proudly, pointing at the ground.

Carter glanced sharply at McCoy. "Do you hear that, McCoy?"

Gib nodded, wishing Kuchana hadn't said it. "I do, sir." He held her gaze. "What makes you think it's Geronimo?" he asked her.

"The horse he rides has a large chip out of its right front hoof." Kuchana dismounted, gesturing for McCoy to come and look.

McCoy got off his horse, moving to where Kuchana crouched. Her thick black hair hung around her shoulders and breasts as she leaned down, pointing at the print. Kneeling, he studied the hoofprint. Sure enough, it was of a hoof that had a crescent-shaped piece missing. He looked up and gave her a quick smile.

"Good work."

The praise made her feel wonderful. "Thank you."

McCoy straightened and walked over to Carter. "I think we ought to make camp at the base of the mountains, sir. We should be there in about three hours. Tomorrow morning we can start tracking Geronimo through those high canyons."

Carter nodded. "Excellent, Sergeant." The idea of only three more hours riding in this brutal oven appealed to him.

Kuchana swung back up onto her horse. For the rest of the day she would continue to track until they halted to make camp. Uneasy with Two Toes, she'd barely slept the past four nights. His eyes told her that he was waiting for an opportunity to send her to the Big Sleep.

Kuchana sat tensely on her blanket. She had settled herself next to the horse line, knowing that Wind would alert her if someone approached. Two Toes had made camp with the other scouts far enough away, but she didn't trust him. The stars blinked in the coverlet of Father Sky, and Mother Moon moved silently from the eastern horizon, nearly full.

Grateful for the light, Kuchana sat with her legs crossed, listening to the murmurings of the soldiers down below her. Carter had chosen to make camp just at the foot of the wild and rugged mountains. By the end of the day, four horses had died, and those men would now have to walk. Carter was furious, and she wondered if the man ever spoke in a normal tone of voice. He had screamed at the four soldiers for losing their mounts. It had not been their fault. Carter had pushed the column too fast and not given the animals enough rest.

Several other cavalry horses were becoming lame because the heat of the desert was too much for their hooves. Unlike the hardy mustangs who were raised in the arid wastelands, the Eastern horses bought by the army were practically useless in the desert. This was Kuchana's third expedition, and she knew that by the time it was over, at least half the column would be returning on foot.

The other problem was metal, of which the equipment had a considerable amount. During the day, it became too hot to touch and it was easy to burn one's skin. Even the Springfield rifles were impossible to handle. Carter was discovering that expeditions were a daily nightmare of problems that had to be faced and solved.

A noise made Kuchana jerk her attention to the right, her hand automatically moving to the butt of her knife. Out of the darkness she saw McCoy approaching. Her heart beat harder, but not out of fear.

"You move almost as quietly as an Apache," she told him in a low voice, as she got to her feet.

Gib noted she had taken off the army jacket. "I purposely made noise. I didn't want to scare you." He halted, less than a foot between them. In the starlight he saw the glow in her eyes and smiled. "How are you doing?" He was worried about Two Toes.

She shrugged. "Better than the dark-skinned ones." Kuchana gestured at the encampment below. Most of the men had fallen into an exhausted sleep, except for the guards who patrolled the perimeter. "Carter is still braying like a mule."

McCoy chuckled softly. "He's been upset since this expedition started. I don't think he's going to change. He's the kind of man who wants a soft life, not a hard one, like this." He looked longingly at her smiling lips, remembering the molten kiss they'd shared a week earlier. He hadn't been able to erase the torrid memory from his thoughts and his appetite for Kuchana had only sharpened as a result.

Drowning in the look he gave her, Kuchana felt shaky. A strange, uncoiling sensation began between her legs, a feeling of pleasure coupled with an ache. How could just his heated, silent gaze make her feel like this? She stared at his mouth, wanting to taste him once again.

Reaching out, Gib threaded the thick strands of her hair through his fingers. "I just wanted to tell you how pretty you are."

Kuchana absorbed the tremor in his husky voice. "Your eyes speak of what lies in your heart," she breathed softly.

Gib moved closer, trying to fight his need. Her lips had parted, and the whisper of her words had grazed his body like a lover's caress. "And I see the happiness in yours," he admitted, settling his hands against her face. Her eyes were lustrous as she looked up at him. "I can't get the kiss we shared out of my mind," he told her thickly, needing to feel her mouth against his once again.

Lifting her hands, Kuchana placed them against his chest. "I dream of it," she admitted, tilting her chin upward, silently asking him to do it. She saw Gib smile.

It was wrong to kiss her, but Gib didn't care. Their time together was nearly nonexistent. Every day, the eyes of those who wanted to hurt Kuchana followed her every move. Only in the cover of darkness could he steal precious moments with her. Leaning down, he whispered her name against her mouth. The texture of her lips became firm as he claimed her hungrily. Their first kiss a week ago had been tentative. This time, he felt her unbridled, heated response, her lips molding and moving against his, signaling a hunger that matched his own. Surprised and yet pleased, Gib felt a savage heat building in his loins as she stepped closer, pressing her body to his.

Kuchana moaned as his mouth claimed hers in fiery adoration, his tongue tracing her lower lip, biting it gently and then soothing it. A storm burst within her, and her breathing became ragged and shallow as he continued his tender assault. Her senses reeling, she tasted the sun on his mouth, the saltiness of his sweat, and inhaled his odor, which only heightened her need of him.

"Easy, easy," Gib crooned against her wet, full lips. She was trembling, and he moved his hands from her face to around her body, bringing her against him. Like water cupped in his hands, Kuchana spilled against him, her brow resting against his jaw. He slid his hand slowly up and down her spine, trying to steady her. Inhaling her wonderful fragrance, he detected the lavender scent. "Settle down, my wild, beautiful woman," he coaxed thickly.

Kuchana could only breathe raggedly, holding on to Gib for support, afraid of falling. Her knees felt weak in the aftermath of their kiss. Just the soothing touch of his hand on her back stabilized her spinning world. "I feel as if the Thunder Beings struck me," she managed in a quavering tone.

Chuckling, Gib agreed. Thunder Beings were the creators of storms. "I feel as if I've been struck by lightning, too." She was incredibly pliant in his arms. He hadn't dreamed of holding her, not yet. Now, here she was, clinging to him, trembling, and he could feel her womanly curves fitting against his body. "It will pass," he told her, his mouth near her ear. "Just rest on me and I'll hold you until your knees get a little more solid under you."

"How do you know of my knees?" She was amazed.

Smiling, he pressed a chaste kiss against her hair. "Because mine feel the same way."

Laughter slid up her throat, and Kuchana buried her face in the damp folds of his shirt, aware of the tensile strength of his chest beneath her cheek. She felt Gib's silent laughter in return, and in that moment felt happier and more alive than she had in all her life. The darkness enfolded them like a mother with her children, hiding them and what they held in their hearts for one another. For once, Kuchana was grateful for the night.

After another five minutes, Kuchana was able to stand on her own. Gib allowed her to step away from him. He saw a sentry coming their way and knew he had to leave.

"Tomorrow," he told her seriously, gripping her shoulder, "be careful. I'm going to order Chee and Big Elk to scout, but I want you to stay behind me. If Geronimo is around, he might try to kill you if he recognizes you."

She basked in his concern. "Geronimo will not kill me. Remember? I am already dead as far as he is concerned."

McCoy wasn't so sure. The sentry was nearly upon them and he let his hand slip from her shoulder. "Just stay close to me tomorrow, and stay out of Carter's way."

Understanding, Kuchana nodded. "I will."

He smiled, noting the softness in her face. "I'll see you tomorrow morning."

The prints that Chee picked up on Geronimo's group led up a steep wall of a cliff. Kuchana saw the scouts far ahead, climbing slowly on the winding trail. She had used the rocky path many times in the past, but it was dangerous, and if man or animal was careless, they could plunge to their deaths.

Carter's hands were white-knuckled on the reins of his horse, who was stumbling over the rocks on the eighteen-inch-wide trail. One side was the cliff wall. On the other, a thousand-foot drop to the floor of the canyon. His eyes were huge with fear, and he sat frozen on his horse.

McCoy placed the reins of his horse on its neck. If the horse stumbled, the animal would need the length of the reins to use his head to regain his balance. Carter was speechless in front of him, holding his horse's head tight. The fool. Gib twisted around in the saddle to look at Kuchana, who rode behind him.

"How long is this trail?"

"Another mile and then it opens up into a new canyon above us."

"Does it get any narrower?"

She nodded. "Yes, up ahead."

McCoy grimaced and looked beyond her. The men of the Fourth were struggling up single file, their faces filled with tension. "Don't look down!" McCoy shouted back at them. "Look in front of you!" He saw several of his men jerk their heads up and stare ahead. There was no way Gib was going to lose one of his men to vertigo. It had happened before, but not to an expedition he was in charge of.

The heavily laden mules brought up the rear of the struggling column. Although the animals were more surefooted than the horses, Gib worried about them. Carter had ordered heavier than normal loads for them and they were top-heavy. If they lost their equilibrium, there was no way they could right themselves. Damn Carter and his shortsightedness. Gib had tried to argue with him at the post while the mules were being loaded. He'd warned the officer that if the column were caught in narrow confines, the mules would get in trouble. If even one mule was lost, the expedition would have to be shortened. There would be no way to retrieve the food, water and grain the mule carried. The only people who managed to survive in this kind of climate without supplies were the Apaches, who had learned to live off the land and to teach their horses to eat cactus.

Just as Kuchana predicted, the trail narrowed. Carter was taut in the saddle, a cold sweat pouring off him. His eyes were shut tight against the sight of the dizzying height. His gelding was stumbling badly. Every time the animal faltered, the officer yanked hard on the reins. Three times, McCoy had told him to let the reins drop but Carter just kept pulling harder, forcing the horse's head down practically against its chest.

Suddenly a shout went up behind McCoy. He heard the braying of a mule. Twisting around, he saw the lead mule leap backward. He spotted a rattler on the trail in front of the animal. Damn!

"Let him go, Corky!" he shouted at the man holding the mule's halter rope. If he didn't the man would go down the canyon with the tottering mule.

Kuchana watched in horror as the column froze on the ledge. The mule brayed again, the cry cut short as the load he carried shifted to the right, destroying his balance. Her hand flew to her mouth as she watched the mule tumble over the edge, legs flailing as it plunged downward. The animal's last bray echoed like a scream off the rocky walls. Kuchana shut her eyes, unable to watch the impact.

"My God," Carter whispered, his eyes enormous. The mule lay unmoving far below. Shaking, he gripped the pommel of his saddle. "G-get me out of here, McCoy!" he shrieked.

Gib saw that the officer was panicking. Quickly dismounting, he edged along the wall of rock.

"Take it easy, Carter," he called. "Just sit still."

"I-I'm going to fall! I'm going to fall! I'm going to fall!" Carter was hunched low on the saddle, his fingers digging into his horse's mane.

The idiot! Gib thought, as he saw the horse begin to shake in fear. "Shut up," he hissed to the officer. "Shut up and sit still." Flattening his back against the jagged rock, he eased himself between the horse and cliff. One wrong move, and they could all wind up over the edge.

McCoy crooned to the frightened horse. Carter held the reins so tightly that the animal's mouth was open and bleeding. Moving slowly, McCoy reached up and wrapped his fingers around the reins in Carter's hands.

"What are you doing?" Carter whined. "Don't loosen the reins. Don't—"

With a powerful jerk, McCoy stripped the reins from Carter's gloved, sweaty hands. Finally free, the horse whinnied and raised his head, relaxing. Glaring up at the officer, Gib put a hand on Carter's elbow.

"Get down," McCoy growled. "Nice and slow. We'll walk our horses up and out of this."

Panicking, Carter raised his knees and jammed them into the horse's sides. The animal grunted. Unable to leap forward, it jumped sideways, trapping McCoy.

Gib groaned as the horse pinned him to the wall. Son of a bitch! His ribs hurt and the rocks ground into his back. The animal was wild-eyed, hugging the cliff as Carter began to shriek again.

"Shut up!" McCoy roared. Swiftly, he lifted the toe of his boot, sinking it deep into the horse's belly. The animal jerked away. Instantly, Gib dropped to his hands and knees. The horse pulled back against the safety of the wall, scrambling for footing. Gib crawled around the horse's quivering legs, then slowly got to his feet. Holding his aching ribs, he glared up at the officer.

"Get the hell down off that horse. Now!"

His mouth working, Carter stared down at him. "I—I can't move. If I do, I'll fall."

"If you don't climb down out of that saddle right now I'll push you off myself," Gib snarled.

Kuchana watched tensely. McCoy's words rolled like thunder down the canyon. Carter jerkily dismounted and pressed his back to the cliff, breathing hard.

Murmuring to Wind, who had often negotiated these dangerous trails, Kuchana dismounted. She turned to watch as every man in the column followed suit.

"All right," Gib ground out, grabbing Carter by the collar, "you lead my horse up. I'll take yours."

Shaking his head, Carter babbled, "Y-yes, you take my horse, McCoy. I-I'll take yours."

Cursing roundly, McCoy moved in front of the gelding. He picked up the reins and clucked to the horse, and the animal followed placidly at his heels. The sooner they got off this trail, the better, Gib thought as he kept a sharp eye out for any more rattlers. He wouldn't be surprised if another one crawled up on the trail to bask in the sun.

Kuchana breathed a sigh of relief when at last they reached the end of the trail and entered a second canyon. This one was long and narrow with cliffs rising on both sides. Their yellow ocher color was dotted here and there with scrub. The column had made the rest of the trek without further incident and now Carter sat on a rock, his head resting in his hands, his face still waxen with fear.

Gib moved among the men, complimenting them on their courage under the circumstances. He had the mules and their loads checked. Everyone needed a rest, and taking over command, he ordered the column to halt and rest for half an hour.

Kuchana was taking a sip of the precious water from her canteen when she heard rifle shots ringing through the canyon. Sucking in a breath, she whirled around, looking for McCoy. His face was dark and tense.

"Geronimo!" she whispered, capping the canteen and throwing it back on the saddle.

"Mount up!" McCoy roared to the troop.

Carter shakily got to his feet. What now? The gunshots were continuing. The scouts must have run into Geronimo.

He climbed into the saddle, disoriented. The sounds of fighting were coming from every direction. At first, he thought his cavalry was being fired upon, but it wasn't. He watched the troop of Negroes quickly remount.

"Sergeant, get this column under way," he squeaked. There was no way he was riding in front. "Kuchana, take the lead."

"No!" McCoy roared, riding up to him. He glared at the officer. "I'll ride front. You stay back, Lieutenant."

Relieved that McCoy was taking over, Carter gladly acquiesced.

McCoy ordered the bugler to sound the charge. He urged his horse to the head of the column, drawing his pistol from its holster. As the notes of the bugle sounded, he spurred his horse forward at a gallop. The gunshots weren't that far ahead, and his two scouts would need reinforcements right away.

The thunder of horses' hooves echoed through the canyon. As Gib swung his gelding around the curve of the sandy-floored canyon, a horse came up abreast of his.

Jerking a look to his right, he saw the rider was Kuchana. "Get back!" he yelled at her. Dammit, he didn't want her in the line of fire.

"No!" she shouted, urging Wind to keep pace with his horse.

Gib swore under his breath. There was nothing he could do. Speed was of the essence. Part of him wanted to punish her for her foolish decision. Another part of him admired her for her courage under the circumstances. A fierce love welled up in Gib as he held her defiant gaze. God, how he loved her. And right now, the world was being torn apart all around them.

Chapter Ten

M<small>c</small>Coy bit back a curse as they rounded a large pile of towering rock. His eyes narrowed. Chee and Big Elk lay unmoving on the canyon floor, blood staining their clothes. Above them were a group of fifteen *soldatos* and Indians. His disgust turned to anger as he raised his hand, a signal for the column to halt.

"Stop shooting!" he shouted at the *soldatos* in Spanish. Automatically, he gestured sharply for Kuchana to remain behind him. *Soldatos* were the worst of the Mexican army. They were more scalp-hunters than trained military men. The Indians they used as scouts hated Geronimo and all Apaches with murderous intensity.

The leader of the *soldatos,* a huge, dark Mexican with a black mustache and sombrero, signaled for his men to hold their fire.

Gib spurred his horse forward, dismounting and dropping to Chee's side. He turned the Indian over. He was dead. So was Big Elk. Damn! McCoy straightened, glaring at the leader who had come forward while the rest of the group hung back among the rocks. "These men were army scouts."

"We thought they were Geronimo's warriors," the big one argued, gesticulating with his hand. "We had every right to kill them."

McCoy was breathing hard, trying to harness his fury. "They were wearing U.S. Army jackets. Are you all blind?"

Stung, the leader surveyed the column. "They sneaked up on us. We didn't know. One moment we were peacefully eating our meal, the next, we were being fired on."

Gib knew it was a lie. Scouts would never fire on anyone. They were sent out to spot the enemy and ride back as quickly as possible with their report. His gaze ranged over the ragged, dirty group. They looked more like animals than men. At least the scouts with the U.S. Army kept themselves clean and neat.

Carter rode up, thoroughly angry. "You tell those stinking bastards to get the hell out of here! Who do they think they are?"

"The *soldatos* will kill anyone who has black hair, Lieutenant," McCoy answered. "They get paid twenty-five dollars a scalp when they take them across the border and give them to a scalper. It doesn't even matter to them whether they kill an Indian or a Mexican."

"Didn't they see our scouts wearing our uniforms?"

"Sure they did. But they didn't care." Grimly, McCoy looked down at Chee and Big Elk. It was obvious that the two men had been bushwhacked. "And there's nothing we can do to bring them to justice. We're in Mexican territory."

With a wave of his gloved hand, Carter snarled, "Tell the stupid bastards to leave."

McCoy nodded, repeating the order in Spanish. He noticed the leader looking beyond him. Turning, he saw Kuchana sitting on Wind, her face filled with hatred. She could have just as easily been killed if she had been scouting. The thought of losing her struck him so hard that he closed his eyes for a moment, unable to wrestle with the feelings the realization cut loose within him.

"They lie!" Kuchana suddenly exclaimed. "Chee and Big Elk were innocent. The *culo-gordos* are murderers."

Carter turned his head, appraising Kuchana's taut, flushed features. She was angrier than a stirred-up hornet. He'd have been far more upset if one of his soldiers had been killed. Scouts were easily replaced.

The leader of the *soldatos* bristled at Kuchana's outburst. His round, sweaty face grew furious. "You tell that slut to shut her mouth or I'll blow her head off. No redskin speaks of us like that."

McCoy jerked his pistol from its holster, cocking the weapon and aiming it directly at the leader. "You even look like you're lifting that rifle in her direction and you're dead," he said roughly.

The leader glared down at McCoy. "You wouldn't shoot a *soldato*. We are partners. We are on your side."

Gib's finger brushed the trigger. He wanted to make sure they all understood him. "Get the hell out of here. Now."

"Geronimo is not here!" the leader cried. "You search in vain."

"Leave," McCoy ordered, the barrel of his pistol never wavering.

Stung, the leader gestured to his men. "Come, our friends will not share their food or fire with us." He glared at the officer. "We intend to report this to our superiors. You will be in much trouble."

McCoy said nothing as the group retrieved their horses and mules hidden behind the rocks and mounted. The last *soldato* to file past the waiting column took his whip and struck one of the pack mules on the rump.

The mule leapt forward, startled. The handler yelped, the rope singing out of his gloved hand. The mule, freed and heavily loaded with a day's supply of food, galloped down a trail that led to another part of the canyon.

"Dammit!" Carter shrilled. He jerked a look over at McCoy. "Send Kuchana after that mule. I will not lose another day's supplies."

Holstering his pistol, Gib held Carter's angry glare. "I'll go with her, sir. Our scouts aren't safe in this area alone.

And I'll be damned if I'm going to see another one of our people shot and killed.''

Shrugging, Carter dismounted. "I don't care what you do," he answered irritably. "Just find that damn mule and be back here by dusk." All Carter wanted was to rest in the shade. He gave orders to have the men bury the two scouts and set up camp.

Kuchana nudged Wind forward, still trembling from the encounter with the *soldatos*. She and Gib took off down the trail at a steady trot, disappearing quickly from view.

When they were alone and able to ride side by side, Kuchana spoke up.

"The *culo-gordo* murdered Chee and Big Elk."

"Yes," McCoy said evenly, "they did."

"You will not avenge their deaths?"

Gib shook his head. "We cannot. There is no way to dispute the *soldato*'s story, Kuchana." Without thinking, he reached over and gripped her hand. "I just thank God it wasn't you."

Kuchana was shaken by the raw emotion in Gib's voice. His fingers were firm against her hand. Shyly, she returned the squeeze. "Painted Woman watches over me," she returned. "She knows I have a promise to fulfill. She will not allow me to die before I can make sure my people are safe on the reservation once again."

"I'm not trusting anybody with your life," he groused, releasing her hand. "Not even Painted Woman."

"You protect me like a mother bear protects her cub," she chided.

Grimly, Gib nodded. They returned to the business of tracking the fleeing mule. The ocher-yellow walls of the canyon rose hundreds of feet around them.

"I know this area well," Kuchana began, as she pulled her sweaty mare to a halt, wiping her face free of perspiration with the back of her sleeve. She longed to get rid of the heavy wool jacket, but she knew Gib would insist she continue to wear it, especially now.

The shadows cooled them considerably, and Gib waited for Kuchana to tell him more as his gaze scanned the canyon.

"This trail the mule follows leads to a water hole," she explained.

"A water hole?" Gib had been in these mountains off and on for the past four years and had never seen any sign of water.

She smiled. "Yes, it's partially hidden in a cave at the end of a box canyon. The mule has picked up the scent of the water and is heading toward the hole."

"I'll be damned." Gib took off his hat, rubbing the sweat off his brow with his gloved hand.

"This water hole is one of two that Geronimo found for us. It is fed by an underground spring and half of it sits in a cave." She smiled. "There are even cottonwood trees and grass near it." Patting Wind affectionately, she added, "The horses will like it."

Grinning, Gib settled his hat back on his head. "I think I'll thank that *soldato* for causing the mule to bolt."

"I would like to bathe before we go back to camp."

McCoy nodded. "All right, but let's see if the mule's there first," he muttered.

Smiling confidently, Kuchana said, "He will be."

McCoy gave a low whistle as they rode to the end of a small box canyon. There, beneath an overhanging cliff, was a blue-green water hole. It wasn't large, but the cool colors of the water looked incredibly inviting against the yellow stone. The errant mule gave a bray as the two riders approached, lifting his head for only a moment before returning to his foraging along the bank.

Kuchana tilted her head, waiting for Gib's reaction.

"You were right," he said, laughing. Suddenly, the events of the past few hours slid off his shoulders. "This is incredible," he admitted, pulling his thirsty horse to a halt at the edge of the water.

Dropping the reins, Kuchana brought her leg across the front of her saddle and slid off. Wind promptly buried her nose in the water, gulping loudly. As Kuchana looked around, a sadness filled her. Many times they had camped nearby, waiting for the deer and bighorn to come down and water. It had been one of the few places they could get fresh meat for the starving group.

Dismounting, Gib saw her eyes grow dark as she looked around. He unbridled his horse, tying the headstall to the pommel, and let it drink its fill. None of the animals would stray from the water or grass, so it was safe to allow them to graze without hobbles. Coming around the horse, he crossed to Kuchana who was studying the rocky terrain.

"Memories?" he asked her quietly. Her hair was hanging in long, blue-black sheets, and he longed to reach out and run his fingers through the thick strands.

"Yes..." She looked up into his shadowed, sweaty features, thinking how handsome he was. "The animals come here to drink," she began softly, needing his nearness. "I can remember many times lying up there on that ledge, hidden, and waiting for a deer or bighorn."

"To feed your people."

She nodded, unexpected tears coming to her eyes. She turned away and her voice grew strangled. "Being here hurts my heart. It brings back so many memories of my family, of Ealae and her children..."

Gib settled a hand on her shoulder, gently pulling her around. He saw the tears begin to track through the dust on her cheeks. "Listen, why don't you bathe? I'll keep watch while you do. And then I'll wash while you stand guard."

Sniffing, Kuchana stole a look at him. "I should not cry. It is not right."

"I don't mind your tears," he whispered, removing them with his thumbs.

"You have said that before."

Gib held her troubled gaze. The last time he'd kissed her, the gold in her eyes had burned like sunlight. He longed to see that lustrous look in them once again. "Some *pindahs* don't consider tears as bad, or a sign of weakness."

"But, I am a warrior."

McCoy was in a dangerous situation. It had been so easy to erase Kuchana's tears, to cup her face, but as he stared down at her trembling lower lip, the heat in his loins exploded with violent intensity, and he ached to make her his. "In my eyes," he told her in an unsteady voice, "your tears don't make you weak, Kuchana. They bring out the softness in you. You walk in two different worlds," he went on quietly. "One expects you to be a warrior, but the other knows that you are a woman, something you've learned since coming to the post."

Kuchana nodded, closing her eyes, feeling protected and cared for by Gib. "I see the women wearing dresses, and I wonder what it would be like to wear one. Nettie wears pretty ribbons in her hair. And Poppy uses a water that makes her smell like flowers."

"Perfume," Gib said, gently caressing her high cheekbones. "All those things are about being a woman, Kuchana, but they don't make a woman what she is."

Opening her eyes, she met his gaze. "I do not understand."

Forcing himself to break contact with Kuchana, Gib allowed his hands to fall to his sides. "Melissa wears dresses all the time, has her hair done and wears sweet perfume, but that doesn't necessarily make her a woman."

Stymied, Kuchana lifted her shoulders. "Then what is a woman in your eyes?"

He smiled, caressing her hair. "What lies in her heart makes her a woman. You have that quality, Kuchana. You always have." Gib was moving onto dangerous ground. Ever since the first kiss, Kuchana had made a commitment to him, or she never would have allowed it. Each time they were alone like this, all his good intentions dissolved. Clearing his throat, he continued, "You've been a woman in my eyes since I met you. Nothing changes that."

"And you like my tears?"

"I like sharing what lies in your heart. When someone is special to another, these kinds of things happen naturally. It's a good sign."

Kuchana stood still, unsure what to do or say next. She saw the burning blue fire in his eyes, as she had seen it previously whenever he was about to kiss her. She longed to reach out and place her hand on his chest where his heart lay, but she fought the longing. *Pindahs* had different and confusing rules where a man and woman were concerned.

McCoy saw the darkness returning to her eyes. "Go bathe," he urged, wanting to somehow bring that smile back to her beautiful lips. He was rewarded instantly as her delight shone on her face.

"And then I will guard you?"

He nodded. It wasn't easy to let her go when what he really wanted to do was take her in his arms. "Yes, my turn next."

Kuchana watched as McCoy walked back to his horse and unsheathed the rifle. He turned his back to her and took a position that gave him a good view of the area. Once he had sat down on a rock in the shade near the pool, she eagerly stripped off her damp, dirty clothes.

As she stepped into the cool water, memories of the many times she had bathed here before surfaced. The women enjoying the deeper water while the children played in the shallows. As she dipped beneath the surface, she could almost swear she heard their laughter. Swimming to the edge, she waded out of the deeper part. Scooping up a handful of the sand on the bottom, she began to scrub her flesh until it was free of the sweat and dust of the expedition. Next came her hair, which she washed with renewed fury. Each night she would run the comb that Nettie had given her through her thick, black hair. It kept the strands free of the endless, blowing sand. Clean, she went to the bank, grabbed her clothes and washed them, too. The only thing she didn't wash was the army jacket. At least she would have clean clothes against her skin.

Placing the damp shirt and trousers on the rocks to dry, Kuchana turned and went back into the pool one last time. She paddled through its center, moving toward the half that was overhung by the ocher rock. For a few minutes, she played, diving, turning and gliding through the water.

McCoy heard her splashing and wanted to turn around and watch, but he knew how embarrassed Kuchana would be if he did so. The mule and horses munched contentedly on the grass, remaining beneath the flowing branches of a huge cottonwood tree. This place was a little slice of heaven, Gib decided. More than anything, he wanted to strip naked and join Kuchana in the pool.

Shaking his head, he tried to concentrate on keeping watch, constantly perusing the cliffs above. He heard Kuchana splashing toward him again.

Moving to the edge of the pool, Kuchana sat down on a flat rock to dry off in the sunlight. She ran her hands up and down her arms, brushing off excess water. She glanced over at Gib, noting his strong back and broad shoulders. He was sitting no more than ten feet from her.

"Poppy said you never married," she began. "Many of the soldiers do not have women."

Gib's rifle rested comfortably across his thighs. Kuchana was so close. He liked the huskiness in her voice. Swallowing hard against a dry throat, he tried to sound conversational. "The West isn't a place for most white women, Kuchana. They can't take the weather or the loneliness. That's why most of the men don't have wives."

"Poppy has a husband who's a lance-corporal," she pointed out, running the comb through her hair. "She followed him out here."

"Poppy and a lot of the laundresses did come West with their husbands."

"The dark-skinned women are courageous compared to *pindah* women."

Gib chuckled. "You might say that. Although, I've met some very brave *pindah* women, too. Most of them are married to ranchers. They're very special ladies."

Kuchana frowned as she moved the comb slowly through her thick hair. "You are a good and kind man, Gib. I know there are not many *pindah* women here, but I think you could have married and had a family."

He shrugged. "I've just never found the right woman, I guess." *Until now.*

"What must this woman have to be right for you?" she asked hesitantly, amazed at her audacity.

Gib thought for a moment, enjoying her searching question. "She must have eyes that glow with the gold of sunlight. Her laughter must take away pain. She must share her tears with me and hold me when I want to be held." He ran his hand down the barrel of the rifle, Kuchana's face hovering sweetly in his mind and heart. "She must possess the courage of a cougar and the sensitivity of a deer."

Kuchana's hands stilled as she savored his low, husky voice. How could she possibly be such a wonderful woman? She was not all those things. Gib had admitted that his intentions toward her were honorable, but did that mean he wanted to marry her? She didn't know, and now that he had just told her what he wanted in his woman, she was afraid to ask. It was impossible to be all those things, she decided, her heart breaking a little at the thought.

McCoy waited as the silence grew. He had tried to put what he felt in words and images that she would understand, perhaps finding herself in the picture he painted. "What kind of man would you want to marry?" he finally asked.

Kuchana stared out across the pool, her skin dry now and her hair barely damp. She tried to think, but her heart ached with pain over McCoy's earlier words. "I have not thought much about the man I will marry."

"It's important for me to know, Kuchana."

With a small, defeated shrug, she tried to put her feelings into words. "He would be a man who speaks from his heart and not lie or only tell part of the truth. He would be gentle with me, and proud of who and what I am. He would not ask me to change. His heart would be like the bear, powerful and protective." She licked her lips, frowning as she searched for more words.

"What about children?"

"Of course." She turned to stare at his back, longing to place her hand on his shoulders and feel his strength beneath her fingertips. "I hope that our love would be shown through the children I would bear him."

"So, someday, you want to have a family and not always be a warrior?"

Kuchana stood up, feeling the heat of sun on her skin. It was a good feeling, and she smiled. "Of late, I have been dreaming of a wickiup and children."

"Oh?"

"Yes." Kuchana splashed out of the shallows and placed the comb next to her dried clothes. She picked up the lavender calico shirt, shrugging it on and buttoning it. "I used to have nothing but dreams of fighting and battles. Now, since coming to the post, I have dreamed of a home and many children laughing and filling my arms."

"Is that a good dream?" Gib knew the Apache put great stock in their dreams.

With a small laugh, Kuchana said, "Very good." She pulled on the nearly dry trousers. Picking up the red cotton sash she used as a belt, she tied it around her waist. "I am dressed now," she informed him.

Gib rose and turned around. Kuchana's hair was sleek and heavy, shining from the recent combing. She was pulling it from beneath the collar of her shirt, allowing it to drape around her like an ebony cloak, her movements fluid and graceful.

Placing the rifle on the rock, he stepped toward her and put his hands on her shoulders. A look of surprise and then

You may be the winner of the

MILLION DOLLAR
GRAND PRIZE!

TO BE ELIGIBLE, AFFIX THIS STICKER TO SWEEPSTAKES ENTRY FORM

$1,000,000.00	**MILLION DOLLAR GRAND PRIZE**	$1,000,000.00
	SWEEPSTAKES ENTRY STICKER	
$1,000,000.00		$1,000,000.00

FOR A CHANCE AT THOUSANDS OF OTHER PRIZES, ALSO AFFIX THIS STICKER TO ENTRY FORM

TO GET FREE BOOKS AND GIFTS, AFFIX THIS STICKER AS WELL!

OVER EIGHT THOUSAND OTHER PRIZES

WIN A MUSTANG BONUS PRIZE

WIN THE ALOHA HAWAII VACATION BONUS PRIZE

Guaranteed **FOUR FREE BOOKS** No obligation to buy!

Guaranteed FREE VICTORIAN PICTURE FRAME No cost!

Guaranteed *PLUS* A MYSTERY GIFT Absolutely free!

ENTER HARLEQUIN'S *BIGGEST* SWEEPSTAKES EVER!

IT'S FUN! IT'S FREE!
AND YOU COULD BE A
MILLIONAIRE!

Your unique Sweepstakes Entry Number appears on the Sweepstakes Entry Form. When you affix your Sweepstakes Entry Sticker to your Form, you're in the running, and you could be the $1,000,000.00 annuity Grand Prize Winner! That's $33,333.33 every year for up to 30 years!

AFFIX BONUS PRIZE STICKER

to your Sweepstakes Entry Form. If you have a winning number, you could collect any of 8,617 prizes. And we'll also enter you in a special bonus prize drawing for a new Ford Mustang and the "Aloha Hawaii Vacation"!

AFFIX FREE BOOKS
AND GIFTS STICKER

to take advantage of our Free Books/Free Gifts introduction to the Harlequin Reader Service®. You'll get four brand-new Harlequin Historicals® novels, plus a lovely Victorian Picture Frame and a mystery gift, absolutely free!

NO PURCHASE NECESSARY!

Accepting free books and gifts places you under no obligation to buy a thing! After receiving your free books, if you don't wish to receive any further volumes, write "cancel" on the shipping document and return it to us. But if you choose to remain a member of the Harlequin Reader Service®, you'll receive four more Harlequin Historicals® novels every month for just $2.89* each—$1.06 below the cover price, with no additional charge for delivery! You can cancel at any time by dropping us a line, or by returning a shipment to us at our cost. Even if you cancel, your first four books, your lovely Victorian Picture Frame and your mystery gift are absolutely free—our way of thanking you for giving the Reader Service a try!

This lovely Victorian pewter-finish miniature is perfect for displaying a treasured photograph. And it's yours FREE as added thanks for giving our Reader Service a try!

Harlequin Reader Service®   Sweepstakes Entry Form

This is your **unique**
Sweepstakes Entry Number: 1W 233745

> This could be your lucky day! If you have the winning number, you could be the Grand Prize Winner. To be eligible, *affix Sweepstakes Entry Sticker here!* (SEE OFFICIAL SWEEPSTAKES RULES IN BACK OF BOOK FOR DETAILS).

> If you would like a chance to win the $25,000.00 prize, the $10,000.00 prize, or one of the many $5,000.00, $1,000.00, $250.00 or $10.00 prizes…plus the Mustang and the Hawaiian Vacation, *affix Prize Sticker here!*

> To receive free books and gifts with no obligation to buy, as explained on the **opposite page,** *affix the Free Books and Gifts Sticker here!*

Please enter me in the sweepstakes and, when the winner is drawn, tell me if I've won the $1,000,000.00 Grand Prize! Also tell me if I've won any other prize, including the car and the vacation prize. Please ship me the free books and gifts I've requested with sticker above. Entering the Sweepstakes costs me nothing and places me under no obligation to buy! (If you do not wish to receive free books and gifts, do not affix the FREE BOOKS and GIFTS sticker.)

247 CIH ACHP
(U-H-H-04/91)

YOUR NAME	PLEASE PRINT	
ADDRESS		APT#
CITY	STATE	ZIP

Offer limited to one per household and not valid for current Harlequin Historicals® subscribers.
© 1991 HARLEQUIN ENTERPRISES LIMITED.
Printed in U.S.A.

Harlequin's "No Risk" Guarantee

- You're not required to buy a single book—ever!
- As a subscriber, you must be completely satisfied or you may cancel at any time by marking "cancel" on your statement or returning a shipment of books at our cost.
- The free books and gifts you receive are yours to keep.

If card is missing, write to: Harlequin Reader Service, 3010 Walden Ave.,
P.O. Box 1867, Buffalo, NY 14269-1867

Printed in U.S.A.

pleasure danced in her uplifted eyes. "A year ago," he began thickly, his hands cupping her shoulders, stroking her gently, "I bought a piece of land thirty miles from the fort. Half of it is prime grazing area. The rest is woods, so there's plenty of lumber and fuel for the winters."

Her lips parted as she was drawn into his hypnotic burning gaze. She was wildly aware of his fingers on her shoulders, stroking her flesh as if she were a treasure of incalculable worth. "This land," she whispered with feeling, "was this a part of your dream?"

Gib ached to draw Kuchana against him. He wanted to feel her curves once again and run his hands over her tall, proud form. "Yes, it's part of a dream I've had for a long time." Since meeting Kuchana, the urge to get the cabin finished and start a better life for himself had filled every waking and thinking moment.

"This land has your heart?"

He nodded. "On the few days I get off every month, I leave the post."

Kuchana drew in a deep breath. "Yes, I've watched you ride away—by yourself."

The loneliness in her tone rippled through him, and fanned the fire in his loins. He held her firmly by the shoulders, realizing that Kuchana didn't understand the implications of his buying the land. The Apaches wandered across Arizona and New Mexico. There was no one piece of land where they made permanent wickiups. "When a man is getting ready to settle down, to take a wife and have children, he buys land and then builds a home."

"You have been building this wickiup each time you leave the post?"

"Yes." Gib searched her clear, trusting features. There was such beauty and life in her brown eyes. The gold of longing was there, too. Unconsciously, he pulled her forward. She came willingly, like a windflower bending to the unseen hand of a breeze, only this time it was to his will, his need.

"Your eyes are like gold fire," he said huskily, sliding his hands across her shoulders, feeling her rest against him. Gib could smell the clean dampness of her hair, and he threaded his fingers through it, smoothing the thick, heavy strands away from her upturned face.

Kuchana drew in a ragged breath, holding it as she saw his blue eyes turn predatory. His fingers kneaded her scalp gently, sending wonderful jagged streams of sensation through her. "You said you searched for a woman who had eyes of the sun," she said hesitantly, resting her palms against his chest, aware of the strength of his muscles beneath the sweaty shirt he wore.

"You've always been my sun woman," he whispered against her lips.

A softened moan rose in her breast as his mouth claimed hers, and her knees buckled. Gib's arm went around her waist, holding her tightly against him. She could feel the thundering of his heart, and the responsive flutter of her own. His strong mouth taught her how to kiss him in return. She tasted the salt of his perspiration, inhaling his male scent. The world as she knew it spun wildly, tilting her off balance, and she clung to Gib, lost in the bright splendor of his mouth. She felt lighter and dizzier than the dust devils that spun across the desert in the hottest part of the day.

His fingers framed her face, tilting her head back even more. She hungrily responded to the invitation of his teasing lips, wanting to drown within the beauty of his powerful kiss. As his tongue skimmed her lower lip, probing the corners of her mouth, she trembled violently, a stormy ache uncoiling deeply within her, crying out to be released.

"Open your mouth," he whispered thickly against her lips.

Kuchana responded, trusting him, spiraling more wildly into a world where she was aware only of their twin heartbeats pounding like urgent drums against one another. She clung to him, her fingers digging into his hard shoulders. As his tongue tentatively caressed hers, a whimper issued from her.

McCoy felt as if he would explode if he couldn't bury himself in Kuchana's hot, excited body. Kuchana was wild and uninhibited, not afraid to meet and match his ardor. She was as primal as the harsh land he had grown to love. Her unfettered ability to feel her womanliness and express it to him with such eagerness made him desire her even more. "Easy, easy," he crooned to her, placing small kisses at the corners of her mouth.

Kuchana's world spun as she kept her eyes closed, absorbing the feel of Gib's body against hers. His mouth was worshipful, each small kiss telling her of his need for her. As she lifted her lashes, reorienting herself to the present, she wondered if in some small way, she was like that woman he had described earlier. Her fingers tightened on his arms as she strove to stand on her own feet.

McCoy kept his arm around her waist, watching a rose flush stain her cheeks in the aftermath of their fiery kiss. Her eyes, if possible, were a deeper molten gold than before, as she stared up at him with a dazed look. Her lips were pouty and glistening. It took what little control he had left not to tell her he loved her. God, how he wanted to, but he didn't dare.

Kuchana was about to speak when she heard the snort of an approaching horse. Quickly, she stepped away, not wanting to be seen in Gib's arms. Whoever it was would appear soon. Sitting down on a rock, she pulled on her boots, then stood. Gib had already walked over to the rock and picked up his rifle. He cocked it, watching the long shadow of a horse and rider appear.

The pound of Kuchana's heart took on another beat as Two Toes rode around the end of the rock formation. The scowl on his thin face focused on her, and she wondered if he knew of the kiss she had shared with Gib.

"What's going on?" McCoy demanded, walking up to the scout.

"Lieutenant Carter tells me to come here." He gestured to them. "The lieutenant wants us to kill meat and bring it for the men. He says not to return until we have deer or bighorn."

Gib nodded, swallowing his disappointment. He glanced behind him, noting that Kuchana was glaring at the Yavapai. He would have no time for a quick wash now. "Kuchana knows this area. She'll tell us where to hide so we can pick off the game when it comes down to drink at dusk."

Their time together had been spoiled, and the kiss seemed to have robbed Kuchana of words, as well as thoughts. Picking up her rifle, she forced herself to move, for Two Toes was sitting there, a bored look on his face, his black eyes filled with hate. She was safe as long as Gib was with her. The Yavapai would not lift a weapon against her. Studying the rocky walls, she pointed out two different locations.

McCoy ordered Two Toes toward the eastern location and told Kuchana to come with him to the second spot situated in the northern area of the box canyon. It would mean hours of lying quietly without speaking, patiently waiting for game to appear. As he made eye contact with Kuchana, he saw that she was just as disappointed over Two Toes's arrival as he was. Taking a deep, controlling breath, Gib wondered if it was Providence in disguise. This last kiss had unstrung him to the point where he was losing control. *Not yet,* he reminded himself sharply. *Not yet . . . .*

Chapter Eleven

December, 1885

"Uh-oh," Nettie warned, up to her elbows in suds, "here comes trouble, Mama. Miz Melissa's heading our way."

Kuchana, who was sitting inside the tent out of the rain, looked up. It was drizzling outside, and she had just come over to help Poppy iron clothes.

Poppy's broad, sweaty brow wrinkled. She set the heavy iron aside on a board. "She's up to something, then," she muttered. Giving Kuchana a significant glance, Poppy gestured for her to stand up. "Git away from the iron. You're not supposed to be doing this. If Miz Melissa sees you, she might try to write you up on report."

Nodding, Kuchana rose quickly and ambled toward the opened flaps, stopping next to Nettie, who was working over a hot tub of water. Melissa was dressed in a dark blue velvet dress, a black, billowing cloak covering her from head to toe. She looked so beautiful, Kuchana thought, watching the woman daintily pick her way across the muddy expanse.

"She's up to no good," Poppy grumbled. "She's got that look on her face."

"The dress she wears is beautiful," Kuchana noted wistfully in a lowered voice.

Frowning, Poppy said, "Chile, clothes don't make a person. In her case, they just cover up the bile she has toward anyone who crosses her path."

Nettie continued to scrub the clothes against the washboard, her hands red and wrinkled from the hours spent in hot water. "She never comes here, Mama."

"Not unless she wants something." Poppy stepped out front, as if to protect her daughter and Kuchana.

Melissa forced a smile as she approached Poppy's laundry tent. She saw Kuchana standing in the darkened depths of the tent, no expression, as usual, on her face. Hate rose in Melissa. The past month had been a disaster for her plan to get rid of the Apache savage. Kuchana led a charmed life, it seemed. She could do no wrong—at least, she couldn't be caught breaking any army regulations. Well, this time, Melissa had the perfect plan to drive Kuchana off the post and back to the reservation once and for all.

"I declare, it's a miserable day out, Poppy," she said to the laundress, stepping within the confines of the tent.

"It always rains in December, January and February, Miz Melissa," replied Poppy.

Shaking the water droplets from the hood and pushing it off her hair, Melissa smiled at Nettie and then Kuchana. "My, you ladies seem to be busy despite the weather."

Nettie smiled nervously, scrubbing the clothes in the tub even more vigorously. "Yes, ma'am, we're always busy."

Melissa held Kuchana's stare. She saw the Apache savage ogling her velvet dress. It was a beautiful creation that Clarissa had made for her. "You seem to like my dress, Kuchana," she noted sweetly, pulling off her white cotton gloves.

Flushing, Kuchana nodded, always tongue-tied around Melissa. The *pindah* woman spoke such fluid, musical English that she felt her own attempts at the difficult language an embarrassment in comparison. "Your dress is like Father Sky," she whispered.

Melissa clapped her hands delightedly. "Oh, you have such a strange and wonderful way of saying things, Kuchana." She noticed Poppy had placed her thick, fat hands into her ample hips, eyeing her with veiled distrust. "I just came over to invite you to the Christmas dance, Kuchana. I felt that you would be a wonderful addition to our plans for celebrating the holiday season."

Poppy's mouth dropped open. "But, Miz Melissa, she ain't got no gown."

Smiling coyly, Melissa shrugged. "I'm sure that Kuchana will find one. Won't you, dear?"

Kuchana shrugged. "What is this dance?" The dances that her people held were sacred rites, linking them with Painted Woman and Usen. Was this *pindah* dance the same thing? A sacred celebration?

"It's a wonderful time where we women waltz on our men's arms and chat with all our neighbors," Melissa said. Reaching over, she gripped Kuchana's arm, even though she hated to touch the savage. "Oh, please, do say you'll come. It would mean so much to me, to the other women here at the post. We felt, since you were our only woman scout, that you would be lonely on Christmas Eve. A dance is a wonderful way to celebrate, laugh and enjoy yourself. I can count on you to show up, can't I?"

Swayed by Melissa's excitement and generosity, Kuchana nodded hesitantly. "You want me to come?"

"I won't take no for an answer." Melissa put on her best pleading smile. "It will be held at the supply building on Christmas Eve. We'll have music, food and punch."

Kuchana looked beyond Melissa. Nettie was shaking her head from side to side. Poppy looked angry. But for so long, she had been an outcast at the post. She had been hoping that the *pindah* women would eventually accept her presence instead of openly making it known that she was to be avoided. Against the laundresses' silent messages of warning, she said, "Yes, I will come."

Nettie was almost bursting to say something, but she wisely waited until Melissa had left. "Kuchana, you just got trapped by Miz Melissa."

Kuchana sat back down, placing the iron on the small wood stove to reheat it. "What are you saying?"

Poppy sat down with a grunt opposite Kuchana. "Chile, you just walked into a trap she's got set for you."

"I do not understand."

Nettie flew back into the tent, drying off her sudsy arms and hands. "Oh, Kuchana, that Christmas dance is for officers, their wives, and the ranching families from around here. Not for us."

"What do you mean, not for us?"

Poppy made a gesture for Nettie to stop hopping from one foot to another and sit down. "Listen to me, chile. That woman is plotting against you. I've been here five years and there ain't never been a colored, Mexican or scout invited to their dances."

Frowning, Kuchana digested their statements. "But she wanted me to say yes."

Nettie made a groaning sound and came over to pat Kuchana's shoulder. "Oh, Lordy, Mama, what are we going to do? If Kuchana turns down the invitation now, Melissa will make it look like Kuchana's insulted her."

"She's got you boxed in, chile." With a ponderous shake of her head, Poppy picked up an iron and began to press a pair of trousers. "Let me think."

Suddenly Nettie's eyes opened wide. "I knows, Mama. I have that purty red dress I was saving for my marriage someday. Kuchana and I are almost the same height, and I can fix it so she can wear it for the dance."

Kuchana looked up at her. "I must wear a dress?"

With a snort, Poppy growled, "You can't go looking like that, chile. You need a dress, slippers and your hair fixed up."

Delighted with her idea, Nettie moved to the other end of the tent, where there was a cedar trunk that held their few valuables. Opening the lid, she reverently picked up the red dress in her arms and brought it over to Kuchana. "Look at this dress, Kuchana," she whispered, laying it across the woman's lap. "Why, this is the finest cotton. Mama made this for me two years ago."

Poppy looked up as the Apache woman ran her fingers lightly across the carefully folded dress, awe in her eyes.

"This feels so soft," Kuchana breathed. She looked up at Nettie, who was glowing with pride. "Are you sure I should wear this?"

"Oh, I'm positive. Mama, ain't she going to look purty in this?"

Disgruntled, Poppy muttered, "Girl, you're plumb blind. That dress ain't nothing to wear to that dance. It's too plain."

Crestfallen, Nettie crouched down, keeping a hand on the dress. "But Mama, can't we gussy it up? I know!" she exclaimed, her brown eyes sparkling. "Tansy has some green and white ribbons." Picking up the scoop neck of the dress, she pointed to the bodice area. "Why can't I sew those ribbons around here? Wouldn't that gussy it up a bit?"

"I suppose."

Nettie beamed at Kuchana. "Why, Mama, we could get Clarissa to do her hair. Wouldn't she look purty as all git out with red ribbon braided into her black hair?" She touched Kuchana's slender throat. "And we could tie a ribbon around her neck. That's what all the ladies do. They wear a ribbon with a locket on it from their man."

"Well, that sounds better," Poppy admitted heavily. "But you're forgetting Kuchana don't know the first thing about manners or dancing!"

"Well, we can teach her all that, Mama," Nettie said smugly, rising.

Completely lost, Kuchana asked, "What must I learn?"

Poppy gave her a sad look. "Chile, you a lamb going to slaughter. I just can't stand this. I'm going to find Sergeant McCoy. He's got to know what's going on. You'll be the laughingstock of the post, and I'm not going to let that happen." Rising, Poppy put the iron aside. She gave both young women a stern look. "You two stay here until I get back."

The rain had become a steady downpour by the time Poppy returned with Gib. Kuchana was busy ironing, and Nettie had gone back to her washing.

Gib ducked under the flap of the tent and sat where Poppy indicated. His heart sank when he saw Nettie's dress. Poppy had told him everything. He knew the whole matter was a trap to embarrass Kuchana. Yet, one look in the girl's wide, trusting eyes, and he realized there was no way to dissuade her from going. Poppy sat down next to him.

"Look, Gib, is this dress not beautiful?" Kuchana held it up for him to inspect.

"Yes, it is pretty." Off and on the past few months, Kuchana had discreetly asked him about the dresses the women wore. He knew she wanted one, but he'd tried to get her to understand that the women of the post would only use it as a cruel tool to whisper even more behind her back.

"I hear you want to go to the Christmas dance," he said.

She smiled. "Nettie said she would teach me how to curtsy and how to dance a waltz."

Poppy gave McCoy a look that spoke volumes. Gib nodded, aware that Poppy knew exactly what Melissa had done. But there was no way to explain to Kuchana about prejudice or the fact that Melissa was trying to publicly embarrass her. In Kuchana's world, such an act was unknown.

"Nettie, you shouldn't be telling her that," her mother scolded.

Chastened, Nettie shrugged her thin shoulders. "Oh, Mama, Kuchana's so excited about wearing my dress and going to the dance. How could I tell her no?"

Gib shook his head at the girl's innocence. Nettie was too young to appreciate Kuchana's delicate position at the post. She saw her as being accepted as white because she was a scout, not a common laborer such as herself. Clearing his throat, Gib realized there was little he could do but help at this point.

"Would you like an escort?" he asked Kuchana.

"An escort?"

"I'd like to take you to the dance."

Kuchana's heart pulsed strongly in her breast. Her dream was coming true. She would wear a dress like the *pindah* women of the post, and she would be with Gib. "Yes!" she answered.

McCoy wanted to throttle Melissa for her cruelty. If he couldn't stop Kuchana, he could at least be at the dance to try to protect her. He managed a small smile and stood up, focusing his attention on Poppy's unhappy features.

"You've got two weeks. Think you can teach her all those things, Poppy?"

The laundress sighed heavily. "I think so."

"I'm sure you'll do fine," Gib said. Seeing Kuchana's face glowing with excitement made him sad and angry at the same time. Damn Melissa.

Three days later, Kuchana hurried from the scout area after just coming back off patrol around the general vicinity of the fort. Nettie had been working every night by candlelight to sew the green and white ribbons around the bodice of the red dress. They had also taken Kuchana's measurements so that Nettie could alter the garment to fit her. The day was blustery and cold, and Kuchana was glad to be wearing the heavy blue army jacket laced with yellow piping and brass buttons.

McCoy was gone for the day up to his cabin, and she missed him. Since Melissa's invitation to the dance, he had appeared deep in thought and even more quiet than usual. The gray clouds rolled sluggishly across the valley. Ordinarily, at this time of year, Kuchana was deep in Mexico, warm and safe from the chill weather. Shivering, she made her way quickly through the rows of tents. Although it was dusk, a number of women, their sleeves rolled up above their elbows, were still working to get the day's laundry completed. She waved to each woman as she went by and they greeted her in turn.

Nettie was holding up the red dress when Kuchana announced herself at their tent. The girl turned with a big smile on her face. Kuchana stood just inside the closed flaps, staring at the dress.

"Ain't it something!" Nettie crowed proudly, holding it up for Kuchana's inspection.

Whispering words in her own language, Kuchana stepped forward, nodding deferentially to Poppy, who was ironing. Nettie had painstakingly sewn the green and white ribbons together and then gathered them in a continuous row around the neckline. Kuchana lightly touched the wide, shining ribbons.

"You have done well."

With a sigh, Nettie said, "I sure did. Mama knows how I hate sewing, but I got so excited over this I outdid myself."

"Try it on," Poppy urged.

Eagerly following her suggestion, Kuchana sat down and wrestled her feet out of her damp boots. In no time, she was standing naked in front of the two women. Nettie provided a white cotton chemise and Kuchana pulled the floor-length piece of material over her head.

"Why do I need to wear this?" Kuchana wanted to know as Nettie retied the small ribbons on the chemise.

"Because ladies always wear this under their dresses," Nettie said. "You're skinny compared to me." Each tie had to be tightened in order the make the undergarment hug Kuchana's body.

Fretting in the uncomfortable chemise, Kuchana said nothing. Her heartbeat picked up when Nettie brought the red dress over her head. Carefully, Kuchana felt her way into the yards of material. To her shock, the neck was extremely low, exposing her collarbones and the slight swell of the tops of her breasts.

"Ohhh," Nettie whispered, standing back after she had buttoned the dress from behind and tied the sash into a bow, "you look so purty."

Poppy stared at the Apache woman. "Chile, that dress makes you look more beautiful than any white woman on the post," she declared.

The cotton material felt sleek beneath Kuchana's fingertips as she smoothed the dress down across her hips. "Truly, this dress is magical." The small puffed sleeves sat on each shoulder and hugged her upper arms. It was the low-cut bodice that made Kuchana fret. She kept trying to pull the dress higher, but it refused to move an inch.

Poppy chuckled indulgently and slowly got to her feet. "Chile, quit picking at that dress or you'll have it shredded before the dance. That's the fashion, a low neckline." Examining Nettie's work critically, Poppy made sure the dress fit snugly in all the right places. Nettie stood back, her hands clasped against her smiling mouth.

"Mama, ain't she purty? Why, red's her color."

Poppy grunted and reached down, picking up a mirror. "Here, take a look," she invited Kuchana.

Kuchana's eyes widened as she held the mirror at arm's length. The color did indeed bring out the dusky glow of her skin and the blackness of her hair. "I look like another person," she whispered, shocked.

"You sure do, chile. Nettie, fetch my two clean petticoats. She can't go to that dance without them."

Kuchana watched as Nettie pulled out the heavy petticoats. She wriggled into them and Nettie pinned them to her much smaller waist and brought the red skirt of the dress down over them.

"Better," Poppy grunted critically, as the dress blossomed outward from Kuchana's hips.

"What about a bustle, Mama?"

Chuckling, Poppy said, "She ain't got no need of a bustle, Nettie."

"Well, then what about a corset? All the white women wear them."

Kuchana snorted. "I will not wear one. I saw Melissa in hers. It is worse than a horse wearing a saddle with a tight cinch. I would go lame if I had to wear one."

Giggling, Nettie pointed to Kuchana's chest. "A corset brings your breasts up so that all the men can see them."

Kuchana thought that enough of her breasts were bared already. "Among my people, a maid dresses modestly, not like this."

"Leave her alone," Poppy told her daughter. "She looks fine as is."

"Now you've got to learn to curtsy properly," Nettie said. She picked up the skirt of the limp cotton dress she wore and showed Kuchana how to make a deep, graceful curtsy.

Kuchana watched with great concentration as Nettie repeated the gesture. The first time she tried one herself, she almost fell. Laughing, Poppy grabbed her by the arm and hauled her upright.

"Watch where you place your feet, chile. Do it like this."

Kuchana watched as Poppy lifted her huge skirt and placed her feet in the correct position. Kuchana tried again, but this time, when she lowered herself, she pitched forward as the massive volume of material set her off balance. She staggered forward, her foot tangling in the dress.

Nettie reached out and caught her, whooping with glee. "Kuchana, you going kill yourself."

"Now, now," Poppy muttered, coming over and placing Kuchana in the middle of the tent, "don't you be laughing at her, Nettie."

"It is the dress and all the petticoats," Kuchana muttered darkly. "I feel like a mule weighted down with a load."

Mother and daughter burst into unrestrained laughter. Kuchana joined them, feeling the heat crawl into her face. Again and again, they drilled her on how to place her feet, lean forward without falling, and then straighten gracefully up.

By suppertime, she felt a little more confident about her curtsy. She ate with their family, listening to Poppy's husband, Jacob, as he told stories about the South, where they had come from many years earlier.

Kuchana felt almost as if she were home again, and the sharing of food, laughter and stories, made her heart ache for Gib. She wished he were here. Sometimes, he did stop and eat with Poppy's family. But those occasions were rare. Thanking them for all their help, Kuchana undressed behind a blanket Nettie held up, and returned to her scouting clothes. Nettie promised to teach her the box waltz the next evening.

Walking back through the darkness to her tent, Kuchana saw the clouds parting in Father Sky to reveal the stars. She feared the night, believing ghosts ranged over the land in the darkness, hunting for the living to devour. A plan formed in her mind, as she recalled Jacob's excitement over the Christmas holiday. To them, it was a sacred feast, much like those when her people gave thanks to Painted Woman or Usen.

As she lay in her small tent, bundled up in a number of wool blankets to keep warm against the icy cold, she thought of what she might do for the laundresses and enlisted men. Normally, toward the end of each month, supplies ran low. Closing her eyes, she promised herself that she would get up early on the day of the dance and go hunting in the mountains for fresh meat for these kind people. It would be her gift. She would have to be careful, though. If the officers or their wives saw her coming back with fresh kills, the meat would immediately be taken to the officers' mess, instead.

As Kuchana fell asleep, she prayed to Painted Woman to give her good hunting, and to make her invisible to the eyes of the officers in order to give the food to those who really deserved it.

Kuchana wanted to shout her thanks to Painted Woman. Slowly rising to her feet from where she hid near the watering hole high in the mountains, she lifted her arms toward the sky, giving her thanks. Dawn was barely on the horizon, and Kuchana had braved the two-hour ride in the darkness to arrive at the hunting site before the animals came to drink their fill.

Joy moved through Kuchana as she carefully picked her way down the rocky, wet path. Below, three huge bucks lay dead, ready to be gutted and taken back to the post as a Christmas gift. No one knew she had left the post except Charlie, the chief scout. He had given her permission because he, too, wanted some of the fresh kill.

Just as Kuchana made it to the level, muddy ground, she heard a noise. Keeping the rifle ready, she whirled around. Her eyes widened.

"Gib!"

He smiled, pulling his horse to a halt, giving an approving nod at her kills. "Looks like you've been out Christmas hunting," he said as he dismounted. In addition to her army jacket, Kuchana was wrapped warmly in a buffalo robe that Gib had bought for her from a trader earlier in the month. Her thick black hair lay like a cloak around her shoulders, the red cloth around her head a startling contrast to the browns and grays that surrounded them.

"What are you doing here?"

He ambled over, hands on his hips. "I was looking for you this morning and couldn't find you. Charlie told me where you'd gone."

Kuchana had to stop herself from throwing her arms around Gib in welcome. She saw the smoldering hunger in his eyes and yearned to kiss him and to speak of her love. She placed the rifle back in the leather sheath on the saddle of the gelding she rode. Wind had come up lame with a crack in her hoof, and had to rest. Now, she rode a hammerheaded bay gelding. Pulling a skinning knife from her belt, she walked over to the first kill and leaned down.

"Is something wrong?" she asked.

Gib pulled out his knife and began to gut the second kill. Steam rose from the cavity of the animal into the chilled air. "No, I just wanted to see you, that was all." This morning, the need to see her had been overwhelming. Standing with her, drowning in the luster of her eyes, Gib felt his loneliness turn to fiery need.

She met his smile. Above and to the north, she could see dark gray clouds tunneling across the peaks, laden with either snow, rain or both. "We'll have to hurry or we're going to be caught," she said, motioning to the stalking weather.

McCoy nodded. Weather in the mountains above the fort could consist of sunshine, rain, hail, thunderstorms and snow—all within a few hours. He had no wish to get caught in it. "Let's hurry," he agreed.

In a matter of minutes, they had loaded the three gutted deer onto the backs of the patient mules tied nearby. Just as they cleaned off their arms and hands in the icy water, the heavens opened up.

With a muffled cry, Kuchana ran for the nearest rock overhang. Gib wasn't far behind, having untied the blanket from behind his saddle and bringing it along. He grinned and moved beneath the rock, which served as a broad, protective ceiling.

"Come here," Gib said as he sat down on the dry ground, reaching for her hand. Placing his arm around her, he drew her against him and pulled the blanket around them. He tucked it in, then sighed, leaning back against the rock. "There," he whispered.

His unexpected embrace left Kuchana wanting more. The kiss they had shared before simmered hotly in her memory. Lifting her face, she met and held his stormy blue gaze. The wind whipped and howled down through the pass and the rain obliterated the scenery, but the storm around them was nothing compared to what Kuchana was feeling from being held in Gib's strong arms.

She could not admit her love to him yet because of her vow, but she could at least show him how she felt. Leaning upward, she slid her hand along his jaw, placing her lips against the line of his mouth. Gib's response was instantaneous. She felt rather than heard him groan, as his arms tightened, crushing her against him, his mouth hotly claiming hers in hungry abandon. Her breath ripped from her, and she surrendered to his overwhelming strength, eagerly kissing him, exploring him as she had dreamed of for so many nights.

McCoy was drowning in Kuchana's unexpected and eager kiss. He had seen the gold fire in her eyes, but hadn't anticipated her intention. His love for her surfaced fiercely as he molded his mouth to hers. He reveled in her fiery freedom to express what she wanted from him. The musky scent of her body spiraled around him, and he lost himself in the texture of her mouth, tunneling his fingers through her thick hair.

"You are like a wild and beautiful eagle, skimming along on sunlight," he whispered against her lips. He felt her breasts mold against him, and the excruciating longing to caress her eroded his shaken control.

Kuchana whimpered as his hands slid between the folds of her coat, seeking her taut, aching breasts. She parted her lips as his hands reverently made contact with her flesh and felt moistness collect between her thighs. Her breasts strained against her shirt as his fingers moved along their periphery.

Beads of sweat formed on McCoy's furrowed brow. "You feel so good," he rasped, feeling her fingers dig restlessly into his shoulders as he explored her firmness. Savagely, he claimed her wet lips, wanting to bury himself within her giving, loving form.

Kuchana lifted her arms higher, allowing him better access to her breasts. His fingers moved inside the cotton shirt she wore, and Kuchana tensed as his thumb brushed her taut nipple. A bolt of unfamiliar heat struck deep inside her.

Thrashing her head from side to side, she moaned, unfamiliar with the urgency that clamored within her.

Gib pulled open her shirt, exposing her breasts. Her breathing was ragged and her need shattered what little was left of his control. She was writhing in his arms, pressing against him. Her skin was smooth and burnished beneath his trembling hands as he skimmed her rib cage. "Easy," he crooned, lifting her against him, claiming one hardened bud between his lips.

A startled cry of pleasure tore from Kuchana the instant his moist mouth closed around her taut, aching nipple. She threw her head back, her hair sliding like an ebony waterfall across her shoulders and his arm, as lightninglike jolts rippled through her body. The sensation was all-consuming and she moaned and whimpered as he suckled her gently.

Kuchana's sobbing breath close to his ear brought Gib back to earth. What was he doing? Gently, he eased her back down into his arms, closing the material of her shirt, hiding her lovely breasts from his view. "It's all right, all right," he told her in a hushed tone, sliding his arms around her and holding her against him.

While he rocked her gently, Kuchana lay weakly in his arms, trying to regain her composure. As the storm abated around them, her breathing returned to normal. The wind howled through the small pass, bringing flakes of snow with it. Kuchana was warm and happy. Finally she found her voice, none too steady and still husky with desire.

"It felt as if I were flying when you touched me."

McCoy pressed a kiss to her brow. "We're good together." Inwardly, he was chastising himself for what he'd done. He had never meant to go this far. It had been Kuchana's kiss that had thrown him. "I've got to learn to control myself when we're alone together like this," he told her ruefully, watching her eyes open, wide with wonder and desire.

"What I did was wrong?"

A wry smile tugged at his mouth. "No, not wrong."

"I have never seen the *pindahs* hug or touch one another. Among my people, we show our hearts to our husband or wife."

"*Pindahs* aren't as free in showing their feelings to one another as the Apaches are, Kuchana." He raised his hand to remove several strands of hair from her cheek. "I like you just the way you are."

Her worry dissolved, and she closed her eyes. "Our moments are like Holos rising across the land—fiery and hot."

Chuckling, Gib nodded. "You might say that."

Content as never before, Kuchana watched the snow shower gather strength around them. She wanted nothing more out of life than Gib's arms around her. "Often I have wondered about your family. Where they live. And if you miss them if they are far away."

With a sigh, McCoy relaxed, feeling peace feather through him. Kuchana's presence always brought him good, warm feelings. "My parents live in New Orleans, Louisiana. It's a state far from here. I used to have five brothers, but they all died in the war."

"Then you know how I feel with the loss of my family," she whispered, hurting for him.

"Yes."

"What was this war?"

"They called it the Civil War. It was a war between the North and South of our country."

"The *pindahs* fought among themselves?"

Gib nodded sadly. "My five brothers joined the South. I was eight years old when they left. None of them ever came back. At the end of the war, I was twelve. My parents were not the same after that." He absently stroked her cheek, the memories coming back to him. "My mother is a mix of Indian and French blood. My father came from Scotland. By the time I left and joined the army, I was seventeen. I was sent West, and spent the first ten years out on the Plains, learning about the Indians. Later, I was transferred to Fort Apache and got my commission as a lieutenant. The scouts taught me the Apache language, and I tried to learn what I could from them. I didn't want to see their kind slowly starved to death on the reservation. In a way, I don't blame Geronimo for leaving. He was only trying to save his people from death at the hands of those who mismanaged the supplies coming onto the reservation.''

Geronimo's name brought grief to Kuchana's heart. ''I miss my people.''

''I know you do.'' He held her for a long time before speaking again, watching the snow fall. ''Sometimes I see that faraway look in your eyes, and I wish I could do something about it.''

Overwhelmed by his tenderness, Kuchana whispered, ''If it was not for you and the dark-skinned ones, I could not stay here.''

The snow flurry was letting up. Gib knew they should be getting back. If they arrived any later at the fort, Kuchana's kill might be discovered by the wrong people. Easing her from his arms, he sat there, a faint smile on his mouth, holding her warm gaze. ''I'm glad you're here at the post. It was the right thing to do. For yourself and your people. Come on, we've got to get back.''

Bereft, Kuchana bowed to his urging. She took Gib's hand and he helped her from beneath the overhang. Their moments together were so few. Looking at him as he walked toward the horses, Kuchana wondered if she would have to wait another two or three months before being in his arms again—where she belonged.

As she picked up the rope of the mule, her mind moved forward to the Christmas dance. Panic riffled through her as she mounted the hammerhead gelding. Would she curtsy correctly? And would she remember the steps to the box waltz? More than anything, she did not want to embarrass Gib or the laundresses who had worked so hard to school her in proper manners and speech.

As they left the canyon that contained the water hole, Kuchana hung her head. The wind was icy and biting. She prayed to Painted Woman to help her remember all that was necessary so that she would not shame herself in front of the *pindahs* tonight. This prospect was more frightening than fighting her enemies. Much more frightening.

Chapter Twelve

Poppy sat back, her hands resting in her lap, watching intently as Clarissa put the finishing touches to Kuchana's hair. The air of excitement in the tent was undeniable.

"I'm gonna be in trouble," Clarissa said in her birdlike voice. "If I don't git back over to Miz Melissa's in time to make sure her dress is perfect, every bow in place, no strings trailing—"

"Hush, Clarissa," Poppy rumbled. "Miz Melissa is already over at the party receiving the guests."

Clarissa smiled nervously down at Kuchana, who sat absolutely still as a bit of makeup was applied to her face. "You look purty, Kuchana."

"Thank you." Kuchana's heart was pounding. "I hope to remember to curtsy well and dance the waltz properly."

Standing back, Clarissa moved to Poppy's side, her long, dark face sober. "Well, Poppy what do you think?"

Nettie came and stood next to her mother, her hands clasped to her breast. "Oh, Clarissa, you outdone yourself. Kuchana looks beautiful."

"She does," Poppy grunted, getting to her feet. The older woman recognized the look of fear in Kuchana's eyes as she sat there, her slender hands clasped nervously in the folds of her dress.

Snickering, Clarissa packed her brush and comb in a small bag. "Just wait until Miz Melissa lays eyes on her. Why, she's gonna faint dead away."

Alarmed, Kuchana stood, her mouth dry. "Oh, no!"

Chuckling, Clarissa moved to the front flap of the laundry tent. "You're purtier than she is, Kuchana. That's why Miz Melissa is gonna swoon. I'll see you tomorrow, Poppy."

"Thanks," Poppy called out as her friend disappeared into the night. Her heart went out to Kuchana, who moved restlessly about the tent. The Apache woman looked so heartrendingly beautiful in the cotton dress that Poppy felt like crying. She knew that Kuchana would be whispered about, poked fun at, and embarrassed no matter how well she presented herself. The fact that she was more beautiful than the blond-haired Melissa was going to cause quite a stir.

Hovering about Kuchana, Nettie nervously straightened the dress here and there, making sure every wrinkle was smoothed out, every bit of material in its proper place. "Why, you look so changed, Kuchana," she said breathlessly. "Wait until Sergeant McCoy sees you."

"Why?"

Poppy grinned. "Chile, take a look at yourself in this here mirror."

Almost afraid to look, Kuchana took the mirror and lifted it slowly. What she saw made her gasp. Clarissa had trimmed and shaped her waist-length hair. Thin bangs now covered her brow and the rest had been brought into a chignon at the nape of her neck and captured in a knitted red enclosure that Poppy had painstakingly made for her. Clarissa had then brought down wisps of black hair onto her temples, softening her high cheekbones and emphasizing her large brown eyes. The woman in the mirror was someone Kuchana didn't recognize. Someone truly beautiful.

"You look precious," Nettie whispered, wiping a tear from her eye as she stood and surveyed Kuchana.

Lowering the mirror, Kuchana held her misty gaze. "I do not know this woman," she whispered unsteadily, pointing at the mirror. "This is not me."

Poppy took out a handkerchief, blowing her nose loudly and then wiping it. "Chile, it's still you. Putting you in a dress and fixing your hair just brought out what we already knows—that you're beautiful inside and out."

Touched to the point of tears, Kuchana gave them a wobbly smile. "Thank you. Without your work, I would never look like this."

Nettie reached down and picked up a pair of red satin slippers. "You gotta wear these, too."

Pained, Kuchana examined the thin set of slippers. "Not my boots?"

"Heavens no!" Nettie said, crouching. "Now, lift your foot and I'll slide these on."

A slight scratch at the front of the tent caused Kuchana to snap her head in that direction. She watched as Poppy pulled one flap aside. Her breath stole from her as Gib McCoy entered the tent in his dress uniform. His eyes widened—first with shock, and then with pleasure as he studied her in heated silence.

Taking off his hat, Gib smiled and nodded. "You'll be the prettiest lady there, Kuchana."

Heat suffused Kuchana's cheeks. His gaze was filled with unmistakable pride and a fiery, undefinable emotion. She lowered her lashes, unable to meet his look. "Th-hank you. Poppy, Nettie and Clarissa have done this for me. Without them, I would look as before."

McCoy's heart was pounding in his chest. He saw the sly look Poppy gave him. Nettie was enamored of Kuchana's obvious beauty. "Your beauty was already there," he said, coming forward. Kuchana was indeed lovely in the plain red dress. The green and white ribbons around the neckline emphasized her slender neck and collarbones to perfection. Nettie had also sewn the colorful ribbons into the sash around her slender waist. Gib smiled. He was sure the women at the dance were going to be trussed up in their corsets and bustles, trying to achieve the same tiny waist that Kuchana had naturally. Slender as a willow, she stood tensely before him, terribly unsure of herself.

He halted a foot from her, digging into the breast pocket of his dark blue jacket. "I think this will finish off what these ladies have started," he murmured, pulling out a gold, heart-shaped locket on a bright red ribbon.

Nettie sighed, coming forward. "Oh, you got one, Sergeant McCoy!" She picked up the ribbon and locket, holding it before Kuchana. "Look at this! It's the latest from New Orleans. Every lady wears a ribbon and locket around her neck."

Kuchana held out her hands and Nettie gently placed the delicately engraved locket in her fingers. The heart-shaped piece of jewelry had been exquisitely crafted.

"Open it," Gib invited, enjoying Kuchana's response to the gift. She handled it so carefully. He yearned to feel her fingers glide across him in a similar loving fashion.

Gently, Kuchana pried the locket open. Her slight frown changed to one of surprise. Inside was a photo of Gib on one half of the heart. "How . . . ?" she stammered.

Nettie elbowed between them, leaning over, examining it with great pleasure. "You really did it, Sergeant McCoy!" she tittered, and smiled up at Kuchana. "This is a sweetheart's locket. You're supposed to put your beloved's picture in it and carry it over your heart."

Kuchana touched the small photo with her fingertips. "I never expected such a gift," she admitted in a low voice.

"The only thing missing is a picture of you on the other side," Gib pointed out.

Kuchana's eyes widened at the implication. She heard Nettie sigh romantically, then the girl took the locket from her and secured it around her throat.

"There," Nettie said, standing back, proud of her work. "Now you look perfect."

Placing her fingers against the locket that rested at the base of her throat, Kuchana smiled up at Gib. "This is why you were gone two days last week."

He returned her smile, wanting to kiss her full, lush lips that lifted with such dazzling joy. "I had the locket made for you a month ago. I just rode over to pick it up."

"For us."

Gib suddenly wanted to dispense with the dance and take Kuchana in his arms to teach her the beauty of his love. "For us," he agreed thickly.

"You better git over there," Poppy said darkly. "The last guests have probably arrived by buggy. You don't want to be late." She bent down, picking up a long black flowing cloak that Clarissa had loaned them. "Put this on, chile, or you'll catch your death of cold."

Gib kept his hand beneath Kuchana's arm as he led her through the darkness. She was tense and quiet, but he couldn't blame her. Yet, at the same time, he could see the sparkling happiness in her eyes because she felt beautiful. Hell, she was beautiful. The change in her was astonishing in some ways, but he had always been hotly aware of her beauty, regardless of the clothes she wore or did not wear.

"My heart feels as if it will burst inside my chest," Kuchana told him in a wispy voice. Up ahead, she saw the building. Never in her life had she seen so many buckboards and buggies. She could hear the music of a violin coming from the opening and closing door as more guests arrived.

"Just stay at my side and be yourself," Gib told her quietly, holding her dark, liquid gaze. The need to lean down and brush her lips was almost too much for him. Nettie had dabbed some perfume on Kuchana and the scent, light and fragrant, spurred his appetite for her. Her hair lifted off her shoulders gave her a mature and elegant look.

Kuchana's attention was drawn to the exquisite gowns of the women entering the dance. Grateful for Gib's hand on

her elbow, she gave him a smile filled with happiness. "Tonight, I feel as if I am a red bird."

"A lovely red bird," McCoy agreed. Already, his stomach was hardening into a knot of anxiety for Kuchana's
sake. He worried about Melissa. What would the little viper
do when she saw how beautiful Kuchana looked? Automatically, his hand tightened on her arm as they approached the door and entered.

"Look!" Claudia hissed behind her fan to Melissa.
"She's here."

Melissa, dressed in an ivory satin dress imported from
Paris, dropped her fan to her side as jealousy and anger
flooded her face. McCoy looked handsome in his dress uniform, his shoulders broad and held back with natural pride.
His hair was neatly combed, face free of a shadow of a
beard, and his eyes were fixed on Kuchana as he removed
the cloak from around her shoulders.

"Why, that Apache savage looks like a soiled dove from
Jacobsen's Mine, doesn't she?" Melissa said in a voice loud
enough for a number of officers and their wives to easily
overhear.

"To think she wore red." Claudia giggled from behind
her fan. "Why, only women of the night wear that color."

Melissa raised her fan to cover her face until only her
narrowed green eyes were visible. The musicians were playing a waltz, and half the people were on the dance floor. To
her chagrin, she noticed a number of ranchers' sons ogling
Kuchana. The fools, they didn't realize she was Apache, and
one of Geronimo's people. Wait until they found out.
They'd look at her differently then.

She couldn't stand the adoration in McCoy's eyes as he
tended to Kuchana's needs. The bastard was like a lovesick
calf. Noting several ranchers drifting in Kuchana's direction, Melissa decided to break the spell the Apache savage
was creating. She didn't know which bothered her more: the
fact that Kuchana's beauty was creating an instant wave of
excitement through the men at the dance, or the fact that

McCoy liked the little snippet. When she was done with the savage tonight, McCoy would find his arms empty. She'd make sure Kuchana would be leaving the post permanently. Then, perhaps, McCoy would notice her.

"Get ready," Gib warned Kuchana under his breath as he came back to stand at her side. Melissa was heading toward them from the opposite side of the dance floor. Because she was the hostess, as well as the wife of the post commander, all the dancers parted, leaving her an unobstructed path.

McCoy studied Melissa, finding a world of difference between her and the woman who rested her fingers nervously on his arm. Kuchana's natural beauty shone from her flushed face and sparkling eyes. Melissa, on the other hand, had rouged her cheeks and painted her eyes and lips. The dress she wore displayed her ample hourglass figure to perfection and her cleavage was highly visible. He wondered absently whether she'd spill out of the extremely low-cut gown if she bent over.

Melissa's shining gold hair was piled high on her head, and she wore a huge gold locket around her throat, four times the size of the one Gib had given Kuchana. The woman did everything with more size, he thought grimly.

Kuchana blinked belatedly as Melissa glided across the room like a swan on a lake. Never had she seen such wonderful dresses or beautiful women. The men's uniforms sparkled with gold and brass, and the lilt of the music surrounded her. The laughter and talk sounded like a babbling brook. Too late, she noticed that all the women wore muted colors. Hers was the only dress of a vivid shade, and certainly the only red one. There were mauves, mint greens, pale sky blues, lavenders and, of course, Melissa's ivory dress, which glittered with hundreds of bows around its skirt.

Kuchana knew little about clothing material, but again, she was struck by the fact that her dress did not shine as the others did. Every other woman wore a dress of firm material that had a glow to it. Glittering earrings, necklaces and rings flashed like sunlight on water across the gathering. Absently, Kuchana touched her ears, realizing they had no ornaments. And then, her fingers drifted to the locket that meant more than anything in the world to her. Only a warrior who was intent upon marrying a maid would give a gift of such beauty.

"My, my," Melissa cooed, sweeping up to them, a cool smile on her lips, "look who came."

Kuchana automatically started to curtsy, but Gib gently pulled her up.

"You only curtsy to the men, my dear," Melissa informed her, arching one brow.

Embarrassment flooded Kuchana. Why hadn't she remembered? There was so much excitement around her that she was already forgetting her manners. Fortunately, Gib had caught her midcurtsy, saving her from complete humiliation.

"I don't think Kuchana needs any lessons in manners," he growled at Melissa. He kept his hand around Kuchana's waist, wanting to silently signal her that it was all right.

Waving her fan, Melissa zeroed in on Kuchana. "I see you're wearing one of *our* latest fashions from New Orleans."

Automatically, Kuchana's fingers touched the locket at the base of her throat. "Yes."

Scowling, Melissa demanded, "Did one of the coloreds let you borrow it? Although, Lord knows where they got the money for such an expensive piece of jewelry."

"It wasn't borrowed," Gib said, watching Melissa's widening eyes. "I had it made for her."

"And inside is his picture," Kuchana added eagerly.

Gib tensed at the flash of hatred in Melissa's eyes as she stared at the locket.

Furiously, Melissa snapped, "Men give women presents all the time, for different reasons. I doubt McCoy finds anything romantic about an Indian."

McCoy's eyes hardened. He opened his mouth to refute the vicious jab when Melissa rushed on in a breathy tone, "My," she said, pointing her fan at Kuchana's dress, "what a lovely gown."

McCoy's mouth tightened. He wanted to throttle Melissa. Too late he realized that the other women at the dance all wore soft colors. Kuchana would stand out like a sore thumb, easily pointed out and talked about, which was what was happening right now. He saw small groups of women whispering behind their fans.

"Th-thank you." Kuchana smiled, her hand moving in a graceful gesture across the skirt. "Once, I saw a red bird when my people traveled far north. His song was beautiful. This color reminds me of him."

"Yes, well, I must say, it certainly complements the color of your skin. Red skin, red dress, what a lovely combination..."

Gib's nostrils flared as Melissa whirled around, ignoring him, and said, "Come, my dear, let me introduce you around." She glided off.

Hurt jagged through Kuchana as she followed, McCoy's hand at the small of her back. *Red skin...* She looked down at her bare arm.

"Don't let her hurt you," McCoy told her. His hand tightened around her waist, and he directed his attention ahead. Melissa was approaching her husband. "You will curtsy to him," he said under his breath.

Nodding, Kuchana managed a broken smile. "Thank you..."

Harvey, who had already tippled too much, stood with drink in hand. He gawked as Melissa presented the couple to him.

Her palms sweaty, Kuchana picked up the skirt, performing a nervous and less-than-perfect curtsy. As she rose, she heard giggles from several of the women who crowded around them.

"I'm surprised she didn't wear feathers..."

"Or at the very least, a breechclout like the men..."

Kuchana recognized the women as wives of officers at the post. As a warrior, she had been taught that the truth never needed to be defended. She did not have to retort, or protect herself from their taunts. Those who valued the truth would see her for what she was—and what she was not— making no judgment one way or another.

"Good evening, Colonel Polk," Kuchana said, her voice steady and clear.

Taking another hefty swig of his punch, the colonel managed a slight bow in her direction. "Evening, evening." Harvey couldn't believe his eyes as he stared openly at Kuchana. "You certainly look different," he rumbled. Melissa slid her arm around his, giving him a brilliant smile.

"Well, darling, she could almost pass for one of us, couldn't she?"

"Quite," Polk agreed.

"Except, Mrs. Polk," McCoy growled, "Kuchana is just fine the way she is."

Anger rippled through Melissa. The arrogant bastard. Her eyes hardened. "Sergeant, I don't recall asking you what you thought."

"No, ma'am, that's true. But Kuchana didn't ask for what you thought, either."

Uncomfortable, Polk muttered, "Mellie, I would like this dance," and pulled her onto the dance floor.

Melissa gave McCoy a black glare, her lips compressed in a tight, angry line.

The crowd began to dissipate around them as most of the couples moved onto the floor for the next waltz. Kuchana lifted her chin, her eyes shining with pride.

"You are truly a warrior, Gib."

One corner of his mouth lifted as he continued to survey the crowd of two hundred or so people. "Oh? Why is that?"

"You protected me."

With a sigh, Gib returned his attention to her. "I'm sorry they said those things, Kuchana. It isn't right."

With a shrug, Kuchana remained close to Gib, watching the couples prepare to dance. She saw a number of women pointing at her, but kept her head high. Apache warriors took many kinds of attacks, but never allowed the enemy to know their true feelings or fears.

"Feel like waltzing with me?" Gib asked.

The night took on a magical quality as Gib led Kuchana to the edge of the dance floor. "Remember," she said quickly, as Gib got them into position and the violinist prepared to begin the waltz, "I am new at this *pindah* dance."

Chuckling, Gib said, "So am I. My mother taught me to dance a long time ago, but this is the first time in fifteen years I've done it." Looking down at his highly polished boots, he said, "I'll feel good if I can get through this without stepping on your beautiful feet."

A flush riffled through Kuchana at his words. "Then I will watch our feet to make sure."

The waltz began, the music swelling and filling the room. Gib tightened his arm around her, proud of her courage, and of her ability to be childlike and honest under such circumstances. He kept them at the outer edge of the whirling couples, patiently working with her on the simple steps and achieving the necessary rhythm. Gradually, as Kuchana stopped watching their feet, he brought her around in a circle, her red skirt lifting slightly.

The waltz continued, the music gathering force. Kuchana felt bolder as Gib established the dance pattern, and she relaxed in his arms. He was incredibly handsome, his eyes startlingly blue against his deeply tanned face. She saw the reverence in his gaze when he looked down at her. As she swirled, her feet barely touching the floor, she forgot about the whispers and lost herself in the dance and Gib's tender look. His mouth had softened and she ached to stretch up and kiss him. They moved as one, as if their hearts and heads knew the other's steps in advance.

All too soon, the waltz ended. Kuchana looked around, discovering that they were standing in the center of the floor.

How had they gotten there? Laughing softly, she placed her hands on his lower arms.

"I flew like an eagle on the winds of Father Sky just now. I do not even know how I got here," she said.

Her musical laughter went straight to Gib's heart. "We flew here together," he told her, leading her off the floor and toward the tables filled with punch bowls, as well as delectable pastries.

Kuchana was flushed and breathless from the dance. As she looked around, she realized many of the women were staring at her, frowns of disapproval on their faces. What had she done? Was a dance not to be enjoyed? To be flowed into as water bends and caresses itself around the rocks of a brook? Feeling their anger dissolved the joy she had felt in Gib's arms.

"Look at her!" Peggy Judson whispered savagely to Melissa from where they stood behind the rows of punch bowls. "You'd think she owns the place the way she's taken over."

Melissa grimaced. She had watched with envy and then jealousy as McCoy had taken the Apache onto the dance floor. At first, Kuchana had been awkward and unsure, but McCoy was an excellent dancer and she had trusted him enough to follow his adept lead. There wasn't one man who hadn't watched Kuchana's lissome form glide with each whirling movement as McCoy waltzed her around the floor. Kuchana had blossomed with the dance, her willowlike body bending and flowing like a trained ballerina with each pulse of the music. There was an animal grace to her, Melissa decided angrily. How could she match that kind of lustful movement? No wonder McCoy wanted her!

"I say it's a sin," Peggy went on. "First she wears a red dress like a soiled dove, and then she dances like one."

"Did you see that?" Claudia said, coming to their side. "I declare, Kuchana's dancing ought to be condemned."

Melissa stood there, waving her fan more rapidly, watching Kuchana approach. "She's nothing more than a slut," she muttered to the surrounding women.

McCoy saw the tight knot of women as they approached, their eyes filled with jealousy and envy. After locating the punch bowl that contained no liquor, he poured Kuchana a glass. He didn't want to risk her getting tipsy. She needed all her wits about her tonight.

"My, Kuchana, where'd you learn to dance like that?" Melissa asked sweetly, moving to stand just on the other side of the table from them.

"Dancing is sacred to my people. It is a way to give thanks to Usen and Painted Woman," she explained eagerly. Thirsty, she drank the punch. She saw two women watching her and then shake their heads. Too late, she remembered that she should drink the punch in tiny sips. Humiliated, she handed the glass back to Gib. Still, she wouldn't allow the *pindah* women to know of her shame, and she stood with her head held high.

"Sacred or not," Peggy pointed out, "your kind of dancing is lustful. It isn't proper."

McCoy scowled. Peggy was the wife of the preacher, David Judson. "I don't think many people would consider a waltz a sin, Mrs. Judson." He saw the gray-haired woman turn a bright red.

"Sergeant McCoy, I do not approve of her dancing. Women like her ought not be found on a post. They do nothing but create lust in men. She should be in a saloon. That's where she belongs."

Kuchana heard the hatred in Peggy Judson's voice and saw it in her pinched and aged face. Melissa was smiling, as if enjoying the tirade. Claudia stood there nodding her head in agreement with Peggy.

"Mrs. Judson," Kuchana began, stepping forward, "I meant no disrespect to your god by showing my love of dance. Among my people, we dance to honor those who watch over us. It is a good thing we do."

Peggy glared at her. "Savages are heathen. I'd expect little more of you. Who do you think you are? Dressed in a white woman's clothes. That doesn't change what you are."

"Ladies," McCoy said in a grating tone, "this conversation has gone far enough. I'm not going to allow you to cut Kuchana to ribbons just because she danced with me."

"Well, really," Melissa cooed, "any man seen with a woman savage says something about *him,* don't you think?"

"Yes," Claudia put in primly, "white men ought to pay attention to their own kind."

Tears filled Kuchana's eyes as she realized the extent of their hatred. She saw McCoy's jaw harden and felt his hand on her arm protectively pulling her away from the women.

"And that dress," Peggy went on, finding that she had a gathering audience who agreed with her. "Only a soiled dove would wear a color like that."

"Sinful," another man called from behind McCoy.

"Git that redskin outa here," a man with a black beard roared, moving through the crowd, heading directly for Kuchana.

The mood had turned into a violent storm of hatred directed at Kuchana. She took a step back from Gib, squarely facing the huge man who looked more like a hairy black bear. He bore down on her, his small eyes glittering with anger. "That slut has no business being here!" he yelled, raising his fist. "My wife and three young 'uns were killed by Geronimo and his filthy heathens."

Unconsciously, Kuchana had planted her feet apart for better balance as the man shoved through the last line of onlookers. Before she could defend herself, McCoy moved directly in front of her, his fists doubled.

"Settle down, Henshaw," he warned, holding up his hand, as the rancher stumbled to a halt, his face flushed and his eyes glazed. Gib could smell the liquor on the man's breath.

Wiping his mouth with the back of his hand, Henshaw gestured violently at Kuchana. "Who the hell let her in here? She's an Apache squaw, one of Geronimo's own." His voice rose even further. "I ain't gonna allow no squaw of his to stay in the same place with me!"

McCoy braced himself as the rancher hurled his bulk at him. He was furious that Polk or one of the captains hadn't tried to contain the drunken rancher. Drawing back his arm, he took a swing, his fist connecting solidly with Henshaw's face. The jolt traveled up McCoy's arm and he staggered backward. The rancher crumpled to the floor, unconscious.

Gasping, Kuchana gripped Gib's arm, watching as blood purled from the rancher's bulbous red nose. She heard screams behind her and saw several women faint. McCoy's hand was raw and bleeding, but he kept her behind him as he faced the ugly crowd. To her left, she saw Melissa come forward, her once-composed features twisted in fury, reminding Kuchana of an attacking wolf.

"See what you've done!" Melissa screeched, coming to a halt only feet away from Kuchana. "You do nothing but cause an uproar wherever you go. My party is ruined and it's your fault." Tears splattered down Melissa's white cheeks. "Why don't you get out of here? Go back to your own kind! If you think you can come in here dressed like a white woman and expect us to accept you after your murdering ways, you're wrong!"

"That's enough!" McCoy roared, his voice silencing the crowd. He rounded on Melissa, wanting to slap her smirking face. "You invited Kuchana to this party. And she didn't start anything. Henshaw did."

"Go back to the reservation where you belong!" Peggy cried.

"Yeah, send the squaw back!" another man joined in.

Gripping Kuchana's arm, Gib pushed her toward the door, keeping his eyes on the men. No one wore a gun, but he didn't trust any of them. They were getting drunker—and meaner—as the night progressed. Once at the door, he went over to the pegs holding the coats and retrieved Kuchana's black cloak. As he threw it across her shoulders, he saw the crowd slowly advance toward them.

"Get out of here," he ordered her tightly, standing between her and the mob.

Gulping a sob, Kuchana blindly threw herself out the door, tripping and almost falling over the hem of her skirt. Fighting to keep her balance, she picked up the dress and ran down the walk. As she ran, her breath was torn from her in huge, white wisps by the icy-cold night air.

"Kuchana!"

Gib's voice carried across the parade ground, but she continued to run, her tears blinding her, freezing to her lashes and against her cheeks. The ground was slippery as she left the walk. She saw the glare of ice in front of her and veered off to the left to miss it. Before she knew it, she was in front of the stable. It was a safe place to cry, for no one would find her here.

She pushed open the door, and the first sob tore through her. As she ran down the aisle between the stalls containing the horses, she was aware of the sweet-smelling hay. A few of the animals nickered a greeting as she moved through the darkness relieved by moonlight only here and there. Stumbling to a halt, she opened another door that led into the hay mow, a huge room filled to the ceiling with loose, dry hay that would supply the horses with food throughout the winter. Burying her face in her hands, she turned, tripping over the dress. She gave a cry and fell, finding herself in a cushion of hay.

She couldn't even run like a lady, constantly tangling her awkward feet in the material of her dress. She could do nothing right. Nothing! Sobs jerked out of her, and she pressed her hands to her face, the tears leaking through her fingers. To her own people, whom she loved with all her heart and soul, she was dead. To the *pindahs* of this post, she was unwanted. The word "outcast" sat like a huge rock on her slumped, shaking shoulders. She was hated. They wanted her to leave. The sounds coming from Kuchana now were primal, like those of a wounded animal, and they drifted out into the darkness of the silent stable.

Chapter Thirteen

McCoy shut the main doors of the stable so that no one could enter and discover Kuchana. Grimly, he strode down the main aisle through the semidarkness, following the sounds of her weeping to the main hay mow. She sat with her legs tucked beneath her, the red skirt a flowing circle around her. His heart wrenched at the raw pain he heard tearing from her.

"Kuchana..." His voice cracked and he shut the door of the room quietly behind him, then moved to where she sat and knelt by her side. Gently, he touched her shoulder, letting her know he was there. She only cried harder, trying to pull out of his grasp, hands still covering her face.

"It's all right," he whispered roughly, gathering her into his arms. "Let me hold you, sweetheart, lean on me. It's going to be all right..."

The instant Gib's arms went around her, Kuchana ceased struggling and fell against his chest, burying her face in the folds of his uniform. His voice was deep as he tried to soothe her agony. She felt his hand against her head, stroking her hair as if to brush away the pain.

"Oh, Gib," she choked out against his jacket, "they hate me. They want me gone from here..."

"Hush," he soothed, kissing her hair, her damp brow and wet cheek, "it doesn't matter what they want, Kuchana. They can't make you leave, do you understand that?"

The tenderness in his voice assuaged the hurt of the abuse she'd suffered. Kuchana placed her hands on his chest, pushing herself back enough to look up into his darkened, grim features. His blue eyes were shards of ice in the shadows, every line in his face testimony to the pain he'd felt for her. Tears fell freely from her eyes, blurring his features. "Th-they want me to go. But I cannot. I took a vow to bring Geronimo back to the reservation." She gripped his arms, her voice wildly off pitch. "I will not lose Ealae. She is the last of my family."

"You're not going anywhere, Kuchana. You're staying here. I won't lose. Not now."

She saw the tears glittering fiercely in his eyes as he cradled her face between his roughened hands. "I cannot stand to leave you, either," she admitted hoarsely. "My heart is with Poppy and Nettie, too. They have been kind, as the Apache are to their own. They accept me as part of their family."

"Anyone who took the time to know you would do the same," Gib said thickly, drying her glistening face with his fingertips. Her lashes were beaded with moisture, her eyes still full of agony. He wrestled with his anger over what Melissa had made happen. No doubt she'd had someone put a bug in Henshaw's ear about Kuchana, and that's why the man had become so outraged, and charged her. "Listen to me, Kuchana, no one can tell you to leave the post. You're officially paid by the army to be a scout. Melissa was behind that whole incident tonight."

"But, why?" Each stroke of his fingers against her flesh sent a wonderful healing warmth through her. Kuchana saw his face grow tender as he removed a tear from the corner of her mouth.

"Because she's jealous of you."

"Jealous?" Her eyes rounded and she was content to be brought back into Gib's arms, resting her head against his jaw.

Taking a deep breath, McCoy treasured the privacy with
Kuchana. She lay against him, her head buried beneath his
chin, her hands against his chest. "Yes, jealous. Among the
Apache, marriage is sacred, and the man and wife are true
to one another. Melissa is . . . well, she's not faithful to her
husband."

"Poppy said the same thing." Kuchana sniffed, considering Gib's hesitant admittance.

"Since I arrived at this fort, she's been chasing me."
Pursing his lips, he continued to stroke her thick, silky hair.
"I've had women in my life, but never a married one. I
won't lie with the wife of another man. Melissa doesn't
honor that code and has tried unsuccessfully to get my interest." There, it was out. Gib glanced down, studying
Kuchana's shadowy features. Her brown eyes were dark,
and her lower lip was caught between her teeth. "Believe me
when I tell you, I don't want any woman but you, Kuchana.
The day I met you, my whole life changed."

She eased out of his arms, studying him, absorbing the
tenderness in his expression, his voice. "I was so frightened, Gib. I thought one of those men would hurt me."

"So did I." He caressed her cheek. "I don't imagine you
realize just how brave you really are, sweetheart. But I do."
His hand came to rest on her bare shoulder, and Gib was
aware of the warm pliancy of her flesh beneath his fingers.
"Tonight, you looked more beautiful than any woman
there. Red looks good on you, despite what they said. It's a
color of courage and boldness, and you wore it well."

Melting beneath the sound of his vibrant, deep voice,
Kuchana closed her eyes, her breath becoming shallow and
ragged. Each time Gib stroked her shoulder, she trembled a
little more. "And I was proud of you. Those men wanted to
fight their way past you to get to me, but you would not
move."

Leaning forward, Gib brushed her lips. "Not on my life
would they touch you, my sun woman. . . ." He tasted the salt
of her spent tears on her lips as he moved his tongue from

one corner to the other, teasing her gently, letting her know how much he loved her. Resting his brow against hers, he swore he would not let himself lose control as he had earlier that day. Kuchana evoked a primal reaction from him, and God knew, he wanted to love her fiercely, and forever.

A ragged breath escaped Kuchana as she cherished the silence that bound them to one another. She could feel Gib's moist breath against her face, and she smiled. "Your breath is like a gentle rain."

Sliding his hand up her arm and coming to rest on her shoulder, he smiled, content to simply be with her. "You're my sunlight, my laughter. Do you know that?"

Kuchana opened her eyes and saw the softened line of his mouth near her lips. "No..."

"You are," Gib said huskily. "I look forward to the times I can see your face, your dancing brown eyes that hold the fire of the sun within them, and your mouth drawn into a smile..."

Sighing his name, Kuchana tipped her head slightly, pressing her lips to his. She felt his hand tighten instantly against her shoulder, drawing her powerfully against him. Swept into the storm of his responding kiss, she bent like a willow, melting beneath the cajoling strength and tenderness of his mouth.

Whether he wanted to or not, Gib knew he had to stop. He gently broke their fiery kiss. Smiling unsurely, he whispered, "Sun woman, you're my undoing. If I don't get you back to your tent, I will dishonor you." He caressed her cheek with his hand. "You don't deserve that."

Kuchana understood and gave a slight nod of her head. Each time he called her "sun woman," a strange, twisting need moved through her, awakening a powerful aching within. The naked hunger in his blue eyes branded her heart forever. She reached up, touching the locket at her throat. "Even though we sleep apart, you are with me..." The vow must be fulfilled before she could tell him the rest of what lay in her heart, the fierce love she felt for him.

Someday, he would speak to her of marriage, of a life beyond her unfulfilled vow. Her upturned face was pure and clean in the moonlight, her eyes guileless and filled with adoration for him alone. "Come on," he coaxed, getting to his feet and helping her stand, "I've got to get you back to your tent before we're discovered here." If they were, Melissa would fan the flames of gossip, hurting Kuchana even more.

As they walked back, Gib kept his arm around Kuchana. In the distance, the Christmas festivities were still going on, as though the incident involving Kuchana had never occurred. McCoy was sure that Melissa was using the crisis and gossiping about it right now. Was her aim to force her husband to release Kuchana as a scout and send her back to the reservation? Or worse, send her via train to the Florida prison where many of the Apache leaders and their followers had been incarcerated? His arm tightened around her shoulders. He was damned if any of that would happen. He had a plan, and he prayed it would work.

Gib said nothing of his worries to Kuchana. The less she knew about the politics of the post, the better. She'd suffered enough under these people. He'd watch and stay alert for her sake. More than anything else, he wanted to pay Melissa back for her cruelty.

"Harvey!" Melissa said, pouting. She was sitting on the bed watching her husband change into his nightgown. "You aren't listening to me." The dolt, he was drunker than a skunk, and having problems finding the armhole in his nightshirt.

"I heard you pet, but legally, I can't get rid of Kuchana."

Striking the feather mattress with her small fist, Melissa muttered, "You saw what she did tonight, Harvey. Why, she walked into our party as if she owned it. And McCoy lied. I never gave that heathen an invitation. How dare he! Harvey, he's really getting out of hand. He still acts like an officer. He ought to be ashamed of his low morals and values. He courts that heathen woman as if he were intent on marrying her!''

Finally locating the armhole, Harvey shoved his hand through it and staggered across the wooden floor to their bed. His hair was mussed, the silver strands sticking out in all directions.

''You're upset over nothing, Pet. I intend to have Charlie give her extra duty for busting in on your party without an invitation. But tomorrow is Christmas, and I don't want to do it then. I'll wait until the next day.''

Melissa snuggled down in the covers, keeping her distance from her husband. ''What kind of duty? Really, Harvey, she deserves a whipping for that kind of insubordination.''

Grimacing, Harvey turned on his side. ''I'll think about it . . .'' and he started to snore.

Melissa leaned over and blew out the lamp. Moonlight invaded their room, highlighting the lace curtains at the window. Damn McCoy for interfering. She had deliberately had Dodd Carter go over and tell Henshaw that Kuchana was one of Geronimo's warriors. If the lovesick sergeant hadn't stood between the heathen savage and Henshaw, her plan would have worked.

Shutting her eyes, Melissa pondered tomorrow. It was a day of rest and religious gathering at the post. Would Harvey have Kuchana written up? The idea appealed to her. There was nothing that the meddling McCoy could do about it, either—unless he wanted to ruin what was left of his career by stepping in.

Her evening hadn't been a complete loss. The twenty-five ranching families who'd attended the party had all made their strong feelings about Kuchana's presence known to Harvey. Surely that would force him to get rid of her. Smiling, Melissa turned over, barely able to sleep. There had been so much excitement, and there was much more to come.

* * *

As Kuchana hunkered down in front of the food kettle near the scout tents early the next morning, she saw Gib leaving the porch of the enlisted barracks. There was a silent hush across the post with few exceptions, the only people awake being the sentries on duty. Charlie and Two Toes snored heavily in their respective tents, having found and consumed a bottle of liquor between them last night.

Kuchana held the rabbit she'd caught earlier over the fire with a stick, watching Gib's progress. As he approached, she offered him a smile. At times like this, he spoke her language, wanting to practice it at every opportunity so he wouldn't lose it.

He took off his hat and smiled down at her. "Breakfast?"

"Yes. There is enough for two. Do you want some?"

Gib nodded and sat down on a log near the fire. He studied her. Although Kuchana wore her usual Apache clothing, she was still lovely. She had combed out her hair, but had left the bangs on her forehead. His heart warmed as he noticed she was wearing the red ribbon with the locket around her throat.

"Did you take that locket off last night?" he teased, picking up the battered tin coffeepot.

"I will never take it off."

The fervor behind her words made him feel good. Gib poured himself a cup of chicory coffee and set the pot back down on the blackened grate over the fire. Steam rose from the coffee in the cold morning air as he lifted the tin cup to his lips.

"No one is awake," Kuchana noted, turning the rabbit, watching the grease drip into the tongues of flame. The fire reminded her of Gib's kiss last night, sending a wonderful song of need through her.

"Most everyone gets drunk on Christmas Eve," he said wryly. The sun had just risen above the peaks, sending a shower of golden light across the frozen desert landscape, and there were a few high and wispy clouds in the sky.

"It is an odd festival."

"Oh?" He enjoyed watching her do the most simple task. Just the economical turn of her wrist, or the movement of her fingers around the stick, made him long for her touch.

"Yes. The men stagger around drunk on firewater. Yet, your bells ring, calling them all to church." She gestured toward the post in general. "I see no one coming to answer the bell."

Gib sputtered in his coffee and laughed. "I imagine it does look rather odd," he said, once he got his laughter under control.

"The only two people I have seen are the man in black and the woman who said I was lus..."

"Lustful."

"'Yes." Kuchana frowned. "What does this word mean?"

Gib held his cup between his hands, warming them. Kuchana was so innocent. He pursed his lips and thought for a moment. He didn't want to hurt with his explanation. "A woman who is lusty is a woman who is close to the earth. She's warm and unafraid to show her feelings to the man she loves."

Her brows rising, Kuchana sat back on her heels, a pleased look coming to her face. "I am that?"

"Every inch of you," he admitted in a gritty voice. This morning, Kuchana's face was clear of any remnants of the pain of the night before. Gib was grateful. She was strong in ways most white women never were. Apaches, like other Indian tribes, did not put much stock in what other people thought of them. In their eyes, only deeds counted.

Shaken by the vibrancy of his tone, Kuchana's eyes fell to his strong mouth. She remembered vividly how he had tasted, how powerfully he had molded her lips to his. Sighing, she smiled. "You make me feel like a rainbow inside."

Swirling the last of the coffee in his mug, Gib met her smile with one of his own. "I have a Christmas gift for you, Kuchana. After we eat, would you like to see it?"

Her eyes widened. "A gift? A giveaway?"

"Kind of," Gib hedged. "Christmas to the *pindah* is a time of giving and sharing. Some put up trees and hang colored cloth and beads on them, placing presents beneath them to give to one another on Christmas day. I don't have a tree, but I wanted to give you something anyway."

"You have already given me your heart," she protested, motioning to the gold locket. "I need no more." Kuchana placed the rabbit on the grate, pulling the stick out of the well-cooked meat. With her knife, she quickly split it in half, handing one portion to McCoy.

Chuckling, he thanked her, and then sank his teeth into the juicy flesh. "Well, among our people, we give a gift every Christmas."

"Gifts should never be expected," Kuchana said seriously, sitting down next to him. "We were taught that a gift could be a colorful sunrise, or a rainbow after a storm. Our hearts are open to things that cannot be bought."

"You're right," he said. Then he winked at her. "That's why I got you a gift—you weren't expecting it."

After eating, Kuchana rinsed off her hands and face with soap and water, and McCoy led her toward the stabling area. He made sure they walked an acceptable distance apart. Although his men knew he cared for Kuchana, she was a scout and their personal relationship had no place on the post.

"What is this gift you have for me?" she asked excitedly.

"Oh, it wouldn't be fair to tell you ahead of time," Gib teased, smiling at her childlike enthusiasm. Kuchana wore her heavy blue wool coat for warmth. He had also seen to it that she had a pair of beaver mittens.

"But why not?"

"Because, my sun woman, it's not our tradition."

She laughed gaily and clapped her hands together, following him around the end of the huge stable and back toward the corrals filled with horses. Gib halted, pulling off the yellow neckerchief he wore.

"Now, hold still while I blindfold you. This gift was too big to wrap, so I have to wrap you up instead."

Standing very still while he placed the cloth around her eyes, Kuchana was keenly aware of his body so close to her own. She yearned to lean back against him. "This gift is that big?" she whispered, clasping her hands to her breast.

"Sure is." He gripped her hand, giving her a gentle tug forward. "Now, stick close and I'll lead you to it."

Excitement surged through her when Gib finally drew her to a halt. She felt him come around her and loosen the scarf.

"Now," Gib whispered, his mouth a scant inch from her ear, "keep your eyes closed when I let the neckerchief drop."

A tingle fled down her neck as the moisture from his breath caressed her. "I will," she whispered huskily, nodding.

Making sure no one was around, Gib took off the scarf and placed his hands on her shoulders. "All right, now open your eyes."

Tied to the outside of the corral was a gray mustang mare. Kuchana twisted a look up at Gib and then back at the horse, stymied.

McCoy grinned at her confusion. "Since Wind went lame you've been riding that hammerhead gelding," he explained, leading her close to the mare. "And I knew you two didn't get along. So, when I was up at Jacobsen's Mine getting your locket, I met a man who had this mare for sale. She's seven years old and was owned by a Jicarilla warrior who was put on the reservation." Gib ran his hand down the mare's neck, giving her an affectionate pat. "I thought you'd be glad to trade this hammerhead in for her. This is your Christmas gift."

Kuchana turned and threw her arms around Gib. "Thank you," she breathed, holding him tightly, feeling his arms go around her. She absorbed the feel of his hard length against her own for precious seconds before they stepped apart.

Gib stood back and watched as Kuchana excitedly made friends with the mare, a tough, sturdy animal. Kuchana ran her hands down each of the mare's legs, speaking softly to her as she did so. The light in her eyes told McCoy everything. Kuchana was overjoyed with the gift.

"Does she eat cactus, too?" she asked, running her hand across the mare's short, strong back.

"Sure does."

"Good! I was getting so tired of the hammerhead wanting grain and hay. That horse will be a mule in his next life."

Laughing, McCoy leaned against the corral, one boot hitched up on the lowest rail. The happiness faded from Kuchana's eyes as she came around the front of the mare to join him. "What is it?" Gib asked.

With a shrug, she gave him a thoughtful look. "I do not have a gift for you."

He ached to reach out and caress her cheek, but fought the urge. "You're the only gift I'll ever want, sun woman. Don't you understand that?"

Losing herself in the blueness of his eyes, Kuchana nodded. "I will be so glad when we find Geronimo. There is so much I want to speak about with you."

Understanding her frustration, Gib gave her a tender look. "I know, sweetheart. From the looks of things, we ought to get a break soon. General Crook has been pursuing him nonstop. Just be patient."

"Damnation!" Melissa cursed. She stood at the frosty window watching the colored column begin its trek out of the post toward Mexico. "Wouldn't you know it." Turning, she swept across the wooden floor and glared at the fireplace. A courier bearing orders from General Crook had arrived, and on Christmas Day. He was closing in on Geronimo, and wanted the help of the Fourth Cavalry.

Before she could push Harvey into writing up Kuchana on report, the woman had suddenly become the darling of the regiment. Mickey Free, an Apache scout who had ridden with Crook for a number of years tracking down his own people, had told the general about Kuchana. Melissa had stood there as Harvey read the orders to her. Crook had specifically mentioned Kuchana and her importance in helping to locate Geronimo. Tapping her foot as she stood in front of the warming fire, Melissa cursed again. Harvey had muttered that since Crook knew of Kuchana and her alliance with Geronimo, there was no way he could write her up on report.

Judging from how proudly aloof Kuchana had sat on her new gray mustang this morning, Melissa could tell that her plan to embarrass the Indian into leaving the post had failed miserably. She had stood at the window watching McCoy. She still wanted him for herself. No man had ever said no to her charms, and he wasn't going to, either.

"Something has to be done," she whispered fiercely, pacing in front of the fire. Her mind whirled with possibilities. Snapping her fingers, she halted. Of course! Two Toes! The Yavapai hated Kuchana. She would get Dodd Carter to hire the scout to ambush the heathen woman, thereby getting rid of her once and for all.

Turning back to the window, Melissa watched the last of the thirty-five-man column leave the post. The icy weather had broken, the temperature was now in the high forties, perfect weather for riding fast and hard. "I hope Geronimo kills you on sight, Kuchana." The words dissolved into a silence broken only by the crackling of the fire. "If he doesn't, Two Toes will, just as soon as you get back to the post."

Chapter Fourteen

"Geronimo is near," Kuchana said softly. Mickey Free, the other scout, gave a bare nod and shifted the rifle he held in his arms. They stood with a group of army officers near Rio Aros, a massive rock fortress with a number of trails leading in and out of it. It was the same spot where Kuchana had told Geronimo she would be leaving. Memories came pouring back to her, and she was grateful that Gib was standing at her side, silently supportive.

"What do you think?" Captain Crawford, a tall, sandy-haired officer whose lean face was burned dark by years in the sun, asked her. The twilight was fading quickly. Two columns of soldiers waited expectantly behind them.

Kuchana glanced over at Mickey Free. The scout was considered one of the best, but he realized that Kuchana knew this territory more intimately than he did. "I think Mickey and I should follow these tracks just before dawn tomorrow."

Crawford nodded. "Sounds good to me. Sergeant McCoy, get your men bedded down for the night. I'll post my scouts who won't be tracking tomorrow as sentries."

"Yes, sir." Gib saw from the anxiety in Kuchana's eyes as she watched the captain that there was something she wanted to ask him.

"Captain Crawford, do I have your word you will not kill my people like the *culo-gordos*?" Her throat ached with tension. Since joining up with General Crook's most favored column from Fort Apache, she had come to like Crawford, who appeared to respect her people just as McCoy did.

With a brief smile, Crawford answered, "Kuchana, my orders are to bring Geronimo and all of his people in alive. I realize your sister is with his group. I don't want any bloodshed."

"Then Geronimo must understand that."

"Oh, I think he does," Crawford said with a short laugh. "He's been eluding us for well over a year, but I've had chance meetings with him off and on. Geronimo is a good judge of character. He knows I'm not like the Mexicans. All we want him to do is surrender and come back to the reservation. My lieutenants, Shipp and Maus, will make sure that once the Apaches are on the reservation, they will get food and clothing, as promised in the treaty."

Relief swept through her and she nodded. "You are a man of honor, Captain."

"Just get some rest. You and Mickey will have some hard work to do come morning."

Kuchana was constantly aware of Two Toes being near. Tonight, as always, she slept by her new mare, whom she had named Moon, for her silver color. As darkness fell over the Mexican desert, camp fires dotted the area. She ate by herself, chewing on the deer jerky, thinking ahead to the next day. Geronimo was near. Did he know of their presence? He was a powerful medicine man, and it was possible he knew they were just outside one of his favorite camping sites.

"Kuchana?"

She lifted her head and saw McCoy walking along the horse line toward her. "Here . . ." she called.

Gib gave her a smile as he crouched down by her blanket. "How are you doing?"

Warmth flooded her heart, for she saw the love in his eyes. "A warrior is never afraid."

"I'm talking to my sun woman, not the warrior," he teased gently, forcing himself not to reach out and caress her cheek. Her eyes were huge and shadowed, telling him of her worry about what lay ahead.

With a sigh, she grimaced. "My heart pounds hard each time I think of seeing Ealae again. And then I worry that Captain Crawford, who cares for my people, may not be able to stop some of his other men from firing their rifles."

"Crawford's a damn good man, Kuchana." Gib turned to glance at the huge encampment behind him. "We were good friends up at Fort Apache before I was busted and sent away."

"I can tell. It is in his eyes. He trusts you."

"Emmet and I go back a long way. The two of us have always struggled to expose the white men who stole the food and clothing that was supposed to go to your people on the reservation. It's become a personal battle with him. Only this time, he's got General Crook's power behind him. His two lieutenants, Shipp and Maus, are a lot like him." He smiled fondly. "The four of us raised a lot of hell. The Bureau of Indian Affairs people hated us on sight."

"I feel much better knowing that you trust these officers."

"They aren't like Carter," Gib promised her.

Kuchana wished that Carter had stayed back at the post, and that Lieutenant Lawton had taken over the column. But for whatever reason, Polk had ordered Carter to take command. "He complains constantly like a braying mule," she said.

It was time to go. Gib knew that Carter was watching him closely, and he didn't want him to go after Kuchana as a result. Straightening, he settled his hat back on his head. "Get a good night's sleep. Tomorrow may change history."

It was barely light as Kuchana stood above Geronimo's encampment. After giving a signal with her hand, she leaned against the rocks at her back and Mickey Free moved quietly to her side. He nodded and gestured for both of them to retreat silently to where the columns waited for them.

As she mounted Moon, Kuchana felt the terror in her heart escalate. Somewhere down there, wrapped in her old, thin wool blanket, was Ealae. Or had she been killed by *culo-gordos*? Because of the powerful emotions sweeping through her, it was so hard to concentrate, to do what was expected of her.

Captain Crawford and his officers were waiting for them. Mickey Free reported what they had found, drawing a crude map of Geronimo's camp in the sand at their feet.

"Very good," Crawford commented. He kept his voice low. "All right, men, here's what we're going to do. I want no shots fired. We'll attack the camp from three sides. I want the horses, food and blankets captured." His brown eyes hardened on his sergeants. "Remember, no man raises his weapon. I want to show Geronimo that we can find him, take his food and horses, but not harm his people. Once he flees to the surrounding rocks, he'll have to talk with us."

Lieutenant Maus, a black-haired, green-eyed officer two years younger than Crawford, spoke up. "Let me take Kuchana, sir. She can lead us around to the southern end, and we'll ride in from that direction."

"Good idea," Crawford said. He ordered Mickey to go with his men. "Gib, you take the eastern end."

"Yes, sir." McCoy saw Carter's face go mottled with fury at the officer's snub. But Crawford respected McCoy's knowledge and trusted him to carry out his orders. Gib pinned Kuchana with a look, silently begging her to be careful. No one knew what Geronimo would do when he found out Kuchana was with them, and he was helpless to protect her.

She gave a slight nod of her head, understanding the plea in Gib's eyes, sharing his uncertainty. Crawford had all the men check to make sure that none of the metal fittings in their equipment would clink or cause a sound. The horses' shod hooves were fitted with cloth to quiet their hoofbeats.

Kuchana rode out with Lieutenant Maus and thirty soldiers. Her mouth grew dry as they stationed themselves at one of the three entrances to the camp. Geronimo and his people slept peacefully, their horses hobbled and foraging nearby. When they rode in, there would be only one way for Geronimo to escape: into the cliffs above the camp.

Praying to Painted Woman to protect Ealae, Kuchana saw Maus give the signal. Suddenly, the silence was broken by the thunder of over a hundred horses galloping into the camp from all directions. Kuchana had little time to locate Ealae. She saw the Apaches throw off their blankets and immediately scramble for their horses in confusion. When Geronimo saw Crawford's men bearing down on them, he gave a cry, signaling the families to climb up into the rocks and hide.

Dust clogged the air as the columns converged on the camp. Men, women and children fled, leaving everything behind. To Kuchana's relief, not one shot was fired. Desperately, she tried to find Ealae among those who were climbing into the rocks, but it was impossible. Within minutes, Crawford's plan had been executed to perfection. Kuchana sat in the center of the milling horses, men and mules. Her eyes sought out Geronimo's people, who peered out from their hiding places far above them.

"Mickey, tell Geronimo I want to speak with him," Crawford ordered, moving his horse through the traffic, coming alongside the scout.

Mickey Free nodded. Cupping his hands to his mouth, he called in Apache to Geronimo and delivered Crawford's message. The army men, in the midst of capturing the hobbled mustangs and gathering cooking pots, blankets, goatskins of water and any food they could find—though there was precious little of anything—fell silent.

"I will not talk to him through you, Mickey!" Geronimo yelled back. "You are mule dung."

Mickey Free repeated Geronimo's reply to the captain, who nodded in understanding. Craning his neck, he located Kuchana. "Will you interpret for me?"

She nudged Moon to the captain's side. "Geronimo has pronounced me dead to his people, Captain."

"Try, anyway. My other scouts are Tonto and Yavapai. Geronimo will refuse to speak to either of them. Maybe you'll have a chance."

Frantically, Kuchana looked out through the graying dawn. She knew what her people were feeling, the dread of being trapped like this by their enemy. She cupped her hands to her mouth and shouted, "Geronimo, it is Kuchana. Captain Crawford wants to speak with you. He does not want to hurt you or your people. Please talk with him."

Her voice echoed through the area. The restless snorting of horses was the only sound for nearly five minutes. She sat there, feeling Geronimo's anger and frustration aimed at her even though he had not said a word. Suddenly, several warriors moved toward Geronimo. "I see the subchiefs, Nachiz and Chihuahua," she whispered to Crawford.

The officer's surprise was evident on his face. "This is good luck. All the parties involved are in one location."

"Kuchana!"

Kuchana tensed as Geronimo's voice rolled like thunder down the canyon. "Yes?"

"You are dead in my eyes, but I would rather talk to you than that mule dung, Mickey Free."

She closed her eyes, relief flowing through her. "My chief, these men wish you and our people no harm. Captain Crawford merely wants to talk with you."

"Why should I trust a traitor?"

Keeping her voice steady, Kuchana felt a stab of pain through her heart. "My chief, I am not a traitor. I told you of my intentions to your face. I was not a coward."

Geronimo snorted. "When our talks are over, you will still be dead. Your sister will never speak to you again."

Hope tore through Kuchana. "Ealae? Is she well?"

"Your sister has more courage than you. She rides with us."

A little sigh escaped from between her lips. McCoy reached out, gripping her hand momentarily, the squeeze broadcasting his own happiness that her sister was alive and safe.

Struggling to control her emotions, Kuchana choked back a sob. "My chief, we come in peace to talk peace. Captain Crawford can be trusted. I give you my word."

"Your word means nothing to me. Let me think on this. I will speak to you later."

Throughout the burning heat of the day, Kuchana acted as interpreter for Geronimo. She could see his subchiefs scurrying back and forth as they met and planned with him, shadows against the ocher rock, appearing, then disappearing. The men and animals sought to escape the sapping heat of Holos in the shade cast by the rocks. She worried, knowing that the fifty people with Geronimo had no food or water.

Emmet Crawford leaned against a rock wall, studying the area where Geronimo and his people hid. The day was drawing to a close. He glanced at McCoy, who had remained at his side during the negotiations. "What do you think we should do, Gib? Geronimo can't fade off into the darkness—our men block his only escape routes. Kuchana seems to be getting him to consider the idea of speaking with me. He's been less and less belligerent as the day wears on."

Gib nodded, noting that Kuchana stood alone out in the center of the flat, staring up at the cliff face. Geronimo or any one of the other warriors could have shot her, but they hadn't. "I think that as a show of goodwill to the chief, we ought to leave food and water behind for him and his people."

"Good idea. I'll tell Kuchana to pass the information on to Geronimo."

As darkness fell, Captain Crawford withdrew the men from the area, leaving behind a blanket filled with deer jerky, biscuits and several goatskins of water. Scout sentries were posted out of sight of Geronimo and his people. Knowing how the Apaches feared the darkness, the army doubted that the group would try to steal away during the night.

Kuchana was cutting open a cactus with her knife, slicing the skin and thorns off so that Moon could eat her fill when Gib found her. She appeared tired and drawn from the day's activity. Gib stood nearby, watching her feed the mare one chunk of pulpy cactus at a time from her hand.

"I'm glad Ealae's all right," he said.

"Painted Woman answered my prayers," she responded tiredly, rallying because Gib gave her sustenance and strength simply by being near.

"The talks are going well. Emmet's pleased."

"I was not sure that Geronimo would speak with us," she answered, feeding the last of the cactus to the mare. Crouching, Kuchana rubbed the sticky liquid off her hands with sand. "I pray he will trust Captain Crawford. He must!" she added fervently.

"Emmet is one of the few men I've known here in the Southwest who have fought for Apaches and their rights. But he's made enemies, too."

"Lieutenant Maus said you were always in trouble with the *pindah* from the Bureau of Indian Affairs at the reservation."

Chuckling, Gib nodded. "Yes, we tangled a few times."

Kuchana's eyes shone with admiration as she straightened. Emotionally exhausted by the endless, trying day, she longed to move into his arms. There was a fire burning in his dark eyes, and she was gently cradled by their silent message.

"I must sleep," she whispered.

McCoy nodded, wanting to reach out and comfort her. "Maybe tomorrow Geronimo will surrender. Tonight he'll have a full stomach to think about it. Good night, sun woman."

Responding to his lowered tone, she managed a faint smile.

Gib awoke Kuchana just before dawn, motioning her to join him and the officers at the small, central camp fire. As she rose, picking up her rifle, she noticed everyone else, with the exception of the posted scouts, was still asleep.

Emmet handed her a cup of chicory coffee when she arrived, murmuring a good-morning to her. Kuchana thanked him, her voice still husky with sleep, and crouched down on the heels of her *kabun* boots.

"Why couldn't we have made plans last night?" Carter muttered irritably, his eyes barely open.

Lieutenant Maus sat next to Kuchana, and McCoy on her other side. "Emmet, how do you want to handle the talks with Geronimo this morning?" he questioned, ignoring Carter's remark.

Before Crawford could speak, a hail of rifle fire erupted from all three entrances of the canyon. Kuchana dropped the tin cup she was holding and lunged for her rifle.

"Son of a bitch!" McCoy snarled, leaping to his feet and drawing his pistol as a troop of Mexican militia rode into the canyon. Gib saw two of the army scouts fall, killed by the Mexicans.

"Stop! Stop!" he shouted in Spanish, racing down the path toward the Mexicans.

Crawford was on his heels, calling out in Spanish that the Indians were scouts, not Geronimo's men. Drawing his gun, he drew alongside McCoy as they ran down the rocky path.

"Don't shoot, we're Americans," Emmet yelled above the gunfire.

Kuchana couldn't believe her eyes. The militia had killed the scouts. She feared for McCoy and Crawford, who were way ahead of her. Behind her, the entire army camp leapt to life, men scrambling for their weapons and horses plaintively whinnying as bullets sang through the dawn air.

Diving behind a huge boulder, Crawford kept hollering the same message, that they were Americans. Finally, the shooting stopped. Cautiously, Emmet came out from behind the boulder. He holstered his pistol and, holding up his hands, walked out between the Mexicans and his own men.

"Don't shoot! We're Americans! Can't you see our uniforms?"

McCoy, behind another boulder, let out a curse. The Mexicans and their Tarahumara scouts were jumpy, their weapons held ready. Emmet was pushing his luck.

Kuchana was suddenly beside him. "Stay down," he ordered her harshly. "Those are Tarahumara scouts with the Mexicans. They hate Apaches."

Breathing hard, she nodded and kept her rifle ready. She saw a number of the militia men slowly coming out from behind the rocks. "Crawford is taking a chance," she gasped, placing the rifle to her shoulder. "They don't believe him."

"There isn't enough light to see his uniform," Gib growled. "That's probably why they opened fire on the scouts." McCoy slowly got to his feet, exposing his head and shoulders.

"Don't go any closer," he shouted to Crawford. "They're jumpy as hell."

Emmet waved his hand, acknowledging Gib's warning. Continuing to speak in Spanish, he climbed up onto a huge rock. Pointing to his uniform, he shouted, "We're American soldiers, your friends. Put down your—"

A nervous Mexican soldier fired his rifle and Crawford was cut off midsentence. His knees buckled and he fell backward off the rock.

With a cry, Kuchana scrambled to her feet. Crawford's head was bloody, his body limp on the desert floor.

Anger rippled through the cavalry and remaining scouts. Mickey Free leapt to his feet, firing at the man who had shot his captain. More rifles opened up, and in seconds, fifteen Mexican militia had been killed by the volley.

Sobbing for breath, Kuchana ran from rock to rock, avoiding being shot as she made her way to where Crawford lay unmoving. Lieutenant Maus and Shipp were shouting at the top of their lungs to cease fire, trying to restore order. Falling to her knees, Kuchana threw her rifle down, hooked her hands beneath Crawford's armpits and dragged him behind a rock to safety.

"Dammit!" Gib snarled, running to her side, "you should have stayed put!" He dropped his rifle, yanking his bandanna off his neck as Kuchana gently turned Crawford's head to one side, exposing the wound.

She gasped as she realized the extent of the wound. "They shot him when he was trying to make peace. The *culogordos* are murderers."

His hands shaking, Gib applied the bandanna to Crawford's wound. Kuchana held the captain's limp shoulders, fighting back her tears.

Gasping for breath, Gib said, "You go get help. Emmet's bleeding heavily. Tell Lieutenant Maus he's got to take command." He reached out to grip her wrist as she started to rise. "And be careful. I won't have you getting hurt. Understand?"

Kuchana saw the fear and agony in Gib's narrowed eyes. His mouth was pulled into a tortured line of pain. Emmet was his friend of many years, and her heart bled for him. "I will be careful," she said, picking up her rifle and leaving.

The next hour was chaos, broken by angry words in English and Spanish. Crawford's wounding had been avenged, as far as Kuchana was concerned. Lieutenant Maus struggled to calm his troops and the Mexicans, all the while trying to keep an eye on Geronimo and his people who had witnessed the entire tragedy.

Deeply shaken, Maus ordered Kuchana to seek out Geronimo. "Tell him nothing has changed. Tell him we must still talk."

Kuchana did as she was told. McCoy went with her, staying close by to guard her.

Geronimo listened intently to her, then conferred with his subchiefs and finally shouted, "I will talk to General Crook after I meet with Gray Wolf at El Cañon de los Embudos in Sonora."

When Maus heard Kuchana's interpretation, he scratched his sweaty jaw. The sun had just come over the rugged peaks. "Gib, what do you think I should do? No one knows Geronimo like Emmet does."

McCoy found it hard to concentrate on the matter at hand. His mind was on Emmet, who lay in a wagon being tended to by one of the cooks. The head wound looked bad, and he had lost a lot of blood. "I think we ought to ask Kuchana," he began heavily. "She knows Geronimo even better than Emmet does."

Maus looked in Kuchana's direction. "What should I do? Should I agree, or should I try to wait him out here?"

Torn, Kuchana thought long and deeply of the two alternatives. The army could conceivably starve Geronimo out, but that might take a week or more. She didn't want the women and children put under that kind of terrible strain. They were on the edge of starvation already. "Geronimo has given his word, Lieutenant Maus. I believe he will meet with you after speaking with Gray Wolf."

Carter snorted. "Lieutenant Maus, you can't possibly take her word for it! I don't believe Captain Crawford would allow—"

Maus glared at Carter. "Mister, when I want your two cents' worth, I'll ask for it."

Shocked, Carter snapped his mouth shut. His hatred focused on Kuchana. He couldn't talk back to Maus or Shipp, who had longer tenure as officers than he did. Uncomfortable that Kuchana's word carried so much weight with the other officer, he vowed to get even. Melissa was right. Kuchana needed to be gotten rid of once and for all.

"Kuchana," said Maus, "tell Geronimo I agree to the terms he's set. Tell him I'll give him back all his horses and goods, and we'll leave his people enough food and water to make the trip to Gray Wolf.''

Stunned by Maus's compassion and understanding, Kuchana nodded. For the first time in her life she was in the company of men who treated her people as human beings, instead of animals. The realization made her feel good about her decision to become a scout. With compassionate men such as this, she knew Geronimo would consider returning to the reservation. As she spoke to Geronimo, she saw her chief smile for the first time. Her heart lifted and she wished that she could speak to Ealae, hold and embrace her. But that was not possible. Already, Maus was ordering a small contingent of cavalry to escort Geronimo and his people out of Rio Aros. The Mexican militia was being detained, their weapons taken and heavily guarded until Geronimo left. The army would return to the fort and wait.

Kuchana was able to get one glimpse of her sister as the Indian woman climbed cautiously down the face of the cliff toward the waiting horses. Ealae appeared thin as ever, though in good health, but she did not lift her head to look for Kuchana. Turning away, Kuchana headed toward the wagon that bore Emmet Crawford. Perhaps she could help tend his wound and care for him until the two cavalry units split up north of the border.

McCoy watched Kuchana walking away from the group. He was proud of her courage and stamina under the circumstances. Once again, he had come close to losing her. No one was more anxious than he was to see Geronimo give up and go back to the reservation. He was also bothered by Carter's hatred for Kuchana. The officer had been relegated to silence because he had so little experience in Indian affairs, or delicate negotiations. What would he do once he was back at the post? Would he continue to harass Kuchana?

Chapter Fifteen

January 2, 1886

"Get rid of her once and for all, Dodd, or you'll never see me again."

Dodd Carter gave Melissa a pleading look. They stood together in the supply office, away from the prying eyes and ears of the men who worked in the building. Making sure the small room's door was shut, he shook his head.

"Mellie, what can I do? Right now she's the apple of General Crook's eyes. Kuchana was responsible for persuading Geronimo to meet with Lieutenant Maus in three weeks." His voice hardened. "And that goddamn McCoy..."

Dressed in a warm, fur-lined cloak, Melissa swept toward Carter. "You want to be rid of McCoy. I want that woman heathen gone. Your career is overshadowed and upstaged by both of them." Her eyes narrowed with ruthlessness. "Think, Dodd. If you get rid of Kuchana, then General Crook would look more favorably upon you." She gripped the front of his uniform coat. "Without Kuchana, McCoy is no longer as important to Crook. Lieutenant Maus and Shipp have the same amount of knowledge of the savages as he does. Kuchana is the key here. If you get rid of her, your career will shine."

Carter considered her fervent argument. "I've been thinking about it, Mellie. The question is, how?"

"You know that Two Toes hates her. Why couldn't you pay him to do it? Send them out hunting together and he can push her over a cliff or something. With the snow up in the mountains, that would be easy to do. By the time her body is found in the spring, the wild animals will have destroyed any evidence. And even if there's an investigation, there won't be enough left of her to prove anything." Her eyes shone with excitement. "Dodd, this is the perfect plan."

Mulling it over, Carter broke free of her grip and paced the perimeter of the room. "Then I'll have Two Toes left. What's to say he won't tell someone here at the post? If he does, my career is destroyed."

"It's easy enough to shoot him while you're out on expedition. Choose the time and place and put a bullet in his back when he's not looking. We lose plenty of scouts to the *soldatos*. Blame it on them."

"And what do you get out of this, Mellie?"

"Whatever do you mean?" she asked with a smile.

Carter held her gaze. "McCoy's the only man to have successfully ignored your considerable charms. With Kuchana out of the way..."

Shaking her head, Melissa moved back to Carter's side, sliding her hand around his arm, pressing her brow to his shoulder. "Dear, dear Dodd, it's you I enjoy spending my time with. This arrangement suits both of us. Claudia and Harvey ought to be married to one another—neither of them enjoys the pleasures of the matrimonial bed." She squeezed his arm gently. "Neither of us can afford to divorce our partner, so we will continue to meet when we can to satisfy our needs. McCoy means nothing to me. You do."

"He used to mean something to you. All you ever did until Kuchana arrived was try to lure him into your arms."

With a delicate shrug, Melissa murmured, "He's only a sergeant. You're an officer. There's such a difference between the two of you, Dodd. You have culture and a good upbringing. He's an animal with only a veneer of civilization. I'm not the least bit interested in that country bumpkin." That was a lie, but Dodd didn't need to know that. Melissa was furious with McCoy's continued interest in Kuchana. Once she got rid of the redskin, he'd turn to her, realizing she was a far better catch. After all, she was a white woman.

"Kuchana is the cause of all our problems," he admitted darkly. "All right, I'll order Kuchana and Two Toes to go hunting together up in the mountain canyons. Two Toes will be happy to do it for five dollars."

"Give him a bottle of whiskey. He'll like that better."

"No. I don't want him drunk and wandering around the post bragging that he killed her."

Melissa nodded. "You're very cagey, my darling. And right."

Slipping his arms around Melissa, Carter drew her to him, covering her lips in a long, passionate kiss. She moaned, artfully pressing herself to his length.

"Oh, Dodd, darling," she whispered breathlessly, "let's celebrate as soon as Two Toes returns without her."

Blood was pounding heatedly through Carter. He smothered her mouth in another wet, demanding kiss. "Yes," he muttered, "yes..."

Kuchana was saddling up Moon when she saw Gib enter the stables. His face was grim as he approached.

"I heard from Charlie that he's sending you and Two Toes up into the mountains to hunt."

"Yes." There were other soldiers in the aisle, cleaning out the stalls, so she kept her distance from Gib, even though she longed to be in his arms. "Lieutenant Carter wants fresh meat for the officers and their families."

"I just checked the officers' larder. They've got plenty of meat." He rested his hand on Moon's neck, watching Kuchana work. Her fingers moved gracefully over the saddle as she rechecked both girths and made sure the poncho behind the cantle was tied snugly. In the higher elevations, she would need it.

"Lieutenant Carter said to go. I can't tell him no, Gib."

Troubled, but not sure why, he said, "Carter has just ordered me to take the mules up to Jacobsen's Mines and get food supplies."

"We'll be going in opposite directions."

An orange headband kept Kuchana's thick, luxuriant hair away from her face. Since the last expedition, she had finally started gaining weight and the gauntness was disappearing from her cheeks. Gib suspected it was because she had seen that Ealae was alive and knew that Geronimo was considering coming back to the reservation. A powerful hunger gnawed at him as he studied her pursed lips. Wearing the buffalo jacket on top of her dark blue cotton shirt and trousers, she was well protected against the cold.

"I don't like any of this. Carter is stupid to send you up there today. Can't he see there's a blizzard brewing?" he thought out loud.

"I tried to tell Charlie there was snow coming, but he said it did not matter."

"I wish I was going with you."

She heard the unhappiness in his voice. It had been so long since they had last kissed that she thought she would die for the touch of his mouth on hers once again. "I wish that, too," she answered softly.

Gib saw the luster in her eyes, the gold fire in their depths. Kuchana was like a glowing ember, easily brought to passionate flame. He ached to have her, to show her the true depth of his feelings for her. But none of his dreams could come true until Geronimo was back in the reservation and her vow was fulfilled. "Look, you be careful. Understand? Two Toes hates you. I don't trust him."

"He is a snake," she agreed, pulling down the stirrup to hang at Moon's side. "But I must go."

Glancing around, Gib saw that they were momentarily alone. He reached out and caressed her cheek, pushing thick strands of her hair back across her shoulder. "Just be on guard, sun woman."

Her breath caught in her throat at his unexpected touch. The vibrating warmth of his voice feathered through her, tender with concern, dark with promise. "I will. We should be back by dusk."

"So will I. I'll come over and see you at your tent as soon as I get back from the mine detail."

The wind was sharp and blustery as Kuchana and Two Toes reached the top of a rocky ravine filled with juniper and piñon. The clouds in Father Sky were grave with warning that any moment rain or snow would begin to fall. Shivering from the cold, Kuchana hunched down in her buffalo jacket. She wasn't used to the plunging temperature changes of the mountains, for her body was accustomed to the ninety-degree winter weather of the Sonora Desert.

For four hours, they had wound their way deeper into the mountains. The three inches of snow on the ground had made it easy to identify the freshest tracks. Kuchana had finally come upon recent bighorn tracks, barely an hour old. She pulled Moon to a stop at the top of the ravine, which wound downward in a rugged V-shape with rocky slopes on each side.

"They have hidden in there to protect themselves from the coming weather," Kuchana told Two Toes as he pulled up alongside of her. She gestured with a mittened hand toward the bottom, hundreds of feet below them. The sky was leaden gray, promising to unleash an angry deluge upon them momentarily. Kuchana prayed it would be snow and not rain. If they got soaked and then the temperature dropped and snow began, they might freeze to death.

"Come," she said between chattering teeth, "let us find them."

"You lead," Two Toes growled.

Dismounting, Kuchana saw several caves off to the left of the ravine, lodged in the wall of a cliff. Brush and piñon almost hid them from view, but she could see their dark, gaping mouths etched into the sandstone walls. Unsheathing her rifle, she gingerly moved across the frozen ground. They would have to track the bighorn on foot with the quiet of a cougar if they were going to catch them off guard.

Just as she stepped down onto the steep ravine slope, it began to rain furiously. In minutes, she was soaked to the skin, her hair plastered against her skull. The drops were bitterly cold, and the wind whipped and howled around Kuchana and Two Toes as they worked their way farther down the slope. Shaking, water running down her face, Kuchana had to keep blinking her eyes in order to watch carefully where to place the toe of her boot so that she wouldn't slip and fall. If either of them fell, it would alert the bighorn to their presence, and the animals would flee. The rain was turning to ice the instant it struck the rocks, making the surface hazardous.

Two Toes cursed in his own language as he slipped. He landed on his back, the rifle dropping from his hand. Kuchana whirled around. Giving her a glare, he struggled to his feet.

"Move ahead," he snarled under his breath. "I will catch up."

Nodding, Kuchana turned and focused her attention on the brush that stood a quarter of a mile away. Did the bighorn hear Two Toes fall? The rain was coming down in sheets and it was impossible to see very far away. Releasing a held breath, she realized the rain had also hidden the sound of Two Toes's fall. They still had an opportunity to kill the bighorn.

Watching the Apache, Two Toes smiled to himself. His rifle lay behind him. He went to retrieve it, keeping an eye on her unsuspecting back. This would be an easy kill. The stupid woman who called herself a warrior would die at the first stroke of his blade. Warrior! Ha! She never even suspected that he sang her death song this day.

Moving quietly after retrieving his rifle, Two Toes put the weapon down as he approached Kuchana from the rear. The rain ceased without warning, the drumming sound turning to silence. Cursing his bad luck, Two Toes decided to unsheath his knife and make the lunge that would end Kuchana's life.

Kuchana had crouched down, presenting a smaller target as she carefully made her way closer to the piñon and juniper. Suddenly a feeling of danger rushed over her and she straightened. Her eyes widened and she tensed, assimilating the warning. What had caused it? She whirled around, holding her rifle high across her chest.

His hand raised, Two Toes lunged, his knife upraised. He saw the Apache whirl around. In the middle of his attack, he could not stop his forward motion. With a cry, he brought the knife toward her chest.

A scream lodged in Kuchana's throat. She thrust the rifle above her head. Two Toes's wrist slammed into the weapon. The knife left his fingers, the point sinking deeply into her thick buffalo coat. With a grunt, Kuchana used the rifle as leverage to push Two Toes to one side. The Yavapai fell with a thud, slipping over the icy stones.

"You will die," Kuchana whispered. She was completely unaware that the knife point had sunk into the flesh of her shoulder, just below her right collarbone. Lifting the rifle, she placed it in position to take the Yavapai's life.

Two Toes picked up a rock and hurled it at her with all his might. The rock struck Kuchana in the chest, knocking her backward. Grinning, he leapt to his feet and threw himself at her. Her rifle clattered to the ground as she fell.

Kuchana quickly scrambled to her hands and knees, gasping for breath, her chest aching fiercely where the rock had struck her. The rifle! She lunged forward, hand outstretched.

With a triumphant cry, Two Toes kicked the rifle out of her reach. The heavy rock he now held in his hand would finish her off. He would smash her skull.

Rolling over, her fingers bloodied from the strike of Two Toes's boot, Kuchana looked up into the snarling, deadly features of her enemy. Her hand searched for her own knife. Two Toes's breath came in white, ragged wisps as he placed both hands on the rock and balanced it precariously above his head.

"Die, witch!" he screamed.

Kuchana kicked out, her boot striking Two Toes in the knee. She heard the bone snap. The Yavapai shrieked in pain as the rock hurtled toward her head. Jerking to one side, she heard it smash inches from her temple. She rolled over and came to her feet like a cat, then struggled to find her knife beneath the bulky buffalo jacket. Two Toes had fallen, holding his knee and moaning.

It was a matter of time, Kuchana realized, breathing in harsh gulps of air. Could Two Toes reach her rifle before she could get her knife out to kill him? The Yavapai was in great pain, but not enough to prevent him from grabbing her weapon, which was only inches from where he lay. Her hands shaking badly, Kuchana jerked her jacket above her waist, seeking, then finding the knife.

Two Toes reached out and pulled the rifle into his hands. His eyes glittered with fury and pain as he turned over and raised the rifle in Kuchana's direction.

Kuchana saw the deadly muzzle of the rifle lifting. She saw the hatred in Two Toes's small, black eyes. Opening her mouth to scream, she jerked the knife from the sheath. She would not die without a struggle. No Apache warrior surrendered. Ever.

Two Toes's finger closed around the trigger. He grinned wolfishly and put her in his sights. Simultaneously, he saw her raise her knife.

Kuchana saw Two Toes's finger pull back on the trigger. She was going to die. At the last possible instant, she regretted never consummating her love with Gib. He would never know how much she truly loved him. A terrible sadness paralleled her frustration and anger toward Two Toes, who would take away the only happiness she had ever known. A prayer to Painted Woman was on her lips.

Suddenly, a shot, very close behind Kuchana, barked out into the heavy, icy silence. She gasped as a bullet struck Two Toes squarely in the chest, smashing him backward. The Yavapai tumbled end over end, eventually coming to rest in a tangle of brush at the bottom of the ravine.

Lowering her knife, she whirled around. Gib McCoy stood on horseback, rifle in hand, looking down at her, his face grim. With a little cry, Kuchana collapsed in a shaking heap. McCoy had saved her from sure death. It began to snow, huge white flakes driven by the wind. Sobbing for breath, Kuchana sat there, her head hanging down, her fingers still wrapped around her knife.

McCoy made his way down to her. The blizzard struck with blinding white fury, and he could barely see Kuchana. Heart pounding in his chest, he moved as swiftly as possible, the rock and dirt skidding down around him. At last he was at her side.

"Kuchana..." His voice was raw with emotion. His eyes widened. The butt of a knife protruded from her shoulder, and her left hand was lacerated and bloodied. "My God..." He crouched in front of her. She was pale, her eyes dark as she lifted them. "Don't move," he rasped, "you're wounded."

Blinking, as if in a dream, Kuchana stared up at him. Everything felt as if it were slowing down. Even Gib's voice seemed distant. She felt him take the knife from her hands, her fingers numb and without feeling. "Two Toes," she choked out. "Two Toes..." Then her world grew dark until, finally, she gave over to a power much stronger than she was in her present condition, and lost consciousness.

McCoy crouched by the fire, the light from the flames dancing off the walls of the huge, dry cavern. Outside, the blizzard raged. Worriedly, he studied Kuchana who lay between the wool blankets on the opposite side of the fire. It had been an hour since he'd carried her to the cave, stripped off her wet clothes and bundled her up in the blankets. To his relief, Two Toes's knife had not met its target fully. When he'd pulled the jacket and shirt off her, fearing a deep chest wound, he'd found that her flesh had barely been cut by the Yavapai's blade. There had been a lot of blood, but little real damage.

Shaking his head, he got up and moved to her side. Her hair was still damp. Moving strands of it away from her still face, he studied her. "So close," he whispered, stroking her hair in a caressing motion. "I almost lost you again."

Tears formed in Gib's eyes as he absorbed her features into his heart. If he hadn't followed his intuition, Kuchana would be dead now. He had been in the mountains heading for Jacobsen's Mine when he'd decided to head west and find her. The terrible feeling that she was in great danger had escalated with every mile he'd covered. Thank God he knew where the bighorn usually hid during storms. At the first ravine, he hadn't found them. At the second, he had. If he'd arrived a moment later, Kuchana would have been dead.

Two Toes had superior weight and strength, but she had fought bravely. He smiled faintly, tracing the soft curve of her cheek. "My sun woman has the heart of an eagle." McCoy's hand stilled on her cheek as her lashes fluttered, telling him that she was coming out of the shock she'd suffered from exposure and trauma.

Kuchana recognized the touch of the hand cupping her cheek. She felt herself being drawn out of the warm blackness and pulled toward the light. Gib. It had to be Gib. As she became conscious, she lifted her lashes, staring uncomprehendingly at him for a long moment. McCoy's face was grim, his mouth a straight line. His hair was tousled, his uniform stained. She saw his mouth soften, and his eyes spoke to her of love.

"You're all right, Kuchana," he told her quietly. "Just lie there. There's a blizzard outside. I carried you into this cave, took off your wet clothes and built a fire."

She frowned and moved, feeling pain drifting up her left arm. Her right shoulder was stiff, reminding her of Two Toes' attack. Gib's hand came to rest on her blanketed shoulder, asking her to remain still. "Why are you here?" Her voice was raw, as if she had been screaming. The rest of her fight with the Yavapai seeped back into her sluggish memory. Closing her eyes, she felt Gib's hand tighten slightly, as if to give her support. "Two Toes," she croaked. "He tried to kill me...."

McCoy whispered her name and pulled her into his arms, the thin blankets the only barrier between him and her naked body. "You remember?" He held Kuchana gently, allowing her to huddle against him, her head buried beneath his chin.

"I...yes..." A tremor quivered through her, and although she was warm, a terrible cold inhabited the pit of her stomach. "You saved me life. If you had not come, I would be dead...."

McCoy ran his hand down her damp hair, inhaling the sweet scent that was only her. "I'm glad as hell I turned around to find you. Something told me you were in danger." Her left hand was bandaged to the wrist, but she slid it upward across his chest and around his neck. Kuchana was beginning to tremble in earnest, as if reliving the fight with Two Toes.

"Is he...is he dead?"

Nodding, he kissed her damp hair. "Yes. I tied him on one of the mules outside. When this storm lets up, we'll take him back to the post." Gib closed his eyes as she burrowed more deeply into his arms, barely able to think, much less talk. "God," he whispered thickly, "I've been so afraid of losing you, Kuchana...."

She clung to him, resting against his chest, allowing the solid beat of his heart to steady her own. His hands moved gently up and down her spine, stroking her, bringing warmth back into her soul once again. "When Two Toes lifted my rifle against me, I had only one thought," she said, pressing a kiss to his chest. Gib's arms tightened around her, and Kuchana nuzzled him, rubbing her cheek against the damp wool of his shirt.

Groaning, McCoy leaned down, kissing her wrinkled brow, her closed eyes and finally her cheek. He was shaking, too, but not out of shock or fear. It was out of need of Kuchana. "What was your thought?" he asked hoarsely. Sliding his fingers through her hair, he felt her arch against him.

Kuchana slowly lifted her lashes and stared at the brightly burning fire nearby. Her voice was low and husky. Risking everything, she slowly sat up and faced Gib. "That you would never know of my love for you. That I would never know what it would be like to be your woman." Gib's eyes burned with a dark blue flame that sent a yearning hurtling through her. The blanket across her shoulders parted, revealing the cleft between her breasts.

"Sweet God," McCoy breathed, cupping her face with his hands, holding the look in her wide, adoring eyes.

Trembling, Kuchana knew she was naked beneath the blankets. She leaned forward, her breath suspended, and pressed her lips to the line of his mouth. "Make me your woman," she pleaded. "I have always been yours...."

Her actions were completely unexpected as her seeking lips sought and found his mouth. Moist breath fled across his face as her mouth moved with sweet innocence across his. Just the slight brush of her breasts, the nipples insistent against his shirt, shattered Gib's control. The last hour of his life had stripped away any pretense of how he felt toward Kuchana. As she pressed herself to him, he humbly realized that she was being more honest than he was. Nearly dying had brought her in touch with what was most important in her life.

Kuchana felt a driving need to prove that she was alive. The gathering storm within her demanded that she move out of the darkness of the uninitiated woman and walk into the sunlight of being complete. As Gib's mouth claimed hers, she gave herself over to the man she had loved from the moment she had met him. There was great tenderness in his hands as they moved almost worshipfully across her shoulders, the blanket pooling around her hips and legs. A little cry escaped her as he cupped each of her breasts, moving his thumbs in feathery circles across the taut, begging nipples.

As he bent his head to pull one nipple into his mouth, Kuchana closed her eyes, surrendering to him in every way, trusting him, allowing her womanly instincts to guide her.

Gently, Gib lowered her to the blankets, her black hair a halo around her, shimmering with blue highlights in the light of the nearby fire. He held her gaze as he unbuttoned his wool shirt then tossed it to one side. Her beauty made his blood pulse through him until he thought he'd burst, and her body, lovingly shadowed by flames, reminded him of her innocent offering to him.

Kuchana's eyes widened as she watched Gib shrug out of the suspenders and pull the blue kersey shirt back to expose the breadth of his dark-haired chest. She had never seen Gib unclothed, and an ache centered hotly between her thighs as she gazed up at him, drinking in his powerful body. Longing to slide her fingers through his curled hair, she lay there watching as he got to his feet, removed his trousers and underwear.

Her lips parted as McCoy stood highlighted by the snapping, crackling fire, and her heart began to pound wildly in her breast. His hardened body reminded her of a lean cougar. His legs were long, thighs powerfully muscled. Kuchana was barely able to think as he lowered himself to her side. She had no idea that a man could look so ruggedly beautiful.

Gib had seen the surprise in Kuchana's eyes as he'd undressed. He knew that an Apache maid was not told of men or of coupling until the day of her marriage. Further, the bodies of Apache men were hairless. He had seen her eyes widen when he had pulled off his shirt to expose a chest covered with a thick mat of hair. And later, he had seen her eyes move lower to stare at him. There had been fear in her eyes at the sight of his need of her.

"You are my sun woman," McCoy breathed huskily, covering her mouth with a long, exploratory kiss. Automatically, her lips parted, allowing him entrance, her breath becoming a sigh as she slid her arms around his shoulders, accepting him. Shaken by her trust in him to do the right thing, to introduce her to a world of beauty, to make her his woman, Gib placed a savage grip on his own need as he continued to ease the fear from her.

As McCoy's lips moved with sureness across hers, Kuchana was reminded of lightning striking, bolting jaggedly down through her, again and again, increasing the ache between her legs. Moving restlessly, pressing her nakedness against his, she didn't know what she needed, only that Gib could give her relief from this sweet ache.

"Easy, easy," he crooned against her wet lips. Each time she moved against him, his hips making contact with the rounded firmness of her belly, he trembled, his control disintegrating. Kuchana was moaning, her fingers alternately digging into and then moving restlessly across his shoulders, pleading with him in a woman's silent language to consummate the fire that burned between them. As he tasted the sweetness of each nipple, she writhed, moaning his name over and over again. The urgency mounted within him as he slid his hand across the gleaming expanse of her belly. Bracing himself for her to tense as he approached the most sacred area of her body, McCoy was surprised as she willingly opened her thighs to give him entrance.

One look into Kuchana's wide eyes, now gold with longing, and Gib understood the power of her needs. Her actions were an honest, unfettered expression of what she felt in her heart. As he lay on his side, absorbing the incredible beauty of Kuchana's eyes, he slid his hand across the dark carpet to discover if she was ready to accept him.

A ragged cry tore from Kuchana's lips as she felt his hand slide between her taut, straining thighs. The moment he touched her moist, sacred womanhood, she thrashed her head from side to side, feeling tiny, jolting eruptions occur with each stroking, caressing movement. The world exploded within her, and she closed her eyes, her cries of pleasure echoing like a song throughout the cave. This was the beauty of love, she thought disjointedly, feeling McCoy's long, hard body covering hers. As his hands settled on either side of her head, she opened her eyes. His face was tense and covered with perspiration, as if he were in some terrible agony. Lifting her arms, she placed them around his neck. His lips drew away from his clenched teeth as she felt him press through the doorway of her sacred womanhood. She waited, breath snagged, hands tightening around his neck, silently begging him to complete their union.

The adoration in Kuchana's gold eyes gave him the courage to move into her slick, moist depths. A groan tore through McCoy as he sheathed himself in her. He met the wall within her that proclaimed her virginity. For one split second, he felt her tense, and then, she instinctively raised her hips, helping him break through the thin barrier, welcoming him into her. Her act brought tears to his eyes. Hands forming into fists, he strained forward, taking her, moving within her, reveling in the coupling that would bind them to one another forever.

The momentary pain dissolved in a flood of new and awakening sensations for Kuchana. With each slow thrust, she moaned with mounting pleasure. Glorying in their mating, she imitated McCoy's movements, bringing herself and him even more heady and fiery gratification. He was a powerful stallion, sleek and strong. Tumbling on storm clouds, each stroke reminding her of the joyous secret of being a complete woman, Kuchana closed her eyes and surrendered to the fire that had ignited between them.

McCoy felt Kuchana tense. A sharp little cry came from within her as she arched upward, their sweaty bodies melded to one another. Sliding his hand beneath her slim hips, he

prolonged the feeling for her until she suddenly went limp
in his arms, almost faint in the aftermath. Humbled by her
ability to be a woman in ways many other women would
never become, he felt the last of his control disintegrate. A
low animal growl rumbled out of him as he brought his own
life into her. The moments spun together for McCoy, sunlight and storm, fire and water.

The sacredness of their act overwhelmed him. He moved
onto his side and brought Kuchana into his arms. He held
her in a crushing embrace, never wanting to let her go.

Chapter Sixteen

❝I feel as if the sun and I are one,❞ Kuchana whispered, nuzzling her cheek into the damp hair on McCoy's chest. A soft smile lingered on her lips as he caressed her shoulder and back.

"You are the sun," he told her thickly, his voice rough with emotion. Each time he tunneled his fingers through her heavy, silky hair, she purred. "You're mine," Gib told her in a low, vibrating voice. "You always were."

Kuchana was too weak to move, fulfilled as never before, in the arms of the only man she would ever love. "My heart has known since the day I met you."

Regret came to Gib's voice as he laid her down, her head resting on his arm. Her eyes were guileless, filled with such overwhelming love that it made his heart wrench. "The only thing I wish is that we could have been married first."

"In the eyes and hearts of my people, we are married," Kuchana answered, reaching up to slide her fingers along his cheek, feeling the bristly growth of beard beneath them. By late day, Gib's face was always shadowed, even though he shaved every morning. His blue eyes were cobalt, and she saw the joy in his face, even though there was lament in his tone.

"But not to my people." Gib shook his head, unable to stop himself from stroking her hair or her satiny skin, so firm and supple beneath his fingers. "I'd made plans for us, but things got sidetracked," he told her with a wry smile.

His smile went straight through Kuchana, dazzling and warming her. "What plans?"

"I wanted to wait until you fulfilled your vow before asking you to marry me."

Touched by his whispered admission, Kuchana traced the outline of his mouth. "Thank you," she whispered. Her vow was important to him, and Kuchana felt moisture gather in her eyes.

"Tears?" Gib asked, gently wiping them away. Right now she looked like a Madonna, her face clear, eyes glistening with the trust she held for him alone and the pleasure of discovering the joyous wonder of becoming a woman. Gib was grateful that the experience hadn't been a terrible nightmare for Kuchana, as he had often heard it was for new brides.

Managing a wobbly smile, she whispered, "You have always honored the road I walk, and never tried to tell me I should do differently, as the *pindahs* have."

Leaning down, McCoy caressed her soft, lush lips with his own, tasting her sweetness all over again. "I love you just the way you are, sun woman. Don't ever forget that."

A cocoon of warmth descended around Kuchana as Gib brought her into his arms, rolling over on his back and covering them both with the blankets. Suddenly, she was exhausted. Closing her eyes, she snuggled close to him, her head resting in the hollow of his shoulder, arm across his chest. Gib loved her. That was all she needed to know. Whatever lay ahead for them she could face, knowing that. Their love would see them through these last weeks until Geronimo went back to the reservation.

"Where the hell have you been?" Lieutenant Carter snarled as McCoy and Kuchana entered headquarters the next morning. His temper was frayed because McCoy hadn't shown up, and he was worried that Two Toes might have gotten into trouble. Now, seeing Kuchana standing there defiantly, he grew even more afraid.

McCoy threw his beaver mittens on the corporal's desk. "Two Toes tried to kill Kuchana, Lieutenant. If I hadn't detoured from going to Jacobsen's to find her, she'd be dead now. A blizzard hit minutes afterward, so we holed up in a cave and waited it out until morning."

Furious, Carter glared at them. He saw Kuchana's left hand was dressed in a bloody bandage. Otherwise, she seemed all right. Damn! His whole plan had been destroyed by McCoy. Hatred wound through the officer as he glared at the grim sergeant who stood between him and Kuchana. "Sergeant, you've disobeyed a direct order. I told you to go to Jacobsen with those mules and get food for the post."

Kuchana stepped forward, her eyes wide with disbelief. "Lieutenant, Two Toes tried to kill me. If McCoy had not been there—"

"Shut up!" Carter roared. And then he punched his finger into McCoy's chest. "You've disobeyed my order for the last time, Sergeant. Corporal."

McClusky leapt to his feet. "Yes, sir."

"Call the guards. Put Sergeant McCoy under arrest and take him to solitary. Then write him up for disobeying a direct order. He'll answer to Colonel Polk for what he's done."

"No!" Kuchana shoved the officer away from Gib. "He saved my life!" she cried. "How can you do this? He should be honored, not punished!"

"Kuchana," McCoy whispered, his voice vibrating with anger, "don't say anything else or he'll write you up, too." He took her by the arm, moving her to one side. His fingers tightened around her arm. "Listen to me," he said harshly in Apache, "if you say anything else, they'll write you up and kick you out of the army as a scout. And then you'll be sent to the reservation or to Florida. You don't want that, Kuchana. You must fulfill your vow. Think of that.''

Glaring at Carter who stood there with a smug look on his young, pale features, Kuchana took in several gulps of air, trying to understand what was happening and why. She saw the pleading look in Gib's narrowed eyes.

"Trust me," he coaxed gruffly.

Nodding, Kuchana stepped out of his grip. McClusky ran out the door, yelling across the parade ground for a pair of guards. It hurt to stand there watching Carter barely able to fight a smile while they waited for Gib to be placed under arrest.

"Well, Sergeant, how do you feel now?" Carter gloated, moving around the desk and jerking open a drawer. He pulled out several papers. "This insubordination ought to cost you your stripes and what's left of your less-than-glorious career. If I have my way, you'll be dishonorably discharged and kicked off this post in a few hours, mister." He slammed the papers down on the desk.

"What about Two Toes's trying to murder Kuchana?" McCoy rasped. "Aren't you at all concerned about that?" Gib knew he wasn't. Carter hated Kuchana almost as much as he hated him. Stunned by the events, Gib had never thought that Carter would write him up for saving the life of a scout. Worse, if Carter claimed he was deserting because he hadn't returned to the post last evening, the charges would send him before a firing squad. Deserters weren't tolerated in the army at all.

Gripping an ink pen, Carter sat down. "Sergeant, from this moment on, what you think or want is of no concern to me. Put your gun and holster on the desk." Savagely, the officer began to fill out the report form.

Gib unbuckled the holster, trying desperately to hold on to his temper. "You still haven't answered my question about Kuchana and the fact that Two Toes tried to murder her."

"Two Toes is Yavapai. She's an Apache. They never did get along. I consider it nothing more than that."

With a little cry of frustration, Kuchana moved to the desk. "But McCoy saved my life. Two Toes sneaked up behind me while we were hunting bighorn. How can you do this to him?"

Carter lifted his head and sneered, "Frankly, Kuchana, I don't care what happened."

"I killed Two Toes," McCoy growled.

A slow smile crawled across Carter's face as he assimilated this latest piece of information. "You killed him?"

Fighting back a sob, Kuchana realized that Carter had wanted to hear that admission.

"That's right." McCoy held Carter's narrowed gaze. Killing Two Toes would bring one more charge against him. Even if he could clear himself of the first charge, he could never the second one. Any soldier found killing a scout employed by the army could be sent to his own death, or at the very least given a dishonorable discharge. Carter had him right where he wanted him.

"No!" Kuchana sobbed, jerking open the coat she wore. "Look!" She tore at her shirt, a button flying off, exposing the wound on her shoulder.

Carter looked at the wound, thinking that Two Toes had almost made good his promise to kill her. What a shame. "Cover yourself up," he muttered, bending his head, continuing to add the new charge to McCoy's report.

Closing her shirt with a trembling hand, Kuchana stood in shock and humiliation over the lieutenant's brusque attitude. Only her collarbone and the top of her breast had been visible, but he had reacted with disgust. She felt Gib's hand on her arm, propelling her toward the door.

"Get out of here," he told her in Apache. "If you stay, Carter will find a way to put you on report. You're upset. Go to Poppy. Tell her what happened. Stay with her."

Looking up into McCoy's taut features, she saw the thundercloud anger in his eyes. "But what of you?"

"I'll be locked up in jail until I come to trial. Carter will probably convene one for me tomorrow morning." He softened his tone, pleading with her. "Please, Kuchana, stay away. He's gunning for both of us. I want you to be able to get your sister to safety. Hold on to that above everything else. Remember your vow..."

Poppy shook her head from side to side. She was up to her elbows in hot water and soap suds, scrubbing a shirt in the tub. "Chile, you stay here with us. That Carter is up to no good."

"And so is Miz Melissa!" Nettie added, looking up from her table where she was ironing. When she saw her mother give a warning shake of her head, she fell silent and quickly resumed her ironing.

Morosely, Kuchana sat near them, her hands hanging loosely between her legs. As soon as she had appeared at Poppy's tent, she had been welcomed with open arms. When they'd discovered her injuries, both women had stopped their work and dressed her wounds. A bowl of deer-meat stew had made her feel slightly better, but she was still worrying about Gib.

"What will they do to him, Poppy?" she asked finally. The huge washerwoman's skin was like polished ebony from the moist heat in the tent.

"Knowing the army, they'll yank the stripes off his arms, play the trumpet and break his sword."

"That's to show everyone at the post that he's no longer a soldier," Nettie added sadly. "Oh, Mama, Sergeant McCoy don't deserve this. Isn't there something we can do?"

"Nothing, Nettie. Now hush up. You're making Kuchana cry."

With a sigh, Nettie set the iron down and got up, moving to her side. "Oh, Kuchana, I'm sorry," and she wrapped her arms around the Apache woman.

Sniffing, Kuchana uttered thickly. "Warriors don't cry...."

Poppy dried off her thickly muscled arms and came over, sitting down opposite Kuchana. She handed her a freshly pressed linen handkerchief. "Chile, a part of you is a warrior. But a bigger part is a woman, and you love a man who's in trouble. You cry all you want."

More tears fell and Kuchana buried her face in the linen handkerchief. When Poppy placed her hand on her shoulder, a sob was wrenched from Kuchana. "How do you know of our love?" she asked in a choked voice.

With a chuckle, Poppy patted her shoulder gently. "Chile, Nettie and I have known for a long time. Ain't nothing wrong with it."

"Why," Nettie added softly, her hand around Kuchana's waist, trying to comfort her, "everyone here knows you love him. Sergeant McCoy is a fine man, Kuchana. We all hoped you would git married after you fulfilled your vow. That's what Sergeant McCoy was waiting on, we thought."

Blowing her nose, Kuchana looked at the tears in both women's eyes. It struck her hard that they would cry for her. "Yes, he was. And you cry for me?"

Poppy gave her a game smile, brushing the tears from her plump cheeks. "Chile, you're a kind person who puts the welfare of others before yourself. How can we not love you for that?"

"I do not know what to do, now. How can I help Gib? A warrior fights on, no matter what the odds. I must fight for him."

"Chile, you can't take on the whole army," Poppy said. "Colonel Polk will hold the court-martial. He's the only man who can decide Sergeant McCoy's fate. All we can do is pray—hard."

Prayer was something Kuchana understood well. Painted Woman had always answered her prayers. Nodding, she wiped the last of the tears from her eyes. "How will we know about Colonel Polk's decision?"

"Easy enough," Nettie said. "If the trumpet calls all the men to the parade ground for inspection, then we know Sergeant McCoy is going be drummed out of the army."

"Well, if that happens," Poppy said with a grunt, standing, "it's a better sentence than to have Sergeant McCoy shot for being a deserter. So, it's a blessing in disguise."

Nettie sat there, her jaw jutting. "Mama, I just know Miz Melissa's behind this."

Kuchana frowned. "What?"

"Hush up, Nettie."

"How can Melissa be a part of all this?" Kuchana demanded, watching Poppy move back to the tub of clothes.

"Never you mind, chile. Nettie spoke out of turn."

Nervously, Nettie got up, moving back to the iron and sitting down. "Kuchana, you better get some sleep. You're going need it."

What did Melissa have to do with this? Kuchana studied Poppy and then Nettie. Neither woman was willing to say anything else. Exhausted by the morning's events, she got to her feet. "Thank you for all your help," she told them.

"You come straight here when you wake up," Poppy said. "I don't want you alone if they decide to discharge Sergeant McCoy in front of the whole post."

Nodding, Kuchana slipped outside, closing the flaps behind her. The air was chilly, and Father Sky was filled with clouds that threatened more rain. Holding her head high, Kuchana walked through the laundry area and the tents of the many families. As she entered the scout area, she saw Charlie sitting by the fire with a glum look on his face. He stared at her, but said nothing. Now the post had only two scouts left. Tiredly, Kuchana slipped into her tent, tying the flaps shut and crawling under the blankets.

She lay there shivering, but it wasn't from the cold. It was out of fear for Gib's life. The prayers she began to chant within her head and heart continued until she fell into a deep sleep. Dreams embraced her, dreams of Gib holding her, whispering words of love to her. And then, they turned into nightmares. Poppy's words haunted her. Would the army call Gib a deserter and shoot him? If they did, her life would also be ended.

Harvey Polk sat in his chair reading the report that Carter had filed on McCoy. The sergeant stood at stiff attention in front of his desk, while Carter stood at ease beside him. By noon, everyone on the post had known of the report and the fact that McCoy was in jail. Rubbing his double chin, Polk dropped the report onto the desk, scowling heavily. Inwardly, he didn't want to lose McCoy's services. The man knew the Apaches and had been instrumental, along with Kuchana, in locating Geronimo. Of late, Polk's career had taken a positive swing, with General Crook sending weekly dispatches to him, keeping him involved in trying to capture Geronimo. No, McCoy was too important to his career to let him go. But how the hell, under the circumstances, could he not discharge the damn fool sergeant?

Clearing his throat noisily, Polk glanced at Carter, who was barely able to keep from smiling. "Lieutenant, I find your charge of desertion by Sergeant McCoy to be a bit much."

Dodd glanced down. "What? But, Colonel, he openly admitted he turned away from Jacobsen's. Who's to say he wasn't going to meet Kuchana up in the mountains and keep heading west?"

Drumming his fingers on the desk, Polk looked at McCoy through his thick brows. "At ease, Sergeant McCoy. What's your side to this story?"

Gib placed his hands behind his back. He then told Polk everything, except the fact that he had made love with Kuchana in the cave. Carter was sneering as he finished.

"And so it was a gut hunch that made you turn and go back to find her?" Polk asked.

"Yes, sir."

"That's because he's in love with the heathen," Carter accused.

McCoy pinned Carter with a black stare. "My feelings aren't a part of this hearing, Lieutenant. I acted on a hunch and it proved to be correct."

Nostrils flaring, Carter paced cockily in front of the desk. "Colonel, with all due respect, this man has a known history of bothering married women. That's why he lost his commission at Fort Apache. Now he's philandering with squaws."

Gib froze. "Lieutenant, don't you ever refer to Kuchana in that way again."

Startled by the threat in McCoy's voice, Carter paused. "Well, I—"

"Lieutenant Carter," Polk interjected with a sigh, "let's stick to the charges listed here. What Sergeant McCoy does in his off time, and with whom he does it, is not my concern. Nor should it be yours."

Chastened, Carter felt his face grow hot. "Well," he muttered, moving close to the desk, "you have to consider my charge of desertion against him."

McCoy watched the colonel. Something wasn't right. He sensed Polk's hesitation. Gib had been in the army long enough to know the games the officers played in order to curry favor from the generals they worked under. Right now, Polk's career had been resurrected because General Crook was impressed with his and Kuchana's success in finding Geronimo.

Gib relaxed slightly and said, "Sir, there was no intent to desert on my part."

"You deserted when you escorted the wife of the post commander to that stage line, McCoy!" Carter cried.

"Dammit, Dodd, settle down," Polk grunted, glaring up at the young officer. "Just stand there and be quiet. I'll ask the questions and make the assumptions."

"Yes, sir."

"Sergeant, I don't believe you were deserting," Polk began heavily. "But the charge of disobeying a direct order stands."

"Yes, sir."

Carter grimaced, wanting to speak up. If he could only get Polk to label McCoy a deserter, the sergeant would be shot before sunset.

"I'm sorry we weren't more aware of the tension between Two Toes and Kuchana."

"I reported it a number of times, sir." Gib glanced significantly toward Carter. "Apparently, the lieutenant saw fit not to act on it. Now, we're down to only two scouts and we need at least four more."

Polk nodded and slowly sat back in his chair, scratching his long white sideburns. "Dammit, Sergeant, my hands are tied. I can't ignore this report."

"I realize that, sir."

Sighing, Polk leaned forward, putting his signature on the report. "Lieutenant, gather the men of the post at 1400 hours. At that time, you will strip Sergeant McCoy of his stripes, take his weapon and break his sword. Your pension will be canceled and a letter sent to Washington, notifying them of your dishonorable discharge. In the eyes of the army, you walk out of here with the clothes on your back, nothing more. Your horse, your weapons and anything else owned by the army remains behind. Do you understand?"

"I do, sir," McCoy answered, girding himself. The humiliation of being stripped of his rank, weapons and worst of all, the breaking of the sword that he had owned for seven years, would be devastating. But as he stood there, Kuchana's beautiful, smiling face lingered in front of him, and he knew that he had made the right decision. Without Kuchana, he had no future. His present might be taken from him, his years in the army ended in shame, but that didn't matter. Somehow, he told himself, he would survive this. His only real concern was that Kuchana would have no one at the post to protect her against the likes of Carter and Melissa. The last thought left a bitter taste in his mouth.

Polk handed Carter the signed report. "All right, Lieutenant, get on with this ordeal."

Carter was stymied by Polk's unhappiness. Why wasn't the colonel elated? "Right away, sir."

"Carter!" Polk's voice rolled across the office as the lieutenant reached for the brass doorknob.

Shaken, Carter jerked to a halt and turned. "Yes, sir?"

"I'm relieving you of command of the scouts. From here on out, Captain Lane will take over the duties. I'm disappointed that you didn't listen to Sergeant McCoy in regard to Two Toes' hatred of Kuchana. Without that woman, we wouldn't even be close to Geronimo. As it stands, this compounds our problems in getting to the chief, but you don't see that, do you?"

Confused, Carter shook his head. He saw a smile edge McCoy's mouth. The son of a bitch. "Uh, no, sir, I don't."

"Get the hell out of here, Carter," Polk said irritably with a wave of his hand.

The two guards came in the door once Carter left. Gib snapped to attention and did an about-face. Polk was very unhappy and he knew why. As he was walked out under armed guard, McCoy breathed a sigh of relief. At least Captain Jason Lane would do a much better job of handling the scouts than Carter had. Thank God something was going right today. As he stepped off the wooden porch, Gib realized that, in a few hours, he would be relieved of duty and kicked off the post. Somehow, he had to get word to Kuchana.

"Private Ladler," he said, looking over at the young soldier.

"Yes, suh?"

"I need to see Poppy. Can you arrange for her to come to the jail to see me?"

Ladler nodded. "I'll do what I can, Sergeant."

McCoy smiled slightly. "Thanks, Private. I appreciate it."

Poppy was huffing like a runaway horse by the time she arrived at the jail. Private Ladler had escorted her across the off-limits parade ground and now opened the door to the structure. Inside, in the dim light, she could see McCoy sitting on a wooden bed inside the cell.

"You've got ten minutes, Miz Poppy."

"I knows, Lemuel. Just wait outside."

The private shut the door, leaving them alone. Poppy waddled over to the cell. "Lordy, Sergeant McCoy, you're in a heap o' trouble."

Gib rose from the cot and stood, his hands wrapped around the cold iron bars. "It's not as bad as it could have been, Poppy. Thanks for coming."

"Your lady ain't doing so good."

Frowning, Gib's hands tightened on the bars. "Kuchana . . . how is she?"

Poppy's grew misty. "Sergeant McCoy, she cried herself all out."

Gib winced, his mouth pursed. "I know. Look, I need you to be with her this afternoon."

"They going to bust you so soon?"

"Yes."

Poppy shook her head. "Oh, Sergeant McCoy, what's wrong with these people? I know Miz Melissa and Lieutenant Carter are behind this. They're bad people. It's all over the laundry—Miz Melissa is so happy, she's dancing around in her house. Clarissa overheard her saying to Carter that she was hoping you'd git shot."

With a snort, Gib said, "I don't care about those two right now. It's Kuchana I'm worried about. Colonel Polk has assigned Captain Lane to the scouts, thank God." He reached through the bars and gripped Poppy's plump hand. "This afternoon, make Kuchana stay with you. The whole post will be there, and she'll be forced to watch. Kuchana doesn't understand or agree with all our rules. She can't afford to interfere. Carter hates her. If she tries to stop the proceedings, he's within his rights to draw his gun." Gib's voice lowered. "Please, take care of her for me, Poppy. Tell Kuchana I'll be back as soon as I can. I've got some plans, some ideas, but it's going to take time to put them into motion."

Misty-eyed, Poppy nodded, patting Gib's strong, darkly tanned hand. "Don't you worry, Sergeant McCoy, I'll take good care of your woman for you."

Gib managed a faint smile, then released her hand. "Poppy, I'll be grateful to you for the rest of my life if you can care for Kuchana until I return."

Sniffing, she blubbered, "This ain't fair. You did nothing wrong. If it weren't for you, Kuchana would be dead. I hate this army sometimes...."

Gib took in a deep breath, holding on to his own anger over the situation. "Carter was waiting for me or Kuchana to make a mistake, Poppy. I played right into his hands, but I'm not sorry."

"I understand," she whispered, wiping the tears from her eyes. Straightening her dress, Poppy whispered, "I'll have Nettie sneak outside the fort just before the gathering. She's got a basket of food, some blankets, our old Henry rifle, and Ned, our horse, for you. She'll meet you down by Draper's Pool."

McCoy stood there, stunned by what she was doing for him. It was thirty miles to his cabin in the mountains on the land he'd bought earlier in the year. And he had been worried about how he was going to make that trek without food or any kind of protective clothing. Poppy was giving him a chance to survive. The horse they owned pulled the laundry cart for them. It had taken Poppy and her family years to save for the old gelding. And he was sure the Henry rifle belonged to her husband.

"Poppy," he rasped, "I'll pay you back for all your kindness. I promise."

She smiled. "Sergeant McCoy, you bring the horse and rifle back when you can. There's no hurry. And we don't want no payment. Consider this our thanks for all the food you have brought to us since you came here. We'll take good care of Kuchana for you. She's like family to us."

Gib watched the laundress leave. Sitting down, he realized for the first time in his life who his friends really were. Right now, he was a pariah; someone to be avoided by everyone on the army post. He didn't feel for himself, but for Kuchana, who wouldn't understand the proceedings, just that he was going to be publicly shamed for saving her life. And it was breaking his heart because of the agony and pain it would cause her.

Chapter Seventeen

The sickening sound of the stripes being ripped from Gib's shirt echoed across the silent parade ground. Kuchana winced visibly as Lieutenant Carter did the deed. Poppy maintained a viselike grip on her wrist, keeping her at her side. Tears blurred Kuchana's eyes at the sight of Gib's impassive face, as he stood at rigid military attention. In front of him were all the officers of the post. Behind them were the hundreds of enlisted men, also at attention.

I must be as brave as he is, she thought, choking back her tears. She stood with her chin held high, even though across the parade ground she could see Melissa and the other wives whispering behind their fans. Her attention was drawn back to Carter, as he jerked Gib's sword from its sheath.

"From this moment on, let it be known that Gibson McCoy is dishonorably discharged from the U.S. Army. He is not welcome at this post, or any other. In our eyes, he's committed a despicable and dishonorable crime." Carter took the sword in both gloved hands, lifting his knee and snapping the blade across it. The sword broke, the crack echoing like a rifle shot.

Carter threw the broken weapon at McCoy's feet. "Dismissed, McCoy. From this moment on, you're no longer a soldier, just a civilian. Walk toward the gate, mister, and don't look back."

Gib's gaze moved left. He saw Kuchana's strained, pale features, her eyes filled with tears. But she wasn't crying. Swallowing hard, he met and held her gaze for a split second.

His fierce love for her welled up through him, erasing the pain he felt. He would do it all over again to save her life, because he loved her. When the drum roll began, he made an about-face, focusing on the gate. His career had ended abruptly, without warning. His parents would be shocked. He prayed they'd understand. His mother would. Gib wasn't so sure about his father. Stoically, as he began to walk, he knew they'd accept it because it was a fact of life. His life.

His thoughts then centered on Kuchana. He hoped Poppy would be able to console her, because he wouldn't be able to. She wouldn't be allowed to leave the post without permission, either. Gib was sure Carter would tell Captain Lane to keep her busy, so that she couldn't leave the post and meet him. No, it would be weeks before he might be able to arrange a meeting with her outside the fort, away from the prying eyes of the officers' wives. *I love you, just remember that, sun woman. Just remember that . . .*

Kuchana watched in abject misery as Gib walked with his shoulders back and head erect out the open gates. The moment he walked through, the drum roll stopped, and silence hung heavily across the parade ground. The huge log gates were slowly pulled shut and locked.

"Regiment, dismissed!" Lieutenant Carter bawled, his voice carrying shrilly over the post.

The rows of men melted into a restless crowd, little being said. Kuchana stood there, staring at the broken sword that lay in the mud in the center of the parade ground. Everyone was walking by it as if it didn't exist. Her breath came in uneven gulps as she watched Carter walk by, smiling. His was the only happy face besides that of Melissa Polk, who stood on the porch looking like a sated cougar.

Without warning, Kuchana slipped free of Poppy's grip, heading directly toward the broken sword. She knew her action was breaking regulations, but she didn't care.

Poppy gasped, too heavy to move quickly enough to grab Kuchana, her eyes rounding as the Apache woman approached the sword that lay in two pieces in the mud. "Oh, Lordy," she groaned, rooted to the spot. If one of the officers saw her, they'd place her on report.

The wind picked up as Kuchana approached the spot. The men had made a path for her. Many of them had saddened looks on their faces, as they met her fearless gaze, murmuring words of apology. They knew Gib loved her.

With a shake of her head, Poppy reached Kuchana and grabbed her by the arm, propelling her toward the laundry tents. "Chile, you come on, before Carter sees you."

Kuchana realized belatedly that a number of men who rode with Gib had spoken to her as they'd left the parade ground. Her heart was torn over Gib's humiliating end to his career. But his men had shown her that Gib was still a man of honor in their eyes.

"Poppy, where's Nettie?" she asked in a raw voice.

"Out," Poppy snapped, moving as quickly as her short, thick legs would carry her, hustling Kuchana along. The sooner she got her away from the officers and their nosy wives, the safer Kuchana would be. It was important she not realize Nettie was already at Draper's Pool, waiting to meet Gib. Kuchana might want to leave and go after him. If she did, Carter would write her up on charges of desertion, and at the very least, she could be horsewhipped within an inch of her life, or shot before a firing squad.

Nettie's eyes were large and filled with fright as she stood huddled next to Ned, their gray gelding, at the bank of Draper's Pool. Her fear of being attacked by a roaming band of *comancheros,* Apaches, or *soldatos* made her uneasy. She kept her thick wool shawl pulled tightly around her shoulders.

"Nettie."

She turned, gasping. "Mistah McCoy!" she yelped happily, dragging Ned along by his reins.

Gib walked down the path to the pool and smiled at the thin dark girl. "You're a sight for sore eyes."

Happily, Nettie dragged a heavy buffalo coat off the saddle and handed it to him. "Put that on or you'll catch your death of cold."

"Thanks," he said, shrugging into the coat. Gib saw two huge sacks of food hanging on either side of the saddle, and the Henry rifle in a sheath beneath the stirrup.

Digging in the folds of her sash, Nettie dragged out a small leather purse. "Here, Mama said to give this to you. She was afraid you didn't have any money, Mistah McCoy. Said for you to head over to Jacobsen's, rent a room, and stay the winter. There's enough money here to get you by."

Gently, Gib held the well-worn purse made from cow leather. He opened it, finding two fifty-dollar gold pieces in it. "Where'd she get these?" he asked in amazement. Poppy was always squirreling money away.

Bashfully, Nettie murmured, "Mama was saving them for my wedding." And then she grinned, her eyes twinkling with amusement. "There isn't a man taking a shine to me yet, so I figured you could use them better than me."

Touched beyond words, Gib closed the purse. Poppy was one of the hardest-working women he'd ever met. She must have saved for ten or fifteen years for these gold pieces. And for Nettie to give him her wedding gift so that he could survive touched him deeply. "Nettie," he said, "I can't take them," and he picked up her hand, placing the purse back in it.

"B-but, you have to. How will you make it through the winter?"

He leaned over, pressing a kiss to Nettie's furrowed brow. "I've got a rifle, thanks to you. The cabin's finished enough for me to stay warm and safe. And I'll hunt my food."

Worriedly, Nettie ran her slender fingers over the purse. "Are you sure, Mistah McCoy? Mama would never forgive me if I let you starve."

With a chuckle, Gib embraced her. "I won't starve, Nettie, so stop worrying." It was almost dark. He'd take Nettie back to the post, drop her off, and then fade into the night, heading for the cabin. Mounting the gelding, he held his hand down to her. "Come on, I've got to get you back to the post, or Poppy will skin me alive."

Beneath the cover of darkness, McCoy was able to get within a quarter mile of the post. The fort didn't have a wall around all of it, just one section, near the headquarters and the officers' billet. The rest of it was spread across the valley, and mounted sentries slowly rode the perimeter. The moon lent enough light to allow Gib to identify one of the main paths that led to the laundry tents.

The sentry had just ridden by and wouldn't return for at least another twenty minutes, so Gib relaxed as he pulled the gelding to a halt. Nettie, who was afraid to ride, had her spindly arms wrapped viselike around his waist so that she wouldn't fall off.

"We're here, Nettie," he told her in a low voice.

"Lordy, I'm glad!" She unlocked her hands and pulled them back into her lap.

"Before you go, will you take a message to Kuchana for me?"

"Sure, Mistah McCoy."

He turned around in the saddle, holding Nettie's solemn gaze. She was a pretty young woman, and Gib knew that Private Ladler was trying to build up enough courage to start courting her. But Nettie didn't know that yet.

"Tell her she has to obey army regulations. I'm not going to be here to protect her any longer, and I know Carter is still gunning for her."

"He sure is!"

Nodding, Gib added, "Tell her that I'll be safe up at my cabin, and that I'll have plenty of food. She's to let things settle down around here. In about three weeks, I'll try to contact her. To do it any sooner will be inviting trouble, because Carter and Melissa know I care a great deal for Kuchana. I'm sure Carter will tell Captain Lane not to grant her any off-post privileges, keeping her a captive, in a way. Tell Kuchana not to fight them. Sometimes a warrior has to be patient."

Nettie grinned. "She'll understand, Mistah McCoy."

"You're like family to her. Kuchana trusts you. She'll listen to you." He frowned. "I love her, Nettie, and I'm worried that because she loves me, she'll want to leave and stay with me. That can't happen. You know what they'd do to her. If she breaks the law, I'm helpless to protect her. She has a fine line to walk at the post."

"Ohh, Mistah McCoy," Nettie sighed, "you finally told her you loved her."

A faint smile touched his mouth. "I suppose you and Poppy knew all along?"

Pressing her hands to her mouth so that no one would hear her giggle, Nettie nodded her head vigorously. Her eyes danced. "We was hoping all along you loved Kuchana. It was easy to see she loved you. Now, don't you worry about a thing. We'll take care of Kuchana."

"Thanks," Gib said, meaning it. "You'd better get down. I'll stay here until I see you get to your tent."

Grateful, Nettie struggled down off Ned, glad to be back on the ground again. She arranged her cotton skirt, trying to smooth out some of the wrinkles. She lifted her hand in goodbye, then trotted down the well-worn path.

McCoy sat there, watching Nettie's slim form retreat. The scout area was only a few hundred yards away. It would be so easy to slip in and see Kuchana. If he was caught, though, all hell would break loose and he'd be putting Kuchana at risk. Nettie made it back to the tent, and Gib turned the tired old horse around and headed back toward the mountains. More than anything, he wanted to see Kuchana. He tried to prepare himself for the fact he wouldn't see her for a while, but it was hard.

He couldn't stop worrying about her. He knew the military system, and understood how it worked. She didn't. Carter or Melissa could lure her into a trap, humiliating her, or worse, putting her in real trouble with the army. His only hope was Poppy, who could guide her through the treachery with a degree of safety.

It wasn't fair that after the night they'd made such beautiful love they be torn apart like this. As Ned picked his way between the cacti, Gib felt a wounded-animal cry gathering deep within him. He wanted to howl like a wolf who has lost its mate. There was nothing he could do. Not yet. Geronimo had promised Lieutenant Maus to meet General Crook. Would the chief finally come back to the reservation? If he did, that would mean he could marry Kuchana and she could quit as a scout. She would be away from the post and in the safety of his arms. If only Geronimo would return to the reservation.

"Goddammit!" Polk swore fervently. He launched himself from behind his desk, glaring at Carter. "Geronimo escaped?"

Irritably, Carter muttered, "Yes, sir. We had him. Kuchana and Lieutenant Maus had persuaded him to go back to the reservation. Everything looked good. General Crook was pleased, and we got to San Bernardo Springs. At the camp that night, some American bastard of a trader sold the Apaches mescal, and they got drunk on it. Nachiz, Geronimo, and twenty of his people melted into the night and went back to Mexico. We got the rest though, sir. General Crook wants Chihuahua and the Apache families that stayed sent by rail to Florida. So, it wasn't a complete loss, sir."

Pacing, Harvey shook his head ponderously from side to side. "This isn't good, Lieutenant. The general made it very clear that if I can get Geronimo, I get a post back East."

"Well, sir, Kuchana didn't help matters any." Carter smiled as Harvey gave him a glance filled with surprise. In the last two weeks, he'd been unable to catch her breaking regulations. On the expedition, he'd tried even harder, but she was like a fox, anticipating his moves and neatly side-stepping them. Melissa was trying to snag her, too, but Kuchana had avoided her at all costs since the Christmas party.

"What?"

"Yes, sir. When Geronimo was roaring drunk, she just sat there. The other scouts, including Mickey Free, tried to talk him into staying."

Rubbing his chin, Harvey went back to his desk. "Bring her to me, Lieutenant. Right now."

"Yes, sir." Gleefully, Carter spun around, mentally rubbing his hands together and congratulating himself. Of course, he'd lied to Polk, but the colonel wasn't going to believe Kuchana's story over his. Officers had honor and integrity. Scouts were considered little more than necessary, and because they were Indian, certainly incapable of telling the truth.

Polk looked up when Kuchana arrived fifteen minutes later. Her face was stoic, and her eyes dark and unfathomable as she entered his office. "Come in, Kuchana," he said, motioning her toward a wooden chair on one side of his desk. "Sit down."

Having braced herself for censure, Kuchana swallowed her surprise as she sat down, holding herself tensely.

"Tell me about Geronimo's unexpected departure."

She faithfully repeated the story, telling her part in trying to stop him. "He was weaving around, Colonel, and I could barely make him understand that General Crook and yourself would help him. He wanted to know why McCoy was not there and he said he didn't trust the *pindah*...er, the army."

Harvey nodded, leaning back in the chair. "Geronimo trusts you and McCoy more than anyone, doesn't he?"

She nodded. "He has known McCoy for many years, and has found him to be a man of his word." Just the mention of Gib's name sent a shaft of pain through Kuchana's heart. It was so hard to know that Gib lived only thirty miles away in the mountains, where she hadn't been allowed to hunt. Kuchana had been sorely tempted to slip out at night, leave the post without authorization and find out if he was all right. Only Poppy's continued warnings kept her here. Melissa was stalking her in earnest once again, and she knew never to trust her.

"I thought so," Harvey grunted. He sat back up, the chair squeaking in protest. Pulling out an order form, he began writing. The scratch of the pen filled the silence. Five minutes later, he was finished. "Here, take this out to the corporal. These are orders for you to locate McCoy and bring him back to the fort. I understand he has a cabin up in the mountains. Tell him I want to offer him a job as a civilian scout for the army."

Heart beating hard, Kuchana stood, her hand trembling as she received the orders, barely believing her ears. "You want McCoy back?"

"I need both of you," Polk stressed mildly. "If the damn fool hadn't disobeyed Carter's order, he'd still be with us. McCoy's a good man, and I hated to lose him, but there was little I could do. But I can offer him a civilian job. Do whatever you can to persuade him to come back here, understand?"

Joy raced through Kuchana. She felt as if she had been jolted out of an unending nightmare. Her prayers to Painted Woman had been answered. "But...Lieutenant Carter said that I was in trouble."

"Eh?" Polk waved his hand. "Carter doesn't know what he's talking about. Now, go on. Those orders don't specify when you have to return. It may take days, even a week, to convince him. Stay until he agrees to come back with you. Tell McCoy I need him."

Trying to still her happiness, Kuchana nodded. "I will come back with him," she promised.

"I'm offering him damn good money, too. Chances are, he's in need of some."

Barely able to think, Kuchana left the headquarters, walking directly to the stabling area. The day was warm and clouds like horses' tails swept the blue sky. Her heart lifted in joy. Two of the worst weeks of her life were behind her.

Poppy had assured her that Gib was fine and she prayed that it was so. Finding Moon, she quickly saddled the mare and trotted off toward Poppy's tent to tell her the good news. Poppy and her family would be happy for them. She would then leave the post, aiming for the rugged blue mountains in the distance. She would find Gib and bring him back.

McCoy had taken off his shirt in the warm sun. Hefting the ax over his head, he brought it down on a huge log. The rhythmic sound of the ax biting into the felled fir echoed through the forest. His arms and shoulders had filled out with even more muscle as he worked morning until night, cutting, chopping and shaping logs. High on the hillside, he could see his cabin sitting at the edge of a huge, oval meadow with patches of green coming up through the snow. He was sweating in the mild January weather, his skin glistening in the sunlight.

Kuchana pulled Moon to a halt. Her keen hearing had picked up the sound of chopping. Was it Gib? No one knew exactly where his cabin was located, so it became a matter of finding, then following the hoofprints to locate him. The early-evening sun slanted through the forest as she moved her horse at a slow trot. Twice, she had run into miners, but they had put their weapons down, recognizing the blue army coat she wore and allowing her to pass in peace.

Her heart began to pound once again, as it had twice before. Kuchana prayed to Painted Woman that this time it was Gib. The sound of chopping became louder, and she saw the woods thinning out into a small meadow ahead. As she pulled Moon to a walk, she still couldn't see where the sound was coming from. She had learned from experience that miners would often shoot first and ask questions later, if they saw an Apache. Taking no risks, she kept Moon inside the treeline down the slope until the man came into view. Her heart leapt violently.

Gib was straddling a huge log, deftly skinning the bark off with his ax. He was stripped to the waist and she marveled at his beauty, unable to take her eyes off him. She remembered the power of his arms around her, the strength of his hot, worshipful kisses. As she sat on Moon, she went weak and shaky inside. His skin was deeply tanned, each grouping of muscles sheathing into the next, taut and glistening as he worked down the log, shedding the bark.

All her worry dissolved. How could she have thought Gib wouldn't survive? If possible, he looked even fitter than before, having put on some weight. The time away from the grueling demands of army life had been good for him, she thought, feeling the prick of tears in her eyes. His dark hair was still short, strands of it plastered against his broad brow, sweat running down the planes of his face that were tight with concentration. Heat pooled and gathered between her thighs as she took in the sight of Gib in those precious seconds.

McCoy heard Ned whinny. Immediately, he stopped chopping, turning in the direction Ned was facing. Up here, miners were known to steal anything they could get their hands on. And they weren't opposed to killing a man to get his rifle, food or any money they could find on him. As he turned, his eyes widened.

"Kuchana!" The word slipped from him in a hoarse whisper. She sat astride Moon, tall and proud, her eyes filled with tears. Gib dropped the ax and took a step toward her. His shock was swept away by terror. Had she deserted the post and run away? He deepened his strides toward her.

Slipping off Moon, Kuchana dropped the reins and ran across the meadow, her arms wide. She saw Gib's sweaty features grow tense with worry as she threw herself into his welcoming embrace.

"Gib!" she whispered, burying her face against his neck. She felt his arms tighten like powerful bands around her, drawing her hard against his body. She moaned as his mouth found hers, and she drowned in the splendor of his long, heated kiss.

"Kuchana," he whispered roughly, gripping her by the shoulders. "You didn't run away, did you?"

Laughing, she tipped her head back, her hands sliding around his corded neck. "No, beloved. I was sent here by Colonel Polk. He wants you to come back to the post and become a civilian scout for the army."

Stunned, McCoy stood there with Kuchana in his arms. She looked incredibly beautiful, but far too underweight. Running his hands down her long, shining hair, he devoured her hungrily with his eyes. "Just as long as you didn't run away," he muttered.

She smiled, lost in the dark blueness of his eyes. His hands caressed her back and hip, and she ached to be one with him again. "Colonel Polk has forgiven you. He told me to stay as long as I needed in order to make you come back to the post."

Grinning, McCoy slid his hands across her shoulders to her face. "He did, did he?" Her eyes were golden with joy, and Gib felt as if his heart were going to burst. How had Kuchana grown more beautiful? Gib didn't know and he didn't care, drawing her to him, claiming her smiling lips. He felt her weaken and lean against him, a sweet crying from within her. She tasted of pine and desert, her mouth moving in hungry abandon against his, matching his need in every way.

Swaying, McCoy took a step back, dizzied by their kiss. His laughter filled the surrounding forest as he held Kuchana tightly against him, rocking her. "God, I missed you, sun woman," he rasped unsteadily.

Tears squeezed from beneath Kuchana's lashes. "I have lived in the darkness without you."

Kissing her hair, temples and damp cheeks, Gib whispered, "I know you have. Come on, I've got something to show you."

The grittiness of his voice unstrung her, and Kuchana felt her entire body respond to him. She never wanted to leave his embrace again. Gib placed his arm around her shoulders, keeping her close as they walked down through the meadow.

"So Geronimo is still on the loose?" he asked.

Kuchana told him of the meeting. "I think Colonel Polk believes that he may come in if you are there with me."

McCoy nodded, leading her out of the meadow to a path along the hillside. "I hope he's right. You came close to getting him back to the reservation."

"I was praying," Kuchana admitted softly.

"And Ealae, your sister, is she well?"

"Yes, she is fine. I got to speak with her this time."

Delighted, Gib listened as he led her up the path. At the top of it was a meadow. He heard Kuchana gasp as they traversed the snowy expanse toward the cabin.

"This is all yours?" she asked in disbelief. A large, roomy cabin sat to the left, along with a barn that was still under construction. To the right were huge holding corrals for livestock.

Gib halted at the steps to the cabin. "Yes." He gave her a wry smile. "I've been busy up here for a year." He gestured toward the corrals. "I'm planning on raising horses for the army. I've got a deal worked out with Jacobsen himself, and I'll be picking up thirty head from him this spring. I figure to breed the Eastern mares with the mustang stallion I captured last week."

Kuchana gasped as she noticed the horse. "He is beautiful!"

The blood-bay stud stood in a seven-foot-high circular corral. "He was tough to catch," Gib said wryly.

"Good straight legs," Kuchana said.

Squeezing her, Gib motioned toward the cabin. "And this is for you."

"Me?"

Gib turned, placing his hands on her shoulders. Her red shirt and the dark red cloth that encircled her head emphasized her dark beauty. "Yes, you." When he saw the confusion in her eyes, he explained. "In my culture, when a man loves a woman, he marries her, Kuchana. And then he provides a house for her so they have a place to live." His voice grew low. "A place where they can raise a family."

Her lips parted as she held his tender gaze. "We will marry?"

Fingers tightening on her shoulders, he said, "Just as soon as Geronimo comes back to the reservation, I'm scaring up a preacher, and we're going to be man and wife, Kuchana. The army will discharge you if you get married, so you'll be out of Carter's and Melissa's clutches." Gib gave her a slow, heated smile filled with promise. "I love you, sun woman, and I intend to have you as my wife. This cabin is for you."

Tears started in Kuchana's eyes as she surveyed the well-built structure. There were windows at the front, and the porch was wide and long, with steps and a railing. "All this?"

"Do you like it?"

She sniffed, caressing his cheek with trembling fingers. "I don't know what it's like to live in one place without moving. I have never lived in a house before."

Laughing, McCoy brought her to him, burying his face in her fragrant hair. "God, I love you, Kuchana. Don't worry," he whispered, "you'll get used to living in one place with a roof over your head. In time, I think you'll grow to like it." Kissing her lips tenderly, Gib cradled her cheek with his hand. "I'm going to spoil you, sun woman. You deserve it."

With a little laugh, Kuchana pressed her hands to his. "All I will ever need is your love, Gib. Nothing more."

Inhaling her scent, he kissed her damp lashes, her nose and finally her mouth. "I know," he whispered against her welcoming lips, "that's why I want to spoil you rotten. Come on, I want to show you what it looks like inside."

In one motion, McCoy lifted her into his arms. It troubled him to realize that Kuchana had lost weight in his absence. Her laughter melted away at his look of concern. Her arms went around his shoulders, her brow resting against his head as he moved up the steps and pushed open the door.

"It's proper for a bride to be carried over the threshold," he told her, stepping into the cabin.

Kuchana lay in his arms, surveying her new home. There was a potbellied stove in one corner, a fireplace in another. The amount of furniture boggled her mind. "This looks like Poppy's home in the tent."

McCoy lowered her to the wooden floor, keeping his arm around her. "I've been buying furniture since last year over at Jacobsen's," he told her. He led Kuchana to a large rocker and ran his hand across the top of it. "I didn't buy this, though. I made it myself." He gazed down at her. "It's for you and our baby. I know they liked to be rocked when they're crying, and I figured you'd like to sit down to do it."

Kuchana watched his scarred, thickly callused hand gently caress the highly polished wood. That was how he touched her, with equal reverence and love. The thought of carrying his child made her feel fulfilled as never before. "I had not dreamed that far," she confided huskily. "I was afraid..."

Gib understood. "I dreamed for both of us."

Looking up, Kuchana held his tender gaze. "For how long?"

He managed a one-cornered smile, caressing her hair. "Ever since I saw you riding up to the fort on Wind."

A lump formed in Kuchana's throat, and she stood in the warming silence of the cabin, feeling the blanket of his love surround her. The depth of his feelings left her humbled in the wake of his admittance. "I do not know why I deserve you," Kuchana whispered, a catch in her voice.

"I do," Gib said thickly, gathering her into his arms. As he held her, he fought the toughest battle of his life. He wouldn't make love to Kuchana. That night in the cave he had broken his moral obligation to her. He wanted her more than anything, but next time she would be his wife.

Content in his arms, hearing the thunderous beat of his heart beneath her ear, Kuchana asked, "What else do you dream for us?"

Closing his eyes, Gib reveled in her pliant firmness. "I dream of finding a preacher to marry us just as soon as Geronimo goes back to the reservation. Then you and I are going to start out life as husband and wife. I dream of you carrying strapping sons and beautiful daughters in your belly. Sometimes, when I'm up late at night, I can hear their laughter, and I can see you smiling. This cabin is going to ring with happiness, Kuchana. I know it will.

"I dream of you gaining back your weight, of not seeing those shadows in your eyes, and a smile always on your mouth." Gib nuzzled her cheek. "I dream of being a successful horse rancher, and of our children living around us, learning to be at peace with the earth and the people, no matter what color their skin. Someday, when we're old and gray, we'll sit out there on the porch in our rocking chairs remembering the good times and the bad." His arms tightened around her. "But most of all, we'll remember the love we hold for each other."

Kuchana murmured his name, pressing a kiss to his mouth, drowning in the splendor of his passion. "Our love has strengthened us through these past few weeks."

Gib smiled. "It was a test, Kuchana. It could have torn us apart, but we're tough people, made of good stock. Adversity doesn't destroy us. It only makes us stronger."

Sighing, Kuchana slid her hands upward to frame his face. "Then we must be strong for the future."

"I know." Reluctantly Gib released her. "Come on, let's get ready to go back to the post. The sooner I can sign on as a scout, the sooner we can try and convince Geronimo to go back to the reservation."

Chapter Eighteen

"**Y**ou drive a hard bargain, McCoy," Polk declared, studying the former sergeant from across his desk. Captain Lane was standing to one side, his face carefully neutral.

Gib shrugged. He knew how badly Polk needed him. "The scouts deserve better facilities than tents, Colonel. There're enough billets open over in the enlisted area to accommodate all six of them."

"First you want three times the amount of money you earned in the army," Polk grumbled. "Then you want to raise each scout's pay and put them over in enlisted barracks. That isn't done anywhere else in this man's army."

Curbing his smile, Gib said, "Colonel, if you're paying me to head up the scouts and be responsible for them, I want them to have equal pay and housing just like the soldiers get."

"Er, Colonel?" Lane stepped forward.

"What is it, Jason?"

"I think Mr. McCoy's requests can be met. After all, the contract we want with him will dissolve as soon as Geronimo is caught. After that, the scouts will be my responsibility."

"Very well." Polk studied McCoy. "Anything else you want?"

"Just one more thing, Colonel."

Setting his mouth, Harvey snapped. "What is it?"

"Kuchana signed a six-year contract with the army to be a scout. I want her contract ended when I get Geronimo talked into going back to the reservation."

Harvey raised his brows. Personally, he didn't care if Kuchana remained as a scout or not, once she had filled her purpose. Melissa was constantly needling at him to get rid of her on some insane charge or other. "That's not a problem, McCoy."

"I want it in writing, sir. Today. And before I sign my agreement to be the head civilian scout for this post."

"Fine," Harvey muttered. "Your old room is waiting for you over at the enlisted barracks, McCoy. I'm sure you'll feel right at home." Getting to his feet, Polk offered his hand across the desk. "Glad to have you back."

Shaking the colonel's hand, McCoy gave a curt nod. He was relieved to be back at the post. Now, having full authority over the scouts, he could again shield Kuchana from Carter and Melissa. "Thank you, Colonel." Turning, he left the room, thinking that being a civilian was a far cry from being in the army.

Kuchana was waiting for him at Poppy's tent. By the time Gib got there, at least forty of the enlisted men who used to be under him were waiting for him. Each man came forward, shaking his hand, welcoming him back. When he finally reached Poppy and Nettie, who stood in the background, they had tears running down their cheeks. Kuchana stood in the shadows of the tent, her face soft with the emotions she was feeling. It was one hell of an unexpected welcome back to the post, and Gib took his hat off and gave the two laundresses a warm smile.

"Welcome, welcome, welcome!" Nettie cried, launching herself into his arms, giving him a hug.

Laughing, Gib embraced the girl. "Nettie, you look prettier than ever."

Embarrassed, she stood back, touching her cheeks. "Why thank you, Sergeant McCoy."

"Has that young, good-looking private, Ladler, been by to see you yet?" he inquired. Nettie looked even more embarrassed, and Gib knew that the private must have finally gotten up the courage to let his intentions be known.

"How could you know that?" Nettie gushed. And then she blinked, realizing Gib had known all along. "You sure keep a secret well, Sergeant McCoy."

Grinning, Gib said, "He's a fine young man, Nettie. From the looks of things, you're getting on well with him."

Lowering her lashes, Nettie stepped aside so he could greet Poppy, too bashful to say much else about Private Ladler.

Poppy opened her thick, heavy arms, giving Gib a huge hug of welcome. She stepped back, brushing the tears from her face. "You look better than ever, Gibson McCoy."

Gib glanced at Kuchana, then back at Poppy. "Things are going well for me," he agreed.

"Come and join us for dinner," Poppy urged, gripping him by the arm. "We're celebrating your return." She gave Kuchana a significant glance. "And if I'm right, we got a lot more to talk about.…"

With a laugh, Gib followed her into the tent. The delicious smell of rabbit stew was in the air. No one cooked like Poppy, and he was hungry for some good home cooking. "I never could fool you, could I, Poppy?"

Grinning, she said, "Nope, you never could."

"Happy?" Gib asked Kuchana, holding her in his arms as they stood next to a wall outside the darkened barracks. It was nearly midnight, and the party at Poppy's had been an endless evening of laughter, stories and men dropping by to get some of her famous walnut muffins she had baked specially for Gib's return.

Nodding, Kuchana was content to remain in his embrace, wanting nothing more of life at the moment. "So many are glad you have returned," she said softly, sliding her fingers along the cotton shirt he wore beneath the leather vest.

"I never would have imagined it," Gib admitted with a chuckle.

"No one at the post felt you deserved punishment."

"That was Carter's doing. And Colonel Polk couldn't drop the charge. He wanted to, I think, but couldn't."

"Carter is a snake!"

McCoy nodded grimly. From his position, he could see anyone coming, but at this time of night, only the sentries were active. Still, he remained alert, not trusting Carter or Melissa. Pressing a kiss to Kuchana's hair, he asked, "Has Carter bothered you since I left?"

Shrugging, Kuchana muttered, "He has been like a dog at the heels of my boots. Every time I ride on an expedition, he blames me that Geronimo is still free."

"He won't anymore," Gib growled. "What about Melissa?" He stroked her hair, threading the thick strands slowly through his fingers. He'd missed these small, yet important moments with her.

"Since the Christmas dance, I know to stay clear of her. Sometimes she calls to me, but I pretend I do not hear and walk away."

"I'll bet that makes her furious," Gib said.

"Carter's wife, Claudia, always calls me names," she added sadly. "But I think Melissa puts her up to it."

"I'm sorry, Kuchana," he said, kissing her temple, feeling the softness of her skin beneath his mouth. The urge to make love to her created an ache in his loins. He didn't know how long it would take to get Geronimo to come back to the reservation, but as he felt Kuchana press herself naively against him he hoped it would be soon. Seeking and finding her lips, he felt them part beneath his own, and he hungrily tasted her moist, welcoming depths. Her fingers dug insistently into his shoulders. She was just as hot and fiery as ever, perhaps even more so now that she had tasted the pleasure of love.

"You always taste like sunlight," he whispered, running his tongue across her lower lip, feeling her tremble in his arms.

"And you are like a rainbow that appears after a soft rain," she sighed, languishing in the strength and tenderness of his mouth.

"Sunlight and rainbows," Gib said hoarsely. "I like what we are together." Reluctantly, he fought the powerful desire to begin kissing her again, exploring every inch of her warm, ripe body that trembled against his. "I don't know how long it will take, but when this is over, we'll get married."

She smiled softly, contented as never before. "As long as I can be at your side, I will wait." Her eyes darkened. "I never want to be apart from you."

"That," he promised thickly, "will never happen again."

Their moment together was coming to an end. Kuchana would go to her new room in the barracks and have a bed to sleep upon, thanks to Gib's agreement with the colonel. As she pulled away, Kuchana caught the flash of a skirt in the darkness near the stabling area. Shivering, she blinked. Was she seeing things? She knew that ghosts walked the night and, possibly, that is what she had seen. Following Gib into the barracks, she shrugged it off, feeling safe in the building and knowing he was sleeping nearby.

"Dodd! How did this all happen?" Melissa demanded breathlessly, sweeping into the room in the stables, which was their favorite place for trysts. She shut the door, holding the lamp in her hand.

"I didn't let anything happen. You're married to that old bastard," he muttered darkly, watching her march imperiously over to him. "Didn't he say anything about hiring McCoy back as head scout?"

She hung the lamp carefully on a nearby hook. "Of course not! Harvey doesn't talk to me when he comes to bed. He just falls asleep and snores outrageously."

"Well," Carter warned, "McCoy's got the upper hand now." Then he proceeded to tell her everything.

Melissa stood there, angrily tapping her foot. "I thought we were rid of him."

"I almost had that new Yavapai scout talked into trying to kill Kuchana in a hunting accident. Now that he knows McCoy is back, he won't. He's scared of McCoy because he knows he killed Two Toes."

"Hellfire and damnation!" Melissa spat, her eyes glittering with frustration.

Surprised by her outburst, the officer stared at her. Normally, Melissa didn't lapse into cursing like a mule skinner. "Why are you so upset? Your husband says he'll get orders for the East as soon as Geronimo is caught. McCoy guarantees that will happen. He and Kuchana are the team that can bring the chief to us."

Muttering under her breath, Melissa gritted out, "Dodd, sometimes you are thick! I want Harvey here! He can run for governor of the state. I'd much rather be the wife of a governor than the wife of a general. There's much more power out here. Back East, Harvey will just be another general."

Shrugging, Dodd opened his hands. "Well, either way, you win."

Glaring at Carter, Melissa tried to sort things out. McCoy had been welcomed back to the post with open arms. The only thing missing was a military band. Dodd was weakening, backing down, and she was furious with his spinelessness. "I'm going to wait and watch those two. And you make sure Kuchana obeys regulations." Balling her small hands into fists, Melissa whispered, "I don't care how long it takes, I'm going to do everything in my power to make them miserable!''

With a snort, Dodd walked toward the door, his amorous intentions wilting beneath Melissa's maniacal barrage. ''There's very little I can do. McCoy's a civilian now and answers directly to your husband, Mellie. I have to be careful McCoy doesn't get me into trouble. He could ruin my career, and the bastard knows it.'' His hand on the latch, he studied her in the shadowy light. Her lips were pouty, like those of a spoiled child.

''Put a bullet in both their backs! I know Harvey is planning one expedition after another, rearranging new meetings with Geronimo. Kill them when the opportunity arises.''

With a shake of his head, Carter muttered, ''Mellie, you aren't being realistic.''

She glared at Dodd as he slipped out of the room. Stamping her foot, she stood there, her mind moving over many options and possible plans. The key to getting to McCoy was Kuchana. That much she was sure of. Walking over to the lamp, she picked it up, then waited five more minutes to make sure Dodd had left the stable. It wouldn't be wise to be seen coming out of the building together. As it was, Harvey was still over at headquarters, planning the next expedition.

''There is a bad feeling in this place,'' Kuchana told McCoy as they rode side by side into the Mexican town of Fronteras. Behind them was Lieutenant Gatewood's expedition from Fort Apache. They had been tracking Geronimo for several weeks and, needing more supplies, had detoured to the small town of shacks and one central well, to buy what was needed for the hundred or so men and their animals.

McCoy squinted against the overhead sun, feeling the tension as the villagers, mostly women and children, came and stood outside their adobe huts along the main street of the small community. "The people look scared. Geronimo is probably in the area."

Kuchana nodded. Ahead, she could see a short man with a protruding belly come out to greet them. His hair was slicked back with bear grease, and his eyes were small and greedy.

"Welcome! I am Don José Mateus, the prefect of this district."

McCoy raised his hand and then motioned for Lieutenant Charles Gatewood to come forward. Gatewood, a tall, spindly officer with walnut-colored hair, nudged his dusty gelding forward. Like Gib, the officer knew Spanish, as well as Apache, having been in the Southwest nearly five years.

Mateus scuttled forward, his official coat gilded heavily with gold braid and medals. "This is an unexpected surprise," he told Gatewood after introductions.

"My men need water, and if we can buy supplies from you, we'd be grateful," Charles told him.

Just then, two Indian women at the end of the street caught Kuchana's eye. She recognized them instantly and gasped. They were Geronimo's warriors. McCoy tensed, glancing at the warriors and then back at Mateus, who had a stricken look on his face.

"What's going on?" Gatewood asked.

"Don't know," McCoy said, "but keep your weapons holstered. Kuchana, ask them to come nearer. Tell them we're the ones who are to meet with Geronimo."

Nodding, she nudged Moon away from the group, raising her hand in greeting. To her joy, she recognized Shanaei and Raven. Both women drew to a halt, surprise on their faces.

"Ho!" Kuchana greeted. "Why are you here?"

Shanaei hesitated. She sat on a starved-looking bay mustang, covered with dust. "Don Mateus invited Geronimo here. We did not know you were coming," she said, gesturing to Gatewood's column.

Kuchana shrugged. "It was agreed we meet Geronimo. Lieutenant Gatewood speaks for General Miles."

Raven, who was barely seventeen, looked around, her eyes suspicious. "Mateus promised Geronimo food and celebration. I do not see any of it."

Before Kuchana could reply, thirty *soldatos* raced from hiding places on either side of the street and surrounded the three women. Moon moved nervously, and Kuchana reined in the mustang. The other women stared at the rifles aimed at them. It was a trap! Kuchana opened her mouth to tell them not to fire when McCoy's voice thundered down the street.

"Put those rifles down! These women are a part of our column!"

The *soldatos* looked nervously at one another as the cavalry moved down the street toward them, rifles and pistols drawn. McCoy arrived first, glaring at the *soldatos*.

"If you want trouble, just keep pointing those rifles at these women."

Don Mateus panted, coming to a halt, waving his arms. "Stop, stop! This isn't them, you fools! This isn't Geronimo! It's two of his warriors!"

Shanaei glared at the prefect. "You lied! You said Geronimo was welcome here." She jerked a look up at Kuchana. "He has set a trap for all of us who ride with Geronimo. Last night, he promised us food and water if we would come back today."

Wringing his hands and sweating profusely, Mateus pleaded, "No, no! That isn't true. I meant what I said. We'd welcome Geronimo and his people."

"Ha!" Shanaei spat, jerking her horse around. "You are murderers, Mateus! You want our scalps so that you can sell them for money."

Kuchana reached out, grabbing Shanaei's arm. "Tell Geronimo we won't allow this *culo-gordo* to hurt anyone."

McCoy added in Apache, "Tell Geronimo we'll meet with him. Lieutenant Gatewood wants to talk. He has brought gifts of food and blankets for your people."

Dying to ask about Ealae, Kuchana knew it was the wrong time. Shanaei was upset, but she knew the woman warrior would carry the message back to her chief. The two women left, galloping out of the town, quickly disappearing into the sagebrush hills that surrounded the town.

Gatewood ordered supplies be bought. The men dismounted, giving their horses a well-earned rest from the afternoon heat. Kuchana remained in the saddle, not trusting the *soldatos* who slunk back to the buildings, their rifles at their sides, watching the cavalry sullenly. There was no love between the Mexican army and the U.S. Army.

Gib saw the anguish in Kuchana's eyes. He rode over to her side. "We're getting closer," he told her softly.

"If we hadn't come here, Ealae might have been dead before the end of the day if Mateus had lured Geronimo into the town."

"But he didn't." Giving her a slight smile, he said, "The time's drawing near. I can feel it."

"Geronimo wants to talk," Shanaei told Lieutenant Gatewood. They stood near the riverbed of Bavispe, the canebrakes a waving, green wall outlining the rare water source in Sonora. She pointed to Kuchana. "He wants to speak to her only."

McCoy thought over the request. Kuchana's life might be in danger. There was no way of knowing. "No. I'll go with her."

Gatewood seconded it. "Shanaei, these two act as my emissary from General Miles. You must take both of them."

Nodding, Shanaei ordered them to get rid of all their weapons. When she was satisfied both were unarmed, she gestured them to follow her out of the bed of the damp river sand and into the canyon high above, where Geronimo was waiting.

The sun was low. In another hour, it would set. Kuchana's heart beat hard in her breast. She prayed to Painted Woman that this meeting, which could bring peace to the Southwest, would occur. Once, Gib reached over and caught her hand, giving it a squeeze and then releasing it. Heartened by his gesture, she managed a smile for him. She could see his love for her in his eyes. No one wanted this meeting more than Gib.

As they wound their way slowly through the canyon with its towering ocher walls, Kuchana tried to focus on the present, not the uncertain future. Geronimo had evaded them, playing hide-and-seek with the army across the border. She wondered how many of her people were left.

Geronimo sat before a fire roasting a rabbit when they entered his camp. Kuchana looked quickly around. There were seventeen warriors now, and fewer women and children. To her great joy, she saw Ealae sitting wearily on an old wool blanket spread across a rock in the shadows of the canyon. Fighting back tears, Kuchana reined in her horse and dismounted.

"The ghost is back," Geronimo growled. He sized her up. "Army life suits you, Kuchana. No longer do you look like a gaunt cougar roaming our lands."

"If you would return to the reservation, my chief, all your people could eat well."

His eyes glittered. "Wormy biscuits and moldy bacon rind?"

McCoy stepped forward. "Lieutenant Gatewood and General Miles have promised fresh meat for you and your people, Geronimo."

With a shrug, the chief glared up at McCoy. "I trust only the two of you. Lieutenant Crawford was a good man, but he is now at the Big Sleep."

"Gatewood is just as trustworthy," Kuchana quickly put in.

A number of male warriors came down by the fire and watched McCoy with guarded interest. Gib now wished he had a weapon; he didn't like the feelings surrounding the meeting. Was Geronimo going to kill Kuchana because she had left him? The powerful chief got to his feet. "I do not trust Gatewood," Geronimo hissed. He jabbed a finger at McCoy. "Go. Tell him that. I will keep Kuchana as hostage."

"No!" McCoy started forward, only to realize too late that two Apaches had walked quietly up behind him. They pinned his arms behind his back, forcing him to stand in place.

Kuchana started to protest, but Shanaei warned her to be still. "No harm will come to you if you do not fight us, Kuchana," she said.

Her eyes widening, Kuchana saw Gib's face turn stony with anger. She held up her hand. "Geronimo will not hurt me," she said. "Do not fight."

Ceasing his struggle, McCoy glared at Geronimo, who was smiling. "If you touch her—"

"I will speak to her about this Gatewood tonight," Geronimo snapped at him. "You bring this officer here to me tomorrow morning. She is my prisoner, ensuring my people will not be attacked by the army during the night."

Breathing hard, McCoy jerked out of the hands of his captors. His nostrils flared. "Remember what I said. Kuchana is not to be harmed or you'll deal directly with me."

The Apache chief held the man's glare. "I trust you, not her. Not Gatewood. Only you have remained true to your cause, McCoy. But I will not harm her. Go now, and tell Gatewood what I demand."

* * *

McCoy met the sunrise with bloodshot eyes. Gatewood rode at his side, grim and worried. Behind them was a mule laden with gifts for Geronimo. Gib anxiously searched the canyon, realizing that Apache warriors had melted, hidden and armed, into the rock walls.

All his thoughts centered on Kuchana. Had Geronimo kept his word? Had he harmed her? Gib had seen the torture that the Apaches could inflict, and his stomach rolled. God, he loved her. He couldn't lose her now. Not like this.

As they rode into the meeting place, Gib saw Geronimo surrounded by several of his best warriors. Shanaei stood by Kuchana, who appeared strained but unharmed. As they drew to a halt, Gib anxiously sought out Kuchana's gaze. She barely nodded in his direction, her eyes dark with exhaustion.

Lieutenant Gatewood dismounted and walked up to the chief. "This mule is loaded with tobacco, food and blankets for your people. We come in peace, Geronimo. I am here to speak for General Miles."

Geronimo motioned for them to sit at the small fire. "I accept your gifts," he grunted, sitting down.

"First, I want Kuchana back with us," Gatewood said, motioning toward her.

With a shrug, the chief said, "She is yours."

Shanaei released Kuchana, motioning for her to take her place alongside the two men. She moved to Gib's side, seeing the relief in his expression. The air of tension built as Geronimo sat there, watching the mule being unloaded by several men, the various gifts laid out on a blanket to one side. After it was done, Geronimo returned his attention to the sweating Gatewood.

"I trusted Lieutenant Crawford. He was a man who spoke with one tongue and one heart. I do not know you.

Kuchana speaks highly of you, saying that you walk in Crawford's shadow. What do you have to say for yourself, Gatewood?''

The officer cleared his throat, obviously nervous, but prepared to stand his ground with the fierce Apache. "I am General Miles's emissary, Geronimo. I speak for him to you and your people. The gifts we bring today show our good intentions. If you give up and come back to the reservation, you will save your families and children. We want no more bloodshed. General Miles wants peace. If you don't agree, he will continue to hunt you down until every last one of you has gone to the Big Sleep."

Kuchana knew Gatewood spoke the truth. She was rigid with the desire to cry out and beg Geronimo to come back to the reservation. The chief rubbed his square jaw, holding Gatewood's gaze.

"What else?" he demanded.

"If you come back, you and your families will be sent by train to Florida for internment. You will be fed and well taken care of."

Angrily, Geronimo got to his feet. "My home is here," he exclaimed, jabbing his finger down at the ground. "You expect me to go to Florida? I will not! You will take us back to the reservation, or we will fight!"

McCoy saw the warriors grow restless. Nachiz, a sub-chief, quickly came forward, holding his hands up in a sign of peace.

"You are safe here," he assured the soldiers. "We will not harm you. Geronimo does not want to be sent to Florida."

For the next hour, Geronimo snapped question after question at Gatewood about General Miles. For years, General Crook had chased Geronimo and tried to parley with him. But when Crook failed to bring the chief in, Miles had been given the task. Geronimo knew little of this Miles, so he hammered Gatewood for information. Gatewood stood there, sweat running down his face, answering each question thoroughly and completely, trying to gain Geronimo's trust.

Kuchana moved restlessly, knowing that Geronimo might run once again. If only Gatewood's earnestness and integrity would win her chief over. She saw Geronimo waver, and she stepped forward between the men.

"My chief, Gatewood is like Crawford—a man of honor. You can trust him." The plea to save her sister and those few Apaches who were left remained within her. Kuchana stood tensely, her hands open in supplication.

Finally, after long minutes, Geronimo stood up. "Consider yourself not a white man, but one of us, Gatewood. Remember all that has been said today and tell us what we should do."

Eagerly, Gatewood said, "Come with us back to the reservation. You and your people will not be sent to Florida. I promise you. We will protect you as we travel through Mexico. No harm will come to you."

Geronimo gave the officer a steely look. "We do not surrender to you," he growled. "I have agreed to come back to the reservation only if things improve for my people."

Gatewood nodded. "No, you're not surrendering."

Pleased, Geronimo said, "Good, it is done, then."

The canyon swirled with stunned silence. Kuchana turned and looked at Gib. Finally, her prayers had been answered. Geronimo wasn't surrendering to the army, but merely negotiating a peace. Ealae would be safe. Kuchana's vow was fulfilled. Suddenly her knees were wobbly, and she locked them into place, not wanting to show what a terrible strain the whole ordeal had been for her.

McCoy saw her waver slightly. He moved to her side, his hand wrapping about her upper arm. As she lifted her head, he saw tears in her eyes. Tears of relief. Managing a slight smile, he whispered, ''It's all over. Now, we can go home and get married.''

Chapter Nineteen

"Ealae, will you be all right?" Kuchana stood holding her sister's hand. Geronimo had given her permission to speak with her sister as the cavalry unit helped to gather up the few items and place them on the backs of supply mules.

Wearily, Ealae smiled, squeezing her hand. "I will be fine now that Geronimo has said that you are back from the Big Sleep."

No one agreed more, Kuchana thought. To her relief, the chief had changed his decision, making her a living person to the tribe once again. But her sister was gaunt, and Kuchana was worried about her. "Is there anything I can do for you? For our people?"

"You have done it, sister." With a sigh, Ealae looked around at the seventeen warriors and what was left of the women and children, a mere handful of the once mighty and free Chiricahua tribe. "I prayed for you the months after you left us. For a long time, I did not even know if you had survived the trek across the desert, or if the army had accepted you."

Kuchana nodded. "Painted Woman kept me safe." She hesitated and then said in a low voice only her sister could hear, "I've fallen in love, Ealae."

"The man in the deerskin jacket?" she guessed, a smile coming to her dark eyes.

"Yes. Gib McCoy was the man who saved my life when I rode up to the fort to offer my services as a scout." Her voice quavered with emotion as she sought out the approval of her older sister. "I want to marry him, Ealae. Will you bless our union?" It was important that the family, even if it now consisted of only one person, bless the arrangement.

Pushing a strand of black hair away from her face, Ealae said, "That means you will not be living on the reservation."

"No. He has a cabin up in the mountains above the fort."

"A good place to raise children?"

Her hand tightening around Ealae's, Kuchana answered, "Yes, a place filled with peace. Gib will raise and breed horses and, perhaps, run some cattle."

"Then," Ealae whispered, her voice filled with emotion, "I bless your marriage to this man. McCoy has always been respected by Geronimo. He is a man of truth and honor."

Closing her eyes, Kuchana threw her arms around her sister, holding her tightly. "Thank you," she choked, "thank you."

"I will miss you, my sister." Ealae began to weep. "These months without you have been lonely."

Kuchana pulled away, wiping her own tears from her cheeks, not caring if the other warriors saw her crying. "Gib said that after we are settled he would ask the *pindahs* to release you to us. That way, you could be free, Ealae, truly free."

Smiling through her tears, Ealae managed a softened laugh. "I do not think so, my sister. You see, I have fallen in love with a warrior." She motioned to several Apache warriors standing near Geronimo. "Tall Elk saw my suffering after you left. He is a gentle man, Kuchana. There were nights I did not want to live through, because everything had been taken from me—from us. Tall Elk would come and sit by me, without touching me, or saying anything. He would simply sit there. During the day, if he wasn't out hunting or protecting the families from *soldatos,* he would ride at my side."

Joy raced through Kuchana. She knew of Tall Elk's integrity. The man was honored among her people as a fierce warrior, but also as a good provider to what was left of his family: his mother and two sisters. Smiling, Kuchana whispered, "Then I am happy for you, Ealae."

"And do I have your blessing?"

With a little laugh, Kuchana hugged her sister again. "Of course you do." As she held Ealae, she wondered how the news of her marrying Gib would be met at the fort.

"Mellie, Mellie!" Claudia Carter entered headquarters, her face flushed.

Melissa looked up from reading the report that Gib McCoy had just placed on the corporal's desk. The man had merely tipped his hat, uttered a polite "Good morning," and left. The arrogant fool.

"What is it, Claudia?" she asked.

Claudia shut the door, her gloved hand across her lips. The corporal had left for the moment, so she raced over to Melissa. "You'll never guess what just happened."

"What now?" Melissa asked irritably. It was bad enough that Geronimo was now on his way back to the reservation with Lieutenant Gatewood. Harvey was walking on air, anticipating a meaty assignment in Washington from General Miles as a result. All her plans for him becoming governor of Arizona had been smashed.

Gripping Melissa's wrist, Claudia leaned over and whispered, "McCoy has gone to the Reverend Judson and asked him to marry them."

Startled, Melissa jerked her chin up, glaring at Claudia. "Them? What are you talking about?"

"McCoy is going to marry Kuchana! Can you believe it? Why, the post is raging with talk over it. Imagine him marrying that savage! Why, it's un-American! No white man worth his salt would stoop to marry a heathen woman.''

The report dropped from Melissa's fingers as she stared at Claudia. "No!"

"Isn't it terrible?"

Standing, Melissa stalked to the door. "That bastard is not marrying that whore on this post! Not as long as I have something to say about it!"

Gasping, Claudia stood there. She had never heard the colonel's wife talk in such an unladylike fashion. Melissa jerked open the door and hurried along the wooden walkway. Blinking, not wanting to be left behind, Claudia picked up her skirts to follow.

The early afternoon was cooler than usual because of the clouds across the turquoise sky. Melissa, white-faced, her green eyes glittering like shards of glass, ignored the beauty and aimed herself at the chapel, which stood off to one side of the supply building. She saw a gathering crowd of soldiers, laundresses and other assorted rabble. If McCoy thought he was going to get away with this kind of insubordination, he was mistaken! Peggy Judson would demand that David, her husband, not marry the couple. And David, who was a limp shadow of a man, would obey. Still, Melissa wanted to throw her considerable weight into the ring, thwarting McCoy. She wasn't going to let him get away without punishment for ignoring her. Besides, if it weren't for Kuchana and McCoy, her plan to make Harvey governor would have worked. Her mouth tightening, Melissa was carried along by her anger as she swept into the tightly knit crowd around the door of the chapel.

"Let me by!" she shrieked.

Instantly, the soldiers leapt aside, recognizing her voice. The laundresses moved less quickly, giving Melissa sullen looks as she elbowed through the sea of faces toward the open door of the chapel. Once inside, Melissa jerked to a halt, breathing hard. She waited, allowing her eyes to ad-

just to the dimness. The chapel was filled to overflowing.
Soldiers who had just come off the expedition were standing at the pews, along with wives and children. Even the
aisle was filled, and Melissa began to elbow through the
sweaty men who stood in the stifling heat.

"You will not marry her here!" Peggy Judson announced. She snapped a look at her husband, who stood tall
and thin in his black coat and trousers.

"Mrs. Judson," Gib began, trying to be reasonable, "I'm
a Christian of the same faith as you. It's my right and priv-
ilege to ask the Reverend Judson to marry me and the
woman of my choice."

Peggy's face wrinkled with fury. She glared at Kuchana,
who stood at McCoy's side dressed in her male Apache garb.
"Mr. McCoy, who do you think you are?"

"A man in love with his woman. I want to make her my
wife." Gib kept his arm around Kuchana's waist, a protective gesture to try to keep her away from Peggy Judson's
foaming hatred. He heard a murmur of approval from the
men of the Fourth Cavalry. Kuchana's eyes were large, and
she was distraught by the unexpected hatred of Peggy Judson.

"Now, please," David said in a strained tone, the Bible
clutched in one long, thin hand. He gave his wife a pleading look. "Mr. McCoy is a Christian, dear, and—"

"White men ought to marry white women!" Peggy
shrieked.

McCoy glanced behind him, seeing the faces of the Negro
soldiers grow closed as Mrs. Judson's insult struck home.
Anger stirred through him, and he pinned a lethal look at
the small, angry woman who stood blustering like a ban-
tam rooster in front of her shaking husband.

"Mrs. Judson, your remark isn't appreciated by me." His
arm tightened around Kuchana's waist when he felt her
tremble.

"God doesn't let animals of different species crossbreed, so why should we taint our white stock with another color?" the woman continued. "This savage you want to marry is a redskin, in case you've gone blind. The babies she'll have will be half-breeds. Is that what you want?"

Kuchana heard the voices of the men rising behind her and felt the escalating tension in the room. Peggy Judson's thin lips pulled away from her sharp, fanglike teeth. "The children I bear for him will be children of our hearts," she broke in, answering for Gib. She held up her hand toward Peggy. "If you cut my hand with a knife, you will see that my blood is the same color as yours. How are we so different? If you spent time in the sun, you also would change color. Your skin would become dark brown."

Snorting, Peggy muttered, "You simple savage. You don't understand."

"Mrs. Judson," Gib warned, "don't say another word. Kuchana's way of seeing things is the way I see them, too. Every person in this chapel is the same color inside. No one is so different as people like you would like to believe."

Melissa pushed and shoved the last few feet to the front of the church, the men parting to allow her to pass. Gasping for breath, she marched up to where Peggy and her husband stood. "This is insane!" she rattled up at McCoy. "First, you get busted for trying to steal the wife of the post commander at Fort Apache. Then you humiliate all of us by being court-martialed and drummed out of the service. Now you come back to stir up more trouble by wanting to marry this heathen in a place of God. I will not allow you to do that, McCoy. Not now, not ever. You take your precious savage and leave. There's not going to be any marriage performed here today."

McCoy turned to look at Melissa's pale, twisted features. "I'm a civilian, Mrs. Polk. I'm no longer under U.S. Army command, and your orders don't mean a damn thing to me." He turned, nailing the minister with a dark look. "And Reverend Judson has already agreed to marry us."

Peggy gasped, taking a step back from her husband. "David!" she cried.

"No!" Melissa shrilled. This was too much. She lunged for the pistol that hung from the holster of a nearby soldier. Jerking it free, she cocked it and held it up.

Instantly, Gib pushed Kuchana behind him as Melissa lowered the barrel, pointing it directly at him. "Don't," he growled at her.

The entire assemblage froze. Peggy Judson's eyes grew huge as she watched the pistol waver in Melissa's shaking hands.

The Reverend Judson lifted his hand. "This has gone too far," he protested in a high, strangled tone. "Mrs. Polk— Melissa—give me the gun. You don't want to shoot anyone."

Kuchana fought against Gib's arm that held her captive behind him. She was still a warrior; someone who would never hide in the face of danger. Ducking quickly beneath his arm, she moved out of McCoy's reach, leveling her gaze at the harshly breathing Melissa.

"It is me you want, not him," she challenged huskily.

"Either one will do," Melissa spat, dividing her attention between them. "Don't move. I'll shoot anyone who does."

McCoy held up his hand, cautioning the minister to stay put. Melissa's finger was brushing the trigger in earnest, and by the look in her wild green eyes, she was fully capable of shooting whomever irritated her more. His attention was on Kuchana, who bristled tensely, slightly crouched as if ready to attack.

"Kuchana, don't make her shoot," he ordered her in Apache. "She wants to kill."

"It will not be you, then." Kuchana kept her gaze trained on Melissa. "She has always hated me. I will not allow her to kill you," she returned in her own language.

Dodd Carter pushed his way through the people in the crowded aisle, his face red with anger. "What the hell's going on in here!" He stopped abruptly, seeing Melissa pointing the pistol at McCoy.

"Stay where you are, Dodd!" she yelled. "I'm going to get my revenge on this bastard." Swinging her eyes back to McCoy, she grated. "Ever since you've come here, you've ruined my plans. You're nothing but vermin, McCoy." The barrel trembled. "I hate you. And I hate her! Between the two of you, everything's been ruined!" She began to sob, compressing her lips.

Carter sucked in his breath, his eyes widening as he saw her pull back on the trigger. "Mellie, don't!" he screamed, lunging toward her.

The gun exploded. Kuchana was knocked off her feet as Carter flew between her and Melissa. He had grabbed Melissa's wrist just as the pistol went off. A cry tore from her as she saw Carter suddenly buckle in midair and crumple to a heap on the wooden floor. Melissa cried out, dropping the pistol, and backed away.

Cursing, McCoy leapt toward Carter's side. "Get the doctor!" he roared. Instantly, there was movement in the chapel as several of the soldiers ran outside and across the parade ground to find the doctor.

Claudia Carter fainted, caught in the arms of several of the soldiers. Shrieks and cries filled the chapel. Kuchana remained crouched, watching Peggy Judson also faint into the arms of her husband. David Judson sank to his knees, his face pale and beaded with sweat.

Looking up, Kuchana saw Melissa turn on her heel, racing for the side entrance door of the chapel. Instantly, she jumped to her feet in pursuit. The white woman, hampered by the dress she wore, was barely out the door before Kuchana caught up with her.

With a screech, Melissa saw Kuchana coming after her. The Apache woman's face was emotionless, her eyes black and determined. Managing to reach the cottonwood that gave the chapel some shade, Melissa picked up a long branch that had fallen from the tree. Just as Kuchana reached out to grab her, Melissa swung the limb at her head.

Kuchana's head exploded with light and then pain. Melissa had caught her off guard. The blow felled her, and she sank to the ground, trying to shake off the dizziness. Gasping for breath, she watched as Melissa headed for the stables. The woman was wild-eyed. Kuchana realized belatedly that Melissa was a warrior, despite the garb she wore. Staggering to her feet, she kept that in mind as she raced across the parade ground, certain that Melissa was intent on running away.

The soldiers standing outside the chapel were startled by the sudden activity. They stood with their mouths agape as Kuchana raced to the stables. She was within two hundred feet of the open doors when Melissa, astride her favorite bay mare, exploded out of the stables at a full gallop.

Kuchana realized she was the only one who stood between Melissa and her freedom. She saw the *pindah* woman whip the mare mercilessly with her crop as she bore down on her. The look in her eyes was the same one Kuchana had seen in the eyes of other enemies who had been intent on killing her.

The mare's mouth was open, her eyes rolling as she thundered toward Kuchana. There was no mistaking Melissa's intention, and Kuchana stood in her way, unmoving, feet spread for balance, arms away from her body.

McCoy lunged through the men at the door of the chapel. A cry caught in his throat as he saw Melissa and the horse bearing down on Kuchana. Instantly, he realized that Kuchana was going to try to stop Melissa from running away.

He wanted to curse, to cry out a warning. If Kuchana didn't move, she would be killed.

At the last second before the collision, Kuchana gave a deep, warbling war cry. The animal, shaken by the sound, veered slightly to the left. Melissa shrieked, yanking the reins hard to try to get the horse back on its deadly course.

Never taking her eyes off the mare, Kuchana moved with lightning speed. Her hand shot out, seeking, then finding the leather reins. Melissa's crop came down on her head and shoulder, momentarily stunning her, but Kuchana held on, the hurtling horse yanking her off her feet.

Kuchana felt pain explode through her shoulder as she brought the horse's full forward weight up short. Melissa screamed as the horse's head was jerked around. The animal stumbled, its legs crumpling as it was flung sideways, off balance. The animal's nose dug into the sand and Melissa was thrown over its head. Sand flew up into the air as the horse landed on its side with a grunt. Kuchana pulled her hand free of the reins, struggling to get to her feet. Gasping for breath, she saw Gib race by her.

People were running from all directions toward where Kuchana was standing just behind McCoy. She saw Colonel Polk hurrying toward them, too. Bracing herself for more verbal assaults, Kuchana stood watching as Gib helped Melissa sit up.

"Don't touch me!" Melissa spat, breathing raggedly. Her fine silk dress was sprinkled with dust and she began to brush it away in short, angry strokes.

"What is going on?" Polk roared, making his way through the gathering people.

McCoy twisted around, looking up at the white-haired officer. "Your wife just shot Lieutenant Carter," he said, his voice raw. "Melissa took Corporal Evans's gun and held it on Kuchana and myself. When she went to pull the trigger, Carter saved Kuchana's life by stepping in between them."

Polk's narrowed eyes focused on his wife, who sat unceremoniously in the dust at his feet. "Mellie?" he whispered in disbelief.

Huge tears rolled down Melissa's face as she got to her feet by herself. Her breath was coming in ragged gulps as she surveyed the crowd around her. "Shut up, Harvey! Just shut up!"

Kuchana saw the colonel's face grow plum-colored. Without a word, the officer stepped up to his wife, gripping her by the arm. "Come with me," he ground out.

McCoy watched as the rest of the officers followed Polk and his wife. He moved to Kuchana's side. She was covered with dust from head to toe.

"You took one hell of a risk," Gib told her roughly, moving his hand across her hair. "Are you all right?"

As she nodded, Gib studied her. He saw the mark of Melissa's crop down her neck, the red welt disappearing beneath her shirt. "You're not all right."

McCoy was interrupted by the minister, who came up to him, his face white with shock.

"I think," Judson said in a quivering voice, "it would be best to marry you now, and then both of you can leave. Once the colonel realizes what his wife has done, and the price that will be paid, you will be nothing but a reminder of his pain."

Gib nodded. "Then you'll marry us?"

The Reverend Judson nodded, shakily opening the Bible he still held. "Right here and now."

By the time they reached the cabin in the mountains, it was dark. Kuchana rode in silence at Gib's side. Behind them was Wind. Kuchana had wanted her mare brought along. She would be bred to the mustang stallion and become one of the mares in his band. Above them, the stars hung bright and silent, reminding Kuchana that Father Sky throbbed with life. Rubbing her brow, she spoke. "I pray our wedding day is not a symbol of things to come."

Gib reached over, capturing her hand and giving her fingers a gentle squeeze. The simple gold wedding band on her left hand glinted dully in the starlight. "What do you mean?" After the brief ceremony, Poppy and Nettie had hugged them, promising to come for a visit soon, after the shock of Carter's death had worn off.

"*Pindah* ways are odd. Among my people, days are spent in preparation for a marriage. There is always much feasting, dancing and joy."

"I know," he comforted, wanting to take away her pain. "I'm sorry it had to be this way, Kuchana. It was my fault. I didn't realize there would be so much opposition to my marrying you. Especially from the Reverend Judson's wife." He sighed and shook his head. "I should have figured on it. She was the one who openly attacked you at the Christmas party. I'm sorry."

"I do not blame you, my husband. I only pray that unhappiness does not follow our days together."

He smiled. "It won't. That's a promise."

Kuchana lifted her chin, watching the silhouette of the log cabin grow larger and larger. Suddenly, home sounded good to her. Her heart lifting from her worries, she saw that Gib was equally touched with the realization that they were coming home—together. As man and wife.

Gib dismounted and went around, lifting Kuchana out of the saddle. The realization that, today, she could have died two different times, shook him deeply. When her feet had touched the ground, he framed her face with his hands, gazing deeply into her eyes, which burned with the golden promise of their future. "Go on inside. I'll get the horses stabled for the night."

His touch sent tingles of pleasure through her, erasing the darkness of the day within her heart. "I will await you . . ."

Placing a chaste, swift kiss on her parted lips, Gib released her.

Inside the cabin, Kuchana lit several of the lamps, sending light throughout the room. The mountain air was cool, but not cold. Pouring water into a huge tin basin, she took off her clothes and washed herself. She padded through the cabin and found their bedroom, with its brass bed covered by a colorful quilt. Shivering, Kuchana slipped between the covers, sinking into the feather mattress, with a moan of pleasure. As she snuggled down between the mattress and quilt, she felt safe and happy as never before.

Her eyes were drooping closed by the time Gib came in. She heard him in the other room, pouring water and washing himself. Exhausted by the events of the past two days, she fell asleep.

The far-off call of a coyote, yipping at the approaching dawn, awakened Kuchana. At first, she couldn't recall where she was. The strength of Gib's body resting against hers was all she knew. And then, as her lashes lifted, she inhaled softly, recalling that now, she was home. A real home with her husband, and a life of promise suspended gently before her.

She raised herself on one arm, her hair a black sheet sliding across her shoulder and breasts, and gazed down at Gib as he slept. Her heart sang a joyous song to Painted Woman, because she had more than answered all her prayers. "You are my husband, a part of my soul now," she whispered to him, resting the curve of her palm against his bristly growth of beard. In sleep, the corners of Gib's eyes and around his mouth lost their lines of tension.

Looking up, Kuchana watched as Holos rose, his strong rays slanting through the window behind their bed, creating rectangular squares of light on the opposite wall. The lace of the curtains broke up the light, revealing intricate, shadowy patterns within the squares. Was not life like that?

Kuchana thought, gently pushing the strands of hair off Gib's brow.

Leaning down, she followed her heart, pressing a kiss to his brow, her lips trailing from there to his cheek and then molding gently to his mouth. A quiver raced through her as his mouth claimed her tentative exploration, and she sighed, allowing Gib to pull her on top of him. The hardness of his body sent a sheet of delight through her as she felt her body molding and giving here and there.

"You're so sweet," Gib whispered thickly, sliding his hands upward to frame her face. Kuchana's firm body was hot against his. The smile she gave him reminded him of a rainbow after a storm. This morning, her eyes were clear and all the worry that had shadowed her was gone. If he read her correctly, there was nothing but joy in the present and hope of a better future in her warm liquid gaze. "My sun woman," he murmured, capturing her lips, savoring the fire she shared so willingly and trustingly with him.

The world spun slowly to a halt as Gib ran his hands down the sides of Kuchana's trembling form. His fingers caressed her and she responded, pressing her hips into his. His groan reverberated through her, heightening her senses, stirring her womanly yearning to bright new life. As he turned her over on her back, his hands stroked and touched her in reverent adoration, weaving a soft web around the both of them.

His mouth descended to pull the peak of one of her nipples into its moist interior, and bright lights danced beneath Kuchana's closed lids. As he suckled her, a stab of longing bolted through her. The need to couple with him, like Mother Earth welcoming the seeds dropped by a tree, nestling them within her fertile soil, became dominant.

Shifting, Gib slid his hand between her strong, curved thighs. Her eyes, a dazed gold, reflected how he felt as he positioned himself over her, placing one hand beneath her slender hips. This time, he wanted the lovemaking to be slow and good for Kuchana. The way she parted her lips, the way the corners moved upward as he came into contact with her hot, moist core, told him that she welcomed him into her.

Closing her eyes, she moved her hands across his powerful shoulders and felt the muscles tense. As she instinctively lifted her hips to welcome Gib deep into her body, she understood that together, they formed a circle of life. As he thrust into her, a moan rose in her throat, a song of fulfillment long sought and found with the man who held her in his arms at this moment. Her lashes fluttered as she absorbed his strength, marveling at his tenderness as he kissed her eyes, nose and lips, holding very still so as not to cause her discomfort.

She moved her hips, silently inviting him more deeply within her. The sliding, heated friction built within her, and she reveled in the pleasure each slow thrust gave her. Her lips parting, she cried out his name, a sacred sound as the fire within her exploded and she arched her back.

Moments later, she felt him release. Smiling languidly, she took his full weight, satisfaction pulsing through her as never before. He was the sky, she the earth. They had come together as one. And now, as she ran her fingers across his damp back, she prayed to Painted Woman that a child would form in her womb to symbolize the love they had for one another.

McCoy smiled as he gently turned onto his back and pulled Kuchana on top of him. Her black hair pooled in sheets across his chest, strands of it clinging to her brow and cheek. The glow of love in her eyes made him smile. "You were worth waiting for...fighting for," he told her huskily, moving each of the strands off her face.

She rested her brow against his. "I saw Grandmother Spider making her web as we loved one another. Each time you touched me, I saw another drop of dew gather on the silken web she was spinning."

Caressing her cheek, Gib sampled her lower lip, swollen from his kisses. There was an earthy sweetness to Kuchana he would never tire of. "What else?" he asked.

"Within the dew there were rainbows."

"You make me feel that way, sun woman."

She barely opened her eyes, studying him in the warming silence. "You are the rain, and I am the earth. We belong together."

"We always have," he agreed quietly, threading her hair through his fingers. "And, God willing, we'll have many children to show how much we love one another."

"Even now, I pray that I carry the first of many daughters and sons for you."

"I hope it's a girl just like you."

Tears sprang to Kuchana's eyes as she pressed a kiss to his mouth. Among the Apache, the women were seen as the stronger ones. Only they had the ability to have children, to have a monthly moon and give back their blood to Mother Earth. These were the mysteries of being a woman, being close to the veil of unseen life. Apache men held their women sacred. Although Gib was white, he honored her by wishing their firstborn was a daughter.

Gib gently kissed each of her eyelids, then eased Kuchana off him and sat up, bringing her back into his arms. Shafts of sunlight slanted through the bedroom, and he looked down at her, covering her with the multicolored quilt so that she wouldn't become chilled in the cool morning air of the mountains.

"You know," he began softly, tucking her against him, "I never had a dream. I always saw myself in the army, never married, never wanting anything more. And then, when I tried to help Juliet Harper and got busted, everything started going wrong, and other things began to matter. I had just begun changing my life when you showed up."

She lifted her lashes, content to be held, her head resting on his shoulder. "Me?"

"I think I fell in love with you the instant I saw you," Gib admitted, smiling down into her smoldering eyes. "But I didn't realize it until much later." He chuckled. "And then I had to fight myself not to kiss you, touch you or—" he leaned down and kissed her lips tenderly "—love you."

"Painted Woman works in mysterious ways," Kuchana agreed. "I lived only to fulfill my vow to see what few were left of my people spared and protected by the army. I know it is not the best answer, but it was the only one I could see."

"Well," Gib soothed, seeing her brows knit with anxiety, "I think this time around General Miles will make sure that your people are fairly treated. All we can do is hope and pray for that, Kuchana."

She sighed, languorous in his arms, never wanting anything else. "Yesterday, I didn't believe my eyes. How could Melissa kill someone?"

Gib shook his head. "I don't know, sweetheart. She's never been very stable. There's a wild streak in her, and she's been spoiled by men who have given her anything she wants. If she doesn't get it, she throws a temper tantrum like a child. This time, she chose to use a gun instead of stamping her foot and sulking the way she usually does."

"What does this mean?"

Shrugging, Gib muttered. "Carter's dead. His wife will probably go back East to her parents and start all over. Melissa killed a man, true, but still, if there's a trial, I imagine she'll get off without a sentence. Polk's career is washed up, though, as a result. I'm sure the army will force him to retire. What he'll do then, who knows?"

"And when they leave, will you be welcome at the fort?"

"Probably."

Whether he wanted to get out of bed or not, Gib knew there were horses to be fed and watered. Reluctantly, he released Kuchana, threw back the covers and stood up.

Kuchana sat in the center of the bed, admiring Gib's naked body bathed in sunlight. He was a strong, good man in her eyes, and she smiled at him when he realized she was looking at him. "What of Poppy, Nettie and her husband?"

"I'm sure they'll stay at the fort," Gib told her, moving over to the chair where he'd put his long johns. "They have a good life compared to most of the Negroes who live in the South, and they know that. In a couple of months, we'll ride down and see them." He shrugged into the red underwear, then retrieved his pants and pulled them on. Going back to the bed, he sat down to put on his boots.

Kuchana moved over to him, placing her arms around him and resting her head against his back. "Perhaps, in a few months, Nettie will know that Private Ladler loves her and he will propose to her."

Gib twisted around just enough to pull Kuchana into his arms. With a giggle, she came willingly, resting in his lap, her arms around his neck. He kissed her hotly on the mouth and whispered, "Maybe in a few months we'll have good news for them, too," and he placed his hand against her softly rounded belly.

Warmth raced through her heart as she embraced him tightly. "I love you," she whispered.

"And I love you, my sun woman, forever..."

* * * * *

Everyone loves a spring wedding, and this April, Harlequin cordially invites you to read the most romantic wedding book of the year.

With This Ring

ONE WEDDING—FOUR LOVE STORIES FROM OUR MOST DISTINGUISHED HARLEQUIN AUTHORS:

BETHANY CAMPBELL
BARBARA DELINSKY
BOBBY HUTCHINSON
ANN McALLISTER

The church is booked, the reception arranged and the invitations mailed. All Diane Bauer and Nick Granatelli have to do is walk down the aisle. Little do they realize that the most cherished day of their lives will spark so many romantic notions....

Available wherever Harlequin books are sold.

HARLEQUIN
American Romance®

RELIVE THE MEMORIES....

All the way from turn-of-the-century Ellis Island to the future of the nineties... **A CENTURY OF AMERICAN ROMANCE** takes you on a nostalgic journey through the twentieth century.

This May, watch for the final title of **A CENTURY OF AMERICAN ROMANCE**—#389 A>LOVERBOY, Judith Arnold's lighthearted look at love in 1998!

Don't miss a day of **A CENTURY OF AMERICAN ROMANCE**

A CENTURY OF
AMERICAN ROMANCE

1990s

The women... the men... the passions... the memories...

H A R L E Q U I N
American Romance®

THE ROMANCE THAT STARTED IT ALL!

For Diane Bauer and Nick Granatelli, the walk down the aisle was a rocky road....

Don't miss the romantic prequel to WITH THIS RING—

I THEE WED
BY ANNE McALLISTER

Harlequin American Romance #387

Let Anne McAllister take you to Cambridge, Massachusetts, to the night when an innocent blind date brought a reluctant Diane Bauer and Nick Granatelli together. For Diane, a smoldering attraction like theirs had only one fate, one future—marriage. The hard part, she learned, was convincing her intended....

Watch for Anne McAllister's I THEE WED, available *now* from Harlequin American Romance.

ITW

HARLEQUIN'S WISHBOOK
SWEEPSTAKES RULES & REGULATIONS
NO PURCHASE NECESSARY TO ENTER OR RECEIVE A PRIZE

1. To enter the Sweepstakes and join the Reader Service, affix the Four Free Books and Free Gifts sticker along with both of your Sweepstakes stickers to the Sweepstakes Entry Form. If you do not wish to take advantage of our Reader Service, but wish to enter the Sweepstakes only, do not affix the Four Free Books and Free Gifts sticker; affix only the Sweepstakes stickers to the Sweepstakes Entry Form. Incomplete and/or inaccurate entries are ineligible for that section or sections of prizes. Torstar Corp. and its affiliates are not responsible for mutilated or unreadable entries or inadvertent printing errors. Mechanically reproduced entries are null and void.

2. Whether you take advantage of this offer or not, on or about April 30, 1992 at the offices of Marden-Kane Inc., Lake Success, NY, your Sweepstakes number will be compared against a list of winning numbers generated at random by the computer. However, prizes will only be awarded to individuals who have entered the Sweepstakes. In the event that all prizes are not claimed, a random drawing will be held from all qualified entries received from March 30, 1990 to March 31, 1992, to award all unclaimed prizes. All cash prizes (Grand to Sixth), will be mailed to the winners and are payable by check in U.S. funds. Seventh prize to be shipped to winners via third-class mail. These prizes are in addition to any free, surprise or mystery gifts that might be offered. Versions of this sweepstakes with different prizes of approximate equal value may appear in other mailings or at retail outlets by Torstar Corp. and its affiliates.

3. The following prizes are awarded in this sweepstakes: ★ Grand Prize (1) $1,000,000; First Prize (1) $25,000; Second Prize (1) $10,000; Third Prize (5) $5,000; Fourth Prize (10) $1,000; Fifth Prize (100) $250; Sixth Prize (2,500) $10; ★ ★ Seventh Prize (6,000) $12.95 ARV.

   ★ This Sweepstakes contains a Grand Prize offering of a $1,000,000 annuity. Winner will receive $33,333.33 a year for 30 years without interest totalling $1,000,000.

   ★ ★ Seventh Prize: A fully illustrated hardcover book published by Torstar Corp. Approximate Retail Value of the book is $12.95.

   Entrants may cancel the Reader Service at anytime without cost or obligation to buy (see details in center insert card).

4. Extra Bonus! This presentation offers two extra bonus prizes valued at a total of $33,000 to be awarded in a random drawing from all qualified entries received by March 31, 1992. No purchase necessary to enter or receive a prize. To qualify, see instructions on the insert card. Winner will have the choice of merchandise offered or a $33,000 check payable in U.S. funds. All other published rules and regulations apply.

5. This Sweepstakes is being conducted under the supervision of Marden-Kane, Inc., an independent judging organization. By entering this Sweepstakes, each entrant accepts and agrees to be bound by these rules and the decisions of the judges, which shall be final and binding. Odds of winning in the random drawing are dependent upon the total number of entries received. Taxes, if any, are the sole responsibility of the winners. Prizes are nontransferable. All entries must be received at the address printed on the reply card and must be postmarked no later than 12:00 MIDNIGHT on March 31, 1992. The drawing for all unclaimed Sweepstakes prizes and for the Bonus Sweepstakes Prize will take place May 30, 1992, at 12:00 NOON at the offices of Marden-Kane, Inc., Lake Success, NY.

6. This offer is open to residents of the U.S., the United Kingdom, France and Canada, 18 years or older, except employees and their immediate family members of Torstar Corp., its affiliates, subsidiaries, and all other agencies and persons connected with the use, marketing or conduct of this Sweepstakes. All Federal, State, Provincial and local laws apply. Void wherever prohibited or restricted by law. Any litigation within the Province of Quebec respecting the conduct and awarding of a prize in this publicity contest must be submitted to the Régie des Loteries et Courses du Québec.

7. Winners will be notified by mail and may be required to execute an affidavit of eligibility and release, which must be returned within 14 days after notification or an alternative winner will be selected. Canadian winners will be required to correctly answer an arithmetical skill-testing question administered by mail, which must be returned within a limited time. Winners consent to the use of their names, photographs and/or likenesses for advertising and publicity in conjunction with this and similar promotions without additional compensation.

8. For a list of our major winners, send a stamped, self-addressed envelope to: WINNERS LIST, c/o MARDEN-KANE, INC., P.O. BOX 701, SAYREVILLE, NJ 08871. Winners Lists will be fulfilled after the May 30, 1992 drawing date.

ALTERNATE MEANS OF ENTRY: Print your name and address on a 3" ×5" piece of plain paper and send to:

In the U.S.	In Canada
Harlequin's WISHBOOK Sweepstakes	Harlequin's WISHBOOK Sweepstakes
3010 Walden Ave.	P.O. Box 609
P.O. Box 1867, Buffalo, NY 14269-1867	Fort Erie, Ontario L2A 5X3

LTY-H491RRD

Back by Popular Demand

Janet Dailey

Americana

A romantic tour of America through fifty favorite Harlequin Presents®, each set in a different state researched by Janet and her husband, Bill. A journey of a lifetime in one cherished collection.

In April, don't miss the first six states followed by two new states each month!

April titles # 1 - ALABAMA
                    Dangerous Masquerade
                2 - ALASKA
                    Northern Magic
                3 - ARIZONA
                    Sonora Sundown
                4 - ARKANSAS
                    Valley of the Vapours
                5 - CALIFORNIA
                    Fire and Ice
                6 - COLORADO
                    After the Storm

May titles #   7 - CONNECTICUT
                    Difficult Decision
                8 - DELAWARE
                    The Matchmakers

**Available wherever
Harlequin books are sold.**

JD-AR